FATAL FLAW

FATAL
FLAW

J.E. KELLENBERGER

Matador
Unit E2 Airfield Business Park,
Harrison Road, Market Harborough,
Leicestershire. LE16 7UL
Tel: 0116 2792299
Email: books@troubador.co.uk
Web: www.troubador.co.uk/matador
Twitter: @matadorbooks

ISBN 978 1 80514 410 6

British Library Cataloguing in Publication Data.
A catalogue record for this book is available from the British Library.

Printed and bound by CPI Group (UK) Ltd, Croydon, CR0 4YY
Typeset in 11.5pt Minion Pro by Troubador Publishing Ltd, Leicester, UK

Matador is an imprint of Troubador Publishing Ltd

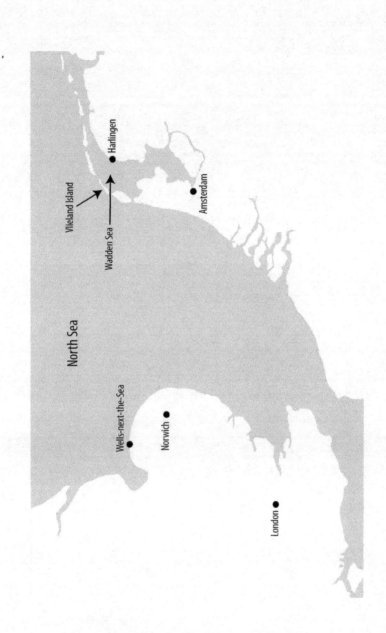

PROLOGUE

1973

The round was going well for Arne Visser until he took his tee shot at the par five sixteenth hole on the South course at the exclusive club which was hosting the region's annual seniors' championship. He had been instrumental in persuading the committee to choose his home club. It would be an advantage over his fellow competitors who played at other courses within East Anglia.

Arne was a good golfer but not exceptional. He had negotiated the preceding holes well and had a good score; very possibly a winning one. But on this occasion his drive was not long and straight; it was low and wayward. It disappeared, lost from view as it hooked into the lefthand tree-lined rough heading for the out-of-bounds markers.

Maybe the tension was getting to him. At just fifty years and a few days, it was the first time he had met the age qualification to participate in the event, and he was psyched up to win. He liked gongs and accolades and a win here would do his standing no end of good, and in addition, divert attention away from his struggling business interests. He was a larger-than-life character and would use the kudos of winning a regional title to his advantage, even if it was an event just for seniors. Currently his business back was against the wall and he was walking a tightrope to hide the indebtedness of his group of companies. As he picked up his tee, he decided that he was not going to allow one errant drive to spoil his day, and no, when asked by his playing partners, he would not be playing a provisional ball as he felt sure that his original had not gone out of bounds.

The sixteenth hole was a dogleg to the right. His playing partners, both in their mid-fifties, had fired their shots up the middle of the wide fairway, positioning them strategically for their second shots around the dogleg curve. Arne's drive was by far the longest, having the topspin that a hook imparts on the ball. He walked quickly to the area where his ball appeared to be heading. He was already in the woods by the time his playing partners arrived at their balls, some fifty yards short of his position. Concentrating on taking their next shots they failed to notice Arne in the wooded rough seeking a suitable spot to illegally drop an identical ball from his hand. It fell with a near-silent plop and Arne adjusted its position deftly with his foot. A quick scan showed no sign of his original ball, and as far as Arne could tell, no sign either of any players on the adjacent fairway of the adjoining North course to spot him cheating. For Arne it was the perfect scenario, and without a hint of guilt he selected a mid-iron and stroked the ball back onto the fairway leaving just a short chip to the green.

Knowing glances were exchanged by his playing partners but after the rebuff on the tee neither had the appetite to challenge Arne's contention that he had scored a birdie four. His prickly reputation as a businessman preceded him. A few remarks tinged with sarcasm which was lost on the Dutchman about the extraordinary luck he had had with the ball hitting a tree trunk, missing a prickly bush, and coming to rest on an ideal lie with a clear pathway to the green was all they were prepared to venture. They knew it was wrong, but they were here to enjoy their day out, and it would be less messy to turn a blind eye now than to get embroiled in an unpleasant saga.

Dogs on leads could be walked on the rather easier North course while their masters enjoyed a few holes of relaxed golf; it was one of the members' perks. Ted, Alistair Drew's Airedale terrier had heard or spotted something and had been straining at the leash to get to the source of his excitement. He sniffed at the object and then growled. Alistair gently stroked Ted's head around the left eye where the cataract was forming as he bent down to pick up the ball which was lying in a tuft of lush grass. It was monogrammed with initials he knew well. He looked across to the adjacent South course as the athletic figure of Arne Visser came into view and appeared to scan the out-of-bounds area before dropping a ball surreptitiously from his pocket. Alistair concluded righty that neither he nor Ted had been spotted by Arne.

Later, in the clubhouse at the prize ceremony, and while Arne was still making his winner's speech, club captain Alistair, a man of modest golfing ability but immense integrity, quietly sought out Arne's playing partners. Just a glimpse of the original ball was all they required to silently confirm Alistair's belief.

Cheating at golf was not honourable, and war hero or not, some form of redress would be natural justice.

Chapter 1

VISSERS

The wider Visser family had inhabited the northern coastal strip of Holland for several centuries. Living up to the English translation of their surname: fisherman, they had sailed and plied the inner and outer waters of the Wadden Sea, separating the archipelago of islands from the Dutch mainland and protecting it from the destructive forces of the North Sea. In simple sailing boats they designed and built themselves, in favourable weather they fished from dawn to dusk in waters abundant with shrimp and sole, and with rainbow trout in the brackish water of the narrow estuaries.

Generations of Vissers learnt by example from their parents and taught by actions to their offspring, with little change of routine or practice from one generation to the next. It was not until the industrial revolution that the extended family, scattered in small settlements along the meandering coastline in small inlets which offered protection for their boats, were they able to gather in the area's modest town of Harlingen. Thanks to new methods, a network of modern minor roads replaced the worn-out tracks which had served the community since time immemorial. Prone to flooding in winter and overgrown with vegetation in summer, these dirt passageways had prevented the fisher folk from exploring alternative lifestyles. Later, an enterprising core of Vissers with skills to teach, knowledge to impart and an intense desire to learn, moved farther afield to Leeuwarden where they set up permanent home away from the sea for the first time in centuries.

By the time Arne's great grandfather was of working age, his line of Vissers had acquired some land backing onto a dike. With easy access to the harbour, sea and newly set-up businesses operating farther along the dike, they had established a boatyard and built a serviceable boathouse. With no room for living quarters in the yard, they had rented a dwelling on the outskirts of Harlingen and for the first time in their lives they would not be living over the shop. They had become full-time boatbuilders and any spare time on the water was strictly for leisure. And only two generations later, Arne's father was studying nautical engineering in the famous German university town of Bremen; a mecca for the latest maritime technology.

Pieter Visser had excelled at school in mathematical related subjects. The world would have been his oyster had he wished to pursue studies in pure mathematics. He would have been welcomed with open arms by elite universities throughout the western world. But his love of boats – their design and construction – would always be his guiding star and no amount of persuasion or financial incentive could be brought to bear to change that fact. He had told his school teacher that he would succeed as a boatbuilder and that someday he would open his own yard and employ master craftsmen to build his designs. There was never any doubt in the teacher's mind that Pieter could fail to achieve his goal.

Since the beginning of time, as soon as the species discovered water, man was building boats. They were crude in form for thousands of years, but vessels became surprisingly refined as the emergence of sophisticated tools transformed building techniques. Craftsmen became masters as they handed down their practical knowledge to the youthful apprentices.

Gradually, centres of learning started teaching how to apply engineering techniques to boatbuilding, and maritime studies developed into an academic subject. Although still in their infancy in the early nineteen-tens, these courses were sought after as the modern man, keen to better himself, moved away from purely physical work. Pieter was the first in his line to contemplate a working life free of manual labour. Having accompanied his father from a young age, he could sail and navigate expertly even before reaching his tenth birthday. Additionally, in the boatyard, he had shown a natural aptitude for working with wood and several suggestions he had made to refine the design had been implemented to much acclaim. With modest savings accumulated from decades of sheer hard work, his parents willingly paid for higher schooling in an institute of technical excellence. A few days short of his fifteenth birthday, he set off by bus and train for the major town of Bremen at the mouth of the rive Wiese, the second largest town in northern Germany. He would be away for three long years while he studied to become a boat designer.

Quiet and thoughtful by nature, Pieter knew well the sacrifices his parents and siblings were making on his behalf. He would apply himself with diligence and return one day to repay his family for the opportunity they had given him. He would lodge with the family of the institute's caretaker and when not studying he would help the caretaker with cleaning and maintenance tasks. The few marks he was allowed per week as pocket money bought little more than a stamp for a letter home to his parents. There would be no return trips to his homeland for short breaks in the bosom of his family.

Adaptation to a puritanical style of life with strict rules of conduct and discipline was a pre-requisite for harmonious living. Unquestioning acceptance of ancient German hierarchical structures and compliance thereto was expected in all strands of German society in the early years of the twentieth century. The more relaxed attitudes of Germany's neighbouring countries were frowned on and no allowance was made for non-German speakers as high German with all its tenses and declensions was de rigueur. It was a lot to learn for a young lad and silent tears ran down his cheeks in bed on many a lonely night. But, not apparent from his mild manners, Pieter had an inner strength and in due course, fuelled no doubt by his love of boats and the prospect of learning modern design, settled down in the caretaker's family who generally treated him well.

After three long years, he had learnt every nugget of knowledge his teachers had to offer, he received his diploma in maritime studies, bade a fond farewell to the caretaker's family and set off by train and bus for his own home. It was now nineteen-fourteen, Pieter was almost eighteen and had become a young man of note. His family welcomed his return as he got down to work at the drawing board in the boatyard immediately. A lot was expected of Pieter and he was happy to repay their faith.

For family Visser of Harlingen, the dawning of the new century brought a whole raft of innovations to which to adapt. Pieter's return had already heralded some major changes in the working practices of the boatyard. But it was the passing of the generational baton in a silent, respectful, and unchallenged manner that would transform their collective future. Now approaching twenty, and with the same quiet and thoughtful demeanour, his leadership qualities were obvious to all. He would guide them in the new era and they would follow.

It was the first sailing boat they built that pointed to their future direction. Many hours had been spent out on the water developing a blueprint and honing the design; simple, basic, and comparatively cheap, a small sailing boat which stood out from the rest due to its sleek and ergonomic looks coupled with the obvious craftmanship of its build. It would be straightforward to sail even as a single-handed sailor. As word spread and interest in the new craft gathered pace with the receipt of orders and special commissions, so it became apparent that the boatyard should concentrate on building vessels for leisure: hand-crafted sailing boats and small yachts fit for offshore sailing. It would be their niche in the market and they would scale down their previous longstanding work in building vessels to ferry people and goods to and from the outlying islands.

Slowly at first, like a large, heavy wooden wheel creaking stubbornly as it resisted yielding from its habitual position, and then with gathering momentum, the proletariat broke away from the constrictions and subservience of their former lives and danced gleefully into the new world order of the twentieth century where achievement beyond rank was possible. The success of the boatyard and the Harlingen Vissers, due in large part to hard work and attention to detail, became a beacon for other families to emulate. The family prospered and the letters between Pieter and Frieda continued their regular, weekly, metronomic exchanges until one day Pieter announced that he would be away for a few days as he was to be married to the eldest daughter of the caretaker in Bremen. It was nineteen-twenty and Europe was again at peace; the interregnum of the war years giving way to the resumption of the new liberal attitudes of the current century. He would bring his new wife back to a country which would show no overt hostility to her German origins. The war was done and dusted and the Dutch had preserved their neutrality throughout the long four years of hostilities.

In December nineteen-twenty-one, their first child was born, a daughter, followed one year later by a second girl. In November nineteen-twenty-three Arne was born. There had been much debate about their son's first name with Frieda keen for him to bear one reflecting her German background which would serve as a reminder to him of his heritage. She was persuaded that Arne, a name traditional to the specific area of northern Europe in which the family lived, and closely associated with a neighbouring Scandinavian country, would fit the bill when Pieter explained that it meant "eagle" and was symbolic of the insignia on the national flag of Germany as it was in that epoch of a black double-headed eagle on a golden background.

Family life was in the main full and happy for both parents and offspring. Unlike his sisters who seemed very much carved in the Visser mould which had been producing well-adjusted individuals for generations, Arne's passage through early childhood into puberty was an unpredictable roller-coaster as he constantly tested the Visser family patience. Frieda devoted her time to the children and running the home while Pieter spent endless hours at the boatyard pouring over his drawing board. He was never happier than when out on the water testing his designs and often accompanied by Arne; just an old salt passing on his nautical expertise to a young apprentice. And by a very early age Arne was almost as competent as his father. It was therefore unsurprising that a deep rapport developed between father and son such that Pieter showed a more lenient and tolerant attitude towards Arne's hot-headedness and fiery temper than to minor indiscretions by his daughters; besides being unfair, they claimed with some justification, a lack of punishment for bad behaviour would have repercussions in later life.

Following in his father's footsteps, and with a certain feeling of relief within the family unit that peace and calm could now be restored, at the age of fifteen Arne took his place in a gymnasium high school in Bremen where he would receive formal training in general maritime studies before selecting a specialist subject to go on to study at Bremen University. It was early nineteen-thirty-eight and although Frieda had grave reservations about her only son, disruptive or not, going to her homeland for educational purposes at a time in history when the continent seemed to be in flux in several of its major countries with aggressive posturing by right-wing parties, and a civil war was playing out across the Iberian Peninsula, she recognised that Arne needed the type of strict discipline redolent of robust Germanic methods. The family had allowed Arne, his mother acknowledged, one too many liberties and to curb his bad behaviour he was now in need of a no-nonsense system that would instil order and respect into his daily life.

As it had been for his father some twenty years earlier, any discomfiture Arne felt at first with the new rules that now governed the conduct of his life was overlooked as he engrossed himself in his nautical studies. In momentary lapses of concentration, he imagined himself in his beloved boat feeling its movement underfoot, listening to the continuous lapping and slapping of sea water against the hull, rolling and yawing with it as the tiny vessel fought to cut a path through the ocean waves and the constant tinkering required with the sails and rudder to keep it on course to his destination. Adhering to the current rules was no more than a means to an end; in time he would emerge as his own man and would meet the world on his terms and apply *his* standards.

Over the course of many months of diligent study and good behaviour, Arne made rapid progress in all subjects especially in engineering and mathematics. His mental agility with compound computations was exceptional especially those nautical problems he was asked to solve of how to get from A to B involving the range of complex and opposing forces of wind speed, tidal flows, directions of currents and water displacement. He became the star pupil of his year and earned an unwanted notoriety that brought him the unwelcomed attention of some of the local supporters of the prevailing extremist political party.

It was nineteen-thirty-nine and thugs and yobs roamed the streets looking to cause trouble. Dressed in quasi-military uniform and fired up by political rhetoric they acted indiscriminately against various sects of society including foreigners. Despite his fluent German spoken with the slight burr of the region, his straight blond hair, his clean-cut Aryan features, and his German-born mother, he became increasingly under the spotlight of these bully boys who would stop him and demand why he was in civilian clothes. Jostled and barracked once too often, Arne finally took the only course available, and with the words of his mother so often written in her letters to him ringing in his ears, fled before it was too late. And if he ever again saw the little shit in his class who was one of them then that little shit would be dead before he knew it.

* * *

He stood motionless at the open door, silhouetted against the mid-afternoon sun.

'Home at last,' said Frieda in a light tone, only the quivering of her voice betraying the deep anxiety she had been feeling for her son's wellbeing.

'Yes, Mutti,' agreed Arne, 'home at last.'

They stood stock-still for some time looking intently at one another. It wasn't the rapturous greeting between mother and son after a long interval apart that many a parent and child would have expected and cherished. Not normally demonstrative by nature, on this occasion Frieda would have wished to have run directly to him and held him tightly in her arms before kissing him several times. Instead, under instructions from Pieter, she said, 'come and sit down, Arne, you look tired. Are you hungry?'

'Yes, Mutti,' he replied, 'I haven't eaten for two days.'

'Then tell me all about how you got here whilst I cook you a hot meal.' She opened the larder door and selected vegetables and potatoes from a shelf. 'You know you're very bad, Arne, not replying to my letters and causing me to worry endlessly about your safety. It has made your father angry,' she added simply.

'I'm sorry, Mutti,' he said awkwardly, his shoulders twitching up and down to indicate some form of regret or bafflement. 'I just didn't get around to it.'

'You're very bad, Arne,' she repeated, 'but I love you.' Finally, she went and stood behind his chair and enveloped her arms in his whilst she kissed him softly on

10

the cheek. It was true. She did love him even though he caused her pain.

As the story unfolded, Frieda became increasingly wrapped up in his escape, for that was what he felt it was. He said he'd been lucky on two counts: he'd been out of the classroom when three officials in military uniform barged in looking for the Dutch student named Visser as they had an order to detain him for questioning.

'And the second count?' asked Frieda, almost forgetting the stew pot on the range.

'One of the students in my class would have given me away and told them that I was on the ground floor collecting some stationary. He is a rat,' said Arne with obvious distaste, 'but by good fortune he was away training that day with some of his Nazi scumbags.'

'So, nobody gave you away,' said Frieda with relief.

'I suppose not,' agreed Arne, 'otherwise I probably wouldn't be here today.' He jerked his head in the direction of the stove where escaping steam was lifting the lid off the pot, and Frieda turned hurriedly to attend to his meal.

When he continued, his hunger eventually satisfied, Frieda learnt of his dash to Bremen railway station and his subsequent theft of a bicycle when he realised that passengers were required to show their identity papers before boarding the train. The bicycle, left leaning against an outer stone wall of the region's main station, looked old and rusty and proved to have a saddle that creaked and groaned with every turn of the pedals, but it allowed Arne to quickly flee the busy town centre via backstreets and alleyways to emerge into the surrounding countryside, mostly rural in nature. Heading west as far as he could

11

judge, a farmer driving in the same direction and without a load offered Arne a lift. He hoisted the bike onto the open flatbed of the lorry and got into the cab. The farmer was friendly and chatted away amiably as they covered many kilometres together along narrow, winding roads. He already knew better than to pry, so when Arne spotted some railway tracks in the distance and said he would take his leave, the farmer, who had never enquired where he was from or where he was going, just waved a cheery goodbye.

It was by a combination of omnibus travel and short train hops from small stations along the line, most of them no more than halts, where the officialdom of the cities and large towns had not yet permeated, that Arne was able to zigzag towards the border where he crossed by foot over fields of planted corn. Once in Holland, he was able to openly beg lifts across the remaining hundred plus kilometres to his home in Harlingen. He feared his lack of money would be an issue but the region was already in turmoil at the prospect of invasion by its aggressive neighbour despite its avowed position of neutrality such that nobody seemed to mind his inability to pay his way.

Frieda shook her head. A large tear escaped over a lower eyelid which she quickly staunched with a corner of her apron.

'I'm glad you're back,' she said, composing herself. 'Your sisters will be pleased to see you.'

'When will they be home?' enquired Arne.

'Evening time,' his mother responded, 'depending on whether they have balanced the books and finished their work.' Frieda was very proud of her girls. They had left the family business to make their own ways in life. At nineteen and eighteen respectively, they had taken up trainee positions in the bookkeeping department of an expanding manufacturing company in Leeuwarden. Mondays to Thursdays they shared a bedsit provided by the company, and travelled home every Friday evening to spend the weekend with their parents. According to their mother, they were good girls who would make much of their lives. It was Friday and they would arrive home soon.

'And Father?' continued Arne, 'will he be back soon?'

'I really don't know,' Frieda said flatly, 'these are worrying times and your father often stays late at the boatyard talking with his men and various friends about what will happen if we are invaded. He fears for our future.' She looked fearful of the future too. She had already detected some change of attitude towards her by local shopkeepers. She now spoke Dutch fluently but with an accent that betrayed her origins. A small change of attitude now might very well develop into open hostility if the worst happened.

'An invasion wouldn't be easy for you, Mutti,' said Arne, stating the obvious.

'We are neutral,' countered his mother without conviction.

'You are neutral by marriage,' agreed Arne, before adding insensitively, 'but not by birth.'

'Life is never easy,' replied Frieda eventually. Her son's words had upset her, but she knew he was right. She removed the empty plate and cutlery; keeping busy with mundane chores was a form of therapy from her anxieties.

As much as was possible in that uncertain period, when the continent was holding its breath while waiting to see what the Germans would do next, Arne settled into helping his father in the boatyard. It was déjà vu for all the hours they had spent together in peaceful times building boats or out on the water running with the wind with the salty spray on their cheeks. The deep respect they felt for one another transcended Arne's waywardness at other times. It was just two men enjoying each other's company.

Few of Pieter's friends had faith that the Dutch army would have the strength or the determination to resist the Wehrmacht, but they believed that any occupation of their country would be relatively benign; their homeland was, after all, neutral. Arne listened intently as night after night they discussed and debated the impending crisis. All had tales to tell about the Great War and how the Dutch diplomats had skilfully negotiated terms with the Axis countries to avert occupation. Isolated as they were for the duration, a buffer between two feuding aggressors, the Dutch learned the art of keeping their heads down and minding their own business. But Pieter was less sanguine about the present position. He felt that this time diplomacy would be swept aside by a wave of unstoppable violence and as the weeks passed and the political scene appeared to be coming to a hiatus there was serious talk amongst the men about escape. When Poland was invaded the writing was truly on the wall. Thoughts became concentrated on survival; which was better: stay or flee?

'Living under the rules of an invading army might

be terrible,' stated Pieter forcefully when challenged by his son, 'but I just can't up-sticks and flee. You must understand that, Arne.'

'I don't see why not,' retorted Arne. 'If they are likely to subjugate and ill-treat our fellow countrymen as some people predict, then leaving might be our best option.'

'You are young, Arne,' said Pieter. He looked sad and wistful. 'Sometimes I wonder where the years have gone. How did I move from youth to middle age without recognising that fact, to find myself head of a family of five, with responsibilities for their care. To house them and feed them and protect them as best I can.' He fell silent, deep in his thoughts. 'You see I love them all,' he said finally, 'and I can't just rip them from the lives they know and lead them into an uncertain future.'

On the tenth of May nineteen-forty, despite their neutrality, the Germans invaded the Low Countries. It was, if the respective populations were brutally frank, just what they feared. That evening, Pieter returned home alone.

'Where is Arne?' demanded Frieda, in a strangled, high-pitch voice. She was sitting at the kitchen table flanked by her daughters. It was clear that she was agitated. The girls looked expectantly at their father who appeared calm but resigned.

'He's gone,' replied Pieter. No other words came to his thin lips.

'Gone. What do you mean?' asked Frieda hysterically.

'Deep in your heart, Frieda,' replied Pieter softly, holding her hands tenderly, 'you know where he's gone.'

'To his boat?' asked Frieda, with a begging look at her husband to tell her she was wrong.

'To his boat,' Pieter confirmed, as the three women most precious to him in life began to cry. 'He has a good chance to survive the crossing. He is an exceptional sailor. I would have done the same myself if I was his age. We must pray for his safe passage.'

Chapter 2

YOUNG ARNE

Throughout the long and arduous journey home from Bremen, Arne's mind had been focussed entirely on one thing: escape across the North Sea to England. It was a plan initially hatched as an amusement; incorporating lots of derring-do. It acted as a diversion from the stuffy lifestyle he was forced to lead in Bremen. It was only as the political situation worsened that his plan, cavalier as it was in its strategy and short as it was in its detail, became his top priority. But its essence was flawless.

Arne reminded himself that his studies had included the solving of endless theoretical problems of navigation from point A to point B and farther. That point A had invariably been Germany's only sea border along the North Sea from where the bulk of the country's commercial shipping and much of its coastal leisure sailing had to begin, was a fortuitous coincidence because the only directions from there were either north towards the Arctic or south around the Dutch coastline into the southern North Sea in the exact direction in which Arne needed to sail. And the details of the tides, currents, winds, shelves, and sandbars to be negotiated across this stretch of water to the East Anglian coast were still fresh in Arne's memory. Arne could only pinch himself at the good fortune as that knowledge could prove a life-saver.

According to rumours, the Wadden Sea and the string of Frisian Islands protecting the flat, easily eroded Dutch mainland coast from the fierce effects of the North Sea, was unguarded by enemy patrols. The Dutch coastguard had kept vigil over the body of water giving credence to the gossip by allowing as much of the normal ferry boat activity to continue between the mainland and the respective islands as possible. In fact, this body of sea water became a hive of activity as it was probed and tested by young men with equally audacious plans to those of Arne. It was a period when life appeared to be stuck in limbo while waiting for a clearer picture of the future to emerge.

Intent on escape, small groups of twos and threes – mostly daredevils but also those who had a particular reason to fear the Germans – began to form. With their eyes steadfastly on those with the means to do so: a boat, Arne was approached by several former school friends wishing to make a bolt for freedom. They would join an army, they had said, and in due course fight to free their own country. But when pressed for a quick answer to join him on the crossing, Arne stonewalled. Such decisions, Arne told them, required careful consideration. It was a brush off that didn't go down well and a decision that would haunt him in the future. Lying in his bed each night, holding off the desire to sleep, he would go through his plan step-by-step. Had he forgotten anything? Could he improve it? How many days were left before the anticipated invasion? What was certain, he was not going to discuss his plans with anyone, not even with his family. He needed a spring tide when the flow into the Wadden Sea between the string of outlying islands would be at it maximum. It would rush in between the islands with force and energy, and he must be there, present, waiting calmly in the lee of his chosen island to catch its ebbing flow which would hurtle him out into the North Sea with great speed giving him the power to navigate across the stream of Atlantic water which flowed in a northernly direction into the English Channel, hugging the continental shelf on its course to discharge its volume in Arctic regions. Without that extra boost he would more than likely be carried or blown off course, to end at an unknown destination half-alive or dead.

The next spring tidal cycle was six days away and he had no other option than to wait impatiently for it. Arne had decided to sail through the channel between the islands of Texel and Vlieland passing as closely to the sparsely populated westernmost point of Vlieland as he dared. From Harlingen harbour he would first set a course for the small, uninhabited island of Griend some eleven kilometres away; passing it on his port side to allow him to swing south in an extended arc so that he could sail the entire length of Vlieland – some twelve kilometres – in its shadow away from prying eyes by hugging the sandy shoreline of its long, finger-shaped profile until he reached its southernmost tip. The island's lighthouse, in constant use for almost a century, posed no threat to expose his presence as it had been ordered by the Dutch authorities to extinguish its two-seconds-on-two-seconds-off signature light that had kept mariners safe from the sandbars that were dotted around the island. Arne knew them well and even in low light conditions he could move his vessel adroitly to miss them. From that point onwards, when he selected the most beneficial moment to round the sandy headland on the ebbing spring tide to traverse the Atlantic flow, his passage across the North Sea would be dependent not just on the forces of nature or on his sailing prowess, but also on factors beyond his knowledge and beyond his control. No boat from Harlingen had ventured beyond the string of Frisian Islands for months on the advice of the Dutch government, and therefore there was no tittle-tattle to relay to those with ambitions to run away about patrolling German vessels, or indeed about what the Royal Navy were doing. Planning an escape, Arne thought wistfully, would have been so much easier at the beginning of the phoney war when little seemed to be happening on the western front and the dividing waters between the continent and The British Isles were probably under minimum observation, but as every would-be escaper knew, to have attempted a crossing in a small sailboat during the winter months when the North Sea was at its most ferocious, would have been tantamount to suicide.

On the tenth of May the Germans invaded, just three days before the spring tide was due. Like every other Dutch inhabitant, Arne cursed. But his curses were not for his country alone, they were mostly for himself, and for his planned departure which was unlikely to be as discreet or as straightforward as he would have wished. The unbearable wait would be for a further three full days plus another twelve hours for the tidal cycle to reach its ebbing stage.

There was no reliable information about the state of the fighting. Dutch resistance, with the sort of token army that only neutral countries boast, lasted little more than three days before their government surrendered. The radio broadcast to its citizens, on radios that were quickly hidden or stored away for the duration in safe places, implored its inhabitants to cease fighting and to stay calm. By the beginning of the third day, enemy motorcycle outriders and foot soldiers were already infiltrating the main towns. Rumour had it that they would soon be in Harlingen. It was, Arne realised, a now-or-never moment.

Despite the dangers, the act of fleeing into an unknown future marked the start of a great adventure for a young man of seventeen, although strangely, the actual moment of decision was marked with a sense of deep loss. Family and homeland ties, engrained in the psyche for so long, could not be swept away as if they had never had a place in his world. In some form or other they would accompany him throughout life whether wanted or not. But now there was no time to be lost on contemplation and no room for sorrows to down his spirit. With a total single-mindedness Arne took the first step of his plan by making his way in an orderly fashion to his boat which he had prepared as best he could for a journey of several days. There could be no goodbyes, and accordingly there were none. In preparation, he had moved his boat a short distance from the family boatyard to a position along the dike where it was partially obscured by a slight bend in its course. If spotted and stopped by some military authority and charged with illegal activity, he hoped that this small manoeuvre might prevent him from being linked with the boatyard as he was concerned not to jeopardise their safety.

For a local, any thoughts of Arne's boat not being instantly associated with The Visser Boat Company of Harlingen were laughable. Arne's boat itself had metamorphosed from the company's first prototype small yacht into the desirable and affordable vessel that the new middle classes could sail with basic skills on inland waters and venture tentatively offshore when more experienced in the knowledge that their boat was both robust and seaworthy. At just twenty-three feet long, it represented a new breed of small vessel that offered the fun of dinghy sailing coupled with the advantage of being able to do a short overnight trip to a chosen destination. Built mainly from teak and ash, the sleek and ergonomic design of the sloop was devoid of any non-functional parts or unnecessary adornments. Classic in its simplicity, it was the forerunner of cabin design in a limited space; the space-wasting companionways of larger vessels being replaced by just a doorway through the main bulkhead. Inside the cabin, use was made of every cubic inch of its cramped area although it fooled the eye by giving the impression of being bigger than it truly was. The bunk on either side ran the full length of the cabin and was built over a good-sized locker. A small, detachable table was stored in the portside locker together with various sea charts and two life jackets. A grappling anchor, an emergency tiller, various coils of rope and a spare headsail were stowed in the locker opposite. The cabin had no pretensions of grandeur but it would be a welcome place to hunker down when the weather changed unexpectedly.

In his original design, Pieter had retained the standard Bermuda fore-and-aft sail rig as it had been tried and tested in sailing boats in all climatic conditions over hundreds of years. By permitting the boat to sail close to the wind, the lift gained could be used to move forward thereby increasing its manoeuvrability in all conditions. Arne felt apprehensive as he approached the boat, but tried to banish any negative thoughts by imagining lowering himself into the small cockpit, releasing the sheets and pushing off from his mooring. He would have liked to have brought some warm clothing and food with him but all he dared to bring was a jerry can part-full of drinking water. He would stow it in a locker immediately he was onboard; it was very precious.

Just a few paces short of his boat, Arne stopped dead. Something was wrong. He sensed it more than saw it. Was the door to the cabin closed properly? Was the vessel sitting deeper in the water than usual? Was he imagining something that didn't exist? As he put a foot on the gunwale, he heard a soft but urgent call for help from within the cabin. Arne felt unnerved; his adventure was only just starting and already it had taken an unexpected twist. He approached the cabin door and the urgent whisper came again.

'The door's stuck,' said the person inside. 'I can't shift it. Get me out of here.'

'Who are you?' hissed Arne, knowing full well it was Jens Leesen, the son of the owner of Harlingen's chandlery.

'Jens. I'm Jens and hurry up,' the boy replied.

'What are you doing on my boat?' asked Arne indignantly, almost forgetting to keep his voice down. But no answer came until Arne repeated the question more forcefully.

'I know you're escaping and I want to go with you.' Jens was whining and Arne had no other option than to help open the door.

'You sodding fool,' snapped Arne when he assessed the situation, 'you've damaged the door mechanism by forcing it. Get off my boat immediately, you useless bugger.'

'I won't,' retorted Jens. He was no longer snivelling. He was now in demanding mode. 'I'm going with you.'

'Oh, no you're not.'

'I have to.'

'Why?' was all Arne could think of in response.

'Because I'm Jewish.' Arne was stunned. A long pause followed the would-be stowaway's announcement before Arne joined him in the cabin and closed the door behind him as best he could.

'I've no more time to waste,' said Arne, now galvanised by the urgency of his departure. 'I don't know your story, but you've got until the Isle of Griend to make it credible to me that your escape from Nazi-held territory is vital. Otherwise, I'm dumping you there.' It was brutal, but it was honest. Within seconds Arne was hoisting and trimming the sails as the boat made an assured and speedy passage out of the harbour and into the Wadden Sea.

It would be near midnight by the time they approached the island. The sky had already lost all its light but Arne would have no difficulty in navigating around its rocky contours as he knew its bleak topography by heart. At a speed of around five knots, it would take them little over an hour to cover the six nautical miles there.

'You've got about an hour or so to tell me why I shouldn't dump you on one of the islands,' said Arne peering at the anxious-looking face of Jens. 'Keep your voice down as noise travels freely over a calm sea.' Jens was anxious because that was true, but he was also indignant at the way in which a former school classmate was giving him orders. His father, the chandler, was as equally prominent and well-respected a figure in Harlingen as Arne's. But where Arne was forthright, Jens was pragmatic and he knew there was no sense in falling out with him.

'Well,' started Jens, 'my family is of the Jewish faith although we are non-practising.'

'So, you're not really Jewish after all,' interrupted Arne.

'It's not that simple,' continued Jens in a steady voice, 'if only it was.'

'Go on,' said Arne a little more thoughtfully. He had to remind himself that it was only a matter of weeks since he had fled Germany in fear of his life. He should hear Jens out. 'Go on,' urged Arne again, 'I want to hear your story.'

Time sped as the story unfolded; a relatively simple story of a religious stumbling block. Jens parents had split away from his father's wider family when he married a young woman from a Christian background. It wasn't a marriage supported by either of their families, and his young parents had felt obliged to move far away where they could start life free of religious constraints. They considered The New World but settled instead for the north Dutch coast. In a happy homelife, neither Jens nor his younger sibling practised any real form of religion although his father and mother separately recognised and respected the special days in their own faith's calendar.

According to Jens, religion had not been an issue for his family until right-wing politics in Germany had swept aside any remaining libertarian views and had led to the spectre of invasion. It was then, Jens had recounted, that attitudes began changing. And his story chimed with Arne as his own mother, Frieda, who had lived in harmony with the Dutch population in Harlingen for almost two decades, had also complained of a change in relationship with her acquaintances. Arne had scratched his head and rubbed his chin and there had been a long lull in conversation while both contemplated the other's circumstances. Eventually, Jens had broken the silence by explaining that some gentiles, to protect themselves, might not overlook his father's facial characteristics. It was food for serious thought on which Arne might have dwelt and chewed over for some considerable time had not an unexpected noise arisen from deep inside the cabin. It sounded like a cough. Arne was quick to react by pushing Jens aside from the cabin entrance. A small figure was huddled on the wooden floor, and even in the darkness he could make out the face of a young girl.

'Who's this?' shouted Arne, forgetting to keep his voice down. He was shaking with rage.

'It's my sister,' said Jens meekly. 'I couldn't leave her behind.'

'Who?' Arne shouted again, incredulous.

'My father told me that I should escape with her as our future in Holland is uncertain. If I could find a way to go then I should go immediately and I should take Annaliese with me.'

Just in time, with a yank on the tiller, Arne saved his boat from a rocky outcrop. He had been distracted at a critical moment in the boat's passage around the northern aspect of Griend. 'I should throw you both overboard right now,' spat Arne. 'You distracted me. You risked my future too.' Jens did not reply; he was busy cuddling his young sister who looked very scared. 'I can't take you both on the crossing and if I don't concentrate right now on navigating around Griend and along Vlieland's coastline, then either we'll be spotted by the authorities or we'll run aground. And that could be the end of all three of us.'

Another hour passed before Arne spoke again. Navigating in the gloom had taken all his resolve. He had brought the boat safely to a position short of the island's southern tip and dropped anchor into the sandy seabed. The southern extent of the island was usually uninhabited and they appeared unobserved. It would be daylight soon but they had no choice other than to wait patiently four more hours before he could position the boat to catch the ebbing spring tide.

Annaliese was nine years old. He had never met her before but recalled Jens talking about her at school. His kid sister. Arne now knew why the boat appeared to be sitting slightly deeper in the water than usual when he approached it along the dike at Harlingen. There were two bodies onboard, not heavy, but sufficient to weigh it down. It had been a recurring question at the back of his mind and now he had the answer. But the question of what to do next remained unanswered. To try to cross the southern North Sea as an experienced single-handed sailor, being responsible only for himself was one thing, but to try with two passengers who had no experience out on the water would surely be disastrous. He would have to make a cruel decision. It would be for all their sakes, he told himself. They would have to take their chances with the Germans and he would have to take his chance with the cruel North Sea. Arne looked at his watch. He judged that the tide would start to ebb in forty minutes, and it would take roughly fifteen minutes to sail around the headland from their current protected position. He must have the boat ready at exactly the right time to take advantage of the tidal surge out into the North Sea otherwise all chance was lost.

It would be the last time, Arne vowed, that he would ever let himself feel guilty about putting his own needs before those of others. When he told them his decision, they had begged him to take them with him. He had explained again and again just how hopeless for them all such a situation would be. But they knew little about the sea and its dangers; they just wanted to evade the Germans and could not understand why he was refusing to take them. They would not be persuaded.

Arne took the boat in as close to the shore as he dared. The sea temperature in May would be chilly but not cold and he gauged the water would come up to Jens's armpits when he pushed him in. He was taller and stronger than Jens and the scuffle was not prolonged. He then gently handed down Annaliese to her brother and stayed until both had waded ashore onto the sandy beach. With instructions to head inland while maintaining visual contact with the sea, he estimated that, despite being on the part of the island that was mostly uninhabited, they would soon find an islander who would give them food and dry clothing. He didn't look back to see the misery etched on their faces as he prepared to sail away, and they wouldn't have seen the tears that flowed freely down his cheeks at the shame he felt for leaving them.

Arne's boat, The Frieda, was hurled forward with a force that had Arne straining to control its dead ahead course. With one hand on the tiller whilst the other fought to hold the sail lines, his passage across the current was both physically and mentally traumatic. It was at a point when, for the first time in his sailing life he doubted his ability to survive, that he remembered some wise words of his father. From a very young age, Pieter had always impressed on him the need to steer the boat using its sails not its rudder. He released the tiller and with a hand on each line, he was able to trim and maintain the sails so that the boat was no longer fighting the elements. She was using them to her greater advantage, and if she was heading somewhat off course then so be it.

It was not until he found the calmer water beyond the Atlantic flow that his confidence returned. Whilst so fully engaged with its traverse and his own survival, not for a single moment had he given any thought to patrol boats or enemy aircraft. It was broad daylight with a cloudless sky. He could be seen for miles from the sky, although from the sea his lowly presence would be harder to spot. The wind dropped and The Frieda stalled. Aircraft flitted about in the sky but without any obvious intention. Arne was hungry and tired. He was also downhearted; he had left his homeland and family. He released his grip on the lines, curled up in the cockpit and fell asleep.

He was awoken by the noise of flapping sails; the wind had got up and the head sail was loose. The Frieda was running hard and it took Arne some minutes to get her under control. The sky had clouded over and there was now no sight of the sun. His watch indicated five in the afternoon; he had been asleep for more than four hours. There would still be daylight for a further four hours, he judged, at this time of year but navigation by the stars would be impossible unless the sky cleared. Rain started to fall, slowly at first and then more persistently and the previously balmy day turned colder. Arne shivered. He had no way of knowing how many nautical miles he had covered and only a rough idea of his course. His previously renewed optimism drained away as he contemplated what to do next.

It was only next morning at first light that he decided to steer against the current. Worried that he had allowed himself to be pushed too far north on a course heading ever more into the vast expanse of the North Sea, he held The Frieda as tightly as he could on what he hoped was a westerly direction. But the day ahead was cloudy with only an occasional glimpse of the sun, and he could do no more than hope that he was steering in the correct direction. Fatigue had set in by the time his watch indicated noon. He had had nothing to eat or drink apart from the water he had brought onboard – which he had shared with Jens and Annaliese – and which had now run dry. The struggle to stay awake was overwhelming and in a moment of clear thought he decided to drop the sails, deploy the anchor and climb into a bunk. Within seconds he was in a state of deep slumber, totally unaware of his good fortune that the anchor had lodged in sand on the top of one of the sandbars lying in a crescent off the Norfolk coast. In the relatively calm conditions, coastguards on shore watched the bobbing but stationary boat. A state of war existed and putting out to sea in any circumstance required permission. Another night passed before a naval vessel headed out to see if there was friendly life onboard.

The coastal vessel approached the Ower sandbar with circumspection. Even at the highest point of the sandbar there would be sufficient fathoms of water below its hull to get in close for a detailed inspection. There was no sign of life on The Frieda. An "ahoy" was shouted through a megaphone but drew no response. An officer with a loaded pistol stood on deck as a seaman hauled himself onto The Frieda as both boats came close together for an instant. From the deck, Arne was just visible sprawled out inside the cabin. With due precaution, the seaman nudged Arne's legs rousing him into a sitting position to look uncertainly at the man standing before him in naval uniform. He looked disorientated. His thin lips were cracked and appeared stuck together. He tried to speak but was unable to do so. The sailor smiled and the moment of high tension passed. A line was attached to The Frieda and the coastal vessel headed back to the safety of its home port with Arne in tow. It would be the job of the intelligence boffins on shore, the officer announced, to determine whether the young man in The Frieda was a spy. Until then, all they had to do, he said, was to give him some water and keep him alive.

With his high-powered binoculars trained on the boat being towed into the harbour of Wells-next-the-Sea, retired Rear Admiral Drew watched the docking proceedings carefully. He was standing in his garden on the only relatively high point along Norfolk's northern coast. He had the time to observe the rigmarole on the dock unfold. A blanket was slung over the shoulders of a young man as he was helped by a sailor to the harbour master's office. He was under guard by the officer who still had a drawn pistol.

The young man, the former rear admiral noted, although looking worse for wear, appeared not much older than his youngest son, Alistair. And there was something familiar about the boat in which he was towed into the safe harbour. It was small but had a certain style with crisp lines and sat squarely in the water. It would probably be fun to sail, he thought. It was, as he turned his attention back to his garden to clearing the red valerian which had unwantedly self-seeded into another flowerbed, that something struck him. He hurried into the house and sat down at his desk in the library. It was *his* room and he had it arranged just as he liked despite his wife's protestations at the increasing number of files and stacks of old newspapers that he kept. Certain areas of the room were off limits to the cleaner and Alistair – now the only one of their four children still at home – was banned altogether. From a stack of various yachting magazines that he had been reading and collecting from the early nineteen-thirties onwards, he sorted out all the editions covering launches into the leisure sailing market of new boat designs, and it was not long before he came across the edition he was seeking. The new boat, pictured splendidly on the front cover in colour, was apparently designed and built by master craftsmen in The Netherlands by The Visser Boat Company of Harlingen. The retired rear admiral felt sure that the boat he had seen being towed into harbour no more than fifteen minutes ago was identical to the one shown in all its glory in the magazine that he was holding in his hand.

Within minutes he was striding out on his way to the harbour master's hut as he felt sure that the information he had might prove useful in identifying the young man who appeared to have been rescued.

'Morning, Bernard,' called out the rear admiral distinctly as he approached the police officer standing on guard outside the hut.

'Good morning, Sir,' replied the constable. Even though the rear admiral was now a retired naval officer all the locals still called him "Sir." 'I'm sorry, Sir, but I can't let you in. I've got my orders.'

'Understandable, Bernard. Got to wait for the correct authorities to arrive, I suppose.'

'Yes, Sir,' replied Bernard, relieved that the rear admiral had accepted his tricky position. They had known one another a long time and played regularly in the same darts team at The Crown & Anchor, and Bernard didn't want to do or say anything that might harm that relationship.

'I think the young man you're detaining is Dutch,' said the rear admiral, flourishing his magazine. 'That yacht he came in on is made in Harlingen by the Visser family, and I'm guessing that he either works for that family or is a son of the owner, Pieter Visser.'

'I don't think the lad speaks English,' ventured Bernard after a lengthy pause whilst he carefully considered what he was allowed to say. He didn't wish to step on any higher authority toes.

'You could give this to the harbour master,' suggested the rear admiral, thrusting the magazine at Bernard. 'It might defuse the situation inside whilst waiting for a translator to arrive.' Bernard looked dubious. 'If the boy recognises the photograph of what I believe is his yacht on the magazine's cover,' continued the rear admiral, 'then you will know that he is Dutch and unlikely to be a German spy.'

'Might prove helpful,' agreed Bernard after another lengthy pause. 'I suppose I could.' He turned slowly to face the hut and knocked twice on its stout wooden door. The harbour master appeared, quiet words were exchanged, and the magazine accepted and taken inside.

The rear admiral strolled along the eastern harbour wall in the hope of a closer inspection of Arne's yacht, but the boat, like its human occupant, was under guard. Wartime regulations were new and rather exciting to the local population and there was a willingness and desire to fulfil them no matter the circumstance. However, despite orders, the young naval rating who had hauled himself onto Arne's boat was soon chatting readily to the rear admiral about the vessel they had brought in. It was, in his words "a cracking sloop" and indeed, from only a few yards away, the rear admiral too could admire the woodworking skills of the builder. There was no doubt about it, it was a stunner. But when asked from where out in the North Sea the boat and passenger were escorted in, the naval rating clammed up.

He thought that would be an end to his little bit of snooping but as the rear admiral passed the harbour master's office on his way home, he was spotted through a window by Clive, the harbour master, who came out and thanked him for his prescience. Apparently, the lad, better for his cup of tea and a sandwich made and delivered by Clive's wife, became very animated when he saw the magazine. And when Clive got out a sea chart of the southern North Sea, Arne's finger quickly pointed to Harlingen. In response, Clive had pointed to Wells-next-the-Sea and Arne had grinned like a Cheshire cat. He didn't speak English except for the odd word or two but as soon as a Dutch translator arrived, Clive believed they would learn the full story. His name, Arne Visser, and that he was the son of Pieter Visser who owned The Visser Boat Company of Harlingen was all that they knew reliably for the moment, and that it seemed unlikely that he was a German spy. He would be locked up in the hut overnight until the authorities told the harbour master what to do with him. Bernard, thought the rear admiral as he climbed up the only gently rising hill for miles around to his house, would have a long and rather warm evening and night to stand guard on Arne's overnight prison.

In the end, it was a Dutchman who had been living and working on The Broads for many years who was first to arrive as an unofficial interpreter. A tired and stiff Bernard had overseen his entry into the hut shortly after Clive's wife had delivered an early lunch with a bottle of beer to wash it down. Clive himself, had taken over responsibility for Arne when the naval officer and rating had been given more important things to do. As the story emerged of Arne's escape across the water in his own boat – waiting in the lee of Vlieland Island to catch the right tide to sail across the Atlantic flow, sailing close to the wind to maintain his course, crossing his fingers not to encounter any German patrol boats, and finally flinging out his anchor in desperation to maintain his position rather than in hope – the tension in the hut eased. There had been no mention in his story about any unscheduled passengers in his boat. Arne had erased them from his memory bank; what was done was done, and as he had earlier promised himself, no sleep would be lost over its morality.

The home in which the Drews lived in some comfort was not a typical seaside-style of house. It was not Art-Deco like some posh houses along the Kent and Sussex coasts, nor was it in the style of Arts and Crafts buildings to be found frequently nestling into the landscape high above coves along the Cornish coastline. It was not even like other simple but functional dwellings, bungalows in particular, which purposely kept a low profile to withstand the severe onshore winds along the long East Anglian shore. Their home was a solid and spacious Victorian stone edifice with a huge bay window overlooking the sea. Thomas Drew had purchased it on promotion to a pay scale that after feeding, clothing, and housing a wife and three children, still left sufficient over to pay the monthly mortgage. He was originally from that part of the world, and although away at sea most of his working life, he had designs on enjoying his retirement in an area he loved. Traditional to their fingertips, husband and wife took afternoon tea sitting across a small table in the bay window in quiet contemplation of the magnificent view. Their three eldest boys had long since flow the nest to various parts of the world. It was only Alistair, their fourth who was born late in life, who was nominally at home, except during term time when he was away at boarding school. He was home now as the recent war regulations regarding schooling decreed. When his father, forty-nine years older than his thirteen-year-old son, recounted the excitement on the quay that day, Alistair was all agog to know every detail. For his father, it was mostly the boat that held his interest, but for his son it was the person who had propelled it to a British shore.

'Tell me about him,' demanded Alistair when he arrived home from his new local school.

'*Please*. Tell me about him, please,' said his mother, reminding her son of the polite behaviour she and her husband valued.

'Tell me about him, please,' repeated Alistair. 'I'm dying to know.'

'He's Dutch, he's young, he's probably about seventeen, he's fair-haired, he's the son of a boat designer, and that's about all I know at present.'

'He must be brave too,' said Alistair excitedly. 'What an adventure. Was he alone?'

'It appears so,' replied his father. 'He must be a good seaman to have crossed single-handed, even if he needed our help for the last leg. I can see from your face that he's already your hero.'

'Where is he now?' asked Alistair, the question tumbling out of his mouth at a rate of knots. 'I want to see him.'

'He's firmly under lock and key until the intelligence people have interviewed him,' replied his father. 'He's off limits to you.'

'What will happen if they can't come for a few days?' asked Mrs Drew sensibly. 'Clive and Bernard can't be expected to monitor him all the time.'

'Can he come here?' demanded Alistair, thrilled at the very prospect. His father did not reply. It was a rather good idea, he thought.

Accommodation in the rear admiral's spacious house had been approved by higher authorities on a "house arrest" basis, to which Arne had agreed. He was given the bedroom of the Drew's eldest son the door of which was lockable with a long, cylindrical key. It was without doubt comfortable, but it was the washing facilities which Arne valued most. In the bathroom mirror, his face looked thin and drawn. The wispy hairs that had started adorning his chin and cheeks over recent months now appeared fully fledged and a razor was required to bring about some semblance of neatness. The salty sea spray that had caked on his forearms into little white mounds and stringy lines required soaking in warm water to soften up before being washed away, and some old clothes were found whilst his own were laundered.

A French and German dictionary sat on a shelf of the packed bookcase in the rear admiral's study; but nothing to translate Dutch. Arne picked up the German dictionary and used the new word in his English vocabulary: "okay." The rear admiral put together some simple questions which Arne was able to answer with much flicking back and forth of the dictionary's delicate pages. When it was realised that Arne spoke fluent German and had been, until recently, at school in Bremen, the rear admiral telephoned the authorities in London who quickly cranked the wheels of the security service. A car arrived in Wells-next-the-Sea the following day bearing a senior intelligence officer and an official translator who set about an in-depth interview with Arne in private and which lasted several hours.

There was time for a drink with the rear admiral, a former colleague when both were on active service, before the intelligence bod departed with his driver for the capital. In true navy custom, several tots of rum were allowed to lubricate the mouths of the former friends as they relaxed. The alcohol had a marginal effect on loosening the officer's tongue too so that the rear admiral learnt that Arne had been able to describe in reasonable detail the layout of the naval dockyard at Bremerhaven, Germany's prime port. All accurate information, gleaned from no matter what source, was now a valuable commodity in wartime Britain, and Arne had done his bit to be helpful. The boy was not an enemy agent, of that the officer was sure. He was like at least a dozen others who had also risked their lives to escape the occupation of their homeland. He posed no threat to the nation's security and their only ongoing interest in him was his fluency in Dutch and German, skills which the officer warned would be needed at some point in the future, especially if Great Britain survived. For all intents and purposes Arne was free to do as he pleased. His options, of course, hinted the officer were limited without money, a job, a roof over his head and the English language to learn.

'That was a whizz-bang idea, Dad,' said Alistair gleefully when his father told him that Arne would be staying with them until he had learnt some basic English and got a job so he could provide for himself. "Dad" was a new terminology that the rear admiral would never have countenanced with his three older boys. He had been known as "Father" to them in an epoch when such vulgar epithets were considered common and not suitable for his strata of life. But war was changing many things and his wife had told him that he had to move with the times, although she had made it clear to Alistair that on no account could he call her "Mum." 'Who's going to teach him English?' Alistair enquired.

'I'm sure I can find a teacher at your new school to come here and give him some private lessons,' replied his father. 'He'll probably pick up the language quickly.'

'But what will he do for work?' questioned Alistair. 'And how will he buy food if he hasn't got any money?'

'Or, more importantly,' continued Thomas, 'how will he buy food without a ration book?'

The summer of nineteen forty brought superb weather with endless blue skies and blazing sunshine. While battles raged on land, sea and in the air, the north Norfolk area remained largely untouched by the vicissitudes of the period. The leisure boats, mostly used for sailing in and around The Wash, had been hauled out of the marina for the duration to make way for small naval coastal patrol craft. The usual summer holiday makers from the Midlands and the London conurbations were absent and the local farmers were having to make do with a greatly reduced workforce to tend the fields, but they were thankful that the reed cutters had completed their winter programme to keep the channels navigable. Despite the summer season, they already feared that manpower shortages on the home front created by a protracted war would, by the following summer, reduce The Broads to a nasty bog.

Arne's first paying job was helping the harbour master to comply with the navy's requirements for the maintenance of the erstwhile marina, now devoid of any signage of its presence. Clive spoke slowly and clearly to his new employee and pointed to the dictionary – on loan from the rear admiral's library – whenever he received a quizzical look from Arne. By high summer Arne's ability to speak English had improved remarkably. He was still something of a celebrity in the small town; news of his crossing of a dangerous sea having been spread throughout the small community over pints of beer drunk in the pub; his notoriety being embellished with every sip of warm beer drunk.

As he found his feet in the new environment so Arne's thoughts turned to the future. His focus had been purely on escape and he had given little thought as to what he would do when he achieved that end. It was obvious that there would be little call for his sailing expertise at such a time and although he had woodworking skills in boat building, it seemed unlikely that the time was right for that either. The harbour master treated him kindly but his job as Clive's assistant was menial and unchallenging. Also, it was his first taste of being told what to do and Arne didn't like it. To be his own boss, Arne decided, would be his goal but doing what, for the present, remained unresolved.

It was Alistair who inadvertently solved the problem one day about their immediate futures by talking about joining up. He was thirteen going on fourteen, but like most boys of a similar age, he was gung-ho to participate in repelling the enemy. His greatest fear was that the war would end before he was old enough to show his fighting credentials.

'You're lucky,' said Alistair naively. 'You're almost eighteen. They'd take you.'

'Lucky?' queried Arne. 'Maybe, but I'm not British.'

'Dad told me,' Alistair said, 'that all the countries that have been invaded are forming armies of their own countrymen who are living here in Britain. You could join the Free Dutch.'

'I could,' replied Arne, his lips beginning to form a smile when he realised that it would be a way out of his present dilemma. And if he could win medals and help liberate his family in Harlingen when the time came, then after the war it would be useful kudos for future ventures in the world of business. He was beginning to savour the taste of acclaim.

Since the order of Arne's confinement to barracks had been lifted, the two teenagers spent the long summer evenings together walking around town and in the permitted areas of the harbour. The little peacetime crafts had been unceremoniously moved to an area where they were made truly high and dry. They were objects of love to their owners who felt the need to check from time to time that they were still there, run a hand tenderly along their timbers, pat them, and talk to them as if they were a treasured pet, and assure them that, in the fullness of time, they would be out on the water again with the wind billowing in their sails.

Arne too loved his boat and felt proud of what he and Pieter had accomplished. His boat stood out from the rest. Musing, he wondered if he might one day sell boats to the rich and famous, or become the captain of a cruise liner, or sail around the world single-handed and win an enormous amount of money and prestige. Alistair called him over to come and have a look at a stray cat and her just-born litter that had set up home in a corner of Arne's cockpit. But against expectation, Arne appeared livid. He reached over the gunwale, grabbed the kittens and chucked them carelessly to the ground. The mother cat hissed and spat and tried to claw him but Arne just laughed.

'You didn't need to do that,' said Alistair, raising his voice slightly. 'They weren't doing any harm. They would have left on their own accord when the babies were stronger.' He bent down and gently picked up the offspring and found a place in another of the beached boats alongside where the mother and babies could safely continue to grow. 'You might have badly hurt the kittens by throwing them so roughly onto the ground.' It was a rebuke, but for Alistair it was also a chastening insight into a possible flaw in the character of his hero from Harlingen. And maybe it was a portent of what was to come.

Chapter 3

ALISTAIR & TED

1970

The alarm went off at six o'clock causing Alistair to stir. It wasn't normally set as he was usually awoken by Ted bounding up the stairs and jumping onto his bed, but this morning he had to leave home earlier than usual and couldn't rely on Ted's services as an alarm clock. Alistair's beautiful wife, Anna, was already up. She was an early bird by nature and although she loved Ted too, the first thing she wanted in the morning was a cup of coffee and not a weighty Airedale terrier pinning her to her bed. After all, he was Alistair's dog and he could take the pain of a misplaced paw in his personal area, not her.

Alistair was "big" in some form of engineering in Norwich. Anna wasn't quite sure what he did there or how important he was when he was there, but it required driving the round trip of seventy-four miles from Wells-next-the-Sea on several days of the working week. Sometimes he would take the train to London and be away from home for a couple of nights. Today he would catch the early morning train for a meeting convened by the Ministry of Transport. He had packed his usual overnight bag and would stay in the same modest hotel – all expenses paid – that was situated just yards from a tube station and which he had used on countless previous occasions.

In their early years of marriage, the couple had frequently debated the subject of moving home. Anna had on each occasion argued the case for a home nearer the capital and nearer for his daily office commute, but Alistair had stood firm and immoveable; he loved it where he was. The house in Wells had been his home virtually all his life and he hoped and prayed it would remain ever thus. Upon the death of his father, the rear admiral, and with the proceeds of his substantial inheritance and the agreement of his siblings who lived on far off shores and who had absolutely no interest in the property at Wells, he had purchased it when it went up for sale to obtain probate. The transition had been seamless and he felt sure his father would have approved. But he did allow Anna to bring some second half of the twentieth century modernity to the property with an interior redesign including bathrooms, kitchen, and decorations. It appeased his wife and by their tenth wedding anniversary she loved the house almost as much as him.

Ted wasn't actually Alistair's dog. They had wavered at the near insistence of their middle-born son who had claimed that the only thing he wanted in the whole wide world one Christmas was a puppy and that, of course, he would feed it, groom it, walk it, train it, and clear up after it. According to him, that was a "given" because if you loved your pet, you would do that willingly. Alastair was sceptical; he'd heard promises like that before. It was the grand guarantee that guaranteed nothing. But Anna felt they should do something special for their middle son as middle sons had a history of being overlooked, and so a puppy was chosen from a local breeder with a good reputation. On Boxing Day, the family picked up Ted from the kennels, their middle son cradling him in his arms all the way home as if he was a piece of fine China. At first the ten-year-old was true to his word and did all the things that he had promised he would, but as the weeks passed the fun of being a dog owner wore off leaving just the daily grind. When questioned by his parents about his lack of interest in Ted, the only response from the pre-pubescent child was a mumbled and unintelligible justification of his inaction and a request to be left alone.

'Ted likes *you*,' said Anna later that evening to her husband as he was sitting reading his newspaper.

'Ted likes everybody,' responded Alistair.

'Yes, I know,' continued Anna patiently, 'but he particularly likes you.'

'So?' asked Alistair, looking over the top of his broadsheet, 'what are you suggesting?'

'I'm suggesting, darling, that you become his master. Ted would love that.' Her husband said nothing. 'Really, Alistair,' continued Anna, exasperated that he could not see what was obvious. 'Ted only has eyes for you.'

'Isn't that a song title?' asked her husband attempting to hum the tune.

'You could take him to the office,' suggested Anna.

'You are the boss there and make the rules. He'd be no trouble. And I could look after him when you're away in London.' There were a few seconds of hesitation before Alistair agreed. He'd known it all along. There had been a bond between the two from the moment they'd clapped eyes on one another.

'You'd be two cool dudes hanging out with one another,' she said mimicking a cowboy accent. 'That one of you is a young puppy and the other is a father of three sometimes human teenagers would make no difference. You're made for one another.'

Summer evenings out walking with Ted along the harbour walls of the restored marina reminded Alistair of his youth. He had been a bit of a loner as both his parents were considerably older than him as were his three siblings. Away at boarding school half the year, he knew few boys of his own age in Wells with whom he could play and explore. When Arne arrived on the scene early in the war, it came as a welcomed surprise; he didn't want the war, but it was nice to have someone of a similar age – Arne was four years older than him – with whom to hang around with and generally get into mischief. Alistair stopped abruptly and so did Ted, who looked up at his master as if to question why the sudden halt, but Alistair was gazing intently out to sea totally unaware of the dog's presence.

The brief memory of Arne had hit him like a blow below the belt. Transient as it was, it had knocked him for six. Those few months with Arne had made a lasting impression on him. Normally mild-mannered and affable, helpful, and considerate, Alistair could feel his blood boil with anger as he thought of what Arne had done. It wasn't right then and it wasn't right now. He felt tarnished by their association as if he too had acted without propriety. Ted waited calmly while the black memory cloud passed over Alistair's head. Soon his master was striding out and chivvying Ted along as they made their way home.

Anna was out that evening with the three boys. She had taken them to the annual cricket match between Wells and Burnham held in the magnificent grounds of Holkham Hall. They had cycled there and were looking forward to the delicious picnic spread that was the hallmark of the long-established event. Available as soon as both teams had completed their innings, the youngsters gorged themselves on an array of tasty and filling snacks. Her boys were also looking forward to cycling home along the windy lanes with just their bike lamps to illuminate the route. She had told them sternly not to go too fast in the faint hope that they would heed her advice.

Alistair sat in an armchair in the bay window with Ted alongside him. He stared out at the panoramic view in the slowly fading light in much the same way as his parents had done some thirty years before while enjoying their ritual afternoon tea. He'd often had flashbacks of his life since those times but this evening's flashback had been different. It had been upsetting, but he couldn't pin down why. He felt his teeth on edge; he couldn't relax fully and Ted sensed his discomfort. He closed his eyes and was transported back three decades to the time when, with his father by his side, he had waved goodbye to

Arne at Norwich station. Arne was going to London to join up in the navy. There was a smirk on his face as he waved farewell from the open carriage window. He parted without a single word of gratitude for all the Drews had done to accommodate and feed him, the job the harbour master had given him, the help from the school teacher with learning English, and the general friendliness of the townsfolk towards his cause. It was, Alistair realised, an astonishing display of arrogance that he simply hadn't been old enough to recognise at the time.

Soon narrow shafts of wavering light from the bikes appeared in his peripheral view as their riders made their way up the drive. A noisy entry into the house quickly brought Alistair back from his reverie, but he knew it was a subject that he would revisit before long.

Anna deliberately cuddled up in bed with her husband that night as she had sensed his melancholia. Ted had been by his side until she closed the bedroom door and shooed him downstairs to his own sleeping quarters. Alistair wasn't normally affected by low morale; he usually kept an even keel through both calm and choppy waters. But tonight, he was in reflective mood and needed some extra tender loving care.

'Penny for your thoughts,' she whispered into his ear. He didn't reply but she felt him shrug. 'You seem down in the dumps,' she continued. 'Can I help?'

'Just a low moment,' Alistair admitted eventually. 'I'm fine now.'

'I don't think so, darling. Want to tell me about it?'

'Not really. Nothing much to say.'

'What caused your low moment?' persisted his wife. 'Trouble at work?'

'No. No, nothing like that. Nothing for you to worry about. Go to sleep.'

'Neither of us will fall asleep until you've got whatever it is off your chest.' She sat up, switched on the bedside light, plumped up her pillow, crossed her arms over her chest and waited for Alistair to come to his senses. 'I'm waiting,' she warned him. He smiled; she could read him like a book. She and Ted had him down to a fine art. No point in pretending otherwise.

'Give in,' he said, struggling to sit up. 'Shall we go downstairs and have a cup of tea?'

The kitchen table had always been their broker in times of discord. It was where they could sit across from one another and comfortably hold hands when necessary. The table was nothing special; just firm and strong and showing the scuff marks of time. And Ted had joined them when he heard the kitchen door creak as they opened it. He lay quietly on its flagstone floor aware somehow not to interrupt. Anna set down the teapot squarely on the table after filling their cups. They sipped the soothing hot liquid for some time before speaking.

'It was one of your important festivals today, wasn't it,' said Alistair.

'Yes. It was Tisha B'Av,' replied Anna looking directly into his pale green eyes. 'It was originally a day of fast to commemorate the destruction of Jewish temples, but it has become associated with other tragedies too. But I'm non-practising as you very well know and with the amazing spread of food at the cricket match, I definitely wasn't fasting. And I have another faith calendar too. Don't forget my mother was Catholic.' She smiled sweetly and squeezed his hand. 'What made you say that?'

'It was Arne. I had a vision of him when I was out walking Ted.' Ted stirred; he'd heard his name. 'It was unpleasant. Silly, I know,' continued Alistair, 'but it brought back memories of dark days. It was unsettling and made me feel at the same time both nostalgic and melancholic.' He pursed his lips and made a goofy face at Anna. 'His image reminded me of the circumstances in which we met. You, your brother, your former friends, your country, all those troublesome events.'

'It could have been a tale of woe. But it wasn't.'

'No, it wasn't, because I met you.' They stared at one another for a while in complete silence before Alistair continued. 'It turned out to be one of the best days of my life.'

'I was Annaliese then,' she recalled, 'and just at the awkward age of sixteen. And you were nineteen and had been conscripted into the British Army as a private.' Anna looked rueful. 'My poor homeland. How it suffered during the war and how wonderful it had been to be liberated. Jens and I didn't know then what had happened to our parents. Of course, we feared for their safety. So many shocking rumours abounded then, but nobody could have predicted the terrible truth. But you already know this, my darling.'

It was the small hours of the morning before they made their way back to bed. There had been a need to rekindle the stories of their past; well-worn stories but ones that resurfaced from time to time as if they needed another airing.

After leaving the sandy beach, the young Annaliese and her brother, Jens, had struggled up the steep face of an imposing dune to a high point where some flatter, grassy land made walking possible. When they had looked back to the sea, Arne was already out of sight. They were on their own, a young man and his even younger sister, and they were dirty and soaking wet. They walked on for what seemed like hours until they stumbled across a small wooden hut; a place of refuge out of the weather. Refuge for whom they didn't know, and didn't care. Jens realised that his sister was near the point of exhaustion, although she had not complained. They sat on the narrow bench and Jens put his arms around her to provide some comfort. The day became warm and they removed their damp clothes and lay them out on the ground to dry properly. By early afternoon they were striding out along a narrow path that had been pounded out by many pairs of boots over the years.

'Someone must use this path regularly, Annaliese,' said Jens.

'To go to the lighthouse?' she asked.

'Probably. But it won't be used now.'

'Because of the war?'

'Yes. No lights permitted in war,' said Jens looking steadily ahead. 'This path should take us to the person who normally maintains the lighthouse.'

'Will he help us?'

'I hope so. I really hope so.'

They must have covered almost nine kilometres of the long, thin island before they encountered someone. He was standing outside a larger version of the previous wooden hut. He was wearing workman's clothes and had a pipe in his mouth. Jens hailed him and he replied with an acknowledging wave of the hand. He didn't look German.

'Are there any Germans on the island?' asked Jens, addressing him in Dutch.

'I think so, but I haven't seen any yet,' the man muttered in reply.

'We're thirsty and hungry,' said Jens plaintively. 'My sister is exhausted and needs to lie down.'

'She can lie down in here,' replied the man after some thought. He beckoned them in and they entered wearily.

They were not far from the only village on the island situated at its north-eastern most tip. He would go in later and buy more food with money given to him by Jens, until then they could share his meagre offerings. It would be best if the villagers knew nothing of their presence until he assessed the situation with the Germans. Jens was relieved that the bread and cheese, followed by a hot but tasteless drink did wonders for his sister. Although still very tired, she now had colour in her cheeks, and was in a talkative mood. Answering her many questions, they learnt that the old man had tended the lighthouse single-handed for almost thirty years after leaving the mainland for a quieter life. Tobacco and his precious radio were his only luxuries although he did have a wind-up gramophone and a box of old records. Dressed in oddments supplied by a family in the village, and lacking any need for personal hygiene, with the passage of time he had become a hermit. He was never lonely, he had told them, because he loved his job and spent most of his time running and maintaining the building and mechanism. He would take the ferry to the mainland when new parts were required but he was always glad to return to the tranquillity of Vlieland. Today, however, he appeared to be enjoying their unexpected company.

He was away for no more than fifty minutes - a period when Jens opened the windows to try to disperse the tobacco fug within – before returning clutching a parcel wrapped in stiff, brown paper. It contained more bread and more cheese, and some evil smelling sausage. He also brought news. By proclamation no inhabitant could now leave the island as the ferry services to the mainland, principally to Harlingen, had been halted by the Germans. The townsfolk were waiting to discover if they would be forcibly evacuated to the mainland. Meanwhile, the Germans were bringing in heavy machinery and were believed to be fortifying the island's defences. The townsfolk were very gloomy, food was in short supply, and their hitherto peaceful world was being turned upside down.

One month later, under guard, a sad and bedraggled band of underfed and anxious islanders, including the lighthouse keeper and his two guests, were marched from the village centre to the ferry dock where they were pushed onto a vessel heading for Harlingen. Holding bags containing as many possessions as they could cram in, they cut a forlorn sight. Some had relatives to find on the mainland, others, like the lighthouse keeper, had no kinsfolk to contact. Jens told him that his family would look after him as he had been generous to them on Vlieland, but when they arrived at the chandlery, their hopes seemed dashed. The door was boarded over, and paint had been daubed across the shop's name of "Leesen & Son." The windows were intact, but bore the word "Jude" in large letters in the same-coloured white paint. Annaliese looked distraught and began to sob.

'Don't cry, sister,' said Jens. 'We will try the back entrance. I have a key.'

'What does the word mean?' asked Annaliese pointing at the window.

'Somebody doesn't like us because our father is Jewish.'

'Why?' she asked innocently.

'I'll explain later. Let's go and see if we can get in,' said Jens sounding more cheerful than he felt. Only the local shopkeepers would have known about the back entrances to the shopping parade. The little party of three trudged round and were relieved to find their door undamaged.

The story might have ended there, but Alistair urged his wife to carry on; something or someone was still bothering him. Anna resumed at the point where Vissers became involved when Pieter had stared through the shop window between daubs of graffiti and noticed Jens inside. He had been desperate for news of Arne, although what he learnt from Jens made for uncomfortable listening. He was sorry, he had told Jens several times, very sorry indeed that Arne had found it impossible to take Jens and his sister with him, but the forces of the sea currents, the waves and the winds would have been against a more heavily laden small boat. As it was, he had no idea whether his son had succeeded in making the crossing. He didn't know whether he was alive or dead or captured, and in that regard neither Jens nor his sister could help him.

There was no sign of vandalism inside the shop or in the flat above where they lived. According to Pieter, it was the Germans who had defaced the shop front and closed it down and he had tapped on the window to warn them that it was dangerous to be seen inside. He was sorry but he didn't know what had become of Jens's parents. It was a body blow for Jens. He was only seventeen and his chin quivered with the news of his missing parents. He was on the point of tears when Pieter suggested that the little party of three could spend the night in his boatyard while deciding what to do, and that his wife would find a change of clothes for all of them and a razor to remove the lighthouse keeper's wayward beard so that he wouldn't stand out from the crowd when going about Harlingen.

'Unsurprisingly, there were no prospects of jobs at the boatyard,' said Anna. 'I watched my brother cover his face with his hands. He was questioning his wisdom about us trying to escape on Arne's boat and knowing that if we had stayed with our parents, we would have been together. And we might have protected them.'

'So much for you to handle at your tender age of nine,' said Alistair reflectively. 'No child should have to be burdened with such worries.'

'When Pieter returned to the boatyard the next day, he brought food as well as clothing. After we'd washed, put on clean clothes, and eaten a filling meal, we felt more positive. Pieter brought news too of our parents. They had been sent to a detention centre in Groningen, the biggest town in our region of Holland. I was too young to understand the implications of this move, but Pieter did and so did Jens.'

'You had nowhere to go and no idea what to do. Two children and an old man who had been living like a hermit for years.'

'But Pieter was a good man and Henrik, the lighthouse keeper, turned into our rock. He wasn't really a hermit; he was an eccentric. He was intelligent and kind, and not as old as he looked.'

'But for them,' said Alistair yawning, 'you might not have survived, my darling, for me to meet and marry you.'

'It's time for bed,' said Anna finally. 'I know now what was bothering you. It's what happened to Henrik, all those years ago.'

'Yes, that's right, I realise that now,' agreed Alistair, 'and to be more precise, it's how Arne treated Henrik when they first met.'

* * *

The offices of Alistair's firm in Norwich – consultant engineers specialising in bridge construction in East Anglia and the Midlands, of which he was the founder and the senior but youngest partner – were not lavish by London standards. His regular trips to the capital for meetings with public and private sector bodies were usually conducted around a table in far plusher conditions, often with presentation material but away from the humbler basic clutter found in most engineering workspaces. Public sector contracts were often big-money, big-ticket deals with umpteen conditions and clauses and Alistair always ensured that he was accompanied by one of his specialist associates in contract law and accountancy.

His father, the now deceased rear admiral, had put aside his disappointment that his youngest son, indeed like his three elder sons, had chosen a career outside the navy. But it came as no shock as it had been apparent from an early age that Alistair was destined for employment in some form of construction. Out on The Wash with his father from time to time, it had been evident that sailing for Alistair had been strictly for leisure. Alistair's real pleasure had been playing endlessly with his Meccano set and showing how well he understood the principles of mechanics long before he received any formal teaching. At school and university, he had excelled in technical subjects, and after his periods of conscription in the army followed by work experience on site, he had quickly learnt the ropes of how to gainfully apply his knowledge to business enterprises.

It was at one such meeting in Whitehall that he was reacquainted with Arne Visser; the first and only time they had met post-war being a brief encounter in Harlingen shortly after the war's end when as young men they had sized up one another and taken stock. Now in his middle to late forties, Arne's accomplishments were the stuff of comic strip derring-do – escaping across the North Sea, wartime service for the Allies, new boat designs for recreation, sailing single-handed around the world in both directions, skippering elite big boat races, and glamorous women on his arm at public events – but in the world of commerce in which he had grown rich, he had the reputation of being a hard-nosed, self-serving businessman with little regard for others. He was certainly no "Mr. Nice Guy."

The best that could be said about their encounter was that it was cordial. Arne, in fact, knew little about the comparatively low-key life of Alistair save that their encounter in Harlingen in nineteen-forty-six had been a matter of pure chance when he was searching for his parents and sisters, and Alistair, as a well-educated conscript private with a formerly high-ranking naval father, had been seconded to an intelligence unit searching for evidence of war crimes. Alistair had noted then the cavalier way in which Arne had dismissed the efforts of Henrik to look after Jens and Annaliese during the long, weary years of war, especially after Pieter's death. It had been Henrik who had befriended the youngsters through those demanding times and their high regard for him was obvious to any bystander. That Arne dismissed him as nothing more than a tramp because of his strange array of second-hand clothes, left a lasting impression in Alistair's memory. It had not only been a hurtful and unnecessary remark to make but had shown an insight into Arne's character; a seeming lack of empathy for a fellow human being. But he gave Arne the benefit of the doubt as Arne had recently learnt from his sister about the death of his father while running messages to the invasion forces, and the unexplained disappearance of his mother, Frieda.

Arne was present at the meeting in the capacity of a representative; a figurehead for a company hoping to secure a contract for the provision of concrete. He had been offered a well-paid non-executive directorship for a few hours of work a month in return for his celebrity status which was deemed likely to grease the inward flow of work into the firm. He knew nothing about concrete but had shown himself to be a canny, wheeler-dealer businessman. His active participation in the meeting was minimal; it was his very presence around the table that turned a prosaic commodity into something far more glamorous. And, as always, Arne had a keen eye for any photo opportunity linking him with the project which might come his way.

Although the venue had changed, Alistair's opinion of Arne had not. After a few hesitant enquiries as to when the two men had last met – an enquiry that Alistair was happy to respond to without too much detail as being a long time ago in their youth and a brief encounter after the war in Harlingen – they had little else to converse about. Regarding concrete, Arne appeared to say all the right things at all the right times in support of his company's bid while deferring to his technical colleagues for in-depth specifics. But as ever with Arne, there was the underlying impression that his true interest in the project lay in self-aggrandisement. Still, conceded Alistair, Arne wasn't the only person in the world to put himself on a pedestal; all sorts did far worse than that, and unkind words unlike murder, grievous bodily harm and sexual assault, were, after all, only words. But he wasn't to know then that it would be a spat with Ted that would show Arne in his true colours.

When proposals were first mooted in the mid-sixties to build a new motorway linking London to Cambridge together with an upgrade of the major trunk road from Cambridge to Norwich – thus providing the motorist, often with a caravan in tow, with an easy run from the heart of the metropolis into the wilds of Norwich and its surrounding pleasant countryside – Alistair and his partners had submitted plans for the refurbishment and widening of several of the bridges along the trunk road which was scheduled to be made dual carriageway along its entire length. The existing bridges were already mandated to be inspected at least once every two years and his firm had held that contract for some time – it had been one of the first significant contracts that Alistair's fledgling firm had secured – and prospects of them winning the new contract were high.

For many weeks on-site inspections became the norm, often with colleagues or technical representatives of other companies involved in the work, but always with Alistair's constant companion, Ted, who usually stretched out in a prone position across the entire width of the back seat whilst the car was in motion. At halts and traffic lights, Ted would raise his head to have a good look out of the back window and to convey to his master by means of a grunt that he was monitoring their progress along the sinuous narrow roads and lanes of the rural countryside. Today, they were to assess the widening of an existing bridge which also spanned a narrow river. Alistair and Ted had been on-site for a considerable time as it was agreed with colleagues that a whole new redesign of the bridge would be more appropriate than a patchwork extension.

It had started raining the moment they had got out of the car, and before long the ground around the abutments and along the earthed-up river bank became boggy under the constant trampling of feet in Wellington boots as the officials completed the survey. They took shelter from the drizzle under umbrellas while discussing some finer points of the proposed new design, with Ted waiting patiently on a lead by Alistair's side. The inclines became slippery as the party moved up from the roadside to inspect the bridge's superstructure. A car drew up on the local road which crossed the trunk road via the bridge, and Arne stepped out. He was a tall man but no longer slim. His fair hair was still abundant and had been expertly cut to complement his strong facial features. He was wearing business clothes with black leather shoes polished to a high shine. When he learnt that the consensus of opinion for the redesign was for more steels and less concrete – a situation with a less favourable financial outcome for the company he represented – he insisted on inspecting the intended areas for the new abutment foundations.

Despite words of caution about the condition underfoot, Arne was not a man to be seen to be deterred. He was sure-footed down the initial steps of the slope, but at a muddier point his expensive shoes failed to gain sufficient traction on the slimy surface resulting in an inelegant slide to the bottom. He had done well to retain his balance although his shoes were now heavily caked in mud. A few expletives in his native tongue escaped his lips, in addition to the sound of some suppressed laughter from the watching group. It was clear to all that Arne was not amused.

It was at moments like this that Alistair's calm approach often saved the day. He had defused potentially tetchy situations in the past by his generally cordial manner and enabled parties at loggerheads with one another or feeling hard done by to resolve matters amicably. Alistair and Ted made their way down the slope with circumspection to join Arne.

'We're obliged to wear hi-vis gilets and hard hats while on-site,' said Alistair evenly, handing the items to Arne. 'Health and Safety rules apply here.'

'Okay,' replied Arne eventually, accepting that it was too small an issue over which to have a confrontation. 'Show me where you intend to replace concrete with steel.'

'We want to avoid the need for a bridge pier between the carriageways for several reasons,' said Alistair, pleased to be back to discussing the business of the day. 'If we beef up the superstructure at this point,' he continued, pointing to a central section of the bridge, 'then it will be possible to do just that.' Alistair looked at Ted who gave his master an adoring look. 'You see,' he continued, turning to face Arne directly, 'a bridge without a central pier with a reinforced concrete foundation will not only be cheaper and quicker to build, but it will also be easier to maintain.'

'I'll discuss it with my technical people,' replied Arne somewhat haughtily, as if Alistair's recommendation could be challenged, although he knew that that was highly unlikely.

If matters could have ended there, no lasting harm would have been done. There would have been some form of tacit acceptance of the proposals followed by handshakes all round and polite goodbyes before everyone returned to his own workplace.

The trouble was not caused by any further loss of dignity negotiating the grassy incline up from the lower roadway, as Arne paid far more attention to going safely up it than he had earlier to going down, and neither Alistair in his Wellingtons with grippy soles nor Ted on a longer lead, had any difficulty whatsoever. But, unfortunately, Arne's arrival up on the flat where he had parked his car coincided with Ted urinating by the driver's door, splashing the perfect metallic paintwork with his bodily fluid and adding considerably to a rainwater puddle just where the driver would need to put his foot when getting into the vehicle. Arne shouted in annoyance and Ted growled at the unfriendly rebuke; he wasn't used to humans yelling at him. Too late, Alistair realised, that the fault lay with him; he had forgotten to shorten the retractable dog lead and with no trees about and the car within range, Ted had used it as a substitute.

'Sorry,' said Alistair immediately, pulling Ted towards him and shortening the lead. 'Apologies for that mishap.'

'You should keep your blessed dog under better control,' snapped Arne, 'or better still, not bring him to meetings at all.' It was clear that Arne was livid. No reply and a hasty retreat, Alistair realised, was the best course of action, but the normally gentle Ted had other ideas. He stood his ground defiantly when Alistair pulled on his lead and snarled at Arne.

'Get your sodding dog away from my car,' demanded Arne. But Ted refused to shift. Arne aimed a kick at Ted. Whether it was destined to hit or was just a warning shot across Ted's bows was unclear.

'Don't hurt the dog,' warned Alistair. 'He hasn't done you any harm. I'm sorry he peed against your car but that's not a reason to shout at him.' Arne gave them both a look that could kill. He opened the car door, and in his fury forgot about the puddle just by the door. The squelch was audible as the rainwater laced with urine rose above the shoe's welt and penetrated the upper. Arne slammed the door, revved the engine, and in a fit of pique, did a dramatic three-point turn in milliseconds in front of them as a mark of his displeasure. There was noise and a spray of loose gravel as he roared away in an almighty temper. Ted whimpered. He had been hit by a flying stone.

'When did this happen?' asked the vet.

'About two hours ago,' replied Alistair. 'I brought him here as soon as I could.' Alistair had driven back to his usual veterinary practice in Wells as quickly as he could.

'You were right to do so. It's a nasty abrasion.'

'Is he in pain?'

'Very probably,' replied the vet. 'Eyes can be very painful, and the cornea in particular. What was it that caused the damage?'

'Most probably a small stone hitting his eye at a rate of knots.'

'So, it wasn't a clean object,' stated the vet. 'I will need to treat him for a possible infection too.' Whilst Alistair held Ted as still as possible, the vet examined Ted's eye carefully with his ophthalmoscope. 'There's a deep abrasion but I'll need to instil a local anaesthetic before trying to clean it. It doesn't take long to work, so if you can just keep him calm for a few more moments then I can get on with patching him up.'

Ted wasn't the best patient in the world. He was still far too young to have developed a sense of seriousness, but together with the nurse, Alistair kept him quiet while the vet performed some delicate work on the injured eye.

'Will the eye recover?' Alistair asked anxiously.

'Time will tell,' the vet replied noncommittally. 'It's going to need a lot of attention to help it heal. Steroid drops every four hours for at least a week and antibiotics too. It's a serious injury, and there's a risk of a cataract developing later.' Alistair looked glum. He stroked Ted and whispered a few words of encouragement in his ear. 'Watch me,' continued the vet, 'I'll show you how to instil the drops so that the cornea gets bathed adequately in the solution. I'll give him some painkillers too to be used as and when needed. Keep him quiet, give him lots of treats and cuddles and bring him back for a check-up next week.'

Ted was at the centre of the Drew family's world for the next seven days. After an initial period when he seemed miserable, his tail finally began to wag. Anna in particular was furious that their beloved family pet had been injured by Arne. She felt he should be reported and prosecuted for causing the injury.

'He didn't do it expressly,' reasoned Alistair. 'It happened as a result of his foul temper.'

'But he was the cause,' insisted Anna. 'If he hadn't been around, it would never have happened.'

'I know, I know,' repeated her husband, frustratedly. 'But he didn't do it intentionally.'

'The equivalent of manslaughter then,' Anna persisted. 'He mustn't be allowed to get away with it.'

'There's nothing we can do,' Alistair declared. 'Different

laws apply to animals. We must concentrate our energy on looking after Ted.' But, although while outwardly maintaining a pragmatic stance, inwardly Alistair was seething. Nothing, his late father had once told him when he was a young boy, engenders more hatred than wilfully hurting a person's beloved pet and even though he accepted that Ted's damaged eye was accidental, he knew his growing hatred of Arne would last forever.

* * *

There was huge excitement in the Drew household as the seasons changed and high summer gave way to late autumn. Anna's brother, Jens, had been promoted to principal consular officer and had recently taken up his new post in London. As a result, Alistair and Anna were invited to attend a gala dinner in the presence of a member of the Royal Family and Her Majesty's trade minister at Mansion House hosted by the Lord Mayor of London. It would mark the three hundredth anniversary of formal trade links between the British Isles and the Low Countries, and its purpose was to further cement the rapport built up over those long years to the benefit of banking, commerce, and joint construction projects between the nations. The Dutch, The Belgians and The Luxembourgers would be represented in numbers by their own trade delegations.

The question of what to wear became a burning issue for Anna. With no close female relatives to consult, she turned to her tennis and social pals for suggestions, but as none of them moved in diplomatic circles, Anna had to resort to photographs in glossy magazines of life in the capital as led by the rich and famous.

'If Jens had married, I would be able to ask my sister-in-law what to wear,' Anna said to her family.

'Sorry, but I can't help you out on that score,' replied a distracted Alistair. 'I know I've got to wear tails. Never worn them before, never been to anything that grand.'

'You men are lucky. All you need do is to hire a set of the appropriate clothes from a high street tailor and job done.'

'Well, what are you getting stuck on? It's bound to be a long dress as I'm wearing tails.'

'But what about the choice of tiara?' she asked in a serious tone. Alistair looked aghast. 'Only joking,' carried on Anna, 'I'll wear the crown instead.'

The Dutch Embassy, located at Hyde Park Gate, was abuzz with the noise of friendly chatter. Alistair and Anna had travelled down to London early to enjoy a few days of visits to the theatre and opera before presenting themselves at the embassy for a cocktail party on the eve of the Mansion House dinner. It would be a wonderful chance, Anna had told her family, to speak in her mother tongue if she could still remember it, and to see her brother for a long chat before the formalities of the following evening. The embassy setting also offered the best opportunities to sound out new business ventures between the Brits and the Dutch, and to share information about ongoing projects; it would be networking heaven. The language of choice was English as few of the British guests – entrepreneurs and directors of industry – spoke

Dutch, but it gave each an opportunity to enter into the spirit of the party by repeating a few hastily learnt words of salutation in an excruciating accent to every person they were introduced.

Jens was greatly in demand that early evening ensuring that the embassy's guests were making the most of the opportunity to rub shoulders with like-minded business people, but as soon as he saw his sister arrive, he was by her side embracing her. It was evident that the bond between them ran deep, and whilst Alistair wandered off to make new acquaintances, the siblings exchanged news excitedly. They were all they had from their roots, one and other. It had taken years to establish that both parents were dead; one a victim of the holocaust, the other the victim of having married a Jew. Of their wider families, they had no knowledge since the fissure had occurred when their parents entered into a split-religion marriage.

'It's time you got married and started a family,' Anna told her brother bluntly. 'You're getting on and time is running out. And I want some nieces and nephews.'

'I'm trying. I'm on the hunt all the time, but so far, no luck,' replied Jens smiling. 'I just have to be patient and so do you.'

'Don't be patient for too long. You may run out of time.'

'I've had some girlfriends but every time a meaningful relationship seems on the point of developing into something worthwhile, I get posted to a totally different part of the world.'

'Not easy for you,' said Anna, giving her brother a

kiss on the cheek. 'It's so lovely to see you and we expect you to come up to Norfolk to spend as many weekends as possible with us.'

'To meet my nephews. Yes, that would be great.'

'And to meet Ted.'

The cocktail party was in full swing when Arne, with a glamorous young woman on his arm, entered the room. There was a momentary hush while the assembled crowd recognised the new arrival. Alistair looked up and swore softly. Arne's presence wasn't a surprise, but he had been hoping, rather unreasonably given that Arne was one of their country's famous sons, that the bad penny wouldn't turn up. Ted was miles away in Norfolk but nonetheless Alistair felt him tense.

After introductions to the ambassador and his wife, Arne became the centre of attention. He wasn't a businessman in the sense that he ran a large corporation, or an entrepreneur in the sense that he had started his own manufacturing company, or indeed a consultant in the sense that he had an eminent scientific background, but with the passing of time he had turned himself into a successful lobbyist of government and big business. For a big dollar he would plead your cause, no matter the subject.

It fell to Jens that evening to ensure that the well-oiled wheels of diplomacy reached every single guest. When it came to Arne, with history between the two men, neither managed more than a frosty greeting, so it was to the lady on his arm to whom Jens turned his attention. Dark haired, olive toned skin, hourglass figure, and almost as tall as her infamous escort, she was not quite as young as she looked on first sight and her apparent glamour was due more to classical good looks than to garish make up. A master of languages, Jens quickly discerned her "Latino" accent when she replied to his greeting in Spanish. It wasn't classic Castilian she had spoken but the more informal Latin version of Spanish.

'Are you from South America?' he asked in fluent Spanish.

'Yes, I am,' she replied, smiling.

'Don't tell me where you are from. Let me guess,' said Jens immediately. 'Somewhere in the south of that vast continent. Argentina or Uruguay, I think.'

'Near the River Plate.'

'Both countries are near the River Plate,' he protested.

'And both capital cities too,' she laughed, displaying dimples in both cheeks.

'I've just completed a posting in Montevideo so I am going to plump for Uruguay. By the way, I'm Jens. And you are?'

'Eva.'

The conversation would happily have continued, but Arne had grown restless. Eva was with him and he was the star, not her. The couple moved on, circulating amongst those who wished to meet Arne. But Jens closely followed their progress as he had every intention of speaking to Eva again. He realised that that opportunity could present itself the following evening if he could liaise with the Lord Mayor's staff to sit next to the lovely Eva while her escort was on the top table. It could be seen as the height of diplomacy to offer to look after her whilst Arne was doing his stuff promoting his country from a position of prominence seated next to the Lord Mayor.

The Mansion House was the grandest of settings for what was, in essence, a trade supper. Pomp and ceremony abounded; outfits of yesteryear were worn by all. There was service by attentive staff who seemed to glide around the grand banqueting hall. With food exquisite in its presentation and taste, speeches amusing and mercifully short, and Anna's question as to whether ladies would be wearing long gloves with sequins was answered. Alistair tussled all evening with his white bow tie which bobbed up and down with every movement of his Adam's apple. He sat next to the lady from Montevideo with Jens a further seat away, but her attention was not turned to him, it was firmly fixed on Jens. They spoke in Spanish which Alistair did not understand, but the words they said needed no translation.

'They seem to be getting on well,' said Anna, nudging her husband.

'I hope Arne is not watching them too intently,' replied Alistair. 'If so, words may not be cordial at the end of the evening.'

'I wonder where they met, and if they are boyfriend and girlfriend.'

'Or is she just another gorgeous woman he is employing to decorate his arm?' he replied. It was a measured response by Alistair. He would have liked to have said something far more cutting. Anna looked at him directly and warned him not to allow Arne to rattle him.

It was Christmas before Jens was free to visit his sister; a heavy workload at the embassy in London and at the Manchester and Edinburgh consulates had limited his spare time. He had spent hours sorting out his predecessor's paperwork and filing methods into a system that made common sense. The ambassador had hinted that one day in the not-too-distant future the embassy would have computers to do all that sort of boring stuff but until then Jens and his clerical staff had just got to process the growing demand as best they could.

His sister had told him that Alistair would meet him at Norwich station, and that she expected him to stay for at least a week. She would not take no for an answer. His nephews were looking forward to seeing him again and the latent excitement had rubbed off on Ted too.

For the normally conventional Jens, his arrival with a woman was wholly unexpected. Alistair had to blink twice before realising that the lovely lady who was walking alongside him was Eva. Both had a suitcase and were smiling radiantly. But it was not that morning's only surprise, for at the house they were welcomed by a very special but unexpected person, Henrik.

'Explanations inside please,' shouted Alistair to the assembled family by the front door. 'Far too cold to hang about outside. Come on Ted, you too.' Grouped around the open fire in the main living room, after embraces, everyone wanted to speak at the same time but it was Henrik who was given centre stage.

The kitchen door was ajar. Through the open aperture Anna could hear Henrik's faltering words of English as he talked to Alistair and the boys. It sounded laboured but was laced with laughter especially when Alistair unwisely contributed the few words of Dutch that he knew. Anna closed the door softly and put her arms around her brother. They had escaped to the kitchen not only to do the washing up but also to catch up with one another.

'What a surprise,' said Anna, giving her brother a wink. 'You turning up with Eva.'

'It is the nineteen-seventies, dear sister,' replied Jens. 'And I do intend to marry her if I can.'

'No need for prudishness then. But I don't want the boys to think that it is acceptable behaviour for you and Eva to share a room before marriage. Fortunately, we have sufficient accommodation for you to have separate bedrooms.'

'You don't mind? My bringing her here.'

'Of course not. I am thrilled that you have found someone at last. I know where you met her, but what about Arne? Was Eva his girlfriend?'

'No, she wasn't,' said Jens, separating the cutlery to be washed from the crockery. 'He'd met her in the days when he was skippering big boat races around Cape Horn. Her boyfriend at the time was a crew member. Those events were also associated with lots of parties and social gatherings before and after the actual races, and Arne always kept tabs on any good-looking women in the entourage.'

'A list of women he could ask to accompany him at special events?'

'Probably. I'm not sure if he had any other intention, long-term that is. Eva thinks he's a loner.'

'So, Eva was just in London by chance when he asked her to accompany him to the Lord Mayor's dinner.'

'No. He knew she was in England because she had split with her boyfriend to pursue a university academic career,' replied Jens. 'In fact, she'd been here several years, firstly in the north and now in London. She is a senior lecturer in South American political studies.'

'Whoa. That's some subject,' said Anna before adding, 'I hope her family has not suffered at a dictator's hands.'

'No, fortunately not, but they are not active political dissidents. It's the reason why she left her homeland though. Fear of an intolerant regime.'

'So, I have something in common with her because I too have left my homeland,' said Anna.

'But for you, it was for all the right reasons.'

'Yes, I've been very lucky. Very lucky indeed,' Anna observed. 'And I hope you will be too, Jens. You deserve it.'

'She's eight years younger than me. She might not want to marry an older man.'

'And not forgetting that she's also better looking than you and taller,' replied his sister playfully. 'But she'd never find a man with more inner strength than you have.'

'Tell me about Henrik,' said Jens, changing the subject swiftly for fear of choking with embarrassment.

'Ah, Henrik. The successful relocation of our dear friend,' Anna declared, 'into the bosom of the Drew family of Wells-next-the-Sea.'

Anna dried her hands and started putting the crockery back into their usual stacks; small plates of the same size in cupboards above the working surface, larger, heavier dinner plates in the cupboards below. Then, seated at the kitchen table, they recalled memories of when they had first met Henrik.

'He seemed like a hermit then,' declared Jens. 'And looked so much older than he truly was.'

'He must have been in his late forties in nineteen-forty, but appeared to us as if he was at least thirty years older than that.'

'We were very young at the time. You were only nine and I was seventeen. Anyone in their thirties would have seemed ancient to us.'

'And the long beard didn't help.'

'It did nothing for his image,' agreed Jens. A long pause followed while they both let their minds drift back to wartime memories of Henrik. 'In a strange way, the war was kind to Henrik,' said Jens contemplatively. 'It rescued him from a life of loneliness with just the physical structure of the lighthouse for company. But you can't hug bricks and mortar.'

'It was quite out of the blue that he suddenly had to take charge of us. And then compulsory evacuation from Vlieland Island to the mainland forced him to integrate with people again.'

'It revealed the true Henrik. A man who was social without being gregarious.'

'And a man of talents,' added Anna. 'He just needed a family with whom he could show off his strengths.'

'And we were it,' mused Jens. 'The would-be hermit cast off his carapace and emerged as a person of resilience.'

'"No man is an island" so an old English saying goes,

77

my eldest son tells me. We were just the catalyst that caused his revival. And Pieter's death …,' she trailed off.

'Pieter's death affected us all,' said Jens solemnly. 'But I agree. It seemed to make Henrik doubly determined to ensure that we survived the war.'

'Your brilliant idea to ask him to run what was left of the chandlery when we learned the fate of our parents, sealed his re-emergence into normal life,' stated Anna. 'And by the time I married and moved away and you had decided on a career in the diplomatic corps and would be away for long periods on postings, Henrik had built an anchor in Harlingen with the shop and the customers he served. He grew into the perfect shopkeeper although he never became sartorially suave,' Anna added giggling.

'But the jumble of clothes he wore suited him,' Jens pointed out. 'He was comfortable in himself and his customers didn't give a damn what he wore because he was always helpful.'

'The years were unfortunately taking a toll, hardly surprising as he grew into his seventies. He couldn't go on forever.' Anna sighed deeply. 'He needed support,' she continued, 'we asked him several times to come and live with us, and finally he agreed. His assistant took over the shop and that was that, although he did have tears in his eyes as we loaded his few belongings into the car and set off for a Channel port.' Ted nosed around the almost shut door and gave Anna the familiar look that he was on the scrounge for a titbit. 'Ted took to Henrik instantly. They're big buddies now although Alistair is still top dog.' Jens crossed his arms and gave his sister a wry grin. He hadn't grown any taller since the age of sixteen. Short in stature, it was his thick, light brown hair cut short and combed sideways from his off-centre parting that people would have noticed. As always, he looked neat and tidy – a necessity Anna assumed, for work in the diplomatic service – but his open face made him very approachable. He was forty-three but would easily pass as being in his late thirties. 'There will be someone to mourn him when he dies, someone to shed a tear, and someone will miss him when he's gone,' Anna went on, 'until then he will remain a valued member of our family.'

'Will you knit him a Christmas jumper?' enquired Jens mischievously, 'just to make him feel truly at home.'

'No, I will not,' replied Anna firmly stressing the word "not." 'I've never learned how to knit and wouldn't have the patience even if I could. But I might buy him one from a charity shop.'

Although still mostly British, this particular year's Christmas traditions were liberally sprinkled with Dutch and Latin American customs. Jens had purchased a child's plastic horn from a toy shop, and in a re-enactment of his country's mid-winter wooden horn blowing by the edge of a body of water to announce the birth of the baby Jesus, it had everybody in fits of laughter as he stood solemnly in the bay window overlooking the sea emitting a tinny screech. Ted looked anxious and hid behind a sofa and didn't emerge until Alistair told him it was safe to do so.

Anna's Dutch offerings were Kerstkranjes; sweet biscuits with a hole in the middle. She had baked them for the first time in years and the boys had pushed the end of the tree branches through the central hole. There had been many breakages with the broken morsels being scoffed in seconds. Biscuits that survived the indelicate handlings of the three young adults shimmered under the tree lights and gave it an unexpectedly homely appeal.

Eva's contribution, she explained, was really intangible. Her country was mostly secular and the twenty-fifth of December was not recognised by the government as an official holiday. But instead, there was its widespread observance as the "Day of the Family." In the southern hemisphere it was mid-summer and families gathered outdoors for steaks grilled and charred on barbecues, followed by sweet dishes prepared by all the family, and young children were allowed to stay up late and enjoy the music and dancing. Alistair found a long-playing record of Latin American music in his pile of record albums, and Henrik with the help of gestures, asked Eva for the first dance, a rumba; everybody joined in despite a lack of knowledge of the steps involved. By the time it was Jens turn to dance with Eva in the more intimate salsa, it was obvious to Anna that the couple would be grateful for some privacy and she invited all those who would like to play the card game "chase the ace" to join her in the library. It was coded language for an instruction they *had* to obey.

* * *

One gloriously sunny day in Wells-next-the-Sea in early spring when the chilliness in the air was still present but leaf buds on shrubs and trees were growing fat and firm with the promise that their grand entrance into the world was just around the corner, Alistair, with Ted at his side, made their way home after an invigorating walk around the marina. It was a Saturday morning and they were at their leisure. As they made their way up the drive to the front door, they crossed paths with the postman. Friendly greetings were exchanged. Ted had his head patted and the wiry fur on his neck ruffled before the postie was on his way again to his next delivery address. Alistair picked the two letters out of the small metal cage attached behind the letter-box on the back of the door; one was addressed to Mr and Mrs. A. Drew, the other to Henrik.

It was Anna who read the letter to the Drews as it was written in Dutch. She became so excited that the words of translation tumbling out of her mouth were jumbled beyond understanding.

'Slow down,' ordered Alistair. 'I can't understand a word you're talking about.'

'It's about Jens,' said Anna, taking a deep breath. 'He's got married to Eva,' she added hastily.

'Wonderful news,' shouted Alistair in delight. 'I know that's what you wanted.'

'He travelled to Montevideo to meet her family, stayed with them, and got married there as soon as they had complied with all the formalities. They are staying on at her parents' home until he has finished his annual leave, before returning to London.'

'On their honeymoon, then. When they return, we must arrange to go down to London for a celebratory meal.'

'I do hope they had some photographs taken.'

'One day we could go on holiday to Uruguay to meet her parents,' Alistair suggested. 'I've always fancied a trip to that continent full of dark intrigue and political skulduggery.'

'You'll have to brush up on your tango.'

The other letter also turned out to be written in Dutch. When Henrik opened it and put on his reading spectacles, he smiled. As a rule, he didn't receive many letters, and those he did were in English and usually of an official nature that he had to call on Anna to translate. He was now in his seventy-fourth year with, according to the local optician, a deteriorating standard of visual acuity. The letter was typed and had a formal appearance, although the sender had handwritten his first name in the opening salutation. With a struggle, Henrik worked out that it was some kind of invitation to Vlieland Island, but asked Anna for clarification.

'Oh. This is exciting, Henrik,' she exclaimed, after carefully reading through the letter twice. 'It's an invitation to the opening of the new lighthouse on Vlieland. Apparently, you are the last surviving keeper of the old lighthouse. The new one is automatic and will only require a twice-yearly maintenance check.'

'It's an invitation to what exactly?' asked Henrik looking puzzled.

'To the official opening. The nine members of the municipal council will be present plus the member of the Dutch parliament in charge of lighthouses. After the ceremony, the mayor requests the pleasure of your company at a luncheon to be held in the main tourist centre on the island.'

'How did they know my address?' he asked quite sensibly, the creases across his forehead squeezing together like the bellows of an accordion when asked to play a high note.

'From their records, presumably,' responded Anna. 'You worked for the municipality. They were your employers during the years you oversaw work in the old lighthouse. Like all municipal employers they were obliged to keep records.'

'But those records must date back to before the war,' he pointed out. 'I haven't been there since we left in nineteen-forty. And never returned even when I lived in Harlingen.'

'When I arranged for you to live with us in England, I had to inform the authorities in Harlingen that you would no longer be liable for taxes in their authority, and I had to supply them with your new address in England. So, that's how they knew where to contact you,' explained Anna.

'Should I go?' Henrik asked Anna uncertainly. He looked nervous.

'It's up to you, Henrik,' replied Anna, sensing a tone of reluctance in his voice. 'You don't have to if you don't want to.'

'Would you come with me if I did?'

'Of course,' said Anna, rubbing his hand comfortingly. 'You can be proud of the years you maintained the old lighthouse in working order. And I'd love to walk along the trodden path, if it still exists, that brought my brother and me to your little wooden hut.'

'If that still exists too.'

From the moment it was delivered, the family nicknamed it "Pandora's Box." Constructed in tin, it was the size of a medium-sized suitcase. There was unsurprising evidence of rust at several of its corners but otherwise it seemed in good condition. An old label on its top, still readable, proclaimed its provenance – it belonged to the lighthouse keeper on Vlieland Island. Whether it belonged to the lighthouse keeper of the day, or to a particular lighthouse keeper was unclear, but Henrik's name was on the delivery label that had been stuck on its top.

After the new lighthouse opening ceremony, the mayor had explained to Henrik that the team in charge of dismantling the machinery in the old lighthouse and clearing away any loose debris had found the tin trunk stowed away in a dark space under the bottom two steps of a stairway. Not knowing if it had any importance, they handed it to the council instead of disposing of it. It was heavy and none of the council members were able to prise open the lid to investigate its contents. The mayor suggested gifting it to Henrik as a souvenir of his days as custodian of the building on the basis that it was unlikely to contain anything of commercial value to the council, but might contain something that had sentimental value to Henrik.

'Looks intriguing,' said Alistair to his family assembled around the trunk.

'Open it up, Dad,' instructed his youngest son, not yet quite a teenager.

'I don't quite know how,' replied his father, running his fingers along the edges of the box's lid. 'There are no apparent gaps.'

'Try the end of a screwdriver,' his youngest son

suggested. 'There must be a place where you can get the tip under the lid.'

'Good suggestion,' Alistair replied. 'You're born to be an engineer,' he added, looking at his son who was beaming with pride.

'I'm not sure it's worth the effort,' intervened Henrik. 'I used to stand on it sometimes in order to reach up to adjust a piece of mechanism.'

'Then you know what's in it,' stated Alistair.

'Just some ballast, I presume,' replied Henrik after Anna had told him the English word for "voorschakelapparaat".

'You never opened it?' enquired Anna.

'No. I don't think so,' said Henrik shrugging his shoulders. 'I wasn't …,' he hesitated while picking his words, 'I wasn't in an enquiring frame of mind in that period of my life.'

'Do you think the Germans would have planted a bomb in it, Dad?' asked his son excitedly.

'No. But if they had, it would have exploded by now with all the humping about that it's had to endure.' Anna winced. She hadn't considered that possibility.

'Dad, I think it's soldered around the top,' said his eldest son, giving it a very close inspection. 'There are no gaps to insert a tool to prise up the lid.'

'Then it's a mystery,' his father replied. 'And I guess that no one will really be content until it is solved. But it's Henrik's property and Henrik has the right to decide its fate.' There was a definite note of ambivalence in Henrik's reply. He pursed his lips, wrung his knobbly hands, and finally looked up to the ceiling for help or for inspiration before giving the go-ahead.

'It would be a pity,' said Alistair, 'to just destroy the box without giving any thought to its history.'

'If it's not too damaged I could put it in your room, Henrik, and use it for storing your extra blankets.'

'If you turn it upside down, Dad, and cut the bottom off with a hack saw then when you turn it right side up, it will still look presentable as a blanket box.'

'That sounds a bit brutal,' responded Alistair with a cheeky smile, 'having your bottom cut off, that is. But if it's necessary then I might try that. What we don't know yet,' he said, rubbing his stubbly chin, 'is to what the ballast is stuck. There was no sound of rattling when we shifted the trunk so this ballast, whatever it is, must be attached to something.'

Alistair started by drilling a small pilot hole at each corner into which he inserted the tip of a narrow-blade saw. Progress was slow as the tip of the saw could get little purchase on the tin as it repeatedly met with a hard, immovable object attached to the trunk's bottom. Alistair scratched his nose, shook his head, and told the family that another plan was needed as this particular one wasn't going to work. The family drifted off leaving Alistair, on hands and knees, holding the proverbial baby.

After Anna gave it a good clean, nothing happened to the box for several weeks apart from being put in Henrik's room with his neatly folded extra blankets being placed on its top. Everybody had other more important "things" to do, and it wasn't until Alistair mentioned it to one of his colleagues at work that another plan emerged; a rotary saw adaptor on a power tool could, with a steady hand, work its way slowly along the solder line separating the top from the rim. And with the borrowed equipment, and when there was a high possibility of no interruptions, Alistair and Ted locked themselves in the tool shed and got on with the job.

* * *

The headline news that evening was about a tragic accident that occurred when the driver of a four-by-four carrying two passengers, when approaching an overhead bridge on a dual carriageway road, was forced to swerve suddenly to avoid a motorcyclist illegally overtaking his vehicle on the left-hand side. In narrowly avoiding contact with the speeding bike, the driver had lost control and his vehicle had slammed into the central pier of the bridge causing unexpected damage to its stability. A coach full of senior citizens on their way home from an outing was travelling at a sedate pace along the minor road which crossed the bridge. The coach driver, a woman with plenty of experience driving coach parties, was unaware of the accident that had occurred two or three minutes previously, there being no outward sign of damage to the bridge structure and no view of the crumpled land rover on the carriageway below. There was nothing to foretell the doom that was about to occur.

When the police and a single ambulance arrived on the scene sometime later – alerted by the driver of another car who had searched and eventually found a telephone box – the true horror of the incident became apparent. The two constables, one of mature age whose lined face suggested he might have a great deal of experience, with his young sidekick who looked fresh out of police college, got out of their patrol car with trepidation and surveyed the macabre scene for some time as if they had been turned to stone by the grisly sights to behold. Minutes passed before the senior man came back abruptly to his senses and radioed into his base for urgent back-up support. When the solitary ambulance arrived, without the urgency of blue flashing lights as the gravity of the accident was unknown, a rapid call for paramedics was made by the crew as they sensed the kind of injuries that they were likely to find.

Over the next many hours, the scene became increasingly chaotic as the various rescue services arrived and swung into action as soon as the senior fire officer who was co-ordinating the rescue effort at that stage said it was safe to do so. Health and Safety officials, together with police photographers, were also in the vanguard of the arrivals with a view to establishing the cause, but meaningful progress was slow while the firefighters inched their way along the length of the coach, a section of which was hanging precariously in fresh air over the crushed parapet. A deathly silence hung over the whole area as workers talked in hushed tones whilst carrying out their gruesome tasks and the number pronounced dead at the scene rose steadily.

The first media representatives were the local journalists who were quick to report to their bosses that the incident was no ordinary minor prang. Notwithstanding communication difficulties with the area scoured for working public telephone boxes, they filed early reports to their editors of the unfolding drama. Shortly, as word spread, they were joined by journalists and correspondents from the national press and television bringing with them all the paraphernalia of their profession. They were held at bay by the police who had already roped off a large area of both roads. Snippets of information were wheedled out of various rescuers inside the cordon and a cohesive story was pieced together from that detail, and by early evening the news slots had a headline story to broadcast that would gather in newsworthiness and momentum in the days to come.

A main source of information was the driver of the four-by-four who had, by the grace of God, secured himself in his seat by means of his seat belt. It wasn't something he did normally, he had told his rescuers as they cut away crumpled metalwork around his seat so that they could extract him without causing further harm to his injured knees; it was just a chance in a million that on that very journey he had belted up. Seat belt wearing wasn't mandatory he had told them, almost as a justification for his two passengers whose deaths he correctly assumed by the lack of medical attention paid to their corpses as the firefighters cut away metalwork to release them from the twisted debris. He'd been doing his sister a favour by taking his niece to her boarding school for the new term; they didn't have private transport and the school was located out of town and not on a bus route. All at once, as if caught up in reality, he put his head in his hands and wept; his sister and niece were dead and he was being comforted by one of his saviours. Later, when encouraged by a police officer to recall what had occurred, he was able to explain that a biker dressed in black with a dark helmet and riding a powerful-looking motorcycle had cut across his path from the passenger side. There had been glancing contact between the vehicles, and together with the unexpected overtaking manoeuvre, it was sufficient to cause him to veer to the right without sufficient time to straighten up before slamming into the base of the concrete pier.

The toll of casualties on the minor road would remain unknown until the coach could be fully investigated. In its present position it was deemed far too dangerous for rescuers to advance to the front of the cabin where most of the dead and seriously injured were likely to be found. Heavy lifting gear was on its way but could only be used on the go-ahead of a specialist structural engineer for fear of further destabilising the structure. So far, thirteen passengers from the back of the coach had been rescued; three totally unscathed and ten with minor injuries. A mobile drinks and food stall had arrived and the rescued were being comforted with cups of tea and biscuits while awaiting first aid treatment. They were all elderly and in shock but at the same time willing to divest themselves of the horror of the accident by telling their stories, which were all roughly similar. With no view of the road ahead, they were unable to say whether the driver would have had any advance warning that something was amiss with the bridge before driving onto it. The first they knew of the impending disaster was when the coach slammed to a halt amid a cacophony of crunching and squealing noises. A section of the bridge's roadway near the mid-point gave way under the weight of the packed coach. As the tarmacked concrete split away, the section fell and twisted, and the front of the coach nosedived into the abyss created by the fracture.

The local authority's chief civil engineer, responsible for the entire range of engineering works within the authority's borders except rail and water infrastructure, was called away with urgency from his evening meal. Later that night, he had alerted his team of bridge specialists to rendezvous the following morning at the site of the accident, and Alistair and colleagues were already waiting when he arrived on site at first light. Inside the cordon, and with the utmost care, they inspected the destruction. Overnight, under arc lights, the coach had been lifted and swung around to sit safely on the minor road. There were no survivors amongst the twenty passengers plus driver still on board; all displayed impact-type injuries, with the driver's body barely recognisable as that of a human being.

It was to the base of the disintegrating pier that the engineers turned their initial attention. Unprotected by any form of crash barrier, it had taken the full force of the land rover's impact. Alistair bent down and scooped up a handful of mortar; stone-sized pieces crumbled in his hand as he rubbed them between thumb and fingers. He looked steadily at the chief engineer. No words between them were necessary to convey the message that the concrete was of sub-standard quality and that there would have be an official investigation into the cause. They were both aware that no matter the outcome of that high-profile inquiry, unless the culprits were discovered and held publicly to account, mud would stick to all the innocent parties involved in the bridge's design, construction, and maintenance.

The broadcasters were the first to air a detailed account of what had happened on that fateful day. They plotted the course on the television screen of the unfolding scenario with maps and diagrams, times and numbers, statistics and probabilities. According to them, two separate factors had caused the enormous loss of life; a speeding motorcyclist who had driven recklessly and who was currently the target of a nationwide police hunt, and a mooted construction fault – with possible criminal intent – in the bridge which was now the subject of intense forensic scrutiny. Alistair ran his fingers through his hair and clasped his hands tightly in his lap. The company that had supplied the concrete mix and reinforcement steel rods was the same company for whom Arne was paid mega-dollars to lobby for contracts. As one of their non-executive directors, he would need to provide truthful answers to any questions posed to him in court.

Chapter 4

ARNE

1972

Arne's response to the telephone call from a journalist asking him how he felt about being associated with an organisation that was being investigated for malpractice in what had been dubbed "The concrete case" by the media was of the "get lost" variety. Although the journalist failed to understand the actual Dutch swear words he used, she did understand the click on the line when Arne slammed down his receiver. Accountability was not Arne's forte and he had been in a foul mood ever since the bridge accident had happened. It wasn't so much the number of dead that bothered him – although he was truly sorry so many people had been hurt – it was a question of how he could justify his non-exec earnings from PerfectMix Limited, if interrogated in court.

The woman sitting on the sofa next to him stirred. She attempted to kiss him on the cheek but was brushed aside. Arne stood up abruptly. He'd come to another pivotal moment in his life. There had been many such moments previously and he had negotiated them successfully, he reminded himself. After a brief goodbye, a promise to get in touch soon, and a parting kiss on the lips, he left her flat hurriedly and made his way home. He would meet the new challenge head on and not worry overly about who got hurt if they got in his way.

He had based himself in Pimlico for the last six years; an expensive area of central London known for its gardens and Regency architecture. Through contacts and networking, he had bought a flat at an advantageous price on the top floor of a four-storey building that occupied a corner plot. Formerly owned by a sailing companion whose family sponsored big yacht events, it was now Arne's only home. Small in size, it had the kudos of a top-notch postal address with charming views over Eaton Square gardens in one direction and the busy Victoria railway terminus in the other, although few friends or acquaintances were invited in to appreciate those views. It was his sanctuary, his den, a place where he could be himself, a shelter in hard times, a place for thought and reflection, and a setting where he could cry his eyes out in private for the loss of his father. Apart from his cleaner-cum-shopper of essential items, the only other person to visit the flat on a regular basis was his daughter, and those visits were rare.

He sat down heavily in an armchair. The unrelenting tentacles of the media had managed to locate him at his current girlfriend's flat, and therefore he could expect nothing less than a constant barrage of annoying calls to his own telephone number. He crossed his legs, stretched out his torso, and flung back his head as if inspecting the state of the ceiling decoration, but there was no inspiration to be had there. He hummed a tune to himself, a favourite jingle from his schooldays, but it did not lighten his mood. If anything, it made him feel more morose. He got up and stood by the window giving views of Victoria station. He stared at the commuters hurrying to catch their trains home, at those who had just arrived and were looking for buses to take them onward to the West End for a concert maybe, at the ever-moving taxi rank as just hired black cabs left full from the front and empty taxis joined at its rear. He wondered if all the people he saw were satisfied with their lives. Had their youthful hopes been fulfilled or had they been dashed against some rocky outcrop? Were they doubting themselves as he was doing now? It was a seminal moment, he realised, and one that made him question just what he had to show for the last thirty years.

The telephone rang. Arne stared it in the face for some time but did not pick up the receiver. Instead, he hastily grabbed his jacket, took the stairs down two at a time and left the building via the service exit. Out on the street, hands tucked in his bomber-jacket pockets, he started walking with no clear thought as to where he was heading. Soon he found himself striding up Buckingham Gate and along The Mall to arrive and mingle with the throngs of humanity always present in Trafalgar Square. He was in the heart of theatreland. He stopped. What was he here to do? He didn't know. The only thought that came into his head was the need to contact his girlfriend the next day to explain his abrupt departure from her flat.

The following evening, they would go out to dinner in a smart Italian restaurant and they would spend the night together in her bed.

He was looking up at the statue of Lord Nelson standing on his lofty perch at the top of a lonely Corinthian column, a man of the seas and the oceans just like Arne, when he became aware of someone calling out his name. He turned in the direction of the sound, scanning faces for one he recognised. Moving towards him was a man short in stature but wide in girth with spectacles and long hair which hung over his collar. He was instantly recognisable as a mariner from his wartime past.

'Hi, Arne,' he said excitedly, clasping Arne's outstretched hand. 'It is you, isn't it?'

'Yes, it is me,' confirmed Arne, somewhat amazed. 'I would have recognised your physique anywhere. What are you doing in London?'

'On vacation with my wife and her sister,' said his former naval senior officer. 'They've gone to a theatre show and I've got the evening free.'

'So, you're strolling around enjoying the sights and sounds of London.'

'And now I'm hoping that we can share a couple of hours together catching up with our pasts,' said Chuck in his distinct American accent. 'It's been too long, Arne, since we swapped stories.'

They were both from similar sailing backgrounds. It had been Chuck's father who had taught him how to sail in much the same way that Pieter had passed on his knowledge to Arne. It was Chuck's father too who had a boatyard on the eastern seaboard near Hampton, Virginia. But apart from their wartime activities when they served together on merchant shipping, their similarities ended there.

'The last time we met, Arne, was at the presentation ceremony of our war medals for working on convoys,' started Chuck, after they had found a relatively quiet restaurant off the main thoroughfares around Trafalgar Square. Chuck was drinking a cold lager, while the mostly teetotal Arne sipped intermittently at a glass of rosé wine. Food had been ordered and they had time to reminisce. 'I keep mine in a silver frame which hangs in our hallway,' continued Chuck. 'The kids wanted me to do so. What have you done with yours?'

'I keep it in a desk drawer,' replied Arne, sounding a little embarrassed and added as way of explanation, 'I've moved around a lot over the last three decades. Home has been a lot of different places since they were awarded to us.'

'Every time I pass mine in the hallway, I feel proud. Proud of what we did. Proud of the hardships we endured. And proud to have served with so many brave men, including you, Arne.'

'They were difficult times,' agreed Arne, 'but we all had a common denominator, our heritage.'

'The Free Dutch. I was amazed that there were so many of us, even if many like me were first generation Americans.'

'We all seemed to be adventurers like Marco Polo, feeling the need to explore the world, yet prepared at the drop of a hat to defend our small land mass on the continent of Europe.'

'How did you end up on convoys?' asked Chuck, who had volunteered as soon as he had seen a newspaper article calling for Americans with a Dutch heritage to form into various fighting units to repel the Germans.

'It's a long story,' replied Arne. He paused whilst wondering if he should stop there or continue. He was comfortable in Chuck's presence and decided to carry on. 'After escaping across the North Sea, I spent a few months with people in Norfolk before being called to London to give as much information as I knew to the intelligence services about the Dutch coastline, its outlying islands and Bremerhaven. They didn't need me as a translator then as many of our diplomats who spoke near perfect English had either elected to stay in London or had been trapped there by the speed of the German invasion.'

'So, you joined up?'

'Not exactly,' said Arne. 'I was told that I could join my fellow free countrymen learning how to fire a rifle and throw a hand grenade, and it would give me a roof over my head while I was training. I didn't fancy that. I told them my skills were in sailing and I would be more useful teaching at a naval college.' Arne shrugged his shoulders. 'I protested when they suggested I would be more suitable as a rating on merchant vessels, but it didn't do me any good. They gave me a train warrant to Liverpool and said they might need me again if Great Britain was not invaded.'

'It was goodbye, then. Hero for crossing the North Sea single-handed but don't expect any privileges.'

'Exactly. But when I joined the SS Serpent and discovered that most of the other ratings were young

Dutch lads who just like me had escaped from the Nazis, I didn't feel so hard done by.'

'The familiarity of speaking in your mother tongue again would have helped you settle down,' said Chuck thoughtfully.

'I put on the ill-fitting and scratchy uniform they gave me, was shown the bunk I would share with another rating who would be on the opposite twelve-hour watch to me, had some hot food in the mess, and by nightfall we had slipped out of territorial waters heading for an assembly area with other merchant vessels,' said Arne. 'There was no going back,' he added ruefully.

'And I was waiting to join your ship when you finally docked in Boston.'

'But there was no going ashore for sightseeing. It was non-stop maintenance work on the ship whilst a shore-based crew loaded the important military cargo.'

'And all hush hush with civilian and military police in charge on the docks,' agreed Chuck. 'I wondered what I had let myself in for. It was only when I met the other guys who had volunteered and were new on board like me that I was glad to be part of the crusade against fascism.'

The remainder of their time together was filled with wartime reminiscences of life on geriatric merchant ships that should have been retired years before, of patching up corroded metalwork, oiling stubborn machinery, fixing broken lights, and being first in line for food when the galley opened. Little was mentioned about the huge dangers they encountered every minute they were in convoy formation, or of pulling sailors who were near exhaustion out of the cold Atlantic when their vessel had been torpedoed.

Unusually, Arne had sipped his glass dry, and Chuck had insisted on a refill when ordering his third lager. The sharp change of subject may have been due in equal parts to an alcoholic lubrication to which Arne was lately unaccustomed coupled with his dejected mood.

'Your life,' started Arne without any consideration for the niceties of privacy. 'Has it been rewarding?'

'Rewarding?' questioned Chuck. 'In what terms do you mean?'

'The last three decades. Are you satisfied with how they have turned out?'

'That's deep stuff,' replied Chuck after some reflection. 'I was happy, basically, just to survive the war. When America entered in nineteen-forty-one, I quit convoys to join an American unit. My father pulled some strings and got me a place in the US Naval College in Annapolis to train fast track as an officer. As you know, I saw active service in the Pacific.'

'And afterwards?' probed Arne, 'have you achieved your goals?'

'I didn't have any goals, Arne, other than to lead a normal life. Thanks to my father, I took over the boatyard and have loved running it ever since. I have a happy marriage and three healthy daughters who I can indulge. I live a conservative life and don't have any goals other than to look after my family. What more would a man want?' Chuck added, turning the tables on Arne.

'You are content,' Arne summed up.

'Damn right, I'm content. Why wouldn't I be?'

It was a question to which Arne had no answer. Chuck finished his beer, looked at his watch, said how much he had enjoyed talking over old times, and then left to wait outside the concert hall for his wife and sister-in-law at the end of the musical show. Arne might there and then have reflected on the values that governed Chuck's life and the contentment that he so obviously enjoyed, but he didn't. Instead, he made his way by foot to Leicester Square and dived down into a members' only club where there was music, dancing, and girls to chat up. His moment of self-doubt had passed and he was ready again to showboat his headlining skills.

If Arne believed that a swaggering approach with reference to his glamorous lifestyle, sporting achievements and war record was sufficient to deflect criticism and third-party responsibility for the bridge tragedy, then he was very much mistaken. The media, as always, took the approach of a dog with a bone, but it was the general public's fixation on fair play that was the real factor. They had lost their appetite for poseurs of any description.

As the weeks passed, and evidence of suspected malpractice surfaced, Arne's association with the concrete supplier in return for a fat fee became an increasing burden. Although it was legally impossible to lay a finger of guilt at Arne's door, his link with the company by association was damning. At such a time Arne did what Arne did best. He scarpered to the southern seas, borrowed a boat from an erstwhile sailing chum and went solo around a sector of the southern hemisphere ostensibly to break some obscure record. It bought time, but it proved to be a fundamental error. By the time he finally arrived back in Pimlico some six months later, his creditors – those who had done him favours of one kind or another over the years so that he could swan around the world and be seen in all the right places – had lost faith in their lobbyist protégé. Their tolerance was running dry and so were his funds, and it was Chuck who came to the rescue with an interesting job offer.

* * *

They stood on the bluff overlooking the broad spur of the Hampton River that after leaving the Atlantic Ocean and snaking around an elongated land mass, travelled northwards to the main marina in downtown Hampton. Recreational sailing clubs and boatyards of various descriptions were dotted along its sandy banks, the largest of which had been the life's work of Chuck's father.

'See,' said Chuck very proudly, pointing at the name in large capitals on the boatyard's main building, Hag & Son – shipwrights.'

'It's impressive,' replied Arne. 'It brings back boyhood memories of my father's boatyard in Harlingen.'

'Boatyards are in our blood, Arne. We were brought up as toddlers with our lives revolving around what was happening in the yard.'

'You're right,' agreed Arne, 'but for me there was no happy ending. When I returned to Harlingen after the war, there was no boatyard left. It had been destroyed.'

'War damage, I presume,' said Chuck sympathetically.

'Bombings and sabotage. Probably neglect too. And

no father either,' said Arne sadly in a tone of voice that would have left no listener doubting Arne's love for his father.

'You never did tell me how he died,' said Chuck after a lengthy pause.

'While you were in charge of a patrol boat in the Pacific,' recalled Arne, 'I had been assigned to British Intelligence as an acting representative of the free Dutch forces.'

'What did you do?' enquired Chuck.

'All manner of tasks: translator, interpreter, supplying geographical knowledge of areas the Allies were considering for clandestine missions, quiet coastal locations to land or pick up members of the Dutch resistance, possible targets for raiding parties, and, of course, everything I knew about Bremerhaven. It was a hectic time and although I was safe behind a desk most of the working day, it was an exhausting time mentally.' He paused for a break as they both watched a wooden boat with classic lines glide gracefully down the slipway of Chuck's boatyard to enter the water without a splash. 'She's a good looker,' said Arne admiringly.

'The job I want you to do is about a vessel like her,' replied Chuck, 'but I'll tell you about that later. Go on with the story of your father,' he urged.

'After the invasion in Normandy, when the allied forces were back fighting on the continent, there was a tremendous demand for information about German troop positions in the Low Countries. The Dutch resistance was providing much of that intelligence by radio, but it was a highly dangerous task for their operators and for anyone found to be associated with them. Those found helping the Allies were either summarily shot, or, far worse, were tortured first for the information they had passed on, and then shot.' Arne sighed deeply. 'I wasn't to know then that my father had been the co-ordinator of the resistance group in the Harlingen area.'

'In the scheme of things, I guess that particular coastal area was very important,' said Chuck sombrely.

'The sea approaches had been heavily fortified by the Germans, but as their requirements for troops in France became more pressing, so the resistance had more freedom of movement and were able to gather information and to report on what was happening in the area.'

'All the valuable observations they had risked their lives to obtain.'

'I feared greatly for my family, particularly Pieter, in those long months between the Normandy landings and the push back of German troops across the Rhein with the eventual capitulation of the Nazis. So many times, I had wondered if my father had got involved with the resistance, risking his life for the cause. It was the sort of thing he would do. Also, I knew nothing of what had happened to my mother and sisters or the boatyard, but I feared the worst.'

'When exactly did you find out?' asked Chuck.

'I was drafted to somewhere in Holland when the need for interpreters became urgent. I was attached to a small unit of the Royal Signals Corps whose chief responsibility was the maintenance of communications with forces up at the front and with the high command situated in various quarters previously requisitioned by the Germans but vacated in double quick time as their armies fell back to safer positions. The local inhabitants were cheerful and so grateful to be liberated but at the same time mindful that the Germans might make a counter attack at any moment,' Arne recalled.

'A nervous period for everybody,' stated Chuck. 'I can't begin to imagine how awful it must have been.'

'One day, I found myself near Harlingen,' said Arne. 'I asked to be excused for the remainder of the day so that I could try and obtain news of my family. The officer in charge not only agreed to my request but also arranged a lift on the back of a motorcycle as Harlingen was at least eight kilometres from where we were.' Chuck said nothing. He waited patiently for Arne to assemble his recollections. 'We approached with caution in case there were any stray Jerries around. The town was calm and on first sight looked reasonably normal. There was bomb damage but most buildings looked intact. Everywhere looked shabby, including the people who seemed to be going about their daily lives as best they could. But they smiled at us when they saw our British uniforms. Then I spotted someone I knew from my school days. He didn't recognise me at first. We were both seventeen when last we'd met, and now we were aged twenty-two and were adults who had been tempered by the vicissitudes of wartime living.'

'You asked him about your family?'

'I did. Immediately,' said Arne, his lips pressed tightly together in a downward curve. 'I knew it was bad news as he was reluctant to tell me. My father was dead, along with some other resistance workers. He had been executed by firing squad.'

'Pour encourager les autres,' commented Chuck in surprisingly good French.

'A warning,' agreed Arne, nodding.

'What happened to his body?' enquired Chuck sensitively.

'Taken away on the back of a lorry according to my former schoolmate,' said Arne, 'together with the others, and dumped in front of the town hall for all to see.' Arne hesitated. 'It all happened at a time when the Germans were in disarray. It was just a matter of time before they were beaten and they knew it. Where once they might have put them in mass graves or sent them to Germany for interrogation, they had to make quick decisions about disposal.'

'They could have burned the corpses, I suppose,' suggested Chuck, who was already feeling a great sadness for his former shipmate. 'A heavy dousing of petrol and there wouldn't have been any identifying evidence left. Just a few odd bits of human bone. What about your mother and sisters?'

'I found our street. Apart from a couple of nearby homes which had been turned into rubble by a bomber which had crashed down after being hit by a fighter, I later learnt, the buildings looked mostly normal. A woman who I didn't know opened our front door when I knocked. I told her I lived here before the war and that I wanted to speak to my mother. She bristled. I pushed inside and called out my mother's name but there was no reply. I asked again about the whereabouts of my mother. She told me to go to the boatyard. I should find my sisters there.'

'She was unfriendly?'

'Very.' Arne's pale blue eyes had lost their sparkle as he recounted the story. 'My mother was German by birth. I wondered if she had been ostracised because of that. She wouldn't have deserved it as she had served the local community well during the years she had lived in the Harlingen region.'

'Did you find your sisters at the boatyard?'

'I found my younger sister there, but it was no longer the boatyard that I had known and loved. It resembled a junk yard and was half derelict. And my sister looked pale and thin and so much older than when I'd last seen her. We'd never been very close,' reflected Arne, 'but we embraced passionately. It was then that she struck me with a further hammer blow.' Chuck waited fearfully, afraid of what that blow might be. It was a warm day but he shivered in dread of what Arne might say. 'My elder sister,' continued Arne, 'had been shot too, and my mother had committed suicide.'

It was the following morning before the two men settled down at a drawing board in the well-equipped office on a mezzanine floor of Chuck's boatyard. The bombshell of yesterday's news had drained both men, and they preferred to concentrate on the job Chuck hoped Arne would do.

'That beautiful boat that we watched slip into the water yesterday, Arne, is the reason why I asked you here,' started Chuck. 'I never had the pleasure of meeting your father, or of visiting the Visser boatyard of Harlingen, but I'd seen the pre-war advertisements for your latest boat in a sailing magazine. The building of wooden boats had been the love and the life of my father and he was so impressed by its looks and its simplified design that he decided to make his version of it. Unlike your father, he wasn't a boat designer, he was an entrepreneur and, at heart, a businessman. He could see the potential of your blueprint. After a long search he found a boat designer who he believed could fulfil my father's criteria and who was keen to do so. That boat we saw yesterday was his version of your original design.'

'There was something familiar about it,' said Arne, 'but it was bigger.'

'Everything in the United States is bigger, including the people,' said Chuck chuckling. 'Our business ventures weren't interrupted until we entered the war in nineteen-forty-one, and by that time we had built and sold a dozen "Serenader" models, as we named them. The one we saw yesterday had come in for a refit. She was still going strong and her owner hoped to continue sailing her for many years to come.'

'Is wood still popular?' asked Arne, 'I thought it had given way to other, synthetic materials.'

'They're lighter, more durable and require less craftsmanship than wood, that's true,' said Chuck, 'but there is still a market for traditional wooden vessels. It's a niche we could successfully fill. You see,' continued Chuck, expressing his thoughts with hand gestures, 'our yard is not big enough to compete in the new market for low-cost vessels that the multitude of weekend, recreational sailors want. You almost need a factory set up for that. But the niche of a smaller market for the older, more discerning sailor who puts quality and style before price is still valuable.'

'And it's where you want to be.'

'Yes. I'm forty-nine, Arne, about the same age as you. My children are girls and they're not interested in anything to do with sailing. They have other hobbies and other plans for their working lives. I can't hand down my business to the next generation in the same way that my father did for me.'

'You will have to sell it at some stage,' commented Arne.

'Probably sooner rather than later, but dependent on the time in the market place being right. So, expansion into another sphere with all the concomitant retooling and the need to learn new methods and craftmanship doesn't seem attractive when you know it's for a shortish time period. I'd rather stick to something that I know will keep us profitable for a good number of years to come. I want to look after my staff too. Without their loyalty the business would never have thrived for so long.'

'And what is it you want from me?'

'Your help and permission to build and market exact copies, with adjustment for size, of your pre-war masterpiece.'

'You mean like the boat I sailed across the North Sea to escape from the Germans.'

'That very model,' said Chuck, guiding him down the mezzanine steps to a corner of the boatyard where a boat lay covered under a thick tarpaulin. I acquired this one from a man in the state of Maine who had bought it second-hand in the early nineteen-fifties. He was elderly and no longer fit to sail it but wanted to find a good home in a maritime museum or the like for classic designs where it could be displayed and admired by other boat aficionados.'

'Is there a story to be told?' asked Arne sensing a certain unease in Chuck's demeanour.

'Yes,' replied Chuck a little reluctantly, 'there is. My father told me that he had purchased and taken delivery of the boat featured in Monthly Sailing just before the war commenced. Soon after, he received an enquiry from someone upstate asking if he would be prepared to loan him the boat until after the war had ended. He too had ordered the same boat but it had not been completed before the invasion.'

'And probably never was,' remarked Arne.

'Probably. The man was rich, and offered my father a generous sum for the loan with a faithful promise that it would be returned as soon as his own boat was finished. According to my father, usually an astute business man, he dithered in the face of a sob story and agreed to the loan.'

'The cash was useful, I presume.'

'At that juncture in my father's life, very useful. And my father felt sure he would have honoured the commitment to return it eventually, but when my father made enquiries after the war's end, he was told that the man had died and the boat had been sold as part of his estate. As my father had no official paperwork to prove it hadn't belonged to this man, he couldn't challenge the legal situation.' After a pause, Chuck added, 'it was his only real mistake in his business life, and one he deeply regretted. But now you know why the timbers under this tarpaulin are so precious.'

'The boat must have had a patent,' suggested Arne, mulling over the story but happy to move on. 'At just fifteen then, I was too young to be concerned with design registrations and the general bureaucracy of bringing a boat to market. But obviously this must have been done. My father was not a businessman but he would have been attentive to such important details.'

'So, who would own the rights?'

'Probably the Visser company, but I truly don't know. I guess you would have to make enquiries with the Patent Office for The Netherlands, although it's probably part of a centralised Common Market body now. And there is no certainty that it survived the war intact.'

'Would your surviving sister know?'

'I doubt it, but she might,' said Arne with a heavy heart. 'When I found her at what remained of Pieter's boatyard, she was in a state of turmoil. She's only one year older than me, and was deeply affected by the loss of our parents and older sister. She was still haunted by their deaths as they had died only a few weeks previously. She could barely talk coherently but it seemed that they were no longer required for the jobs my two sisters had been doing in Leeuwarden at the start of the war, general book-keeping, and invoicing for a manufacturing company. No orders meant no work for most of the workforce.'

'They were laid off?'

'That's about the size of it. It wasn't the company's fault,' Arne pointed out, 'it was the war.'

'Tough to live in an occupied country,' Chuck summed

up with feeling. 'How was your sister surviving without wages?'

'Local people were helping one another by bartering, and some of Pieter's former employees, laid off themselves, rallied round.' Arne looked down at his feet as if in contemplation. 'I had so little time with her then. The corporal kept tugging at my arm to indicate the need to return to our unit. I had to tell her to be brave and that I would return as soon as I could but that might not be until several weeks' time. We embraced again and she cried. I felt wretched leaving her, despite having promised myself when I was escaping across the sea in difficult circumstances that I would never again allow my feelings for someone else to affect my own future.'

'So, when did you see her again?'

'It was much longer than the few weeks I'd anticipated,' started Arne, 'it was several months after the war's end in the spring of nineteen-forty-six, and I had just been demobbed from helping my unit which had been stationed in Bremen as part of the allied occupying forces. I speak fluent German,' he added, 'and there was a great need for interpreters in the early months of peace. The civilian population was in disarray. There was no local government or any services that we usually regard as essential for living. Life for the local civilians was miserable. I was constantly busy translating rules and regulations and acting as a go-between. But when I finally got back to Harlingen, I learned the whole story.'

'Go on,' urged Chuck. It wasn't fiction. It was a true and compelling story about the cruelty of war.

'I went and stood outside our home at first. Nothing

112

appeared changed. A window was open and I was able to peep in. I saw the same woman I had seen previously and presumed that she was living there. She'd been unhelpful before, so I went to the boatyard where I found it humming with activity. Some of my father's previous employees were present. We greeted one another ecstatically as survivors of a terrible period in our history. The boatyard no longer looked derelict. They had repaired or rebuilt whatever they could with materials they had scavenged, and cleaned out the entire yard so that any meaningful work that came their way, whatever its nature, could be commenced straightaway. They too were short of cash and very thin, but their spirits were high.'

'They must have been glad to see you,' said Chuck. 'Someone at last to take charge of the boatyard.'

'Yes, I think they presumed I would. But I was only twenty-three and I realised in that moment that my intentions lay elsewhere. Then suddenly my sister arrived and I forgot completely about the future as all I wanted to know was what had happened to Pieter and Frieda and my other sister. I expected the worst, but in the end even bad news came as a kind of relief. It was the full truth at last.' Arne paused, reliving the emotions he had felt at the time, but when he picked up the story it was in a dispassionate manner. 'When news filtered through to the general population that the Germans had failed to cross the Channel and occupy The British Isles, it gave hope to the people that they would be liberated one day. Resistance groups formed to collect and pass on intelligence. Pieter wanted to help but was given the cold shoulder on account of Frieda being German. When my sisters were laid off and had to return to live at home, they too felt the full force of the locals' censure. They lived through the initial period of the occupation minding their own business. There was minimal interaction with other residents of the town although people were polite especially to Pieter who they knew had been doing his best to find suitable work for his craftsmen so that he could pay them some small portion of their wages. It was Frieda who suffered the most. However loud her protests, she was condemned by her country of birth. She was German and the locals didn't approve. One day she left the house unannounced and never returned. Her body was later found in a canal some distance away. My father was told that it was suicide. Death was ten a penny in those times and no challenge could be mounted to verify the cause, but it was likely to be correct as Frieda's behaviour had become erratic in the previous few months with the strain of knowing that she was the source of her family being shunned. They were all upset, Pieter in particular. Frieda had been a good wife and mother. But they had no course of action other than to be pragmatic. With the removal of my mother, sentiments towards my father and sisters softened. She had been the irritant. As resistance activity increased, so my father's help was accepted. He had a bicycle and couriered intelligence to a radio operator. He was a familiar face about the region and as he was almost fifty, he didn't normally attract the attention of the Germans. However, with the D-day landings, the Germans were on heightened alert and were in no mood for compromise. They located the dwelling of the group's radio operator and Pieter's fate was sealed.

He was killed by firing squad along with other members of the resistance group who had been trapped. When my elder sister tried to recover Pieter's body from the town square where they had been left to rot, she was shot and killed by a German officer with a pistol for attempting to remove his body against his instruction. It was a war crime, of course, as my sister was a civilian and unarmed. I really don't know how my younger sister, Ilse, had the fortitude to carry on. She was all alone but somehow managed to surmount her feelings of desperation and do what was necessary to stay alive.'

'Did she have anyone to support her?' enquired Chuck. 'A former school friend or one of your father's trusted employees?'

'She'd been living and working in Leeuwarden for a couple of years, so she had rather lost touch with school chums, but a man named Henrik who Pieter had befriended, rose to the occasion and helped her.'

'Who was he?'

'He might have been a down-and-out, but I really don't know. Pieter was a good man and it would have been in character for him to show compassion to someone in need. Anyhow, this Henrik had been living with a young couple throughout the war. They had given him a roof over his head and Pieter had been supplying them all with food which was in very sparse supply. In order to bring in some money, Ilse had allowed another family who had lost their own home due to war damage to live in our house. Nearly everything had to be bought on the black market and money was essential for survival.' Chuck looked chastened. He'd had no idea how terrible wartime existence was for the civilian population. In his own country, folks had been able to live off the fat of the land throughout the years of hostilities even when they were involved in fighting in various theatres of war across the globe. Chuck sighed as he realised that what the civilians endured had been worse than his own time on convoys when he and Arne were exposed to short periods of high danger but could relax and enjoy the fruits of life when they were stateside awaiting their next convoy. The contrast was stark. 'Ilse moved in with Henrik and the young couple and they shared the modest rental income,' said Arne picking up the story. 'The four of them got by until the war finally ended. After that, Henrik started working in a shop and my sister was asked to return to her former job in Leeuwarden.'

'But what about the boatyard?' asked Chuck quite reasonably.

'It was a dilemma. Even in normal times her path forward would have proved a real quandary. She knew little about boats, you see.' Arne turned and pointed up at Chuck's office on the mezzanine floor before going on. 'If it had been mostly about book-keeping or general office administration then things might have been different, not just for her but for me too.'

'You could have found a way to work together to keep the Visser boat company alive.'

'Possibly, but we had no paperwork of any description to indicate that Pieter's boatyard had existed pre-war because the small office cum design area within the building where Pieter did most of his work was destroyed by fire when a bomber was shot down by a German gun crew on the ground. Although it didn't hit the building directly, it exploded on impact and, according to those who witnessed it, the resulting fireball engulfed part of the boatyard.'

'No documentation,' said Chuck. 'Tricky.'

'Even in peacetime it would have proved a headache to obtain copies of ownership and the like, but following five years of occupation and the destruction of so many government buildings, it would have been nigh impossible to prove it was ours.'

'But there would have been anecdotal evidence that it existed,' replied Chuck correctly. 'And some actual boats they'd built.'

'Small boats were confiscated and destroyed at the beginning of the occupation. Only those that the boatyard had built for overseas customers would have survived. Tracing those would have been difficult. Pieter would probably have remembered names and addresses of his overseas clients but he was dead and there was nobody else with that knowledge.'

'I see the difficulty you both faced. So, what did you do?'

'For my sister, it was the logical decision to go back to her former job in Leeuwarden. Harlingen and the boatyard held no happy memories for her. She started life afresh and although times were still hard, as restrictions eased and the population got back on its feet, so Ilse's life there blossomed. She became friendly with the firm's accountant and soon after they married, emigrated to Australia, and eventually had children. They were a young family with skills,' said Arne wistfully, 'just what emerging countries in the southern hemisphere wanted. They lived in Perth for five years and I met up with Ilse on several occasions when I was sailing professionally.'

'So,' started Chuck, followed by a long pause as he determined what to say next, 'no chance of getting any official documentation about ownership of the boat's design.'

'None whatsoever in my opinion. Nor any chance of being challenged about your legitimacy to build copies.' After a pregnant pause Arne added, 'we can start with a clean sheet.' Chuck smiled. He could go ahead and build Pieter's super little wooden boat and implicit in Arne's remark was that he would help with the prototype. A silent shake of the hands was all that was necessary to seal the deal.

Arne's brief sojourn in the United States - no more than a few months - had proved both lucrative and convenient as it had allowed media attention surrounding the bridge catastrophe to simmer down. On his return to Pimlico, Arne discreetly severed connections with the concrete company and walked away from the incident as an almost innocent man, his former concrete lobbyist remuneration now exceeded by the deal he had struck with Chuck; a percentage of the sale price of each boat built. It had been decided that it might be a step too far for Arne to associate himself publicly with the launch of the first post-war reincarnation of his father's design. Despite Arne's gung-ho desire for a glitzy advertising campaign, Chuck, with his hand firmly in charge of the tiller, wisely chose a more modest promotion that focussed on the quality of the boat rather than the glamour or celebrity of its aspiring occupants.

With the money supply side of his bon viveur lifestyle seemingly stabilised, Arne's thoughts turned to less prosaic matters: a business empire. His few months staying with Chuck's family, and working with him daily in a calm and progressive atmosphere were responsible for a new line of thinking. He was nearly forty-nine and couldn't expect his playboy image and Nordic good looks to last much longer. As he lay in bed one morning with no reason to do anything or to hurry anywhere, he felt a sense of melancholy. Chuck's laidback attitude to life, with emphasis on a family life and a business which he enjoyed that would adequately, but no more, take care of his wife and children for as long as they needed support, was a lesson to consider. Could he too find happiness and satisfaction in the bosom of his family? Was his personality type suitable to a mundane existence that centred entirely on the humdrum matters of daily living? Nah! But he could and would try to see his daughter and sister more regularly and he would build his own business empire even if he didn't know yet where to start.

It was a holiday in Spain – the new winter playground of the affluent non-skiing middle classes – that the idea for the business empire occurred to Arne. He was on a freebie lodgings holiday in a quiet village on the Costa del Sol. An "old mate" as he referred to his host, Barry, had invited him along with another couple, to spend a few days at his newly revamped villa. Arne had speculatively asked if he could bring his daughter too to make the numbers even. Normally at pains to keep his relationship with her private to shield her from the straightlaced morals of that era when illegitimacy was still regarded as a stigma, it would fulfil a resolution Arne had made to see his daughter more often. Since his host and hostess and the invited couple all knew that he had an illegitimate child and appeared not to mind, it seemed a good way to spend some quality time with her.

One day, leaving the "girls" to continue their sunbathing regime around the pool, the men drove a short distance along the coast to a newly-opened golf course. Affording stunning sea views from several fairways, according to the advertising leaflet handed out at the restaurant where they had dined the previous evening, the men were eager to sample the course's terrain. It was whilst playing one of the sea view holes that Barry pointed out to his playing partners the changes that had occurred in the region since he had bought his villa – then in a somewhat run down state – a few years previously. Extolling the virtues of the winter climate, open spaces, friendly locals, and a helpful regional government willing to consider and support with tax breaks all manner of developments, Barry suggested that the area was an entrepreneur's dream and could easily become a mecca for sporting activities.

'I suppose so,' said Arne without conviction, placing his pitching wedge back into his carry bag.

'You don't sound convinced,' replied Barry, who had made his packet in second hand car dealerships.

'I'm guessing that there's only a limited number of golfers and tennis players who could afford to spend winter weeks or even months on the sunny Iberian Peninsula.'

'But you're not thinking package holidays, Arne. That's where success lies because it opens up a whole new raft of holidaymakers. An enormous market.'

'I thought package holidays were for the working classes in seaside places like Blackpool and Great Yarmouth.'

'You're way out of date,' interjected Barry's other friend, Victor. 'From a slow start in the early nineteen-sixties, package holidays have increased in popularity year on year. And, mark my words, they are about to take off.' Barry sniggered and Victor smiled, but Arne failed to understand the joke.

'Victor,' said Barry, 'is in the aircraft charter business.' Arne continued to look blank. 'You see, Arne, package holidays are moving from the image of coach travel for the working classes to charter air travel for the upwardly mobile classless society of the nineteen-seventies, and Spain is their number one destination.'

'They can get to Spain more quickly and cheaply than a coach ride to Margate,' said Victor, 'and just as importantly, they will be able to show off their suntans when they return home.'

'A status symbol,' added Barry. 'Not to be sniffed at.' It was a choice of words that the Dutchman failed to fully understand, but which prompted him to consider which recreational activities might fit the bill.

'But to keep the cost down, wouldn't people on low wages just go for the sun, sand, and sangria?' asked Arne not unreasonably.

'The vast majority probably,' replied Victor. 'But that's almost the beauty of the situation.'

'Why?' asked Arne.

'Because adding a recreational element to their holiday would elevate it into a posher category. No longer just a cheap, basic package holiday that the masses enjoy, but a vacation with a purpose. And crucially,' said Barry, 'because of mass marketing, still good value for money.'

'The economies of scale,' added Victor cannily, 'because they can use the same facilities as the mass market travellers. They just take a slightly different route when they arrive at their destination airport and stay in a slightly higher-grade hotel. Also, they know that they are going to be mixing with people who enjoy the same leisure pursuits as them.'

'Very important,' interjected Barry, 'going away and knowing you are likely to be mixing with people of similar tastes and interests.'

'Yes, I can see how that could be an attractive prospect,' said Arne, 'but could you really get the necessary numbers and what sports are you talking about?'

'Well, golf and tennis already have more than a foothold in the market. Sea diving and lawn bowling are beginning to make their mark too. The next logical step is sailing.'

'For whom?' asked Arne.

'For both the experienced leisure sailor and for beginners,' replied Victor and Barry, almost in unison.

'I'm sure an avid dinghy sailor who loves being out on the water at weekends would welcome warmer climes. The sea around the British Isles in winter can be mighty chilly. Yes, I can see that could work if there were sufficient numbers,' agreed Arne, 'and I suppose that Spain could be an ideal place for beginners to learn. "Man overboard" would certainly be warmer,' he added laughing.

'Welcome to the bigger picture, Arne,' said Victor smiling. 'It's not a question of "if" sailing activities will take off but "when." Those who get in at the bottom rung will reap the most rewards.'

'Many a business empire has flourished with a simple idea which has been executed well,' contributed Barry. 'Together, we have the knowhow, experience and ability to do just that.'

It took some time for Arne to realise that he had been set-up by two sharp operators, but he soon came to see it as a victory of sorts. He had been looking for a business empire – as if wandering around searching the supermarket aisles and shelves for the location where ready-made business empires were stacked – and they had provided him with one. He could tap into their expertise, their resources, their administration, while heading up a company with his own name: Visser Sailing Holidays. It was a dream ticket permitting him to shed the feckless playboy image for one with commercial gravitas. And along the way he could make himself a fortune as his partners in the umbrella company, Barry and Victor, already had impressive track records in the world of commerce. Moreover, he had literally dozens of ideas to make a sailing week in the sun enjoyable.

* * *

The newspaper was passed across the breakfast table from husband to wife. Eva looked up at Jens enquiringly.

'Two items of interest that touch our family on the same day,' he said. 'Would you believe it!'

'Since I started teaching history and politics,' replied Eva calmly, 'I wouldn't dismiss anything as being impossible.' She searched the broadsheet page without spotting either article.

'There and there,' said Jens pointing at two adjacent columns. 'Alistair and the bridge fiasco, then Arne and the Visser Sailing Holidays company.'

'Two for the price of one,' commented Eva, whose command of the English language had come on in leaps and bounds since her marriage to Jens. They tended to speak mostly in English but sometimes lapsed into Spanish when they wanted a degree of privacy. They were living in accommodation rented by the Dutch embassy for their diplomatic staff. Jens' journey to work was no more than a pleasant stroll on a nice day along a wide thoroughfare followed by a left hand turn into a normally quiet square, while Eva took a crowded route on the tube to the university's main building.

'I feel for Alistair and my sister,' said Jens, after giving his wife time to digest the two articles. 'Alistair's company is a truly innocent party but mud sticks to everyone involved however marginally.'

'Time will pass and memories will fade,' replied Eva encouragingly, 'but it does seem unfair.'

'The public inquiry is not due to report until next year. Alistair and his partners will just have to sit tight and weather the media attention until then, but they will grow tired of it.'

'The article about Arne is confusing,' said Eva

frowning. 'To my knowledge he never had anything to do with running a business. I doubt he has the skills to manage a company.'

'I agree,' replied Jens. 'His character doesn't seem suited to a routine nine to five job, even if he is the boss. After half a lifetime of sailing off into the blue yonder whenever he wanted to fulfil his boyhood dreams, I really can't see how he will settle down to daily desk work.'

'He must have some suitable skills though as he was regarded as a good man-manager when he skippered big yacht races. His crews and back-up staff were always full of praise,' said Eva.

'He's good at things he likes doing, but will he be good at doing boring routine stuff that often seems endless?' queried Jens.

'If he gets a good secretary, he might. One who keeps him organised.'

'And on a tight rein.'

Within months of their agreement to work together, BAV Enterprises, the umbrella company of Barry, Arne, and Victor, was coming under the scrutiny of city traders. In their view the concept of upmarket package holidays might herald an unstoppable bandwagon in the holiday market, and one which would produce a reliable and increasing profit stream over many years to come. While leisure pursuits of a physical nature would get the ball rolling, they felt sure that more sedate hobbies such as cordon bleu cooking, landscape painting, and wine tasting would follow. Night would follow day for some considerable time into the future they all agreed which would lead to an unholy scramble to invest in the emerging markets sector.

Via a plan concocted in advance by Barry and Victor, Arne was allowed a wide latitude of creative innovation under the supervision of a shrewd office manager who they had installed in order to keep tabs on Arne's possible haphazard approach to daily commerce, and in particular to fiscal affairs. But Arne managed to surprise everyone who held low expectations of his staying powers, possibly even himself, by applying the same level of application and energy to new tasks set before him as he had always committed to his racing days. Furthermore, Barry and Victor, together with the office manager who turned out to be Barry's adopted sister, were impressed with Arne's grasp of what was commercially viable, and his ability to make deals with the local business fraternity in the various resorts in an effort to get their ventures up and running.

It had not gone without Arne's notice that the shrewd office manager who had been foisted on him might be reporting back to more than one master. Arne grinned at the thought. There were tricks in competitive sailing to discomfort opponents, and it seemed that there might be ploys in commerce too that he would have to learn pronto if he was to succeed.

Visser Sailing Holiday's stunning early success had little to do with luck or general good fortune. Nudged at times in the right direction by Barry or Victor, the hard work put in by Arne and the insightful and meticulous preparations he'd made, were rewarded by full bookings for the first season with a sufficient level of interest in future seasons to suggest that they would be sell-outs too. For someone not used to modesty, Arne's reaction to this apparent triumph was surprisingly low key. He didn't really know what all the fuss was about when congratulated by Barry and Victor on his master strokes; he was used to winning at sailing, and the holiday company was merely an extension of that beloved pastime. He had told them that achieving goals was what he did and Barry and Victor had nodded imperceptibly.

It was Arne's so-called office manager, Gloria, a chartered accountant who knew the tax laws inside out and who could spot a loophole at a hundred paces, who was able to shed some light on Arne's initial success in the fast-moving world of business. Apparently, he knew everything there was to know about his subject and that, together with a silky tongue whenever he wanted anything, plus with his big image, was all that was necessary to impress the clients. When he wants something, she had told her brother, he has the knack of speaking to you as if you are the most exciting person he has ever met. It was reassuring stuff for Barry and Victor as they had taken a chance getting hitched up in business with a partner who had no track record in commerce.

The gossip spread in the sailing clubs around the cold and draughty winter coastline of England that sailing in warmer climes could be great fun. You no longer had to fit the enjoyment of pursuing your hobby into the seasons of spring and summer. A good value option was now available with decent equipment and a schedule of events and entertainment that would give pleasure, and best of all, the planning and arrangements were all done for you. It had been part of Arne's meticulous preparations that the equipment provided and the marina facilities should be of a decent standard – no leaky dinghies with flaking paintwork or worn ropes or frayed sails, and definitely no marinas with dodgy toilet facilities. The customers were pleased not only with the boats and the life jackets provided, but also with the seamanship skills they were taught which they could practise and show off in each daily mini race culminating in a grand finale on the day before they returned home. Socialising became a big part of the holiday experience as boat crews were changed daily to allow everyone in the holiday group to get to know one another with the midnight oil frequently having to last through into the early hours.

Despite the real-world figure of the tall Dutchman, ageing well and still with a full head of thick blonde hair, but not quite matching his big persona, he seemed at one point to be everyone's cup of tea including Gloria's, who was so very smitten. After several long sessions at their office desks sorting out expansion plans for the forthcoming season, they began to mix pleasure with work. Unsurprisingly, it wasn't long before the odd bit of office banter turned into a full-blown affair. Gloria should have known better. Her discipline in the world of accountancy should have been sufficient to warn her that the path she was treading was strewn with potholes, any of which could cause a big upheaval in her domestic life.

In the early days of her passionate fling, circumspection prevailed. At the end of each working day, Gloria returned home to her husband, and Arne went back to his flat in Pimlico. What brought their working relationship into question were the overnight trips they planned to check-out new locations for Visser Sailing Holidays. The thin lips of Barry, Gloria's brother by adoption, curled up into a snarly shape when he learned of their intentions, but he said nothing. Who was he to sit in judgement on his sister's morals? His partner was a bore and he could understand perfectly well how a bit of romance with a suave operator like Arne could turn a girl's head. But matters came to a head in an untimely way when one morning she woke up in Arne's bed in Pimlico. After an afternoon of unbridled sex, followed by a very filling portion of pizza, they forgot to set the alarm clock for five-thirty so that Gloria could get to Victoria Station in time to catch her normal evening train home to East Croydon. A combination of sex, food and wine had taken its toll. Explanations of a convincing nature were not easy to conjure up, and their hastily concocted story of an electrical fault on the line at East Croydon did not stand up to even basic scrutiny.

Gloria was in a fix and had no alternative than to come clean. She was wise enough to realise that her affair with Arne was just that: a high-octane rip-roaring affair that could endure no more than a further few months before fizzling out in tears. It would never happen again, she told her husband when asking for his forgiveness. She would quit her job at Visser Sailing Holidays with immediate effect and Arne would then represent no more than a person from her past. Well aware of his lack of appeal to the fairer sex, her husband agreed her terms. The couple would carry on their marriage as if the interlude of promiscuity had never happened. It was a blip that would never be repeated, she assured him, in her most engaging manner, whilst at the same time biting her lip at the prospect of living out more boring years with him. And the normally restraint accountant would probably have kept her word if she had not discovered some days later that she was pregnant.

Pregnancy had been at the top of the couple's agenda for most of their married life. Both had wanted children from day one of the marriage, but sixteen years on from their nuptials, the cupboard was as bare as it had been when they had pledged their troths to one another. It was only after getting over the shock of becoming pregnant at forty-two that it dawned on Gloria that a possible solution to their problem of childlessness – for that was what it was – had arrived which may have been heaven sent. After dithering for some days about the most viable course of action to suggest, she announced to her husband that she was expecting. His eyes lit up in momentary delight but turned swiftly to dismay as he realised that the child could not be his. In a heavily sarcastic reply, he asked her what she expected him to do about it, only to be told that they could bring up the baby as if it were their own if he so wished. Gardening was Victor's passion when not auditing profit and loss ledgers. Several hours after her announcement he came in from the garden where he had been diligently weeding and pruning and mulching the plants which meant so much to him. Gum boots removed, dirty gardening gloves taken off and hands washed thoroughly, he sat down at the kitchen table opposite his wife. He was ready to talk.

Over the next few hours, through argument and counter argument, they thrashed out the bones of a plan that would permit them to keep the baby. Details followed of how they would handle questions, if they arose, about the child's height and blondness when they were both short in stature and dark brown in hair colour, or why the baby's blood group was not in sync with that of the father. It would be a deception, they accepted reluctantly, that was against the law but one they regarded as being in the child's best interest as they would combine to give it a happy home. All of a sudden, to Gloria, Victor didn't seem to be quite so boring.

All parties breathed an increasingly deep sigh of relief as the days passed without any scandal surfacing in the newspapers. Arne's renown normally made him an easy target for the social gossip columnists, but on this occasion all parties had acted with the utmost effort to keep matters private. It had been an enjoyable sexual encounter for Arne but nothing more than that, or so he thought; he grinned at the salacious thoughts that ran through his mind, although he would only actually miss Gloria for her office managerial skills. He had to admit that she had been pivotal in the early success of his holiday company steering him along the commercial straight and narrow and guiding him through the labyrinth of regulations to which a modern-day company must adhere. Her work ethic also set an inspiring example which had rubbed off on Arne, but which he now very much doubted that he could sustain without her presence. Whilst Arne was considering how to fill this important vacancy, Barry seized the opportunity to bring financial control of Visser Sailing Holidays under his wing. The only control that would rest with Arne would be nominal, although Barry failed to spell this out when he told Arne the good news that he had found a suitable replacement for Gloria. Just what Barry knew about his sister's affair – he had no evidence, it was just supposition – with Arne wouldn't have convinced a three-year-old, but if a few odd pieces of information were put together, a familiar picture emerged: business trips abroad, sudden resignation from job, new job in Cambridgeshire, proposed move of house to Saffron Walden. They were all strange, but nothing quite as strange as the twinkle in Victor's eye. There was something going on, of that Barry was certain.

Arne was keen to close the chapter on Gloria, as discreetly as possible. His daughter was engaged to be married to a likely high-flyer in the diplomatic service and therefore she had read him the riot act: no adverse publicity, no skeletons to emerge from his cupboard, no childish playboy behaviour, no rumours of unpaid taxes, and absolutely no inappropriate sexual frolics. It was bad enough being his illegitimate child, she had warned him, without anything else detrimental coming to light. This would be his only chance to slightly square his deficit with her so he would have to shape up or take the consequences.

If Arne had been aware of the pregnancy things might have been different, but he wasn't. His daughter's warning was fair enough as he conceded that he hadn't fulfilled his parental responsibilities towards her with any degree of distinction. So long as his daughter's marriage loomed large on his calendar, he resolved to do nothing to upset her special day by getting his head down and channelling all his energies into the holiday company, as if Gloria was still there to regulate him. Business trips to potential warm weather destinations – Mediterranean islands proved outstandingly popular – were introduced into the schedule with flights from local airports featuring heavily. Arne was kept busy recruiting local agents to handle the day-to-day management at each venue. He also held seminars to ensure that the staff on the ground interacting with the would-be holiday sailors knew exactly what was expected of them in order to give the paying customer a holiday experience of real quality. In the same way that he had organised and captained elite professional big boat races in his earlier years involving international consortiums dealing in megabucks, he left no stone unturned.

Over the next eighteen months the business gathered real momentum as a direct result of the carefully created holiday model on offer to a stratum of society that was willing to pay just a little bit over the odds for something special, which was achieved especially thanks to Barry for his skills in persuading a dozen or more one-man outfit diving schools to become part of a bigger picture by joining his company. True to the promise he made to his daughter, Arne managed to stay in the background concentrating on his business, but it was a situation that could not last, although the trigger for the bubble bursting was not directly of Arne's making.

In the small hours of one July morning, a squad of Spanish police raided one of the marinas used extensively by Arne's company. Working on a tip off, they managed to locate and seize banned substances from a sunken wreck off the rugged coastline. The question of whether one particular sunken wreck was quite as it seemed, or had been deliberately scuttled to avoid attention from the coastguards, was answered when a sole diver on the wreck transferred small packages sealed in waterproof materials into one of the holiday company's dinghy-class boats. The dinghy, which happened to be sailing nearby the diving wreck, was later sailed into the marina at the end of the day by one of Arne's holiday makers – complicit in the crime – with the packages stowed in a dry hiding place behind the mast to await an overnight collection by a drug dealer and distributor.

Several column inches in British newspapers were devoted to a report of the raid due to its sheer audacity as it involved narcotics with a street value in the hundreds of thousands of Spanish pesetas. The press also highlighted the ease with which the gang – presumed to have used the same system on several previous occasions – were able to execute their plan. But for the tip off, they might have continued indefinitely. Interpol were keen to identify the sham diver and the bogus sailor who had both used Visser Sailing and Diving Holidays as a means of getting their bounty ashore.

Arne was dragged into the case when his company was asked to produce name and address lists of guests on his package holidays at the time of the raid. When put under the microscope, together with guest lists at the same venue in earlier months, two names stood out as being repeat clients; a man and a woman with different surnames but who had provided the same home address in London. A trawl through Scotland Yard's records for matching names, failed to produce mug shots with any likely resemblance to those choosing sailing holidays abroad. But the London address was flagged up as the home of a couple who both had a criminal record.

It was accepted by the investigating authorities that in no way was Arne, or his company, suspected of being in cahoots with the drug dealers, or have any link whatsoever with them other than by pure chance, but the publicity stirred up some awkward facts. When it came to disclosing their assets and paying their taxes, apparently, Arne's partners were not as pure as the driven snow. As the press gleefully made the most of the story's tenuous link with Arne, his now married daughter blamed her father for allowing unnecessary glare to penetrate once again into her life. Surely, she had said down the phone line in the moralistic voice she adopted when telling him off, that he had not gone into partnership with two people he barely knew other than socially without having done due diligence. Arne was quiet at his end of the line. He had done just that. His daughter seemed to sense his discomfort and in a rare moment of tenderness she told him that she was sorry that they had taken advantage of him, but, really, what could he expect as the world of business was full of sharks. Arne could "see" her waving her hands with frustration at the end of the telephone at his innocent approach to big business. Sometimes she seemed to know more about how the world worked than he did. She heard him sigh and tried to think of something kind to say, but nothing sympathetic came and she'd closed with a simple cheerio.

It was sometime later before they talked again. She had news to impart, and it turned out that he had too.

'Hallo, Arne,' she started softly into the chunky black mouthpiece. She had called him by his first name ever since she'd learned that he was her father.

'Hallo, darling,' he replied in the silky-smooth voice that he always reserved for use when calling her by a term of endearment rather than by her name.

'"We" are expecting,' she pronounced excitedly, 'and I wanted you to be the first to know after my mother.'

'Really?' said Arne, reining back his natural desire to make a quip out of what they were expecting in the post.

'Yes, really,' continued his daughter, 'in about three months' time. We've kept it a secret until now as my husband is in line for promotion and a posting to some country as vice-consul. But I can't hide the change in my figure any longer.' Across the airwaves he heard her giggle with delight.

'Congratulations, darling. Will you still be in England when the baby is born?'

'Almost certainly. Apart from my mother, and now you, the Foreign Office is the only other party to know about my pregnancy and they will allow us to stay put in London until after the birth.'

'Where will you be sent?'

'Anywhere that is English, German, or French speaking. We're hoping for France, but will be happy with anywhere really.'

'Well, I must make sure that I see you before you go.'

'That's why I'm ringing,' she said, hesitating in order to get her practised words in the correct order. 'You will be the baby's grandfather.'

'Obviously,' interjected Arne rather unnecessarily.

'Don't interrupt me, Arne,' she snapped. 'We think it's important that the child should know it's heritage from day one,' she added composing herself again. 'Views are becoming more liberal now.'

'Liberal?'

'Yes, liberal. You know that I mean. Morals aren't as stuffy as they were when I was an illegitimate baby.' She heard Arne shuffle at the end of the line. She knew well that it was a topic he didn't like. 'I want you to…,' she corrected herself, 'we want you to fully participate in the baby's life.'

'What does that mean exactly?' asked her confused father.

'Be at the christening, have photos taken holding him or her. That sort of thing. Sending birthdays cards too. And spending time with your grandchild.'

'Yes, of course,' replied Arne, but without any real conviction. 'I shall be happy to do that, but what about your mother? Will she be agreeable to my presence? She might find the situation awkward. We haven't met for many years.'

'Since conception probably,' said his daughter with a ring of bitterness in her hastily selected words, although she knew that it wasn't actually true. They had met a number of times and her mother had simply dismissed Arne as being unsuitable to father her child, or at that stage in his life, any other child.

'Your mother turned me down as being ill-suited to parenthood,' said Arne. 'She was right at that time.'

'And now?'

'I'm older,' he said shrugging his shoulders. 'Wiser? I don't know.'

'You don't have to be wiser, Arne. You just have to care.' It was brutal talk, but she said it how it was. Maybe it was easier to say upsetting things over the telephone line. No face-to-face interactions to inhibit sensibilities.

She had never known him when he cared for someone. He had only ever loved one person, his father, Pieter. And he'd lived the last three decades without fully knowing how he had met his end. He pursed his lips. Could he love again? He didn't know.

'And you don't have to preach,' retorted Arne, 'I'm your father, not your child.'

'Sorry, Arne. I just want you to be part of my child's family. And if you could genuinely care, that would be ace.' There was a pause; both parties were hanging back wishing to avoid further confrontation. But the jolt of family discord had made them both think. Neither had an unblemished record. Neither had acquitted themselves without fault.

'I shall try to do everything you ask of me,' said Arne finally in a serious tone. 'But no promises. And to set the record straight, I did once care for someone very deeply. My father, Pieter, your grandfather.'

'Sorry, Arne,' repeated Stella lamely. 'I stand corrected.' Switching subjects, she said, 'what was it you wanted to tell me?'

'Nothing as important as you had to tell me,' Arne

replied gallantly. He could talk the talk even if he couldn't walk the walk. 'It was just about my sister. You've never met her and I haven't seen her for ages, probably a decade actually.'

'I forgot you had a sister.'

'She got in touch with me recently,' said Arne. 'After five years living in Australia, she and her family returned to live in Leeuwarden. She had been contacted recently by one of the authorities there.' He went silent for a moment. When he restarted there was emotion in his voice. 'My father is to be awarded a posthumous medal for his work with the resistance during the war.'

'Whoa!' exclaimed Stella. 'But the war was over ages ago.'

'Almost thirty years ago,' confirmed Arne. 'But wheels can grind slowly when it comes to complicated matters like that.'

'Whoa!' repeated Stella. 'That's some kind of news to receive thirty years on.'

'She had been campaigning for our father ever since other members of the local resistance had been awarded citations back in the nineteen-sixties. But until recently she'd hit a brick wall because of various factors.'

'What do you mean?' questioned Stella.

'I wasn't there during the war. I'd escaped to Norfolk. But my sister told me there was a general feeling of dislike amongst my parents' neighbours towards my mother because she was German by birth. And it rubbed off on Pieter too, even though the craftsmen he employed held him in high regard.'

'So, your sister just kept gnawing away at the authorities until they caved in.'

'Not quite that, but on those lines. She was on friendly terms with a man named Henrik. Apparently, my father had shared our family's food ration with Henrik and his friends during the occupation. It was thanks to Pieter that they didn't succumb to malnutrition. Henrik never forgot Pieter's generosity, so when by chance he learnt that my sister had been lobbying for Pieter also to receive recognition of his wartime bravery, he helped her by lobbying too. Their joint insistence eventually proved enough for the authorities to re-evaluate the facts.'

'And they gave way.'

'I prefer to think that their change of heart was due to a recognition that they had unfairly excluded my father.'

'A redressing of the balance.'

'Finally,' said Arne. 'And well deserved. My sister wants me to go with her to collect the medal. There will be some sort of ceremony.'

'And you will go, won't you, Arne,' replied his daughter sharply. 'You *must* go. You can leave your holiday company worries behind for a few days.'

'Of course, I will go. No question. It will be a proud moment for both of us.'

'But you must let your sister keep the medal, Arne. She did all the hard work to secure it. Don't be mean and keep it for yourself. That wouldn't be fair.'

Long after his daughter had rung off, her words about meanness and fairness were still resounding in Arne's head. He didn't know his sister well. He'd grown up with her until his early teens when he left for high school in Bremen. She was only one year older than him, but he really didn't know her at all. And yet she'd shown tenacity in fighting for something that she believed their father deserved. Probably the same sort of tenacity that Pieter showed in the boatyard as he strove for perfection in his designs and for harmony amongst his employees. But his daughter had been able to recognise his sister's character even without meeting her. How could she do that? Was it something that only women could do? An ability to perceive the life that someone else lived through their words and deeds. It baffled Arne. He ran his fingers through his thick hair and shook his head in frustration. Why couldn't he see what was so obvious to her?

Not long after Arne's heart-to-heart with his daughter, it was Barry who awakened Arne to something else he had missed. The senior partner's unexpected visit one sunny morning to the offices of the Visser Sailing and Diving Holidays company situated on the third floor of a rather shabby building in a quiet street south of the river Thames – a location recommended by the Barry and Victor duo as a place where business could be transacted perfectly well without the enormous overheads of a swanky workplace in a posh part of town. Arne had been late to arrive that morning having chosen to enjoy a lie in following his busy weekend with his sister in Harlingen. It was almost eleven o'clock before he emerged from the Elephant & Castle tube station near the Oval cricket ground. His personal assistant – another of the duo's recommendations as replacement for Gloria – scowled as he opened the door onto a large, open plan room with three female typists and one male clerk. The grimace was followed by the twitching of an eyebrow and a slight incline of the head in the direction of Arne's large desk to indicate that there was trouble afoot.

'I've been waiting for you for over an hour,' said Barry quietly but with a hint of menace from behind Arne's desk. He didn't look in a good mood. 'After all the problems the company has had to endure recently with the drugs fiasco, I'd have thought you would have had the common sense to concentrate on your clients and ensure that you give them a first-class service.'

'Good morning to you too,' replied Arne equally quietly but full of sarcasm. 'We can't talk here. No sound proofing behind this thin partition.'

'Right. We'll go to the coffee bar across the road. We can talk frankly there.'

Arne took the coffees to a quiet area of the café while Barry paid. The table top was sticky with spilt liquid. He signalled to the woman behind the counter to come and clean it, but she ignored him.

'I know,' said Arne, starting to use a handkerchief to clean bits of the table so that he could lean his elbows on it, 'it's south London and what can you expect.' His comment had an unexpected effect on Barry who burst into laughter. It broke the tension between the two men.

'Even the table tops in the West End are sticky sometimes,' said Barry smiling. 'The only difference is that in south London they are *always* sticky.' He pulled something out of a trouser pocket. 'My wife makes me carry a paper napkin to do what you've just done with your silk handkerchief. Less washing and ironing to do she tells me.' Arne folded his soiled handkerchief as neatly as he could and stuffed it in a pocket. 'I've just come to find out how you are weathering the drugs scandal storm.'

'I've been in Holland for a couple of days on family business,' replied Arne. 'I need to catch up.' It wasn't the wisest comment Arne had ever made and caused the smile on Barry's face to vanish.

'Keeping abreast of management accounts is at all times a priority for every company wishing to succeed in business.'

'Gloria was in charge of that side of the business,' said Arne, choosing to ignore Barry's rebuke. 'The new man you drafted in should have all the answers if that's what you're after.' Barry tutted. It wasn't what he wanted to hear. He had wanted to be reassured that his junior partner knew every little detail of how the company was proceeding and could correctly recite the company's financial statistics to the nearest decimal point.

'So, you can't tell me how the bookings are holding up post-drugs scandal.'

'Not offhand. But my assistant should have all the numbers.'

'That's not good enough, Arne,' said Barry raising his voice. 'It's your company, not his. You can't lead if you don't know the way ahead.'

'I thought you got the details straight from him,' snarled Arne. 'He is your spy, isn't he.'

'He's here to help you,' said Barry, trying to calm things down. 'He has a wealth of experience in management accounting. He's not an idiot.'

'What, like me? Are you implying that I'm an idiot?'

'You're giving a fair example of one.'

'Well, you know what you can do,' shouted Arne, not caring what the couple at the next table or the three women seated near the counter thought. 'You can get stuffed.'

'And that's exactly what you did to Victor's wife. You stuffed her.'

Arne went quiet. The conversation had taken a worrying turn. He didn't realise that Barry knew about his affair with Gloria. He'd promised his daughter no unseemly revelations.

'Didn't know I knew, did you.'

'No, I didn't,' replied Arne trying not to sound sheepish. 'I didn't know but I'll thank you to keep it to yourself. Others are involved who would be upset.'

'Too right. But you *have* made two people very happy.'

'Who?' asked Arne, a quizzical look on his face.

'Gloria and her husband. They're expecting,' said Barry. 'Against all the odds and years of trying, they are finally expecting.' Barry paused, allowing his words to sink in. Arne said nothing but it was clear he understood the message. The baby would be his.

Chapter 5

HENRIK & TED

Inside the hut nothing seemed to be going as planned. Plan B, heralded as the solution to opening the black tin trunk, was not working. Alistair looked perplexed and Ted was unusually quiet. Work had come to a standstill. Nothing seemed to be happening inside the man-cave when Henrik went to tell Alistair that lunch would soon be ready.

'I'm not making much progress,' admitted Alistair, as Henrik stared at the jumble of equipment on the workbench. 'The rotary saw is ineffective. Its teeth seem to get clogged up with some black goo.' Henrik scratched the top of his head. There were words he didn't understand including "goo", but he could easily see the problem when Alistair handed him the power unit with the saw head attached. Running a forefinger around the attachment's edge, he felt the sticky solution on his fingertips. It wouldn't wipe off and he noted that Alistair's hands were also covered in the "goo."

'I think it is tar,' said Henrik in haltering English.

'Does it smell of coal dust?' Both men spent several minutes sniffing their hands for the tell-tale smell of coal, but "could be" was the best they could come up with.

'If it is tar,' stated Alistair, then we will need a solvent not a saw, and it would explain why I am getting nowhere with a power tool.' Ted appeared to nod in agreement but he was probably only interested in his lunch. 'I'm not a chemical engineer but from what I remember of chemistry lessons, I have a feeling that baking soda might be the answer. It shifts most things. We'd better try it on our hands before we have lunch. Good thing I've got some,' added Alistair, taking a half-used packet off the highest shelf. 'We'll need to mix it with some water to make it into a paste, and then smear it over our hands.'

Over lunch Alistair asked Henrik why he thought the lid of the tin trunk was sealed with tar rather than being welded. Between mouthfuls, Henrik told him that a stock of coal dust had always been stored in the lighthouse. It could be used, he explained, in a runny form as a sealant of narrow gaps in floors or in a stiffer form around the floor edges as they met the circular tower's brickwork, and also as a means of waterproofing some of the small flat roofs which jutted out around the tower. It had medicinal purposes too, but he didn't expand on that.

There was no tarrying over luncheon. Both men were eager to get back to the shed to mix a larger quantity of baking soda paste and apply it liberally around the edges of the box's lid. It was left to Alistair to decide how long to leave it in place. He prodded it a few times, although he didn't know why. Finally, but without any good reason, they cleaned it off, and holding a screwdriver with a thin tip, Henrik started probing for a gap between lid and box sides.

'I think the paste is working,' said Henrik gleefully, 'I've found a little gap.'

'See if you can slide the tip of the screwdriver sideways and increase the size of the opening,' instructed Alistair. 'If you can't then we might have to give the paste a little longer to work.' A little longer turned into over an hour followed by a second coating of baking powder paste. Ted was getting bored, he wanted to go for a walk but neither of his best friends seemed interested. And then, suddenly, with just a minimal amount of leverage with the screwdriver by Henrik, the tin lid flew open. It took both men by surprise, and for a moment they were lost for words.

'Well done, Henrik,' said Alistair. 'Well done. Now let's see what's actually in it.' Both men peered into the dark box. Alistair got a torch to increase the illumination. Nothing was said for some time as they stared at the object inside. 'It looks box-shaped,' said Alistair finally.

'Yes,' agreed Henrik. 'And covered in tar too.'

'As if someone has poured tar in a liquid form all over it.'

'But it must be a very thin layer as it hasn't lost its shape,' Henrik hesitated before continuing. 'The more I look at it, the more it reminds me of the cash box that I used when I was working in the chandlery in Harlingen after the war.'

'I think you're right, Henrik, because there's a shallow recess on the top where a little handle for lifting up the lid would fit. It's no wonder the trunk was heavy, all that tar is very weighty.'

'And it's no wonder,' said Henrik using the same jargon as Alistair, 'that nothing rattled in the trunk. It couldn't because it was firmly stuck down.'

'So,' said Alistair, assessing the situation, 'the tin box inside the tin trunk must hold something valuable otherwise the person who put it there wouldn't have gone to so much trouble.' Ted looked enquiringly at his number one master. 'I'd better take Ted for a walk.'

'Shall I make some more paste and spread it over the inner box whilst you're walking Ted?'

'That would be good, if you don't mind. But I won't be able to help you later as I have some work to prepare for a meeting tomorrow. I'll have to hand over the project to you until next weekend as I'll be busy at the office. Good luck.'

Clearing away and washing up after breakfast had become part of Henrik's daily duties since agreeing to the move to England to live with the Drews. It was Monday morning and Alistair had left very early for the office. The boys were at school and Anna was out shopping. After walking Ted, the pair had returned to the hut in high spirits. It was a fine day and the rickety hut door was left wide open. Soon the gardener would arrive to tend the borders, but for now it was peaceful.

Ted curled up by the open door. He had enjoyed his walk despite the comparatively slow pace at which Henrik walked; Henrik was his second-best friend and Ted was content in his company. Henrik opened the lid of the trunk and stared hard at the smaller box inside. He rubbed his hands, adjusted his spectacles, and started chipping away with an old chisel at the paste covering that had hardened overnight. It broke away easily under pressure revealing the actual box. But the problem of removing the inner, small box from the tin trunk remained unsolved. It wouldn't budge. Henrik scratched his head and rubbed his chin. A layer of tar had been painted on the inside bottom of the trunk before the cash box had been placed on it. There was no way the paste could get at it. It seemed to be another stumbling block until the gardener, with forearms the girth of fence posts and rippling biceps, shoved the tips of his hedge shears into a crevice in the tar and yanked the two apart in a display of superhuman muscular power. Henrik was overawed and Ted, who had watched proceedings with increasing excitement, was slapping his tail so forcefully that he made the hut floor creak.

After a cup of tea to settle his nerves – the Dutch pair of Anna and Henrik had succumbed to the British habit of sipping a cup of tea in times of crisis – Henrik finally removed the cash box from the tin trunk and placed it on the workbench. He licked his lips in anticipation. He had no key to unlock the box if it was locked. He would have to use one of the inventive skills from his past when he was the lighthouse keeper and had to do many jobs without the correct tools. He searched the hut for a short length of thin wire. When he found something suitable, he shaped one end into a hook and inserted the wire carefully as far as it would go into the locking mechanism, and with a deft flick of his wrist anti-clockwise, the catch released. There was no handle to lift the lid. Instead, with the use of a pair of pliers, Henrik managed to get sufficient purchase on one of the fittings into which the ends of the handle would have sat, to waggle the upper section free from its lower portion. It hinged back to reveal, in good condition, a black tray with three sections, all of which were empty. Henrik removed the tray with care to reveal the lower compartment which had been filled in a neat and tidy manner with two separate drawstring bags made from a coarse material, and which laid side by side. Henrik picked out one and eased the drawstring tentatively. The hairs on the back of his neck stood upright and Ted sensed the moment of tension. Turning the bag upside down, the coins dropped onto the workbench with a surprising clang. Henrik stood back abruptly, shocked at what he saw before him. He didn't need anyone to tell him that the coins were made of gold.

Aware that the gardener would soon be putting his tools back in the shed before going home, Henrik counted the coins quickly and put them back in their little bag. Just in time the cash box was stowed away on a shelf behind some old seed boxes, allowing Henrik to close the shed door behind him as they left, the gardener for home, and Henrik for the house as he needed urgent contemplation.

'Are you okay, Henrik?' enquired Anna. 'You are very quiet.' When it was just the two of them, they took pleasure in chatting away in their native tongue.

'When will Alistair be back?' asked Henrik, replying to her question with one of his own.

'He'll be away in London for two nights. The report of the official investigation into the bridge accident is to be announced on Tuesday and he needs to be present with his colleagues to consider the findings. No blame can be attached to them, but the investigating committee will probably recommend changes to avoid any re-occurrence which may affect the whole industry.'

'Oh,' said Henrik, obviously disappointed.

'Do you need to speak to him urgently?' asked Anna. 'You can telephone him in London if you do, although it would be better if you can wait until he returns as he's bound to be wrapped up in the bridge report.'

'Oh, dear,' repeated Henrik, clearly agitated. 'I don't want to disturb him but I need to speak to someone soon.'

'What about me, Henrik? Will I do?'

'Of course, you will do,' replied Henrik, 'I just hadn't expected Alistair to be away from home for so long when I have news of the cash box we found together.'

'Can you tell me the news or is it a secret?'

'It's a sort of secret, I suppose,' started Henrik, 'but in the circumstances, with Alistair focussed on the accident report and the implications for his work, I should probably tell you.' He looked uncertain until he added, 'in a way, it would be more appropriate to discuss the secret with you because it involves something from our homeland.'

'A mystery,' said Anna. 'I quite like those.'

'Just wait. I won't be long.' Henrik marched out to the hut, accompanied by the devoted Ted, to retrieve the cash box. 'It's about this,' he said on his return, presenting it to Anna. 'It was in the tin trunk. We finally managed to open the trunk and extract the contents. But Alistair doesn't know what is in the cash box because I wasn't able to open it until this morning.'

'And it's important?'

'Extremely. I don't know what to do. I need advice.'

'Whatever was in the trunk is yours. It was given to you by the council of Vlieland. It's yours to do as you wish,' said Anna, attempting to reassure him. 'Alistair and I can give you advice, but the trunk and its contents belong to you.'

'I will show you what's in the cash box.' Henrik looked nervous and Ted nuzzled his thigh in a show of solidarity.

'As long as you are sure you want to,' responded Anna.

'I am.' He removed the same bag of coins that he had already opened and allowed them to spill willy-nilly onto the surface of the kitchen table. Anna gingerly picked up a coin and clasped a hand over her mouth. She was shocked. 'I think the portrait on the coins is of our King William III,' said Henrik, 'and I don't need to tell you that the metal is gold. In this bag they are all twenty-guilder coins dated between eighteen-fifty and eighteen-fifty-three. I haven't looked in the other bag yet.'

'My God,' exclaimed Anna. 'Oh, my God. I can't believe it. Gold coins.'

'Dutch gold coins from the previous century, to be precise,' corrected Henrik, looking at his astonished friend.

'I don't know what to say,' said Anna stating the obvious. 'It's an enormous shock.'

'I haven't counted them yet. I'm still reeling from the shock too.'

It took some time before they came back to their normal senses. Under Anna's steady gaze, Henrik started counting the coins again and stacking them into piles of five until Anna suggested that it might be more useful to stack them in piles according to their date. When they were done, they counted one hundred and nine coins, all of which were dated between eighteen-fifty and eighteen-fifty-three.

'It's time to open the other bag now,' said Anna, nervously. 'I wonder what we will find.'

'I hope it doesn't cause us another jolt,' replied Henrik, easing the stiff drawstring with his ageing fingers.

'They're smaller,' said Anna immediately, as Henrik placed the coins, one after the other, onto the table top. 'This one is dated eighteen-twenty and is worth five-guilders,' she went on, inspecting the coin at close range. When all were out of the bag, Henrik stacked and counted the coins as before. There were ninety-seven coins. 'All five-guilder coins and all dated between eighteen-twenty and eighteen thirty-six, except for one,' summed up Anna.

'And all gold,' added Henrik, in a shaky voice.

'Yes, all gold. Apparently.'

'Two hundred and sixteen gold coins in total stored in the small cash box,' said Anna flabbergasted. 'Who would believe it?'

'What shall we do with them?'

'I don't know offhand,' replied Anna thoughtfully, 'but I think we will need to find out some information about them.'

'Some research in the library?'

'Maybe. I don't know my way around the rear admiral's library but I believe he kept a wide range of books. There are probably volumes there which will help us but on which shelves they are stacked I just don't know. We will have to wait until Alistair comes home as I know he wouldn't like it if we just went in and disturbed the books without his permission. The rear admiral's library is something of a hallowed place for him.'

Alistair was tired when he arrived home. Ted scampered down the drive to be the first to greet him; his number one master was home and he was happy to have the gentle touch of Alistair's hands fondling his ears.

'How did it go?' asked Anna as soon as he closed the front door. 'You look whacked.'

'It was part boring and part depressing,' he replied. 'The chairman of the investigating committee allowed an endless number of so-called experts to read out never ending reports which everyone attending knew would result in the same conclusion. The quality of the concrete was the cause due to substandard ingredients and sloppy workmanship.'

'And who was blamed?'

'Public investigations usually skirt around apportioning culpability by claiming it is for the Crown Prosecution Service to prosecute where necessary.'

'That's outrageous,' cried Anna. 'All those people died because of a fiddle with the quality of the concrete, but still their families cannot claim compensation until the case is brought to a court of law. That can't be right.'

'It's the way the system works. Unfortunately, it's not perfect,' said Alistair resignedly. 'I'll go upstairs and change and then take Ted for a walk. I could do with one myself. I won't feel so exasperated after it.'

Whilst dog and master were out walking, Henrik asked Anna when she was going to tell Alistair about the gold coins. It was a load on his shoulders that he wanted to share at the first opportunity.

'I haven't told him yet because he looked all in when he arrived home,' said Anna. 'After supper, maybe, or tomorrow evening when he gets back from work.' Henrik looked disappointed but didn't query her decision. He knew it was right. And in the end, it was the weekend before the right set of circumstances were in place for the subject of the gold coins to be discussed in a fruitful way.

'Henrik managed to get the cash box out of the tin trunk,' started Anna looking at her husband, and as a lead into the subject. 'He wants to tell you about what he found.'

'Um,' murmured Henrik quietly. He was clearly uncomfortable. 'You tell him, Anna. You will do it better than me.'

'Is there a big secret?' asked Alistair smiling, and turning to Henrik added, 'I'm so sorry I forgot to ask you about how you had got on with extracting the cash box. I got wrapped up in the accident report.'

'The gardener helped when I got stuck,' said Henrik shyly.

'Brute force, I expect. That man is built like a tank. Where is the box?' Henrik went and fetched it and placed it on the table right in front of him. 'You've cleaned it up well,' commented Alistair. 'It truly looks like an old cash box now in its mottled grey livery.'

'It's unlocked,' said Henrik. He and Anna held their breath as Alistair hinged back the top. Between them they had cleaned the interior and placed the coins back in the drawstring bags.

'It's as we found it,' interjected Anna, leaning over to remove the empty tray. 'It's what's in the two bags that makes us nervous.'

'Surely not,' said Alistair, confidently opening a bag and allowing some of the content to fall into his palm. An anxious hush descended as he studied several of the coins and the realisation of their probable value began to dawn on him.

'We think the heads depicted are that of William I and III of The Netherlands, and that the coins are cast from pure gold,' said Anna. Henrik blew hard and felt his shoulders relax. He was relieved that Alistair finally knew. 'They are all twenty-guilder coins in the bag you've just opened and are five-guilder coins in the other,' said Anna helpfully. Alistair said nothing and Anna continued, 'we wondered if there are any reference books in the library that might be informative.'

'We certainly need more information, that's evident,' agreed her husband. 'Have you mentioned this find to the boys, or to anyone else?'

'No,' replied Anna and Henrik in near unison.

'You mustn't mention it to anyone whilst we decide what to do. And that might not be simple.'

'We won't, I promise,' replied his wife turning to Henrik who was nodding vigorously.

It was a question of where to start, he had told them, when they sat down to afternoon tea in the bay window overlooking the stunning sea view that his parents had enjoyed for many years.

'It's a tradition I love,' said Anna, pouring the tea into

each cup from a pot with a knitted tea cosy. 'Having a cup of tea and a scone in such tranquil surroundings.'

'We're becoming old fogies,' said Alistair sighing. 'That's what the boys call us. I'm only forty-six but they think I'm ancient. I should mind that they call me an old fogey, but I don't. It's peaceful here and I love it.' With his head slightly tilted, Ted gave him a quizzical look. He was after a titbit even though he knew it was against the house rules. After Anna had cleared the cups and saucers from the low, occasional table, Alistair took up the subject in earnest.

'We know the tin trunk was given to Henrik as a souvenir of his years there as lighthouse keeper, so, nominally, the contents of the trunk also belong to him.' Henrik looked awkward. The coins were worrying him; he wished they weren't his. 'But who do they really belong to and who put them in the tin trunk? I think that should be our starting point.'

'Do you have a theory?' asked Anna.

'If they are Dutch coins,' started her husband, 'as the two of you believe them to be, then the most likely scenario is that they were stolen or looted by the Germans during the war and hidden in the trunk when they were in retreat, with the intention of returning to collect it when peace was restored. Who would have wanted to steal a battered old tin trunk? It should have been perfectly safe in the lighthouse.'

'And it was,' said Anna. 'Perfectly safe for years and years. Safe until the lighthouse underwent major changes and it was found in bizarre circumstances and given to the only living former lighthouse keeper.' Henrik followed the conversation understanding its gist but missing the nuances.

'Presumably the German or Germans who stole and hid the coins died in the fighting as the Allies fought their way to Berlin. That would explain why the loot remained uncollected.'

'So, may we presume that no living person knows about it except us?' asked Henrik, trying to grasp the strange situation.

'Yes, if my theory is correct,' suggested Alistair. 'But it is just a theory.'

'But probably the only viable one,' added Anna.

'Yes. I think we must accept that scenario,' said Alistair, 'but it doesn't throw any light on the *real* owners.'

'Rich people often invest in gold,' offered Anna.

'Eccentrics too,' added Henrik. 'They usually have no trust in the banking system.'

'Or, the coins could have been looted from a bombed-out bank in which case they may have been stolen by someone who was Dutch.'

'But German troops were the only people allowed to cross from the mainland to Vlieland during the occupation,' said Henrik. 'So, it's odds on that the coins were left in the lighthouse by a soldier.'

'We may never be able to track down the original owners,' said Alistair. 'That's something else we will have to accept, but it will make the decision of what to do with them far harder than if we did.'

Despite an outwardly calm appearance – something engrained in him by the rear admiral who had repeatedly told him to be calm – Alistair was feeling the heat of the predicament. The more he thought about it, the more problematic it seemed to become. There were so many questions and so few answers. He was an engineer used to solving mathematical equations, not an adventurer or legal eagle accustomed to making decisions based on raw power or common law. It was Anna who brought him back from his few seconds of reflection by asking about the library.

'I'm sure there will be something helpful in the library about gold coins,' he said, 'but whether we will find something about *Dutch* gold coins, I very much doubt.'

'The value of each coin,' contributed Henrik, 'is likely to be tied in with the daily trading price of gold. I went into the newsagent in town and bought a copy of the Financial Times. Yesterday's fix price was sixty-five American dollars and twenty cents per ounce.'

'You're a marvel,' said Anna, kissing him on the cheek. 'How did you think of doing that?'

'I don't know. It just came to me to do so.'

'Well, that's very useful,' said Alistair, 'as we now know how to get a rough estimate of their worth.'

'Some coins may be of higher value to collectors than their gold content,' said Henrik, and by way of explanation went on, 'not all paintings are of the same value.'

'If you are lucky enough to have a Rembrandt, it would be of considerably greater value than a painting by an unknown artist,' agreed Anna. 'But until we can find some information about our twenty- and five-guilder coins, we will have to treat them all as of equal value.'

'That's sensible,' commented Alistair, thankful to

have some sort of starting point to assess the value of the contents of the cash box. 'But we will need reliable weighing scales to obtain accurate readings.' After some thought he continued, 'I seem to remember my mother using some ancient balance scales for measuring out quantities of flour and sugar for her cakes. Have we still got them, Anna?'

'I have seen them somewhere, but I don't use them. My modern kitchen scale is much handier to use.'

'Well, we could try that first, but I don't suppose its scale measures in grams. Probably just ounces, so it may be rather inaccurate.'

It was Henrik who suggested the obvious of weighing them all together and dividing the weight by the number of coins. His years running the chandlery after the war had taught him many practical ways to circumvent problems. In the kitchen, they stacked all the twenty-guilder coins in the plastic dish and set it back onto the mechanism. The arrow jerked smartly to a high number on the scale before settling down at a lower figure which Alistair recorded. A simple division was all that was then needed. When repeated for the five-guilder coins, and the total gold weight in ounces for both sets of coins finally converted into an approximate figure in sterling, the enormity of the gift to Henrik became apparent. There was unease around the kitchen table and a foreboding that was not readily explicable. Each found something they simply had to do: Anna to prepare lunch, Henrik to sort out the shed, and Alistair to take Ted for a walk. It would be a breathing space for all three whilst they assimilated the facts.

The rear admiral had applied the same sort of discipline to the placement of the hundreds of books on the shelves in his library as he had to the pursuance of his long career in the navy. There was a logic to his methods, but one that had caused Alistair to scratch his chin on numerous occasions when searching for books on a particular topic. Quite what the rear admiral's line of thinking had been was not apparent to his youngest son, as it appeared to him to show no logic at all.

Since his father's death more than a decade earlier, he had used the library more as a study or quiet place when he needed to give deep consideration to his work or to a family matter. It wasn't quite a mausoleum to his father, but he had been wary of making wholesale alterations. It hadn't felt right, until now, to make changes for his own purposes, or, indeed, to allow the boys – now young men with the eldest already at university – to use the room without permission. But in an instance, he could now sweep that aside. Current circumstances had given the library a special purpose and it was right and proper that the room should be opened to the entire family and used for whatever purposes – within reason – they felt necessary. It would function as a family room and be all the more valuable for that.

Apart from the taller books occupying the bottom shelves, after an hour or so of scrutiny and meandering from shelf to shelf, Anna and Alistair agreed that they could find no order whatsoever of the estimated one and a half thousand books arranged on the dusty shelves. No categories were apparent, and there was no obvious grouping together of hardback books in the same colour or of similar thicknesses, or by the same author, or the same subject. Most importantly, no catalogue was found. Alistair was on the point of asking his wife if she could spare some time during the coming week to try to put the books in alphabetical order of author name, but she forestalled him knowing well the implication of the frown on his face. She was going to be particularly busy in town this coming week in the charity shop where she was a volunteer helper, but it would be a super job for Henrik as he could work at his own pace and rest whenever he felt the need.

Ted curled up in his reserve wicker basket which Henrik had dragged in from the hall. He'd already had a walk and now Henrik was buying his good will with a few of his favourite treats sprinkled onto the soft blanket that lined the basket and which he gobbled up in seconds. Settling in for the long haul, Ted yawned and fell asleep, so he missed Henrik working his way along every shelf and removing every book he found with an author's name starting with an "A." And he was totally oblivious to the neat piles of books that Henrik started stacking on the parquet floor in the middle of the rectangular-shaped room, which stacks grew in number and in height as Henrik made his way around the three walls where the almost ceiling-high bookcases stood. It was exhausting work for a man in his mid-seventies and Henrik took several well-earned breaks sitting behind the rear admiral's desk. He had never known him, but the flavour of the man rang out around a room that Henrik felt sure he must have loved. Ted stirred, left his comfy bedding basket, nosed around the stacks, and established that there were no more treats on offer before heading back to his basket for more rest and relaxation.

Unbeknown to Henrik, at some stage in his morning's work, he had handled the very same English-German, German-English dictionary that the rear admiral had used to converse with Arne back in nineteen-forty. Henrik too was a German speaker – as was increasingly the case of the population in northern Holland with the proximity of its larger neighbour and five long years of occupation. He set aside the dictionary and used it whenever he handled a book with an interesting but not fully understood title.

When Anna came home, she found Henrik engrossed in trying to translate the title of Jane Austen's "Sense and Sensibility" into something meaningful to him. Assured by Anna that it was a title with a deep meaning well beyond a straight verbatim translation, they started to clean the shelves of half a century's dust and cobwebs, and the nooks of scurrying little creatures whose homes they were destroying without so much as a warning or an apology. They had decided to start storing the books of authors with an "A" on the shelf at head height in the first bookcase by the door – the two upper shelves would be left empty for the time being and only used if absolutely necessary as Alistair wanted to get rid of the rickety, wooden two-step stool with handrail. Anna donned her yellow washing up gloves and got down to work, with Hendrik in charge of rinsing the dirty cloth periodically in a plastic bucket by his feet. Sorting the "As" into alphabetical order and placing them in their new positions in the library was their last chore of the day.

'We didn't find a single book by an author with an

"A" about gold coins or even coins in general,' said Anna, reporting to Alistair at dinner that evening.

'But we are doing the "Bs" tomorrow,' chipped in Henrik, holding up crossed fingers.

'Stick to it,' said Alistair, 'if there's something there about gold coins, I'm sure you will find it.'

'I've been thinking,' said Anna, a bit out of the blue, 'that the room needs redecorating. Not necessarily modernising, but just being made a little lighter with less of the feeling of male dominance.' Alistair nodded. She was right.

They had to wait for any measure of success until they got to the letter "G." It was whilst sorting them into alphabetical order that Anna questioned the author's name of Goodmann Bell.

'I think this should be amongst the "Bs",' she said looking at Henrik. 'Strange though it is, I think Goodmann is a first name.'

'I know someone in town whose surname is Bell. He's the newsagent,' Henrik replied, turning the book over several times in his hands. 'You might be right.'

'Stop,' cried Anna suddenly. She had been watching Henrik's movements with the book and something had caught her eye. 'In our concentration on author names, we've forgotten to read the book's title, and it just might be what we are searching for.'

Together, they poured over their newly found treasure – "A short history of gold coins of the world" – marvelling that they had spotted it, yet cringing at how they had nearly missed it. They turned the pages slowly, scanning the script carefully and reading the text accompanying the photographs for dates and nationality. Midway through the tome – for that was what it was with over three hundred pages – they discovered a Dutch coin. It was described as a Netherlands Ducat of the sixteenth century and was, according to the text printed below the image, arguably the most important Dutch coin ever produced. The information whetted the appetite but did no more, and although they stuck to the task of filing the books in a recognisable order, their hopes of finding something more useful were dampened.

'I don't think reference books will satisfy our needs,' said Alistair, when Anna told him about their only find in the rear admiral's library, and how they had gleaned nothing helpful from it. They were preparing for bed and he was cleaning his teeth and checking in the mirror that his circular brush strokes were as per the dentist's advice. Wiping some trails of toothpaste off his chin, he added, 'one of my old university friends is a trader in the money market in The City. I plan working in London on Wednesday and Thursday and it occurred to me to suggest that we meet up for a drink after work. I could ask him to do a bit of research on our behalf.'

'Won't he think that a bit peculiar?'

'Why?'

'Won't it be obvious that you are meeting him purely to ask a favour.'

'Well, I suppose so, but he has asked favours of me in the past,' replied Alistair. 'No, I don't think he'll mind if I'm upfront about it.'

'You'll have to think carefully about how you phrase

your request for a favour,' said Anna, 'you can't just say that a friend of yours has inherited a fortune in gold coins and could he tell you how much the coins are worth in the current market. You will need to be a bit more subtle than that and couch your request with care.'

'I see what you mean. I'll have to spin some sort of prepared yarn. Pare back the true story to half a dozen gold coins inherited from a great aunt, something like that,' said Alistair thinking hard.

'I could make a list of every different type of coin we have, not how many,' suggested Anna, 'and then you could ask him to find out the current value of each coin.'

'Brilliant.'

'And that will just leave us with the thorny question of what to do with them. And I will probably want to discuss that with my brother.'

'Understandable,' said Alistair. 'Jens is part of your Dutch family and I'm sure Henrik would be grateful if such an important decision was made with his input too.'

Although Alistair's university chum agreed to help via a network of friends-of-friends trickling down to actual bullion dealers, numismatists and auctioneers, other events overtook its importance. And it was Ted who sounded the warning bell.

'Have you noticed lately how Ted seems to stand guard over Henrik?' asked Anna one Sunday by the by.

'Yes, I have noticed,' replied her husband, shrugging his shoulders. 'He seems very intent on being near him. Dogs can be very sensitive to human frailties, and Henrik is no longer in the first flush of middle age.'

'He's looking tired, I know,' responded Anna sighing.

'We've asked a lot of him recently, probably unfairly. But as you know, he wants to please.'

'Maybe we could get him to see the doctor for a check-up.'

'I can suggest it,' said Anna, 'but he can be very obstinate.'

Alistair rose early one morning to catch the first train to London from Norwich. His chauffeur, Anna, stirred when he got out of bed but he washed and dressed in the bathroom to allow her a few extra minutes of rest. He was surprised to find Ted sitting attentively outside Henrik's bedroom door on the other side of the grand stairway. Ted looked sad and appeared to be crying. He ruffled his fur and stroked his back but Ted only had eyes for the bedroom door. It took a few moments before Alistair realised that Ted was worried about Henrik. He tapped gently on the door and called out Henrik's name but there was no reply.

He opened the door slightly. Ted dived in and scrambled up onto the bed. In the semi-gloom of the early morning and with the thick curtains drawn against the penetrating northern light and easterly winds, Henrik was barely visible in his bed. Alistair called his name again but there was no response. He turned on the light, approached the bed and laid a hand on Henrik. His body was still and cold. Alistair swore. Henrik was dead and Ted looked bereft. Alistair knew he would not be catching the first train to London that morning.

'I couldn't persuade him to consult the doctor,' Anna

said through her tears when she entered his bedroom to find out what was going on. 'I should have tried harder but he was so stubborn. Silly old thing.' Alistair cradled her head in his arms as tears continued to stream down her cheeks. 'I loved him.'

'We all loved him,' said Alistair quietly. 'I think he was happy living here. You'd better wake up the boys and tell them. Bring them in and let them say their farewells to him. They are old enough to see death in the raw. It's all part of life after all,' he added distractedly. 'I'll contact the authorities. A doctor will have to come and pronounce him dead. There may have to be a post-mortem.'

'And I must let Jens know,' said Anna. 'Henrik meant a great deal to him too.'

The death of Henrik led to several unforeseen issues. After the initial practicalities were dealt with, a sombre feeling pervaded the house for days. Ted was off his food and no amount of coaxing could get him out of the house for a walk. The body had been removed and after death by natural causes had been established, a funeral was planned for when Jens could attend.

They formed a small party of mourners at the nearby church. Anna wasn't sure if Henrik had been Catholic or Protestant as she had no recall of him expressing views on religious matters. Alistair said it was immaterial as all that really mattered was that the people who meant something to him were present. Ilse, Arne's only surviving sister, had travelled over from Leeuwarden by car and ferry. She too had known him in wartime conditions when her survival after the traumatic loss of her father and elder sister, was in no small part due to his selfless care. They had corresponded regularly during the period of his life lived in Norfolk and elsewhere. Cards, mostly birthdays and Christmas, with the occasional letter or glossy postcard from a sunny destination where Ilse and her family were enjoying their annual holiday. When Anna contacted her with the news, she was adamant that she would attend Henrik's funeral. The family could manage without her for a few days and she would be very happy to take up Anna's kind offer of a bed for several nights.

After the short service, the party trudged back up the winding incline to the house. There were ten of them in all, including the gardener and Mr. Bell, the newsagent, with whom Henrik had been on friendly terms. Anna had arranged refreshments and drinks which they took in the bay window where comfortable chairs had been moved in especially for informal relaxation. Except for Anna and Jens, there was plenty of chatter as sadness gave way to relief that they had given Henrik a good send off. For brother and kid sister it was a seminal moment. Henrik had come to their rescue and looked after them when they had no one else and he had never flinched from that task. He was their link with their childhood and adolescence in their native country, and now he was gone.

The problem of the gold coins was completely overshadowed by Henrik's demise. The booty stayed locked in the library safe, unloved, and temporarily forgotten, and it was not until Anna checked with Jens whether she needed to contact anyone or any local council body in Harlingen to register his death that she remembered that she had wanted to talk to her brother about them.

'He didn't have many possessions,' said Anna, finding a moment to speak seriously to her brother. 'Barely anything from his former life in Holland save his eclectic set of old clothes, his pipe, and the tin trunk. But he did treasure the Christmas presents that the boys gave him.'

'If you're going to ask me if I'd like a memento of our dear friend, then I would like his pipe,' pre-empted Jens. 'He had the pipe firmly clenched between his jaws the very first time we saw him standing outside his wooden hut on Vlieland. Do you remember?'

'Of course. How could I forget?' Anna replied putting an arm around her brother's waist. 'Just the two of us, forlorn and bedraggled but we had the good fortune to come across the nicest man on the island.'

'All those wartime memories,' sighed Jens. 'It was such a different world then, trying to survive from day to day.'

'The tin trunk,' started Anna, after a pause to recollect those indelible wartime memories. 'I must tell you about it, or rather, what was in it.'

'The one that was given to him by the councillors of Vlieland when the old lighthouse got upgraded?'

'Yes, that one. It has caused a lot of soul searching because there was something valuable in it.'

'Did Henrik have a will?'

'Not to our knowledge, but as I said,' recounted Anna, 'he had few possessions none of which had any intrinsic value.'

'So, there was no need for a will,' stated Jens.

'Exactly. Absolutely no need for a formal will until we discovered what was in the tin trunk.'

'Go on. What was in it?'

'A cash box containing gold coins. Not any old gold coins. Dutch gold coins from the mid-eighteen hundreds.'

'Oh, my word, that's a shock,' said Jens, cupping his hands over his mouth. 'Are the coins very valuable?'

'We've been trying to discreetly find out their value. Alistair has asked an old school friend who works in the financial markets if he can use his contacts to give us a realistic estimate. In terms of bullion weight alone, troy ounces they are called, the value is in the tens of thousands of pounds.'

'Whoa.'

'We have a dilemma, and I wanted to ask you for advice. What should we do?'

'Give them back, I suppose,' said Jens looking uncertain. 'Off the top of my head, I can't think of anything else. I'd have to give it a lot of thought as to the best course of action. And the most practical and the safest. And the most honourable. And you definitely don't want the press to get hold of the story and splash it on the front pages of the Sunday newspapers.'

'It's a dilemma that Alistair and I would rather not have had but we've no option, we have to resolve it somehow.'

'What would Henrik have wanted?' asked Jens rhetorically. 'He was a practical man with no airs and graces. He would probably have liked to use any riches for the benefit of the community.'

'Yes, something like that. He wouldn't have kept any riches for himself.'

'I must think over the quandary seriously,' said Jens. 'Who else knows about it apart from Alistair?'

'Nobody else. When he asked his old school chum for help, he did so very warily. So, as it stands, it is just the three of us.'

'Then it must remain that way until Alistair's friend reports back,' said Jens. 'And we must all tread carefully in the meantime for fear of what the press could do with untrue speculative stories.'

'I agree, but there is also the issue of inheritance,' said Anna. 'We don't know for certain that Henrik has no living blood family, or indeed, any offspring of his own.'

'It was something that he never discussed with us. His life before becoming the lighthouse keeper on Vlieland is completely unknown,' commented Jens. 'That his parents are dead is obvious, but we don't know if he had any siblings and therefore, not just the chance, but the probability of nieces and nephews. It's complicated, that's for sure.'

'We could consider giving them away anonymously,' suggested Anna. 'It might be the safest solution. Alistair definitely doesn't want to be embroiled in publicity. His firm's innocent association with the bridge tragedy was enough for him. And *you* wouldn't want your diplomatic position to be spread over the tabloids either.'

'Yes, you're right,' agreed Jens. 'I don't want to court publicity, quite the opposite. Diplomacy is all about keeping your head down and not making waves.' He paused. 'Even if there isn't a true heir, the sensational stuff published in the press would generate loonies and ill-intentioned people to try to claim it as their own. We could be inundated with claims and the situation could turn into a protracted nightmare of costly legal bills.' He paused again. 'The more I think about it, the more attractive the anonymous option becomes. Let me know when you get an approximate value. The three of us will need to get together to talk it through. In the meantime, I shall give it a great deal more thought.'

'Of course, dear brother, we must all give it serious thought, and who knows, we might come up with a better plan.'

Ted nosed into their tête-à-tête for company. He wasn't his normal self; he was still missing Henrik. Jens stroked his back and told him that he was a good boy, but Ted still looked sad.

'His left eye looks cloudy,' remarked Jens.

'It's a developing cataract,' said Anna, 'the result of an accident caused by Arne. It's growing cloudier all the time and eventually the lens inside the eye will become completely opaque and Ted won't be able to see through it.'

'Is there anything the vet can do?'

'Not really.'

'Poor Ted.'

Wells-next-the-Sea, Ilse had agreed with Anna, when the two of them were alone after the departure of Jens and his wife and Alistair was back in the office, was a very charming seaside location. She had an extra day to spend with the woman she had always known as Annaliese before her own departure to the ferry terminal at Harwich. Anna took her on a walking tour of the small town, accompanied by Ted who appeared less mournful with every passing day. The women were of similar ages and temperament, and were enjoying each other's company.

'There's even a small chandlery,' said Ilse smiling, as they made their way through the heart of the little town. 'It reminds me of our late friend, Henrik.'

'It caters for a much more genteel clientele than in Harlingen,' replied Anna, 'no working boats here, just leisure sailors who like to be called "Captain" and who wear a white hat with a black peak.' They giggled at the image the description conjured up.

'No sailors working for a living?'

'Not along this stretch of the coast, although my late father-in-law, the rear admiral, did get paid for his efforts in wars overseas.' They giggled again. The English class system was still a deep mystery to Anna and was a complete unknown quantity to Ilse. They stopped for a cup of coffee at a café overlooking the marina. 'It was into this marina that the coastguard towed your brother to safety in nineteen-forty,' added Anna. 'The rear admiral always told us the story each Christmas of how he had watched through his telescope the two boats coming into the harbour. Alistair remembers that time well. As a young lad then, your brother's great adventure seemed as thrilling as something from one of his boy's comic strips.'

They chatted on for some time, family talk mostly, but also about the paths they had trodden as their lives had unfolded from childhood to motherhood. 'Before I go tomorrow,' said Ilse, 'I must not forget to give you a bundle of correspondence from Henrik that I collected over the years. It seems that we both valued our written communications sufficiently not to throw them away.'

'I haven't cleared Henrik's room yet,' said Anna, with a reluctance in her voice to remove all trace of Henrik so soon after his death, 'but I do know that he kept private paperwork in a drawer in his room, presumably from you. Would you like them back?'

'No. Generally, I just wrote insignificant cheery news about my family or our holidays. But read Henrik's letters when I'm gone,' urged Ilse, 'you will find them informative and fascinating.'

The house felt desperately quiet with the departure of the final mourner; Alistair was working long hours at the office; the two younger boys were back at boarding school and the eldest far away at a Scottish university. Mostly it was just Anna and Ted at home as Ted wasn't suited to long spells in Norwich. Anna sighed deeply, she simply had to get down to clearing Henrik's room. She knew she mustn't let it become a shrine to him in the same way that the library had been out of bounds to the living after the rear admiral's death. She resolved to make a start that very instant.

Henrik's medium-sized bedroom had a tall window which overlooked the drive and a high ceiling with an ornate rose at its centre. All four walls were papered with a small royal blue-coloured motif on a pale grey background. It was made cosy by the large hand-knotted Persian rug, also with a blue theme, laid out on the wooden floor and the comfortable chair with a large cushion that filled a corner. Its real luxury was a hand basin, towel rail and small mirror allowing the occupant to shave in peace.

Anna sat on his bed for a while not knowing where to start, and if she was honest with herself, afraid to do so. The tin trunk, the focus of the family's gaze in recent times, occupied a place on the floor by the door and in addition to the spare blanket inside, a pair of brown slippers sat proudly on its closed lid. There would be a few items for the charity shop, including the slippers which were relatively new, but Anna knew that most of his clothing would have to be thrown away. The wardrobe contents proved her right; nothing in it was salvageable. It was likewise for the chest of drawers, a stout piece of wooden furniture with sturdy knobs to move the heavy drawers in and out, except for the contents of its top drawer. In it, apart from the cherished Christmas presents from the boys – a bobble hat, a tie, several pairs of thick socks, handkerchiefs, most with sailing motifs of various sorts – was the bundle of letters that Anna had glimpsed once before. She would ask her sons if they would like to keep any of the gifts that they had given Henrik as a reminder of him, and the bundle of correspondence, she would put in the library ready to read through.

It was with a sense of prying that Anna untied the string holding the bundle of letters together. Ilse had warned her that her emotions might be piqued as she read Henrik's handwritten news and tales from post-war Holland, but that she would also feel a sense of pride. Despite the season it was windy and the lashing rain was running down the bay window panes in rivulets, obscuring the fine view out. She weighed the neat bundle in her hands with gravitas and flicked through it like a pack of playing cards. They were all letters in their original envelopes, no cards, or missives of other sorts. She presumed they were in chronological order. She opened the first letter tentatively and noted its date: nineteenth of August nineteen-fifty-two. The paper was of poor quality and had a grey tinge. As she withdrew it from the envelope, it rustled with brittleness against the thicker edges of the wrapper, and unfolded it gingerly. The text was all about the chandlery and the ongoing difficulties in obtaining stock seven years after the war's end. Seagoing activity had recommenced in earnest with the ferries crossing the Wadden Sea to restored pre-war volumes to the islands of the Frisian archipelago. There was a chronic shortage of practically everything as islanders who had been forced to leave their homes as the Germans fortified the islands into concrete jungles gradually returned to their roots. Supplying the ferries with the necessary wherewithal to ply across the Wadden Sea on a daily schedule, with human loads and the resources to maintain them was becoming, according to Henrik's newsletter - for that was what it was – a Herculian task.

Anna removed her new reading spectacles and placed them on the occasional table by the window. Ted had wandered in and out of the room but had not disturbed her as he had sensed her nostalgic mood. She had left Harlingen in nineteen-fifty-two to marry Alistair and live abroad in his family home. It was then that Henrik had started his long monologues to Ilse. She reflected on what her mother had once told her, influenced undoubtedly by her parents mixed religion marriage and the ostracism that it had caused, that in life, when one door shuts another opens. It brought tears to Anna's eyes. Her departure from

Harlingen had caused Henrik pain, and he had countered it with his periodic letters to his dear friend, Ilse, who at that time was living in Leeuwarden. A door had shut on him but he had had the fortitude to open another. He hadn't slipped back into a vagabond lifestyle and it was due in part to the chandlery, the business her father had set up, although she had been too young to know it well when he was alive and working in the shop. She folded the three pages and carefully slid them back into the envelope. The second letter, dated two months later, was in the same vein although it touched on the grand scale of the reconstruction work being undertaken by the council to repair the war damaged dikes and to make improvements that would bring long-term benefits to the residents of Harlingen. The third followed in short order but there was a gap of five months before the fourth was posted to a destination in Australia. It was an airmail letter on lightweight green paper with gummed edges and a pre-printed stamp of Queen Juliana of the Netherlands, and it was the first of a whole wodge of correspondence to Perth, where Ilse and her family had just emigrated. Despite the restrictions in writing space, Henrik was able to cover a lot of ground by adjusting the size of his handwriting. Maybe it was the distance of half a world between them, but there was a sense in his writing of a greater freedom to cover emotive subjects. While in essence it remained a diary of his life as a small-town shopkeeper, the narrative harked back frequently to earlier years to put the current circumstances he described in perspective, ensuring that the reader was in no doubt as to the true worth of the characters involved.

Anna sat upright from her crouched position and stretched her limbs. The rain had stopped and the view through the bay window was once again resplendent. She wondered how many more letters she could read that day before family demands would require her full attention. A rough assessment of the number of letters in the bundle was over fifty and each required a focussed mind. It was the very next airmail letter that gave insight into Henrik's former life when mention was made of an unhappy childhood in Germany. Anna gasped. Henrik was German by birth at least. She had never known him to have any "papers," official or otherwise, and it had simply never occurred to her that he wasn't Dutch. Moreover, he spoke Dutch without any trace of a foreign accent. Reading further, Anna learned that he had been raised in Heerenland, a small town in Lower Saxony no more than a kilometre from the Dutch border and where the local population on each side of the frontier were adept in speaking both languages from an early age. His unhappiness, according to the letter, was due to a rigid upbringing which included extra chores for minor infringements of his father's rules and flogging for dissension. The young Henrik escaped across the border whenever possible to spend time in the museum in Wolden, some three kilometres from his home where he felt safe from the violent moods of his erratic father. He was welcomed there by the old man in charge of the exhibits who in addition to giving him a refuge for an hour or two, taught him all he knew about the artefacts.

The outbreak of the first world war was the impetus for the fourteen-year-old Henrik to make his escape permanent. He stayed in the museum for several months earning pocket money for doing jobs that the kindly old man was too enfeebled to do himself. As relations between the two countries soured, the old man urged Henrik to travel west to seek a job on a farm or in a hamlet, and to make no mention of his German roots. A blaze of small towns and jobs with accommodation ensued until finally, many months later, in a larger town near the coast, he spotted a notice on a local authority board requiring a physically fit man to become the lighthouse keeper on Vlieland Island. The warning of working alone for long periods was a positive incentive to the young man who was happy to be self-reliant and to mind his own business. An explanation at last, thought Anna as she removed her spectacles, of how Henrik's character had been formed and how he had learned to place value on self-support. When they prepared for bed that night, she planned to relate it all to her husband who would be equally fascinated, but Alistair had news of his own to convey. He had received a telephone call at the office from the chairman of the golf club committee confirming that he had been elected club captain and would be due to take up his duties in the late autumn. It would be an even busier time for the Drews of Wells-next-the-Sea, he told her, and he would definitely have to brush up his golf with some lessons from the professional.

It was almost Christmas before Anna returned to the task of reading Henrik's letters to Ilse. She had not felt the need to hurry back to the task as her questions about his early life had already been answered, and she was not expecting any further major revelations. It was the last in the series of his airmail letters to Australia that made Anna sob her heart out, and cause Ted to sit by her side as a sentinel. Later, after getting Alistair to read it too, he remarked that Henrik must have known that Ilse and her family would shortly be returning to live in Leeuwarden so he took the opportunity to relate important but disturbing memories whilst they were still at arm's length in the new world, as if it would touch fewer raw nerve endings that way.

'You see,' said Anna, 'Henrik and Frieda had something in common. They were both German by birth and they were both living in The Netherlands during the occupation.'

'But unlike Frieda,' said Alistair, 'nobody was aware of Henrik's background.'

'Exactly. He didn't have to face the daily hostility that eventually broke Frieda.'

'But he felt the anguish that she suffered,' commented Alistair.

'Exactly. The anguish that drove her to take her own life,' replied Anna. 'As he saw it, his last airmail letter to Australia was his last chance to tell Ilse of the guilt and shame he felt in not openly supporting her mother in her hour of need. She was, after all, just a middle-aged woman who happened to be born in Germany. She had done nothing wrong.'

'But she was just mentally too far gone before Henrik realised the error of his ways.'

'But he had made no error,' said Anna shaking her head.

'In his own eyes he had, and that's what mattered to him.'

'The house is lonely without him,' Anna remarked after a pause. 'The boys are either out, or away, or busy, and Ted is normally with you,' she went on, changing the subject with a certain degree of relief which Alistair noted.

'I think you'll find,' speculated Alistair, 'that there will be no further comments in the remainder of the correspondence between the two of such feelings. He had shared some knowledge with Frieda's daughter because he felt he owed it to her. For some reason, he'd felt duty bound, but in so doing he had finally brought the matter to an end. It might be wise to leave the other letters unread and put the bundle back in the chest of drawers where it will be safe for a good long period.' Anna nodded her approval; Alistair could be very perceptive at times. 'We have a lot on our plate currently and don't need to burden ourselves with overwrought emotions.'

'Let sleeping dogs lie?'

'Yes, but don't tell Ted.'

Alistair's first official duty as golf club captain – a position he would be expected to keep under normal circumstances for a period of two years as his country club with two distinct courses was considered to be one of the finest golfing venues in East Anglia – was of a ceremonial nature. The newly formed committee, along with their partners, would be cheered into the dining hall by the membership for drinks and canapés, and with all expenses paid by the incoming captain, the members would turn out in full.

It would be Anna's first proper encounter with her

husband's golfing chums. The invitations had announced the requirement of the guests to wear formal attire – suits and day dresses were de rigueur – and Alistair had briefed his wife on the type of small talk necessary. It would be boring, he warned her, but she was to steer clear of general discussion about the bridge disaster, her long association with Arne, and on no account was she to mention the gold coins. I will be expected to mingle with all the members but if I see you stuck with a well-known bore, then I will endeavour to rescue you, which remark drew an enigmatic smile from her.

The warning may have seemed over the top at the time, but the subject of Arne was not far from the lips of several of the members. It seemed that Arne had become an object of fascination ever since he had pulled strings to become a member of the prestigious club some nine months previously following his purchase of a holiday cottage near the banks of Oulton Broad. It had easy access to the sea at Lowestoft and was within range of several highly-rated golf courses in the area. He was regarded as a local hero and some stardust appeared to blow off on them when they rubbed shoulders with him in the locker room.

'It was a good thing that you warned me about Arne,' said Anna at home later that evening. 'Some of your chums seem mesmerised by his antics.'

'Some people have their heads turned easily.'

'Will he cause you trouble?' asked Anna.

'Probably. He has a habit of doing so whether it is intended or not,' replied Alistair bitterly. 'He's such a wind-up merchant.'

'You mustn't let his prickly personality get under your skin,' warned Anna. 'It will serve no purpose other than to upset you.'

'You're right, of course. But people can be so blind, they think that all that glitters is gold.'

'But we know that all that glitters is rarely gold,' replied Anna, 'except in Henrik's case when he was the recipient of a gift of two hundred and sixteen coins of almost pure gold.'

'Then we'd better have a toast to Henrik,' said Alistair. They raised their coffee cups to "cheers" and "proost," and to their dear, departed friend.

Chapter 6

JENS

To the Drews, it seemed like an extraordinary amount of time passed before Alistair's friend finally reported back on the value of the coins, and even then, the valuations were approximate. Alistair was on the point of losing patience with his wife after having had to explain to her on numerous occasions that she needed to show a supreme amount of tolerance as there would be a chain of people involved in drilling down to find the right expert to give a realistic estimate of worth, and as they would all be doing favours for someone, nobody could be asked to "hurry up."

Jens arrived in Wells-next-the-Sea by car from the embassy's Manchester consulate where he had been working for a fortnight getting to know new staff, and contacting local prominent Netherlanders. He would stay a couple of nights in Norfolk before returning to London. He had no need to dash back home as Eva was away visiting her parents in Montevideo for several weeks. Together with his sister and Alistair, they had decided not to burden Eva with the knowledge of the gold coins. The less she knew about it the better; it concerned something from their shared past which they had to sort out themselves.

'As you've come alone, I've put you in Henrik's old room,' said Anna, guiding her brother to the left at the top of the grand stairs. 'You will be comfortable there, and we have just had it redecorated.' They stopped in front of the bedroom door and gazed at the wooden plaque announcing that it was "Henrik's room." It was dangling on a cord from a black, flat-headed screw. 'I couldn't bring myself to remove the sign,' explained his sister. 'It was made by my youngest son in one of his school woodwork classes. He probably had a lot of help with the engraving, but essentially, he made it and Henrik was thrilled.'

'You must leave it where it is,' said Jens immediately. 'It *is* still Henrik's room and always will be.' A toot from outside the window announced the return of Alistair from the office and Ted was seen scampering down the drive even before his master had reached the front door.

Cool beers were drunk on the patio in the fading sunlight before the men changed into casual clothes and wound down from the day's affairs. No mention was made of the reason for the conference until after dinner. Relaxing in the sitting room, each with a large whisky in hand, Alistair broke the news of the gold coin valuation to Jens. He explained how he had deliberately given his friend no idea of the quantity of coins they held, only a detailed description of six of them.

'How did you decide on which coins to give detailed descriptions?' asked Jens not unreasonably.

'Most of the twenty-guilder coins, which represented about half of the entire collection, had the same date, eighteen-fifty-three,' replied Alistair.

'And as we found out that they were only produced between eighteen-fifty and eighteen fifty-three, and we had at least one from each of those years,' chipped in Anna, 'it was easy to tell Alistair's friend that we had one twenty-guilder coin from each year of production.'

'But when it came to the five-guilder coins it proved much trickier,' continued Alistair. 'Again, many of them shared the same date but there were several that didn't.'

'And it was a different monarch,' said Anna chipping in again. 'They portrayed King William I.'

'After a lot of serious thought,' Alistair went on, 'and bearing in mind that we had to be cautious, we took the joint decision to only ask about the value of two of the five-guilder coins.'

'Are you going to tell me that you hit the jackpot?' asked Jens nervously.

'It would seem so,' replied Alistair, 'because alongside one of the many coins with the same date, we chose the oldest dated coin of William I's reign.'

'That would have been eighteen-fifteen,' said Jens. 'As I work as a representative of my country in my day job, I have to know my Dutch history well.'

'You're right. Eighteen-fifteen was his first year of reign. He abdicated in eighteen-forty and was succeeded by his son. But unlike you, Jens,' said Alistair grinning at his brother-in-law, 'I had to consult a book to find that out whereas you had it all in your head.' There were broad smiles around the table before Alistair continued.

'It appears that one coin may be worth almost as much as the entire collection of gold coins because of its rarity value. Very few five-guilder coins were minted in the first few years of his reign, and consequently these early coins have a worth that far exceeds their intrinsic gold value.'

'Jackpot,' stated Jens.

'And what's more,' continued Alistair, 'my friend tells me that at auction, if two rich collectors vied against one another, the sale price of the coin could be astronomical.'

'But does the value of the collection really matter to us?' intervened Anna. 'We haven't any plans for using it. Quite the opposite. We've only considered giving it away anonymously.'

'I've given it some serious thought over the weeks, but I haven't come up with an acceptable alternative,' Jens declared. 'If we were people with different morals and different attitudes, then we might have done something with it ourselves.'

'Such as?' his sister enquired.

'Such as using the money raised at auction to build a small, basic hospital in some remote area in a third world country, or installing the necessary infrastructure to provide clean water for the residents of a rural African village. You know, those sorts of things.'

'Use it to do something useful for those in need,' said Anna.

'It's a nice idea,' agreed Alistair, 'but not practical as we now know that the value of Henrik's gift from the council in Vlieland is worth at worst a six-figure sum and at best something in the millions. And there would be all manner of legal loopholes to stop us in our tracts once we allowed the information into the public domain. We would be receiving begging letters in their hundreds, just like the "Football Pools" winners when they go public. Yet not one of us wants the publicity that such wealth brings, nor do we want to be drawn into litigation by false claims of kinship with Henrik.'

'You're right, Alistair. An anonymous donation is our only option,' said Jens, 'and on that score I have an idea.'

'Good, glad to hear it,' responded Alistair immediately, 'because Anna and I have failed to come up with anything satisfactory.'

'Well, it's just an idea,' said Jens, pursing his lips, 'you may not find it satisfactory either, but it does reflect Henrik's working life, and I'm sure we can all agree that whatever we chose to do should have a real link with Henrik.'

'Is it to do with a lighthouse or a chandlery?' asked Anna.

'You're very perceptive, dear sister,' said Jens. 'It can be either, but I think the refurbishment of a lighthouse somewhere along the Dutch coast would be my choice. Keeping mariners safe from the North Sea would reflect what Henrik did for the best part of three decades.'

'Most of them are automatic now. Unmanned. And although I like the idea,' said Alistair thoughtfully, 'if I was to play devil's advocate, I'd be concerned about exactly how we could pull that off without jeopardising our privacy.'

'It has an Achilles' heel, I grant you,' replied Jens, 'but the alternatives of just handing over the cash box to a charity from an unidentified source and allowing them to do whatever they want with the money they raise from an auction may not suit us. The money might be squandered or used for some quasi-political project.'

'And we wouldn't like that,' stated Anna unequivocally. 'Absolutely not, nothing political.'

'And hopefully nothing lost to corruption either,' added Alistair.

'That would be the beauty of using the money for a project that we select. We could mostly avoid politics and corruption by having control over the finances of the project,' said Jens, 'the only question in my mind is how we can achieve it without giving up our anonymity.'

'That's the burning issue,' responded Alistair, 'to get something useful done without anyone associating it with us. In principle, Jens, I agree with your idea, but we are stuck in limbo until we have worked out exactly how we can do it.'

'Time is on our side,' said Anna cheerfully. 'Rarity values usually go up with the passage of time.'

Jens had a great deal to consider on his drive home to London. His mind drifted constantly from the job in hand of driving his car safely along the narrow, twisty roads of East Anglia towards the busy streets of the sprawling capital, to the issues raised by his stay in Norfolk. How was he going to make his glimmer of an idea work to achieve something worthwhile with the gold coin booty? It would require a great deal of careful consideration and he wouldn't be able to share his thoughts with his wife, Eva. He was longing to see her again after her weeks away in Uruguay visiting her parents during the university summer vacation, but their reunion would be tinged with his need to keep it secret. The complication of Arne buying a holiday home in the vicinity and joining the golf club where Alistair had just been elected as country club captain were further factors to mull over. He shook his head in wonder. It seemed that no matter what he and his sister did in life, Arne would always be present, popping up at inconvenient times to complicate matters.

Work at the embassy took the lion's share of his attention. At times, he and his wife would pass like omnibuses in the street, each headed in opposite directions, Eva to her job at the university and Jens to his office. There was little time to spend on contemplation of the dilemma that was posed by Henrik's cache of gold coins or how he might make surreptitious use of diplomatic channels to manoeuvre the chess pieces to fit the desired outcome. It was certainly food for occasional thought, but other issues of greater import were breaking ground as before long Jens learnt that he had been promoted to his first position as ambassador and would be heading to Switzerland within weeks, and not long after that relocation he would become a father for the first time at the age of fifty. Amid the congratulations of family and friends, and the upheaval and elaborate preparations necessary for their new lives both as parents and as the foremost representatives of The Netherlands in the historic Swiss capital, Bern, matters less pressing were suspended indefinitely. Jens realised that it would be some time before something tangible could be made of Henrik's treasure, but as his sister had pointed out, time was on their side.

Adapting to living in the Bernese Oberland within sight and easy reach of snow-peaked mountains, glaciers, lush alpine pastures, and heavily forested hills was a daily wonder for Jens and Eva. The geographical flatness of their own countries was replaced with stunning views of a countryside which never failed to lift morale. It was the country's capital city, yet with a population of less than a tenth of that in Montevideo and almost less than a hundredth of that in London, there was a small town feel to life in Bern. Thanks to the clockwork running of trains and trams, the dense traffic and pollution in their own capital cities was replaced by clean air and a freedom for the inhabitants to move about their memorable town in a relatively safe and relaxed manner.

Eva's first pregnancy at the age of forty-two was strictly monitored by the Swiss doctors; the shock of their regular bills causing Jens a degree of concern. With his wife no longer working, the salary he earned as a diplomat had to cover all their expenses and although it allowed for a comfortable existence there was no margin for excessive living. He wondered if the extra allowance he received for living in one of the most expensive countries in the world would cover the cost of nappies; he hoped so. It might have been all the changes occurring in her body that made settling down difficult for Eva. She was of a Latin disposition from her painted toenails to her fingertips. Gregarious by nature, and with a certain volatility of temperament, she was used to a style of life that included her wider family. While living in London, lingering over dinner under warm, starry skies with her extended family had not normally been possible, but the wrap around feeling of community had been replaced by the non-stop hustle and bustle of one of the world's largest cities. The small town of Bern, with its mostly sedate inhabitants whose approach to life was in the main far more insular, may not have been the ideal location for Eva's touchy-feely personality. Moderation was the key to a contented way of life in the well-ordered capital of Switzerland.

It was not long before the language barrier became a real issue. Although Jens spoke fluent German, he struggled with the Bernese dialect, one of the most intractable variations of Swiss-German. But as his ear adjusted to the unfamiliar sounds, so his confidence to mimic them grew. However, for Eva, a non-German speaker, most conversations had to take place in English, and whilst this was facilitated by a population adept at switching from one language to another depending on the country of origin of the tourist involved, for her it became an irritating factor. Whereas her English skills allowed her to express herself fully, conversations with those with restricted abilities, often resulted in a discourse severely curtailed of true meaning. It was something Jens could do little about and he had to be stoic in the face of her complaints that she was misunderstood. Surprisingly, it was her ante-natal classes that brought some relief to them both when Eva was introduced to a young woman with a husband also in the diplomatic corps.

'I'm so pleased to meet someone at last who speaks proper English,' said the young woman as they were seated at an outdoor pavement café after their class.

'Despite my Spanish accent?' ventured Eva.

'Despite that,' responded Stella, smiling broadly. 'You understand my meaning and that's what matters.'

'I feel the same way too. It's almost as if I have no tongue to express myself when I speak in English to those with limited vocabularies. And I have found very few native Spanish-speakers here in Bern either. It's a joy to have a chat with you when we know that the true nuances of our words will be understood. And what a surprise to learn that your husband, like mine, is a diplomat.'

'But unlike your husband, mine is presently only serving in a junior capacity.'

'My husband had to start on the bottom rung too, he was younger then of course. This is his first posting as ambassador and he's now fifty.' They sipped their drinks and agreed that citron tea was perfect for the time of day. 'Will it be your first child?' enquired Eva.

'No, my second. We already have a toddler,' said Stella. 'We're lucky to be serving in a country with first class health facilities. There are places in the world where I wouldn't wish to be giving birth. Know what I mean?'

'Absolutely. And especially at my age,' replied Eva. 'First baby at forty-two is slightly frightening.'

'I'm sure it must be, but now that we've met, we can give each other moral support. Which embassy does your husband represent?'

'The Netherlands. And yours, I presume, is the British.'

'Yes. We are having a cocktail party soon for some of our compatriots who live in Bern, although there are not many of them because of the cost of living here. It's an annual event, and a chance to meet diplomats new to Bern who are also invited. I'm sure that you and your husband will receive an invitation. Do come if you can, and then we will be able to enjoy non-alcoholic drinks together.'

The British Embassy in Bern was situated in a quiet, tree-lined street of substantial-sized mansions that had formerly been owned by families who had become successful over the years through banking and commerce. The eclectic mix of architecture coupled with mature gardens gave the street an impressive air. But as the needs of the twentieth century metamorphosed from grandeur to more prosaic requirements, so the buildings took on new roles as office space.

The garden party, as it was termed on the invitation, would start mid-afternoon, and end promptly at seven in the evening. With a small but well-maintained formal garden, the British Embassy's annual bash was always well attended. Amongst the throng, the two pregnant wives soon found one another and after performing the niceties of supporting their husbands, chose a shady bench on which to relax as best their physical shapes would allow. They were getting to know one another and to enjoy each other's company. Relaxed and with her guard slipped momentarily, Stella revealed that her father was Dutch. It was a subject that she normally treated as taboo; Arne was her real father, but she was his illegitimate child. In diplomatic circles in that epoch, such matters were kept strictly "entre nous." The news of a Dutch link aroused Eva's curiosity. She went on to enquire about various details of her father's Dutch identity including family surname. Stella sensed that she was on dangerous ground but felt the need, for the sake of politeness, to reveal that her father's surname was Visser. She realised that Eva's questions could not in any way be regarded as probing, but nonetheless, Stella was grateful when her husband appeared suggesting that it was time for them to take their leave.

For Eva it was an uncomfortably warm night. She tossed and turned in her endeavour to find a position in which her body felt at ease. The lightweight duvet was tossed off frequently with the annoyed flick of a foot, only to be reinstated by Jens whose patience was wearing thin.

'What's the matter?' asked Jens finally, turning on the bedside lamp.

'I can't get comfortable,' replied Eva, with a distinct note of frustration in her voice.

'It won't be long now,' said Jens, trying to say something soothing.

'No, it won't be long now until morning. You're damn right.'

'I didn't mean that and you know it. I meant until the baby is born. It's just a matter of holding on for a few more weeks and then it will all be over.'

'It's easy for you to say that. You haven't got to put up with this,' said Eva crossly, pointing at her large belly. 'It's all right for you.'

'I've just got to put up with sleep deprivation instead,' replied Jens caustically. 'How I'm going to get any work done tomorrow, I just don't know.'

The bad-tempered night turned into a frosty breakfast and a swift departure to the office for Jens, leaving Eva to reflect on their overnight quarrel. She was fiery and he was restrained. They were at the opposite ends of the personality spectrum, and unless the baby was born soon, she was afraid that it would all end in tears. Her thoughts about the tears turned out to be prescient as later that day, while chatting with Stella on the telephone, Eva fell silent and failed to respond when Stella asked her down the telephone line if she was okay. When Stella heard a clatter as if the receiver had been dropped, she knew it was time for action and alerted an ambulance to attend urgently at Eva's address. It was her quick thinking that saved the lives of both mother and unborn daughter as Eva was having a pre-eclampsia seizure, and her blood pressure had rocketed almost off the scale. Thanks to the medical care and a few restful days in a plush suite in the hospital, Eva was able to return home in a better frame of mind. Fortunately for Jens, he was able to take a day off work to welcome home his wife and cater for her every need, and it wasn't long before Stella came visiting.

'You're looking so much better than the last time I saw you,' said Stella, addressing her friend from the other end of the sofa. 'I'm so pleased to find you in better spirits.'

'I had a bit of a meltdown,' replied Eva, using a turn of phrase she had heard used on numerous occasions by her students. 'But I'm feeling so much more at ease now.'

'And she's got some colour back in her cheeks,' chipped in Jens. 'Mother and child are back from the brink, thank God, although she's got to have her blood pressure checked daily.'

'Well, that's not so bad. All's well that ends well. One of my favourite sayings,' said Stella.

'And the title of a play by Shakespeare that Eva and I went to see at the Old Vic in London,' added Jens.

'Did you know, my love, that Stella's father is Dutch?' It was a remark that set a ball rolling. 'Her father's surname is Visser,' she added.

'Visser?' questioned Jens, looking intently at Stella for confirmation. 'It means "fisherman" in English. Where does he come from?'

'Somewhere near the coast, I believe,' answered Stella, hoping that the conversation would not go any further.

'I knew a family named Visser when I lived in Harlingen,' said Jens after some thought. 'They built boats.' He didn't want the conversation to go any further either but he felt he had to exclude Arne from being her father. 'Pieter Visser and his son, Arne.' But he didn't get a straight answer as Stella's reply was nuanced. She knew her father only by his nickname, she said, but Jens recognised her answer for what it was: a sidestep.

The work of an ambassador in a long-established country such as Switzerland was rarely dramatic. It had its highs and lows – trade missions, hosting political talks between senior foreign affairs ministers, economic forums, international environmental symposia, elite sporting finals involving host and embassy nations, and volumes of paperwork – when the embassy staff and the ambassador were rushed off their feet glad-handing the delegates, but generally, they worked to a tedious routine. As if by good planning, no major "events" were scheduled to be held in the period after the birth of their daughter although Jens and Eva had had no hand in the fortuitous scheduling since the doctors had prescribed a Caesarean delivery before full-term when Eva's irregular blood pressure once again became a source of danger. Jens cleared his throat – a trick he had learnt from one of his senior colleagues in an earlier posting "quelque part" to get the attention of an audience without having to tap on the microphone and ask if he could be heard – as a prelude to announcing to the assembled embassy staff that he had become a father the previous morning, and that both mother and daughter were doing well. Congratulations were expressed, a glass of red wine from Uruguay imbibed by everyone with a generous slice of Edam cheese. It represented, he told his staff, a union of their two countries.

Even with a live-in nanny hired by Jens, the happy parents barely had a minute to themselves. The baby generated a whirlwind of new activities in the home.

'How lucky we are that you and the baby are well,' said Jens, reflecting on recent events late one evening.

'How lucky it was,' pointed out Eva, 'that I was on the phone to Stella when I had my seizure and that she was sufficiently alert to understand what was going on.'

'Not quite a chance in a million, but not far off.'

'I will say a prayer when I go to church on Sunday.'

'Yes, we are now a threesome thanks to Stella. We can't thank her enough.' After some reflection, Jens remarked that she had been cagey about her father on a previous occasion when the subject arose.

'Cagey? Stella?'

'Yes,' confirmed Jens. 'As if she didn't want to acknowledge who he was.'

'Are you sure?'

'I'm as certain as I can be. She flinched when I mentioned the name Arne. Yes, I'm pretty certain that Arne Visser, originally from Harlingen in north-western Holland, is her father,' said Jens summing up. 'She shares some facial characteristics with him and she's also tall. Yes, I can see a likeness.'

'Why does that worry you?' asked Eva intrigued.

'Unhappy memories, and he keeps turning up like a bad penny.'

'You don't like him, that's obvious,' said Eva, 'but why do you think Stella doesn't want you to know that he is her father?'

'To my knowledge Arne's not married and never has been. I might be wrong,' said Jens, crossing his arms, 'but if I am correct, then Stella will be his illegitimate child.'

'So what?' demanded Eva. 'Surely that's not a reason for hiding your parentage in this day and age.'

'Not for her possibly,' replied Jens insightfully, 'but for her husband's sake.'

'What's he got to do with it?'

'He's a diplomat. Like me, probably like diplomats the world over, they don't wish to be involved in any form of scandal. And having a wife who is the illegitimate child of a notable Dutchman smacks of scandal, and that's without mentioning his holiday company's innocent association with drugs. Mud has a knack of sticking even if you are totally blameless,' added Jens.

'So, you think that for his sake she is trying to keep it quiet.'

'More likely for the sake of her husband's career in the diplomatic service. Yes, that's what I think.'

'And I think that's a ridiculous attitude to hold.'

'Stella's husband is what the British call "old school",' explained Jens. 'He comes from a family with a long heritage of ancestors who held and observed traditional standards. Children born outside of marriage were considered as below par, although everyone knew that society was riddled with such offspring.'

'So, she's not prepared to acknowledge her real father. That is so very sad. Not to have the benefit of the friendship and love of your father just to fit in with some silly, outdated rule.'

'It may not make sense to you, but it does to many,' said Jens, 'and you mustn't forget that Arne may not have wanted her. If I know Arne at all, his first consideration would have been whether a baby daughter would have cramped his style or spoiled his golden image. And if he thought it did, then he would have had no compunction in ignoring her.'

'Another single parent child,' said Eva exasperated. 'You Europeans can be awfully cruel.'

'Let's hope she has a really loving relationship with her mother. By the way, when is her second child due?'

'In a month or so. And I hope that the baby's arrival will be a lot more straightforward than was ours.'

'I wonder if Arne will make a visit to Bern to see his second grandchild,' mused Jens.

'Second?' There may be others too.'

Stella's baby was born naturally without any form of alarm some five weeks later and mother and child returned home the following morning. When Eva visited her, they were quickly back into their normal rhythm of pleasant chitchat despite the need to continuously rock the baby in their lap and staunch its dribbles. The difference in age between the women – almost twenty years – appeared to cause no hindrance to their enjoyment of each other's company.

Eva was under strict instructions from Jens not to pry into Stella's life, nor to try to fill any gaps in the scenario speculated by him. Inquisitive by nature, Eva had wondered in advance how she would rein in her desire to know the back story of her friend's life. But the scene did not play out as expected when Stella chose to confront her difficulty head on.

'I made a faux pas the other day,' started Stella awkwardly. 'Sorry, an unintentional mistake,' she said correcting herself quickly when she realised that Eva didn't understand the meaning of the French words hijacked by the English as part of the lingua franca. 'It seemed silly to me afterwards to pretend that I didn't know my father's first name or where he was born.' She readjusted the position of the baby on her knees, gave it a light kiss on the side of the head and continued. 'My father, Arne Visser, was born in Harlingen in The Netherlands. In his younger years he was a sailor of great repute.'

'I know,' said Eva, trying to make her friend's confession as easy as possible. 'I met him many years ago when his sailing was based in Montevideo. It's on the River Plate and provides perfect competition conditions and safe harbours for expensive yachts.'

'Oh,' responded Stella, 'you've taken the wind out of my sails.' She laughed. It was an unintended pun. 'I had no idea you knew him.'

'I didn't really *know* him. I'd just met him on a few occasions. My boyfriend at the time was a crew member, so that's how we came to meet. But once my boyfriend and I parted company, I never saw your father again.'

'Well, in terms of time I have spent with him, I don't know him deeply either. You see, I have lived most of my life with my mother. She and my father were never married. They had an affair and I was the result.'

'Neither Jens nor I are stuffy about that sort of thing.'

'But most people still are.'

'I come from a part of the world where the whole family is far more important than the circumstance of how they came to be part of it.'

'But it's not like that in most of the world, especially in Europe,' said Stella shaking her head. 'Heritage counts. I'm like a piece of antique porcelain with a dodgy provenance.'

'Not in my eyes.'

'Attitudes are changing, but very, very slowly and in the world of diplomacy, sometimes they seem to be going backwards.'

'I know what you mean,' said Eva nodding. 'Tell me about your mother. Is she as splendid as you?' But they never got round to discussing her mother as the babies went into a joint, ear-splitting wail and the mothers agreed that any further attempts at conversation would have to wait to another day.

With her baby daughter safe in the hands of the live-in nanny, Eva, now feeling fit and restored to her natural exuberance, had free time to explore the charms of Bern: the famous clock tower, the museum, the minster, and the assortment of fountains scattered throughout the town. The tramway reached out as far as the botanical gardens where Eva wandered round admiring specimens from all over the globe. She heard the chatter of Spanish from a group of ladies standing next to a large plant looking splendid in bloom; Ceibo, the national flower of Uruguay. Hearing her native language spoken in the dialect of her home city, Montevideo, was too much for Eva to allow to go without comment. After introducing herself, she joined them for a cup of coffee in the café and was soon enrolled into the women's Uruguayan society of ex-pats. The society opened many doors to socialising, and rather unexpectedly, to voluntary work, such that it was some time before Eva was able to learn more about Stella's upbringing.

Stella had been anxious to see Eva again for several reasons. She felt sure her friend would not disclose the sensitive nature of the information she had revealed, but still felt the need to impress on Eva that the revelation had been without her husband's knowledge. The insidious spread of tittle-tattle like a stealthy snake approaching its prey, was not something he would welcome. Moreover, Stella had felt relieved to have unburdened herself to someone with empathy and who she liked. She would happily tell her about her mother. That chance came as a direct result of the voluntary work Eva now did in the Catholic church hall at lunchtimes on Mondays and on early Wednesday evenings. She taught beginners Spanish and the history of her continent to everyone who came along no matter their age or status. Whenever time permitted, Stella joined them; her mother being of

Hispanic descent. She knew sufficient basic Spanish to get by, but it was the political history of that vast continent that intrigued her. From the tropics at the equator to the frigid tips of land at Cape Horn, the continent was still populated by representatives of the indigenous peoples from the ancient civilisations who were eventually converted to Christianity by the Spanish and Portuguese colonisers. From slavery on the plantations to the setting up of independent states, internal strife and conflict, the rise and fall of military dictatorships, right wing juntas, the detention of thousands of political prisoners and international indebtedness, South America had it all. Stories of the fabulous continent with its dark history enthralled her congregation.

'They are so attentive,' said Eva one Wednesday evening after a class when she had time to enjoy a glass of wine with Stella in a street bar in the centre of the old town.

'That's because you make it so interesting. I'm hanging on your every word most of the time, almost fearful of what's coming next.'

'It's strange,' admitted Eva, 'but I feel freer to talk truthfully about the dark side of my continent here in Switzerland with just kids and pensioners as an audience than I did in London in the university milieu. I don't feel hampered by political correctness. Within limits, I can say things as I see them without fear of sanction.'

'That's what makes it so interesting. You touch the nitty-gritty.'

'Nitty-gritty?'

'Yes. The essence, the fundamentals, the nub of the

matter. It shines out loud and clear and we are transported back in time to sample life as it was then.'

'I'm so pleased it's enjoyable.'

'Your parents,' said Stella, 'are they from an indigenous tribe?'

'I like to think so, but pure-blooded indigenous people go back to the fourteenth century, and after that blood lines were adulterated by the colonisers from the Iberian Peninsula. Whether I would even be one percent indigenous now is unlikely and there would be no way of checking.' It was the perfect opening to allow Stella to continue the story she had previously seemed so eager to tell of her parentage. With her jet-black hair and olive skin tone, Stella shared only her tall height and a certain facial resemblance with Arne, so Eva was expecting her mother to have had her origins in a country with a warm climate.

'The other day, you were going to tell me about your mother,' Eva said sensitively.

'My mother. Yes. My mother is a lovely lady. She's here in Bern. She's Swiss. You met her at the recent cocktail party. She's a widow now but was formerly married to a member of the Swiss government.' It wasn't the sort of response that Eva had been expecting and it was clear from Stella's tone that that was all she was going to get. For one reason or another, on this particular subject, Stella had clammed up.

* * *

Jens was working at his desk when his personal secretary placed the diplomatic pouch squarely in front of his blotter. It was made of thick, black leather with an official crest etched into its face, and had the shape of a slim holdall. He knew what it meant: a lot of work. The delivery of the pouch was a routine occurrence to which he had not yet adjusted. When he finished his task in hand, he readied himself to attend to the contents of the pouch, but something made him pause. He sat back in his chair and studied the bag. It wasn't the subject of customs controls or to any intervention by the host country. Anything could be put in it and would travel in perfect safety. It was rumoured that during the second world war, Winston Churchill received his supply of Havana cigars by way of a diplomatic bag. For an instance, Jens allowed himself to daydream with a "what if." If Havana cigars could get from Cuba to wartime London courtesy of diplomatic channels, could Dutch gold coins from a previous century be moved from a small seaside town in Norfolk to a leading auction house in Amsterdam with instructions that the proceeds should be used to renovate a lighthouse along the Frisian archipelago. And all done anonymously. But it was just an odd moment of reverie. Jens snapped out of his daydream when the bustle of his secretary brought his focus back to the mundane communications from his masters in The Hague. The ritual of the diplomatic pouch, as his secretary opened it and laid the correspondence in his "in" tray for attention according to the priority stamped on each set of documents arrested any further thought of gold coins or of their possible charitable use.

It was Wednesday evening, and his working day having been run, he left the embassy in the safe hands of the night porter and security guard. Usually, he would have caught a tram back to the apartment and been happy to spend some time watching over his slumbering daughter, but it was a balmy evening in late summer and he decided to enjoy the short walk into town to join his wife and Stella for a drink at the bar they frequented after Eva's class. He sat down wearily after greeting the women and ordered a round of drinks. The women were in good spirits and their chatter was lively. An upcoming trade "do" at the German Embassy would be a meeting point the following week for Jens and Stella's husband and a chance for the two couples to socialise.

'Arne will be visiting them next week,' said Eva, as a first comment after they had taken their seats on the tram. It was information Jens chewed over before replying.

'To do what?' he asked. 'Arne never does anything without a motive.'

'To visit his daughter and meet his new grandchild, presumably.'

'Via invitation? I very much doubt that,' said Jens, answering his own question. 'And certainly not if what you have mentioned of Stella's view of him is true.'

'Well, maybe he's a reformed character now.'

'You mean, an updated version of himself, all sweetness and light. No, I don't buy that. An ulterior motive is far more likely.'

'But you must give him a chance. Stella must too,' insisted Eva pleading Arne's case.

'He never gave my sister and me a chance.' There was a bitterness in his voice that Eva accepted she was unlikely to alter.

'He must have hurt you deeply, my love.'

'He is a man who has no time for anyone other than himself. It's as simple as that.' Eva thought that was the end, but Jens added, 'and he's now causing grief at the golf club where Alistair is captain. He went over Alistair's head to arrange to get the East Anglia seniors' championship played there later this year. His action, as the British would say, was not cricket.'

As the chilly evenings of autumn and approaching winter drove the diplomatic fraternity indoors, so the patisseries and restaurants took on the role of meeting and socialising venues. After a midday class in the church hall, Eva stopped for lunch at a small eatery in the old town to meet two of her new Uruguayan friends from the ex-pats' society. Seated at a table for two, she spotted Stella talking animatedly to another woman. She looked familiar, but it took Eva several minutes to place her. She was Stella's mother, of that Eva felt sure, but she was also a prominent figure on the political stage. In her early fifties, she cut a distinguished image with her fine bone structure, short grey hair expertly styled, an upright back, and a slightly haughty air. Just like Stella's father, her mother too had presence.

As the pair left, Eva fought back the desire to go over and introduce herself. Presumed mother and daughter were still engaged in fervent conversation and Eva doubted they had even noticed her presence there. Back in the apartment, and with her five-month-old daughter having a welcomed nap in the cot, Eva cast her mind back to her home city on the River Plate. By boat, Montevideo was no more than a hundred nautical miles from the

Argentine capital, Buenos Aires, where so many of the elite sailing crews had their base. It was also the seat of political turmoil and social tumult; sailing and politics seemed bound together by some sort of umbilical cord.

Jens put his feet up after dinner, unwinding from the rigours of his demanding job. Occasionally, he enjoyed a small cigar. Eva didn't encourage smoking in the apartment but found the rich, pungent smell of the cigar agreeable. It was their time of day to relax in each other's company and after relaying to Jens what his daughter had got up to during her waking hours, she moved on to politics, or more precisely, to Stella's mother.

'Stella's mother,' started Eva, only to be directed immediately by her husband to add the word "presumed." 'Okay, Stella's *presumed* mother,' said Eva trying again. 'If I cast my mind back to the time when my then boyfriend was crewing in elite sailing events, I can vaguely remember her sitting with small groups of other women activists in open spaces around the harbour wall, ardently discussing politics.'

'With their intensity, they would probably have failed to register the exciting situation around them; the virile and muscular young men crewing the yachts. So, what makes you vaguely remember her?'

'Life was very political in those times. Daring to speak one's mind openly on many subjects was, literally, life-threatening. It was brave to express views that opposed military rule, but foolhardy in the extreme. My parents drummed into me the need for caution. They told me that abiding by the harsh rules set, didn't mean that I agreed with them. They didn't want me to disappear overnight from the face of the earth and never to be seen again as happened to so many people who dared to challenge the junta. Young people in particular were prone to do so, and their distraught, wailing mothers could be seen in public squares in hundreds begging for news of their children.'

'That must have been distressing. Are you suggesting that Stella's mother was a malcontent?'

'A militant? Yes, I believe she was.'

'But you say that she's Swiss.'

'She must have been Argentinian at the time, but probably fled the country when she gained the unwanted attention of the junta. Maybe she became Swiss through marriage,' said Eva, shrugging her shoulders. 'I don't know.'

First sightings of Arne were amongst the assembled crowd at the German embassy a few days later. What role he was playing to be invited to attend what was essentially a huge advertisement for the German motor show to be held later that month in the German industrial heartland with networking on the side, was unclear. He was neither diplomat nor industrialist, but as ever, wherever he went, he was unwilling to take on any part as a shrinking violet. Jens, supporting a Dutch delegation of automotive experts, stood back in free moments and observed the interaction between Arne and his son-in-law, a junior British diplomat. The scene appeared to act out as an acceptance on the son-in-law's part that Arne was a figure who would loom large over his life and that he would have to find a way to nullify any detrimental effects that his association with Arne would have on his diplomatic career.

'What's Arne up to?' asked Eva.

'Nothing in particular, just general self-promotion. See and be seen,' answered Jens tersely.

'Does he realise that he's making the occasion uncomfortable for his daughter and son-in-law?'

'Probably.'

'And what about the mother of his daughter over there,' said Eva pointing to a group of five standing round in a closed huddle.

'I don't believe that they are talking about the trade incentives the Germans are offering. Most likely, something far more adventurous.'

'Oh.'

'Rumour has it,' said Jens whispering into Eva's ear, 'that she's still involved as an activist in fighting the junta in her real homeland.'

'Really?'

'You must keep that quiet,' said Jens. 'I'm sure the Swiss authorities wouldn't approve. They are very strait-laced about such matters.'

'A country still cloaked in neutrality,' said Eva, and after a pause added, 'a South American activist with a Swiss passport and a husband engaged in the European Court of Justice. Yes, that really would make for an interesting conversation. But your secret is safe with me.'

It was Anna's first visit to Switzerland. She had delayed visiting her brother in his new post in the hope that Alistair would have sufficient time to accompany her. The fallout from the bridge accident had had so many ramifications in the world of civil engineering and particularly in bridge construction, that as senior partner, and coupled with his captain's duties at the country club, he decided that Anna would have to go alone. She had been itching to see her brother and new niece and he didn't wish to delay her any longer. After an initial burst of hugs and kisses, sightseeing rose to the top of the agenda. Growing up in the flat land of her native country and living her entire married life on the low-lying Norfolk coast, Anna marvelled at the rugged beauty of the distant mountains and the picturesque dwellings with roofs shaped to protect the occupants from heavy snowfalls. According to her brother, it was not a place for bicycles. They all laughed. She'd never had a bicycle herself but the wartime memory of Pieter arriving at their temporary lodgings in the boathouse on an ancient-looking bike was a recollection etched into her mind that she would never be able to dispel just like the smell of varnish in the near-derelict boatyard which lingered long after the wood of the last boat had been protected from the elements. She inhaled the crystal-clear air and pronounced that it was the best she'd ever tasted. They all laughed again. It was good to be reunited once more.

'It's a shame that Alistair hadn't the time to come too,' said Jens, after they'd enjoyed a cheese fondue in a restaurant specialising in Swiss fare. Washed down with a local white wine in liberal quantities, their journey back to the apartment by tram was all that they could manage.

On Anna's penultimate day abroad, a Sunday, Jens planned a hike up to one of the popular viewing platforms in the Jura foothills from where a spectacular vista of the countryside was available, free of charge and without any time limit to take in its magnificence. Following a well-worn trail suitable for most robust, leisure walkers, they arrived at a viewing point puffing and panting from the exertion of a five hundred plus metre climb. The wooden platform had been erected skilfully to bridge a chasm in a rocky outcrop of Jurassic geology. The lookout had a way in and a separate way out. Several hikers were standing immersing themselves in the breath-taking panorama or looking at the points of interest highlighted on the large-scale display map. As they approached the safety railings, Anna stiffened. A tall man with his back towards her was pointing out to a companion by his side the demarcation line of the French-Swiss border which was straddled by the sub-alpine range. Anna didn't need to note the blondeness of his hair to know who he was. Arne announced in English to his companion that they would climb higher to the lookout atop the Chasseral peak, and they soon departed unaware of the presence of Anna or of Jens.

'What's the matter?' Jens asked.

'That man over there,' she replied, looking over in the direction of the couple following the signs to the way out. 'I only saw him from behind but I swear that was Arne.'

'How could you tell?'

'His posture. It was …,' she hesitated as if searching for the right word, 'it looked arrogant.'

'How can a posture look arrogant?' asked Jens slightly irked.

'He wasn't just standing there, he was posing.'

214

'That's Arne then. A leading member of the worldwide society of poseurs. Who was he with?'

'A man, but I don't know who. I wasn't concentrating on him. I overheard Arne tell him that they were going up to the Chasseral lookout.'

'That's at the summit, another seven hundred metres or so higher than here.'

'I can't go any higher,' said Anna firmly, thinking of her already aching legs. 'This is high enough for me. And anyhow, why would we want to discover who he is?'

'Why indeed?' replied Jens thoughtfully. 'But somehow our lives seem to be inextricably intertwined with his, and therefore keeping one step ahead of him might be in our interest.'

On the descent, with talk of Arne banished from their thoughts, they chatted away happily in Dutch about domestic issues and other factors that impinged on daily life. Whenever alone together, Jens fell back automatically into calling his sister Annaliese. Although now completely converted to being known as Anna since her marriage, being called by what she regarded as her proper name, always touched a tender spot. There was nothing quite like the special rapport that being addressed by your real name engendered.

Back in the apartment, Eva was not surprised when she learnt that they had spotted Arne at one of the viewing platforms. She had spoken with Stella on the phone earlier in the day to seek assurance that her infant's slight cough was nothing to cause great concern. Stella had mentioned that her father was also out hiking in the Jura foothills although she made no mention of doing so with her own husband. It wasn't until a photograph printed in the local weekly Bernese newspaper – in essence an advertising medium for the regional tourist industry and which was always keen to make a link with any well-known personality visiting the area – showed a beaming Arne at the Chasseral viewing platform on a day when the weather conditions were picture perfect for extolling the virtues of the landscape, that Eva recognised a face in the crowd.

'That's Stella's husband,' said Eva, pointing a well-manicured fingernail at a bystander caught in the picture.

'So it is,' agreed Jens, after donning his reading spectacles. 'I told you he was up to something.'

'But what?'

'Well, there's not much ocean sailing to be done in Switzerland, so it must be something of a dubious nature.'

'Or just his inner need to continually fill the limelight.'

'A junior diplomat needs to tread warily at all times lest circumstances overtake discretion,' said Jens tellingly. 'His boss might remind him that a place in the shadows is the perfect place for a diplomat to occupy.'

Anna bent over the pram and gently kissed the fair, downy hairs on the side of her niece's head. The family had come to see her off at the railway station. It was an early morning start with a fast train to Zürich, a flight to Heathrow followed by a long train journey home to Norwich where Alistair would meet her. She hugged Eva and thanked her for an enjoyable stay. When the train pulled into the station, Jens hefted her suitcase into the carriage and found her a window seat on the side of the train which would afford the best views of the countryside.

'If I put the case in the overhead rack, will you be able to lift it down?'

'Stop fussing, Jens. I shall be able to lift it easily.'

'And have you got your ticket ready for inspection, Annaliese?'

'Yes. Stop mothering me, Jens. I shall be fine. And don't forget that I can speak German just as well as you,' said Anna with mock indignation.

As the hands on the station clock ticked round to the departure time, Jens warmly embraced his sister before alighting from the train to stand next to his wife and child on the platform for a farewell wave.

A man sitting farther down the carriage overheard snippets of the conversation including the name Annaliese. Arne rolled the name around on his tongue. It was not an uncommon name but not a fashionable one either. Thinking deeply, he realised that he had only ever known one Annaliese, and that had been a very long time ago. He resolved to pay attention to the woman when the train arrived at the terminus in Zürich. There was something about the way in which her name had been spoken. A rhythm, an inflection in a voice that he knew well from his boyhood days. It was, he felt sure, an accent from a region in northern Holland. A native can usually spot another native a long way off.

The infant's cough was slow to clear. Several consultations at the doctor's surgery became necessary including a far more worrying overnight stay in hospital. Jens loved his daughter but there were times when he questioned their wisdom in having a first child at ages forty-two and fifty. Even with a live-in nanny it was not easy. Eva could cope, but could he? Overcome by tiredness and anxiety to do the right thing, he had felt the need to delegate some of his ambassadorial duties; a situation he would never have guessed would be necessary. The weekly diplomatic pouch was delegated on a temporary basis to his senior assistant, a man in his early thirties who seemed to have supreme confidence in his own ability.

'Where are the contents of the diplomatic pouch, Karl?'

'There was nothing in it that required your personal attention, Sir,' Karl replied.

'Even if, in your opinion, there is nothing in the pouch of importance,' said Jens firmly, 'I need to know what it contained. In future, please write a summary of the contents and put it in my in-tray.'

'Certainly, Sir,' said Karl, although his body language didn't reflect his words. 'I have already distributed the correspondence to the appropriate departments.'

'Thank you, Karl.' It was as far as Jens could go to control the methods of the flighty Karl whose self-assurance he considered was often misplaced. When Karl left his office, Jens muttered to himself that recruitment and training of staff had gone downhill since his days. He returned to the job in hand of writing a brief for the forthcoming visit of a government minister, when he would be required to produce facts and figures for the minister's use. Assembling such detail didn't come naturally to Jens, but while persisting with pen in hand, he was seized by a moment of clarity as to how the diplomatic pouch could be used anonymously to get Henrik's coins to the auction house. But it was what Eva had to recount later that evening that proved even more startling.

The tall, distinguished-looking woman in her late forties, sat attentively in the church pew as Eva continued that Wednesday late afternoon with the history of her country, Uruguay. She was reviewing attitudes during the second world war and the political maelstrom that erupted on the South American continent in general in the following post-war period, which was marked by coups d'état, imprisonment and torture of dissidents and ruinous inflation. Eva has seen her before but could not quite place the occasion or the location. As her audience filed out slowly after a discreet round of applause, the tall lady with the prematurely greying hair rose to address Eva.

'Your accurate reminiscence of life in those days of turmoil brought back tough memories for me,' she said, with an outstretched hand to shake with Eva. 'I'm Coco Rohner. I don't think we've met.'

'It's a pleasure to meet you,' replied Eva, now realising that she was the person she had presumed to be Stella's mother. 'I believe you are from that part of the world.'

'By birth, I am Argentinian. I married a Swiss man.'

'So, you are a dual national?'

'No. I have forsaken my Argentinian nationality in favour of being unconditionally Swiss.' She smiled. Her fulsome lips quivered betraying some sort of deep feeling for her Argentinian roots.

'But it is still your country,' said Eva perceptively.

'No. It is no longer my country, but it is still my roots,' corrected Coco. She took a seat in the pew and beckoned Eva to join her. 'There is much we could discuss, I imagine.'

'Let off some built-up steam, maybe. The next church service is in an hour or so.'

'Very well,' said Coco, using her foot to move the kneeling pad out of the way so that she could stretch her legs. 'You tell me how you arrived in the Swiss capital and I will tell you my story.'

'Mine is simple,' said Eva, outlining the restrictions her parents had placed on her for her own safety in the politically-charged atmosphere in Montevideo when she was a teenager and young woman. How she had longed to escape, and in meeting her future husband, had found a way to escape to a society where she could speak openly. She missed her parents and wider family enormously, but her future lay in a milieu without fear of free speech. She wasn't in any sense a politico, but she did fervently uphold the need for history to be recorded truthfully. 'It is the bedrock of our lives.'

'Mine is more complicated,' said Coco. 'I was your next-door neighbour in Buenos Aires, but the regime in power was far harsher that in Uruguay. I was young and couldn't keep my mouth shut. I protested in the streets. It was my undoing. In hindsight I can see I was foolish. I thought at the time that I could change the world by protesting in the streets, but all I did was to cause my family anguish.' It was a dignified admittance to youthful inexperience. 'They came for me one day,' she went on, 'I hadn't heeded my parents' warning. Whilst the brutes banged on the front door, I quietly slipped out of the back door of our house near the waterfront with just a small holdall, little more than a large handbag really, that I kept ready just in case. I guess something inside me acknowledged that I was on a dangerous course.' Eva held her breath. Coco was describing a path she might have trodden herself but for her parents' paranoia with keeping her thoughts private. 'I found myself down on the waterfront. I kept looking behind me to see if there were any uniformed men pursuing me. I wasn't sure. I was still shaking. I walked along a wooden pontoon looking for a boat to hide in. When I found one, I jumped in and hid myself in the cabin. There was no one about, apart from a few voices as people passed the boat and the general bangs and scrapes as the boat rubbed up against the moorings. I must have fallen asleep, the terror of the day catching up with me. When I awoke it was dark and the boat was obviously at sea. A man was standing over me and I felt terrified all over again. He said "good evening" in passable Spanish and smirked.

Over the course of the next hour, Eva sat still in the pew, as if glued to the wooden bench by Coco's unfolding story. By noon of the following day, they were out in the throat of the River Plate estuary with land only just in sight. She learned that the tall man who had hovered over her was a Dutchman named Arne. He was participating in a single-handed round-the-world race, the first to be held since the end of the world war hostilities. He'd set sail before sunrise the next day after a final late night out socialising in Buenos Aires where he had put in a few days previously for repairs. It had been a balmy night and he had flopped asleep in the open cockpit, worse for wear. He'd woken in time to catch the early morning tide before he'd discovered his apparent stowaway partially secreted behind a locker in the cabin. It had been a time of quiet assessment for them both; she was temporarily safe from the regime's thugs, and he was still on schedule to complete the race to Southampton Water albeit with an uninvited guest whose presence contravened the race regulations. There had been options for them both and agreement on both sides to respect the other's wish, but an offload of the unwanted passenger along a deserted stretch of the Uruguayan coast had not been chosen. Instead, they would eke out the rations until they reached one of the islands of the Azores where Coco would leave the boat discreetly, and with money supplied by Arne, would catch a local ferry to the main island of São Miguel before making her way to the Portuguese coast to claim asylum. Arne had planned to re-victual in the main island anyhow, so there should only be a minimal loss of time due to the unscheduled course change.

During the long passage from the southern to the northern hemisphere across the Tropics of Capricorn and Cancer – the furthest northerly and southerly latitudes, according to Arne, when the sun can be directly overhead – there was time in calm conditions for introspection. Although he didn't speak Spanish, Arne could "get by" with the words and phrases he had picked up in so many ports around the Americas. Together with Coco's limited knowledge of English – her family's banking background giving rise to the need for the knowledge of certain expressions in English in order to trade successfully with the United States – they managed to pool their Spanish and English sayings sufficiently well in order to converse meaningfully. While Arne sailed the boat and Coco kept the galley organised when not lounging on deck, personal thoughts turned inwards.

As the days grew warmer, life on board grew more peaceful with subdued activity. Entire days passed without apparent need for effort other than to relax in the cockpit observing the odd passing cloud in the azure-tinted sky track its way from the windward to the leeward side of the boat. All that had needed to be said, had already been said. The romance started slowly with a casual arm around Coco's shoulders while they shared the meagre rations from the same plate. Later, the odd kiss on the cheek followed by a sigh marked an unspoken agreement that they would soon become lovers. Thoughts of their individual predicaments were set aside while they enjoyed a dream-like existence far from land and cut off from reality. It was only as they approached the Azores that the practicalities of their impending return to real life kicked in, and their previously vague plans for Coco's secret leave-taking required a translation into workable detail, that their looming separation hit home. They had grown very close over the past few weeks; they would miss one another. For Arne, there had been more than just the satisfaction that he had helped Coco escape political detention and possible torture. His memories of summarily offloading Jens and Annaliese in other circumstances could be balanced against Coco's escape to a better life. The redress was, for him, a rare moment of pride as he watched Coco's tall, languid body wade up the gently sloping beach to dry land holding no more than the small holdall with which she had stowed away. He would shelter the boat from prying eyes in a cove for as long as necessary to watch the inter-island ferry set sail for São Miguel with Coco aboard. She would be safe then and with the money he had given her, she would be able to get to continental Europe to claim asylum where she chose.

'So, you landed safely in Portugal,' ventured Eva. She had not spoken for some considerable time and the words were emitted in a staccato rhythm as they were forced out between her sticky lips.

'It didn't turn out to be as simple as we had planned,' replied Coco, 'there were no scheduled boats to the Portuguese mainland.' She frowned. 'The idyllic days on the yacht gave way to daily survival.'

'What did you do?'

'I stowed away again. A passenger ship was returning to Europe from the West Indies. It stopped in the Azores to refuel and re-supply. My money was running out and I had no real "papers." I attached myself to a group of passengers who were returning to the ship after an afternoon outing. Nobody queried my presence on the ship. In the market, I had bought a souvenir T-shirt with the name of the island emblazoned on it. I looked the part and when I had combed my hair and tidied up in a cloakroom, I looked presentable.'

'But where did you sleep?' asked Eva anxiously.

'I didn't. I had to keep moving until the ship was out of sight of land. I sat in a deck chair for a long time pretending to be asleep. Eventually, as twilight turned to full darkness, I had to go inside. A steward directed me to the purser's office where I admitted that I had stowed away.'

'Gosh.' It was the same word in Spanish as in English. The two Spanish-speaking ladies saw the irony and smiled. 'That must have been a difficult moment,' Eva said.

'Yes, it was difficult but I was hungry and tired. The purser took my details and then escorted me to the captain's quarters. I had something else to tell the captain. I wasn't just an asylum seeker; I was also pregnant.'

'Oh,' said Eva, nibbling the ends of her fingertips with the built-up tension. 'I suppose you *just* knew.'

'Yes. I *just* knew. The captain wasn't pleased but he acted professionally and told me I would be held securely in a cabin and handed to the authorities when the ship docked in Southampton in five days' time. In the meantime, a steward would bring me food and drink and the captain would arrange for the ship's doctor to assess my medical condition.'

'They were decent then,' stated Eva, and Coco nodded her head in agreement. 'So, you landed in the United Kingdom.'

'No, I was landed in France. A storm blew up in the approaches to the English Channel. The ship received a mayday call from a merchant vessel. It was in distress. Under maritime law, ships in the vicinity are obliged to offer help. We were diverted towards the French coastline to assist. Apparently, we picked up several sailors from a lifeboat and then began a sea search for the remaining crew members. The storm became more severe, the maximum force, and our liner put in to the port of Le

Havre for respite until the storm abated. The rescued sailors were ferried ashore and I was told that I had to go with them and make my asylum claim there. France was deemed to be a safe haven and the law apparently stated that I must apply for asylum in the first safe country I reached. I didn't have a choice but I would have chosen France anyhow as I knew that if I headed due south I would come to a Spanish-speaking country.'

'Which would have a more Latin feel,' said Eva. 'One with which you could more readily align.'

'I knew no French but the officials provided a Spanish speaker who was able to help me. But my options were limited, especially since I was pregnant and was not feeling well. I was lost for what to do next. They put me up in a boarding house with other people they described as vagrants. It was horrible there. I felt safer walking the streets. Weeks passed with no offer to travel to Spain and no improvement in my living conditions. I found a map in a library and decided to try to get to Switzerland as I knew it had been neutral during the war. I stole some money, bought a train ticket, and arrived in the border town of La Chaux-de-Fonds the following day where I officially claimed asylum. The officials there were courteous but unfriendly. I was held in detention for several days before my body finally resolved the matter. I was taken ill and gave birth prematurely to a baby girl. She was born in Switzerland and was therefore Swiss allowing everything to magically slot into place. As the mother of a Swiss citizen, I was allowed to stay.' Coco heaved a sigh of relief as if it was just yesterday that her story had happened. 'The baby made it all possible.'

'Relief at last,' pronounced Eva.

'I married the doctor who delivered my daughter. He was considerably older than me. He had never married because of a rare condition which prevented his ability to generate healthy sperm. He considered it would have been morally reprehensible to place such a burden on a wife. We talked frequently as I visited the hospital daily until my daughter was fit to be discharged. He was a dignified man and rather suave, and said he would look after my daughter as if she were his own when he asked me to marry him. The marriage of convenience turned out to be one of love and respect. He was true to his word and when he died, Stella and I were heartbroken.'

Jens stirred in his seat. He had been transported into a past epoch by the story Eva recounted. 'I know,' he said finally.'

'Know what?' asked Eva unbelievingly.

'I knew Ralph Rohner. When he retired from practising medicine, he worked unpaid for a European humanitarian agency. He knew his days were numbered but wanted to do something to improve access to modern medicine in third-world countries. He campaigned in a European forum to introduce laws to provide regular foreign aid.'

'You knew Stella was his adopted daughter?' said Eva incredulously, 'but you never mentioned it to me.'

'I'm a diplomat. My job is not to spread knowledge or gossip where it is not necessary.'

'Even to me?'

'Even to you, my lovely Eva.'

Chapter 7

ARNE & STELLA

Stella's husband, some twenty years plus younger than Arne had been impressed by his agility on the climb up to Chasseral. He had appeared to sprint up the last third of the climb on a track which was narrow and rocky and one which required a certain head for heights. The spectacular view had been well worth the effort, he reflected, but he was dubious about Arne's reason for the outing. As a junior diplomat on one of the lowest rungs of a civil servant's pay scale, and even when his salary was supplemented with some financial assistance from his own parents, he was in no position to afford the services of a live-in child minder. Arne would have known that Stella could not accompany them; she would have had her hands full with an infant and a toddler. So, what was it that Arne wanted when he deliberately separated Stella from her husband? He may not have known him for long, and certainly not willingly, but he was sufficiently astute to realise that behind his actions his wife's father had a rationale.

Talk across the pillow that night, on a subject that required an artful approach due to Stella's extreme sensitivity about her father, was littered with oblique remarks. It was a test of his diplomacy to move crab-like around the subject in the hope of avoiding stepping on his wife's vulnerable toes, but one that didn't pay off as it ended with harsh remarks from both sides, whispered mostly in semi-muted tones to avoid waking the children, but ended on a final note with a crystal-clear meaning about what the hell her father was up to. It was too much for Stella. She wasn't going to share a bed for a minute longer with such an abominable person. In high dudgeon, and with some theatrical gestures associated with a Latin temperament, she wrapped the dressing gown around her slender torso, knotted the belt tightly, and stomped out leaving her husband to rue his desire to know what Arne was about.

There were other parties interested in Arne's affairs too. For one, his business partners, Barry, and Victor – although Victor's interest was strictly confined to whether or not Arne had any inkling that the baby Gloria had given birth to carried Arne's genes. A daughter with fair hair and a propensity to wave her feet in the air whenever she was the centre of attention. She bore the hallmarks of Arne, not of Victor. And for two, a business empire that was on rocky ground without the undivided attention of its figurehead founder, as Barry had to admit that he could not provide the "flair" that Arne could. And for three, added into the smoking cauldron was Arne's apparent acceptance that when circumstances dictated, cheating at golf was a necessary measure.

* * *

Stella was only British by marriage. Her birth certificate indicated that her mother was stateless at the time she popped into the world, although Coco – no family surname was provided due to political reasons – was believed to be Argentinian by birth. When Stella was discharged from the hospital almost three months after her birth, her mother had already married and become a Swiss citizen. No details were submitted regarding her real father; it was only noted that Ralph Rohner had legally adopted Stella as his daughter.

Nationality had been a sticking point for her prospective husband's family. They could trace their lineage back to some obscure monarch in the distant past. And although Stella could speak English without any hint of an accent – due to the foresight of Ralph in sending her to the international school in Geneva as he realised that the language of science throughout the world was English – it wasn't quite enough to assuage the concerns of her husband's stuffy family. Following a row in which Stella's husband-to-be declared that he was going to marry her regardless of their animosity, matters quietened down and were almost completely resolved when, upon marriage, Stella applied for a British passport. Homage had been paid to the type of society in which they wished their only son to live and prosper, and at that point they felt able to extend their welcome into their family of not only Stella, but also to her mother, Coco, who was from a stable country that had no recent history of attacking its neighbours and was very good at making precision watches.

After Ralph's death, when Stella was still a young teenager, mother and daughter formed an inseparable partnership. Family members were thin on the ground and Coco did what she could to instil in her daughter the values of a family. The oft repeated mantra that Stella had a wider family out there in Argentina but they just could not be accessed until a regime change made it safe for them to travel home, was some sort of temporary comfort blanket. It served a purpose up until her late teens, but could not withstand the enquiring mind of a young adult who declined to accept that she would go through life never knowing anything about her real father.

The desire to discover her real father, if Stella was honest, dated back to before Ralph's death but remained latent out of respect until her happy memories of him began to fade. With the backing of her mother – although Stella would have gone ahead anyway – efforts to trace her birth father began in earnest. It might have been an unachievable objective if Coco had not helped her with name, country, and celebrity. She had never disclosed details, neither to Ralph nor to Stella, about the man who had sailed the boat from Buenos Aires to the Azores. She had disciplined herself to refer to Arne as "the good sailor" and had never let slip any other details. Ralph had never inquired. He loved Coco and Stella and that was good enough for him, and he was happy to let sleeping dogs lie. Stella, however, never really believed that her mother knew nothing about "the good sailor" but she was sufficiently smart to know when the time was right to press and when it was not. One evening, whilst dining out at one of the first fast food outlets opened in their vicinity, Stella broached the subject head on.

'You must know quite a lot about him,' said Stella, as she faced her mother across the table. 'It's time to stop pretending that you don't even know his name.' Coco was silent. She had been half expecting some digging from her daughter. It was the lack of subtleness that threw her.

'Are you serious?' asked Coco, pushing away her plate.

'Of course, I am. It's time for me to find my father, if he is alive. If you know more about him than you pretend, you can't deny me.'

'Well,' replied Coco tentatively, 'it's true that I do know a little more about him.' It was a question from her daughter that Coco knew was inevitable. One day, when Stella posed it, she would have to reply. There could be no shilly-shallying around the subject. She would have to tell all that she knew. 'His name is Arne and he's Dutch. He never mentioned his surname but I learned quite some time later that it is Visser, and that he is a famous Dutchman and a celebrity in the world of sailing. He's a few years older than me.'

'How did you find out?' asked Stella in earnest.

'Mostly from newspapers and magazines. He represented his country at the Olympics and won medals. He skippered elite yacht races around the world. He was also known as a playboy in his younger days.' Coco paused. 'About him as a human being, I know little really,' she continued, shrugging her shoulders. 'He was good to me on the boat, I trusted him. He didn't take advantage of me. But we didn't make any long-term plans to meet again. When I waded up the beach in the Azores and turned round to wave goodbye, he was already setting sail. It was as if my presence in his life had never existed.' Stella looked disappointed and Coco reached out to hold her hands. 'That's all I know really, apart from the fact that he truly loved his father, Pieter. That was crystal clear.'

'He doesn't sound as nice as Ralph,' said Stella, 'but even so, I would like to find him and meet him, although I'm not sure why. Does he know about me?'

'I don't think so. I can't imagine how he could know.' It was an answer that deflated Stella. 'I'm sorry, darling, if you find that upsetting,' added Coco quickly when she saw Stella's dispirited face, 'but that doesn't mean that he wouldn't wish to meet you if he knew you were his daughter.'

In the months ahead, many a moment arose when Stella's eyes glazed over as her thoughts turned to her father. He was a subject she pondered over again and again until one day she felt able to be decisive. She had seen his photo in a trendy gossip magazine and something had just clicked in her brain that she could handle his rejection if it came to that. She was now a woman with a purpose and some invaluable experience of life, and it would take more than his rebuff to upset her. A telephone call to the magazine's editorial office resulted in a contact telephone number, Pimlico 7408. There was no reply to the first half dozen calls, but in due course an answering voice confirmed that she had got through to the correct number.

'Am I speaking to Arne Visser?' Stella inquired.

'Yes, you are.'

'I'm a journalist,' she started, reading from some prepared notes, 'and I would very much like to write an article about your single-handed sailing career. Would you be agreeable?'

'Probably,' replied Arne. 'It would depend on the nature of the article. But, probably yes.'

'Good,' said Stella, keeping to her script, 'could we meet for an initial chat to flesh out the style and range of content that would be acceptable to you?'

'Yes, of course,' replied Arne, agreeing a "where and when" before hanging up.

Their first meeting was in a posh café in London's West End. He had been easy to spot with his blonde hair and good looks. He was taller than she had imagined and was informally dressed. She introduced herself as Stella Rohner, which name very obviously meant nothing to Arne. She carried a notebook and two pencils and stuck to the theme of being a journalist. Arne ordered drinks and Danish pastries, and after a few pleasantries enquired about her employers.

'I'm freelance,' replied Stella. 'I can choose my subjects and offer my work to whoever I chose.'

'Why are you intending to write an article about me?'

'Your sailing days around the globe would be of interest to many readers and would bring some added glamour into their more humdrum lives. It would sell well.'

'And you would benefit from that,' said Arne.

'Yes. I have to make a living. But you would benefit too from the publicity.'

'As long as it's the right type of publicity.'

'Is there some reason why it shouldn't be?' asked Stella. She was one step ahead of her father.

'No. No reason at all. It's the slant that journalists put on the information given in good faith that determines whether it is the right type of publicity or not,' said Arne knowingly. 'You haven't written much down yet,' he remarked off the cuff. It was the perfect moment Stella knew, to focus entirely on his passage up to the Azores with her mother on board.

'In particular, I would like to write about your passage from Buenos Aires to the Azores Island of São Miguel in nineteen fifty-one. I believe it was single-handed but that you had a stowaway passenger. Is that correct?' In the circumstance, it was incendiary language. Arne coughed and spluttered and a sour expression developed on his face.

'No, that is not correct. Single-handed sailing means single-handed and I would not have won the race if I had had a passenger on board.'

'I believe her name was Coco,' said Stella, pressing her case.

'I don't know anyone named Coco, least of all a stowaway,' said Arne adamantly. He looked as if he was about to get up and walk away, and it was time for Stella to deliver the coup de grâce.

'Are you absolutely sure?' asked Stella, confronting him again, 'because Coco is my mother and she has told me all about you, Father.'

When Arne had calmed down and settled back in his seat, he ordered fresh coffees. His mood was a mixture of anger and surprise, with a hint of added jealousy. He took his time before telling Stella that she had got him there on false pretences and asking her what she wanted.

'I wanted to meet my father,' she replied. 'Nothing more sinister than that.'

'You *don't* know that I'm your father. You're guessing.'

'A guess that you know is the truth. All the details match. It could only be you.'

'What is it you want?' he asked again. He was clearly agitated.

'I don't want anything other than to get to know a bit about you. But if that is too difficult for you to deal with, then I'll leave it at that.' She might have left at that point had not the waitress interrupted the scene by serving their coffees. It created a short breathing space for both to adjust to the extraordinary meeting.

'If you were my daughter,' said Arne finally, 'then I should have every reason to feel proud of you.' It was a remark totally in character. He could flip from the "don't know, don't care" to the charming and engaging persona that was also part of his personality.

'And there might be reasons for me to be proud of you too,' replied Stella. She had carefully mapped out the preamble to his admittance - grudging or not – that he was her father, but given no real thought as to what she would say or what information she sought after the acceptance that they were father and daughter. She floundered for a moment. 'I believe you did something special during the war. Is that true?'

'Why would you want to know about that?' he countered.

'If I'm to meet you only this once, then I would like to

take away some knowledge of your life up until now. How you have led your life, your ambitions, your values.'

The story was told, from childhood to present times. The account was brief but did not omit the major events of the life of a man on the threshold of middle age. As to whether or not it gave any insight into the morals and standards of the conduct of his life was questionable, but in recounting his past, his mood mellowed leaving Stella satisfied that she had obtained the framework of information about her biological father that she had craved for so long. Strangely, he made no enquiries about Coco or about her, but in parting on good terms if somewhat awkwardly, he had told her that she would be welcome at his flat in Pimlico if and when she was passing. She had the telephone number, and she only had to call. But it wasn't an invitation that she felt the need to take up for several years. For the moment, her thirst for information was slaked.

When Arne hit the headlines for the wrong reasons in the very early seventies – a period which coincided with Stella's first and only big romance – the resulting hoo-ha proved anathema to her. Normally of a conservative nature, she cringed at the thought of being even marginally associated with the tabloids' muckracking. Her father may not have been to blame for the incidents raked over by the press but he was around when the mud was flying and some of it had stuck to him. She made some telephone calls to Pimlico 7408 and a couple of rare visits to his flat to check the situation, and to arm herself with some facts should it come to light that Arne was her father.

The invitation to join him at a house party in Spain came completely out of the blue. Her first instinct was to decline, but further thought led to a change of mind. He couldn't be all bad. He must have some redeeming qualities. And as apparently the other guests knew she was Arne's illegitimate child, there seemed little point in declining, and it proved to be the right decision. Arne was in fine form throughout the period, displaying a capacity for consideration towards everyone. His undeniable charm, when switched on, was the reason for his popularity in social circles and could be deployed to win over even his harshest critics. Whilst the three "boys" went off to golf most days, the "girls" - two wives and Stella – lounged poolside or went shopping. They barely knew Arne, but referring to him as "her father" it was obvious that they enjoyed his company. And it proved food for thought as to whether she might adopt a more liberal frame of mind towards her own illegitimacy. Times were a-changing, and maybe she should do so too.

Stella's marriage was textbook traditional, the ceremony and nuptials being dictated by the in-laws. Coco and Stella looked down from their lofty heights – both taller than the bridegroom and most of his relatives – and giggled. They were to wear, what seemed to them, a form of fancy dress and to sit at long tables covered in heavy duty white mercerised cotton cloth that flapped down to their ankles, and where conversation could only be conducted by raising one's voice to carry the gap between seated guests. Even the Swiss, not known for their flamboyance, had a far more relaxed and fun approach to wedding days which required not a single rehearsal.

If Stella hadn't been truly in love with her fiancé, she might have called the whole thing off. Coco urged her daughter to remember that she would be marrying her man and not his family, and as he had chosen a career in the diplomatic service, the pair would be spending most of their time overseas, well away from family influence, and Stella replied by thanking God for that. With her new attitude towards children born out of wedlock, and the way in which she could escape from her in-laws, Stella thought she had finally straddled all the hurdles in her path. But Stella was mistaken as a further development was about to erupt.

* * *

Smallish, private companies rarely make the financial press, and if Visser Sailing & Diving Holidays had not been a part of BAV Enterprises - the umbrella company of Barry, Arne, and Victor – it would have been unlikely that their trading performance would have come under the scrutiny that it did. The blame could rightly have been laid at the feet of Barry and Victor – although mostly at Barry's size nine feet as Victor's business acumen had gone somewhat out the window since Gloria gave birth, and everyone in the company knew it.

The statutory accounts did not lie. Where Gloria had been able to be creative with the figure work, the new man posted to Arne's company as office manager to ensure that there was no slacking amongst staff of all ranks, had neither the imagination nor the know-how to shuffle the figures to impress both financial journalists and the auditors that all was above board. A senior journalist, whose boyhood idol had been Arne for his daring wartime escape across the sea, had given the accounts somewhat more than a passing glance and realised that they failed to stack up. There was something fishy going on. When he dug deeper, and associated the accounts with the drugs scandal, he realised that BAV Enterprises may not have been a wholly innocent party in the affair as their exoneration by the police had stated. When he started ferreting about, he soon discovered that a couple who had enjoyed a Visser sailing holiday prior to the incident had served time in the past in secure prisons, and that there was more than a hint of a drugs-related association in their crime. With dogged persistence he was able to link the couple, married but using different surnames, to Barry, which opened up another channel demanding investigation.

Barry was an ex-bankrupt. Not once, but twice. He was too sharp an operator, too willing to cut corners, and too clever by far for his own good. It was not until he teamed up with Victor, the steady Eddy of the duo, that he found success in commerce. But once the journalist had found the first news article dealing with Barry's former misdemeanours in the middle section of a local rag, it led to another, and then another, and before long he had a clear concept of Barry's guiding principle in business: greed. With the help of a colleague with skills in formal accountancy, they were able to establish that batches of unaccounted money had been paid into Arne's company and then taken out in varying amounts. The trail of the laundered money ended with its payment into three different private accounts, and it was, according to the accountant, a pound to a penny that these three accounts belonged respectively to Barry, Arne, and Victor. The accountant tut-tutted; his disapproval was obvious. He implied that as a former bankrupt, Barry wouldn't have been able to become a company director, so he must have had a pecuniary arrangement with someone to "use" their name instead. When the financial journalist checked BAV Enterprises' Articles of Association, he found, as predicted, no mention of Barry. Instead, representing Barry presumably, the name of Gloria Newton was included as director of said company.

The sniff of a story with a potentially wider appeal to his readers than just another dry, financial exposé as it appeared to be on the surface, thrilled the journalist. That his boyhood hero was involved was already a plus, but now the discovery of the involvement of a woman could ramp up the level of intrigue and turn it into a blockbuster tale. And the journalist wasn't disappointed when he discovered the connection between Barry and Gloria. She had been, or still was, his right-hand man. Married to Victor, she had recently had a child and was on, what he assumed to be, a version of maternity leave. But his nostrils told him that it didn't have the feel of a bog-standard maternity leave. With Victor and the baby, she had moved away from the London area to a market garden new town well away from the smoke. It seemed a curious thing to do when the basis for their business lay in the metropolis. Lost for a satisfactory answer to this conundrum, the financial journalist fell back onto his staple source of information: gossip. By fair means or foul, he surreptitiously wheedled out snippets of information from work colleagues which suggested that Gloria had had a fling with her then boss, Arne. From that point, it wasn't a huge step of the imagination to question the parentage of the baby. When he learned that Victor and Gloria had struggled for many years to conceive the child they so badly wanted, the bagatelle balls dropped into place. Arne had sired a love child and Victor and Gloria were bringing it up. It made him wonder. Did he have other illegitimate children? Surely Gloria's baby wasn't the only one. He sniggered at the idea of only the one as being inconceivable for a man with Arne's glitzy lifestyle. His idol had fallen, but in so doing, had rewarded the journalist with a scoop.

'Excuse me please for disturbing you,' the financial journalist said politely to the man who opened the front door in response to his resounding knocks. 'I seem to have got lost. I'm looking for Wilton Crescent. Do you know where it is?'

'Wilton Crescent,' replied Victor repeating the street name. 'It rings a bell. It could be the road which leads off the minor road at the T-junction about a hundred yards farther along, but I'm not sure.' He called out to his wife. 'Gloria, do you know how to get to Wilton Crescent?'

'Is someone lost?' she answered. She appeared in the hall holding the hand of a toddler.

'Yes, I am,' said the journalist quickly. 'Sorry for interrupting you. I thought the street was on the map, but I can't find it.'

'Maps can't keep pace with the building going on in this new town,' said Gloria. The journalist knew that and he also knew the whereabouts of Wilton Crescent. The subterfuge and bluff were working.

'And who is this little one?' asked the journalist as the toddler stuck a sticky hand on his trouser leg for support.

'She's Little Marilyn,' said Gloria helpfully. 'Wilton Crescent. Yes, I do know where that is. It's the mirror image of this crescent farther down the street but on the opposite side of the road.'

'Thanks so much. I'm grateful for your help. I'll let you get back to playing with your daughter. She's very cute. How old is she?'

'Almost two.'

'Cheerio.'

He had slipped back to the road later, and from a hidden position behind a parked car, the financial journalist had been able to take photographs of the family as they made their way on foot to the local park.

'It's not our normal line of business,' his editor said sceptically when shown the photograph of Victor, Gloria, and their apparent daughter. 'We report on finance.'

'It is finance. Basically, anyhow,' his journalist replied, 'with some love triangle stuff too. And a larger-than-life personality. But its basis is money.'

'The whole world is based on money,' responded his editor looking up unimpressed from his overloaded desk. 'Nothing new there. So, what makes this story any different from a sleazy write-up in one of the tabloids?'

'They emphasise the sleaze. We would emphasise the intrigue.'

'What intrigue?'

'A famous personality, wartime hero, etc., with at least two illegitimate daughters caught up, willingly or not, in a money laundering crime.'

'Two daughters?' questioned the editor. 'You've only mentioned one so far.'

'Yes, two,' confirmed the journalist proudly. 'I've discovered an adult daughter too. She's about to be married to someone in the diplomatic corps whose lineage is upper crust.'

'Explain, please,' said his editor curtly. He was clearly pushed for time.

'Well,' started the journalist, 'one of the BAV directors, Barry to be precise, appears to have grown rich over the past few years under the clever influence of his co-director, Victor. He had invested some of his, er, let's call it windfall, in a large villa in Spain. He holds house parties there with an eye to business.'

'You rub my back, and I'll rub yours,' ventured the editor.

'Exactly so,' continued the journalist. 'Arne Visser was invited to one of these house parties on the pretext of a golfing holiday with the boys. He took a young woman with him. She turned out to be his daughter, Stella Rohner. It's a long story, but Arne had only recently learned of her existence. The daughter had contacted him to find out some details about her biological father.'

'Why? She could have let sleeping dogs lie.'

'Curiosity I suppose. You can get a sense of a person

from old newspaper clippings, but you can't get the feel of that person.'

'So, she accompanied him to Spain to get to know him better, and in so doing jeopardised the secrecy of her birth.'

'That's about it,' agreed the journalist. 'It might be seen by some as a bit of a gaffe. But she's young and the call of her own flesh and blood was probably overwhelming.' His editor nodded.

'It's still sleaze with a bit of money laundering on the side,' said the editor.

'No, it's more than that,' said the journalist firmly. 'It's the story of the playboy, Arne Visser, and how his frailties have affected the lives of others.'

'We don't do "human interest" stories,' said the editor flatly, 'unless they are of financial significance.'

'Surely, the laundering of drug money is significant,' protested the journalist in an exasperated tone. It was a rebuke that the editor chose not to recognise. He always tried to cut his senior personnel some slack.

'So, what have we really?' said the editor. 'A wartime hero, turned ace sailor, turned playboy, turned businessman, turned father of at least two children born on the wrong side of the blanket, who through sheer naivety becomes embroiled in shady financial affairs that are way beyond his understanding. What do you want your readers to do? Love him or hate him?'

'Well, put that way, I suppose they could do either.'

'You're experienced enough to know that a good story tells the readers to love him or to hate him. It doesn't give them an option.' There was a lull in the conversation. The cogs were whirring in the editor's brain. Finally, he said, 'I won't print it. Go away and dig some more. If you come up with some more connections, especially financial ones, I'll review my decision. Close the door on your way out.' Alone in his office, the editor paused in his work. He had been to public school and then to university with the father of the family into which Arne's adult daughter was due to marry. He wasn't about to cause a rift in that relationship with a bit of cheap scandal. He was part of an old boys' network that had stood the test of time.

When he examined the birth certificate of Little Marilyn, the toddler of just under two years of age, in the rarefied confines of Somerset House, he noted that it bore the names of both her father and her mother: Father – Victor Wremble, company director, Mother – Gloria Wremble (née Newton). It wasn't considered necessary in that epoch to register the mother's working status. He paid for a certified copy to be written then and there, and waited patiently in the spacious waiting room along with many others, for his name to be called out to collect the ordered document from a counter clerk.

He knew it was illegal to falsify information on a document of such importance. He only had circumstantial evidence that Arne was Little Marilyn's father and not Victor. If he was to sway his editor with the value of his story, he would need something more concrete, and that could only be, he concluded, DNA testing. It was a new form of identification, the use of which was becoming increasingly widespread from its purely scientific beginnings during the inter-war years. But to proceed or not, if in fact he came up with a workable plan to obtain the cells, was not straightforward. There was a moral hurdle to be considered. Not all journalists were hard-nosed and without scruples, and he was one of them. His own childhood background of barely knowing his father made him question his right to upset Little Marilyn's world of happiness. Victor would be a good parent whether or not he was her real father. What right had he, a hack, to deny her that? It was a self-imposed question that could only be answered with one word: none. He would have to find another way to use the circumstantial evidence, one that didn't involve breaking Little Marilyn's heart.

Two years after the birth of her second child, Stella's husband was posted to Lyon, France. He had been promoted to the grade of deputy consul general. Husband and wife were delighted, and allowed themselves visions of the occasional long summer weekend spent strolling along the Promenade des Anglais in Nice, a pushchair with two tired girls leading the way, after a mad two-hour dash down through Provenance. Stella would miss her mother greatly, the posting in Bern having given them a few extra years of close contact. She would also miss Eva and Jens and their daughter with whom they had been on very friendly terms. But postings were part and parcel of a career in the diplomatic corps and had to be accepted as a challenge wherever they were sent.

It was nineteen seventy-five and Stella had come to terms with her own provenance. She rarely saw Arne, but when she did, each meeting felt special and she never regretted making the initial contact with him. In a society which was moving with speed from the formal to the informal, she was moving in synch. Although she still wouldn't volunteer information about her roots, if asked directly there would be no prevarication, she would answer truthfully and without any hint of inferiority. She had come a long way, and her husband's promotion was testament to changing values. Life at that point seemed plain sailing. She chuckled at the thought. So, it came as a rude awakening to learn through Eva, that her father, not content with trying to sort out the financial distress of his holiday company, was now making waves in the world of golf and it would be Eva's brother-in-law, Alistair, who would have to sort out the mess. She sighed deeply. If only her father could act responsibly, but it seemed he couldn't. He was now fifty and still acting like an adolescent. But Arne saw the picture very differently.

* * *

The news that was filtering down through the golfing grapevine was of dishonest behaviour. A non-attributable leak suggested that a recent winning score in a regional championship was anything but what it purported to be, the player involved having used some chicanery to achieve it. No names were mentioned – fear of litigation being the prime reason – but sage heads nodded and tongues wagged with speculation as to who the culprit might be, and golfing justice in the shape of a ruling was meted out quietly and firmly from behind closed doors without any need to the recourse of law. It was a burden off Alistair's shoulders. He had dithered while making up his mind about how to handle the situation. The deception had played out in front of his very eyes and Ted had found the ball that had been hit out of bounds. There was no doubt in his mind – or indeed in the minds of his playing partners – that Arne had cheated. Yet for Alistair it had created an uneasy situation. He knew what was morally right to do, but the very idea of snitching didn't sit comfortably with him. The situation had been dumped on him, and whichever way he chose to resolve it, it would leave a nasty taste in his mouth. The non-attributable leak represented the best solution he could come up with, and once set in motion no one was the wiser that Alistair and Ted were witnesses to the events of that day. He could join in the chatter as if he was a complete bystander, although Alistair did fancy that he had noticed a slight acknowledging tip of the head of one of Arne's playing partners on that fateful day. He might have misread the runes, but he didn't think he had.

Arne was in jubilant mood the evening he "won" the East Anglia Senior Men's Championship. There was a lot of backslapping done, mostly by Arne, and drinking by everyone present for the prize-giving. Cigar smoke hung pungently in the air. If the assembled competitors were slightly quieter than usual, Arne did not notice. Indeed, he more than made up for any shortfall in buzz around the bar area by his extravagant gesture to buy everyone a drink. Never shy to recount any of his successes, Barry took the full brunt of a potted version of Arne's latest triumph when he rang Pimlico 7408 the following morning.

'This is not a pleasure call,' opened Barry testily. 'I'm

ringing to find out why you appear never to be in your office working.' He gave Arne no chance to reply before adding, 'your company is in deep financial shit, and unless you pull yourself together rapidly, it will nosedive into oblivion and you will no longer be flavour of the month with anyone.' His words stopped a hungover Arne in his tracks.

'That bad, eh?'

'Yes, definitely that bad.'

'No shit,' swore Arne softly, adding a few more swear words from his Dutch vocabulary. He knew he was guilty of whatever Barry was accusing him. 'I've been busy with other stuff,' he added lamely.

'You stupid git,' shouted Barry down the line. He was enraged. He was an Eastender and Eastenders didn't take that sort of nonsense from anyone, least of all from a workshy toad like Arne. 'I've been telling you for months to pull your finger out. And so has your office manager. And still, you play the arrogant fool.' Arne said nothing. He had no appeasing reply to make. He was guilty as charged. 'Victor and I will be at your office tomorrow morning at nine o'clock sharp. Be there,' commanded Barry before slamming down the receiver.

Victor opened his bulging briefcase and placed the buff files in a neat array on Arne's desk. He and Barry pulled up chairs so that they were sitting within touching distance of their third and junior director of BAV Enterprises. Arne was in for a grilling.

'Nice to see you guys,' said Arne as an opener. It was a poor choice of words as the faces of both Barry and Victor were decidedly stony. There was going to be nothing "nice" about their meeting.

'Forget the platitudes,' said Barry, wasting no time. 'Victor's going to take you through your balance sheet and profit and loss account line by line.' He looked at Victor who carefully turned over the leaf of the top file to reveal a set of sales figures for the second quarter of the current year. Arne blinked. He didn't know if he was expected to say something.

'The second quarter figures in the holiday trade are usually, for historical reasons, a little down on those of the first quarter.' Arne looked expectant but said nothing. 'Your office manager,' continued Victor, 'would have made you aware of percentages that are regarded in the business as normal.' If, his office manager had said something to him on those lines, Arne didn't recall it, thought Arne as Victor plodded on. 'A more useful barometer of financial health is usually a comparison with the previous two years of trading in that same quarter.'

'Pay attention, Arne,' urged Barry, as he noted Arne's look of boredom. 'This is important.'

'This year's figures show a sharp drop off in holiday bookings vis-à-vis the previous two sets of data,' said Victor, 'and this matters greatly as it signals a likely insufficiency in the near future of working capital.'

'Working capital,' repeated Arne, almost dutifully.

'Yes, working capital you numskull,' said Barry, barely able to contain himself. 'A lack of working capital because you contribute sod all. And Victor and I are not putting up with it any longer,' he added in a threatening tone. There was a pregnant pause whilst Barry calmed himself. There was irony too, as the former double bankrupt prepared to tell his junior director that in the event of insufficient funds, he and Victor would not be bailing him out. They would allow Arne to go to the wall.

'You're in serious difficulties, Arne,' confirmed Victor, turning over the next page in the file and allowing their eyes to fall on another set of management accounts. 'They all read the same way,' he assured Arne, 'your company is not generating sufficient sales to cover your overheads. You're heading on a pathway to go bust, and Barry and I are not going to bail you out.'

'When it's picked up by the media, it will be the final nail in your coffin. You won't come back from that,' said Barry ominously.

'You will have a lot of unhappy clients,' warned Victor, 'who won't hold back in dishing the dirt.' Barry flinched. He recalled from experience how much damage they could inflict. 'If you think that your celebrity status will save you, think again. They won't give you an easy passage.'

Later, after their departure, strolling quietly along the streets of south-east London near his office, Arne realised that that had been the moment when reality had hit home. His celebrity status would work against him, and not for him; it wouldn't be just a minor hindrance, it would be a definite barrier.

His flat in Pimlico seemed strangely quiet when he arrived home in the early afternoon. He hadn't gone back to the office after his meandering walk through some shabby streets south of the Thames. By chance, he had come to a tube station, seen the opportunity to hop on a train or two to take him back to his flat. He supposed that such a neglect of his company duties wouldn't go down well with Barry and Victor, or indeed with his office manager, but he had some serious thinking to do. For the moment, Barry and Victor could go to hell.

He sat for some time in his armchair nursing a bottle of tonic water whilst his mind played out the events of the morning. It seemed he had queered his pitch with his business colleagues, especially with the workaholic Barry. His ego had taken a bashing, and although he felt sure he would survive their petty criticisms, they had made him indelibly aware of the financial tightrope he was walking. He pursed his lips and ran through his options. Lobbying on behalf of this or that company was not yielding much in the way of filthy lucre. His association with the concrete company was still playing out in a negative fashion. The returns from after-dinner speaking were holding up, but for how much longer if Barry was about to trash his name. He still had an irregular income from the design of Chuck's wooden boat, but that was dependent on sales, and not really within his sphere of influence. Yes, thought Arne wistfully, his financial situation was looking tricky.

For Barry and Victor, it had been a one-stop journey on the underground back to their office. Barry was the power pack of the partnership providing constant leadership while Victor attended meticulously to the devil in the detail. It worked well, usually. But Little Marilyn was having a major pull not only on Victor's heart strings but on his commitment to work too.

Barry had sensed Arne's inability to grapple successfully with a regular work ethic long ago, almost before the original house party in Spain some three and a half years previously when they had first floated to him the idea of sailing holidays. But he had also appreciated that Arne's flair could open doors in the holiday market in a way that neither he nor Victor could. They needed that charisma to get the ball rolling, and in that regard the invitation to Arne to join them had been a master stroke. But Arne's days of usefulness were now numbered. He had moved from being an asset to becoming a liability. It was as clear as a bell to Barry, and he would have acted sooner to reduce BAV Enterprises to BV Enterprises had not Little Marilyn come on the scene. He'd had the foresight to put into the Articles of Association the necessary mechanism to divest them of any occurring weak link. And Arne was now a weak link. But he hadn't bargained on Victor's apparent loss of appetite for pulling out all the stops in supporting his deals. For Barry, it was a conundrum; his skill set did not include patience.

'Arne has to go,' he announced to Victor as soon as they were seated in his cramped office. 'He's outlived his usefulness,' he added bluntly.

'You're probably right,' replied Victor. 'We need to find another person to front up the sailing sector. Have you anyone in mind?'

'Depends on you.'

'How come?' asked Victor.

'Depends on whether you're fully committed to our partnership.'

'What's that supposed to mean?'

'It means that you are not giving the business your undivided attention at a time when it needs it,' said Barry sternly. 'You are wrapped up in Little Marilyn at a time when our business needs your full attention.'

'Surely, you don't deny me the pleasure of being a parent for the first time.'

'And for the last time,' retorted Barry, his resolve not to bring up the subject of who had fathered Little Marilyn having faltered. It was a crass remark to make and it infuriated his normally docile partner. Victor would have liked to have snapped back with a below the belt remark, but to do so would have been to invite questions he wouldn't wish to answer. Barry's message was clear. He suspected that Little Marilyn's father was Arne. With as much dignity as he could muster, Victor replied, 'Little Marilyn is number one on my song sheet and has displaced BAV Enterprises to the number two spot.' And both men knew that that summation would be an end to the matter, for while there was annoyance on both parts, there was also a degree of trust and respect between them. There would be no further jibes or inferences about her parentage; she would be accepted as a chip off Victor's block. The matter was closed.

'We need a younger person to lead the sailing sector,' said Barry, changing the subject quickly. 'I'm considering a woman.'

'That would be a smart move. Have you anyone in mind?' Barry *did* have someone in mind, but he judged it best to let matters settle before revealing his choice for figurehead.

* * *

The way in which Stella learned of the existence of her half-sister was bizarre. She had been contacted unexpectedly by a journalist requesting an interview. She had initially assured him that he undoubtedly had the wrong person, but when he asked if she was the daughter of Arne Visser, the hesitation at her end of the telephone line as she sought desperately to find a suitable reply, would have been answer enough. She eventually parried the question by asking the nature of his enquiry as she was just a typical housewife and therefore unlikely to be of any newsworthy value. When he mentioned unpaid bills relating to a flat in Pimlico, and that he could easily travel to France to meet her, Stella had no option other than to agree to a time and date for the meeting.

The back streets of Lyon were crammed with cafés and bars. Since moving from Bern, Stella had trundled the pushchair, now with at least one standing passenger – her elder daughter – along the riverside embankments and through the well laid out squares with origins dating back to Roman times, into the city centre where her children loved to watch the daily activity of the inhabitants. Unlike Bern, Lyon was not the country's capital city, but it had an exciting energy that was absent in the Swiss capital. But away from the wide, leafy boulevards of the city centre, the streets narrowed and wound their ways passed statues and fountains and tiny shops whose origins dated back several centuries. It was in this quarter that Stella had found convivial places to enjoy a morning coffee or an afternoon patisserie under the awnings of various street cafés. Her intention was to arrive early to grab a table on the fringe of the outdoor seating area, but as she approached a man stood up and beckoned her to his table. For Stella, it was an unnerving moment and she had to steel herself not to walk straight on by.

'Salut,' said the stranger before reverting to English, 'you are Stella, aren't you?' Stella inclined her head and removed her sunglasses by way of acknowledging that she was indeed his prey. 'Thanks for coming,' he went on, pulling out a chair and beckoning to the waitress for service. 'Coffee?' He was a neat, compact man with short, greying hair, late forties early fifties, a little shorter in stature than her, she judged, and dressed in nondescript leisure wear. There was nothing outwardly to dislike about him but from the start, Stella felt uncomfortable in his presence.

'What is it you want and what is your name?' she asked getting straight to the point.

'My name is easy, David Wilkins, but what I want is more difficult.' An enforced lull occurred separating his reply to her question while the coffee was served and she stirred the contents of the sugar sachet around in the cup.

'I hope it's not too difficult that you can't explain straightaway,' replied Stella frostily. Some of the diplomatic jargon she heard daily was rubbing off on her.

'My interest is in financial affairs,' David explained. 'Particularly when they go haywire, and when the law may be broken in order to repair any damage done. Do you get my meaning?' He was semi-leering and Stella would have liked to have got up and left, but a sixth sense told her she must stay.

'And precisely what financial affairs are you alluding to?' It was the crunch moment. Arne's finances were always in a mess. Under the table, she crossed her fingers in the vain hope that her father had not done anything illegal.

'Your father seems to be ignoring correspondence from the Inland Revenue,' David offered as a starter, 'in addition to the outstanding payments of various utility bills and ground rent on his London flat. In terms of paying what he owes, he seems to have gone to ground.'

'How do you know all this?' asked Stella, 'and how do you know it's true?'

'I'm a journalist. I must protect my sources, but I can tell you that a lot of this information is out there in the public domain, if you know where to look.'

'And what is your interest in exposing my father, if indeed what you say is true. What's it to you?'

'Why am I sticking my nose into your father's affairs when I have, apparently, no connection with him. Is that what you want to know?' said David steadily. 'Well, I'll tell you exactly why, and it's quite simple really. I was born and brought up in Wells-next-the-Sea, a small seaside town in Norfolk. It was a place where little happened. Quiet and peaceful and full of charm. Does that town name mean anything to you?'

'No, I don't think so,' replied Stella truthfully, although there was something familiar about the county of Norfolk.

'My mother was a teacher there in the junior school. She was a widow; my father having died shortly after my birth. It was just the two of us, we were naturally very close. She brought me up. It would have been a tremendous struggle in those days for a woman on her own to bring up a child. Family life operated on having a father figure and a mother figure. Life was regimented. It you didn't fit the pattern…,' he trailed off. Stella stayed silent. She was afraid that this story was leading to an uncomfortable denouement of Arne. 'She taught English,' said David resuming his story of yesteryear. 'When a young man from Holland arrived in the town after fleeing across the sea from an army invading his country, the townsfolk of Wells-next-the-Sea rallied round and did everything possible within their power to look after him.' Stella's body language slumped. Oh, God, it was that story again, one of magnanimity by the givers and a lack of gratitude by the receiver. 'My mother was asked to teach him some basic English. She was a good teacher. It's the reason why I'm a journalist now, she taught me wordsmithing.'

'So,' said Stella almost defiantly, 'you claim your mother taught my father to speak English. So what?'

'The townsfolk were generally disappointed when he left for London without bothering to thank them for all their efforts in looking after him for several months. It was as if he had no appreciation of all they had done for him. My mother had sacrificed many hours to help him with the new language, hours that as a single parent she could ill-afford to forego. She was disappointed in her foreign student but held no grudge. It did not change her life, but later, something with which your father was associated, *did*.' The chilling remark filled Stella with dread. It even seemed to stop the journalist dead in his tracks. Eventually he continued. 'My mother retired when she took her pension at sixty. Although not well off, she had sufficient for living a comfortable life. She deserved it. She joined the Women's Institute and a rambling club. She would go on weekends away visiting stately houses, or a coach outing with her chums to see horticultural gardens in the area.' He paused for breath. Something dramatic was coming. 'Did you hear about the terrible accident that occurred when a car hit the pier of a bridge and it collapsed. The concrete used to construct the pier was sub-standard. It was later shown to be below the strength needed to support a road bridge. My mother was on that coach. She died along with nineteen others in the party and the lady driver. Despite a public enquiry which showed where the blame lay, no compensation has ever been paid to the victims. Your father lobbied for the concrete company involved. He was well paid for his celebrity status. He wasn't directly responsible for the accident, but he was aware that the company cut corners. Ever since the accident, I have taken a great interest in both the directors of the concrete company and your father. I vowed on my knees that I would try to bring some sort of justice to the bereaved.'

Chapter 8

ANNA

Stella had a lot on her mind when she left the café. The hidden life of "Arne the Gladiator" had been ruthlessly exposed by a man who was still grieving for his mother some three years after her death. There were no crumbs of comfort to be found whichever way she looked at her father's history. She was glad that she didn't have her children with her. She could weep openly without their uncomprehending but penetrating stares. She found a seat by the river and sat down heavily. It was yet another time for contemplation even though she had little faith she would find an acceptable way forward. An elderly couple joined her on the bench. They exchanged polite smiles before Stella was lost again in her father's history, a saga of constant transformation as if he was a chameleon changing body colour to suit the background of the day. How could he at times show such sensitivity towards others, and yet treat them so badly on other occasions? Tears slid down her cheeks slowly and quietly and dripped onto her lap. The final straw had been learning of the birth of Little Marilyn, her half-sister. Not just another promiscuous and ill-judged encounter by her father, but one that would result in the issue of a falsified birth certificate. What a mess. The elderly man nudged her on the shoulder and offered her a handful of tissues to stem the tears. The couple looked concerned but Stella mustered a reassuring smile, looked at her watch, pulled herself together and nodded farewell to the couple. She would do as she always did when she felt low, contact her mother for advice.

* * *

Wells-next-the-Sea was shimmering in the early day sun one Monday morning. Anna had driven her husband to Norwich station to catch the London train, and now, almost home, she couldn't resist the opportunity to stop for a few brief moments to watch the small leisure boats bobbing up and down in the picturesque harbour and jostle against their moorings. She wound down the window and listened to the unmistakeable sounds of lapping water and the clinks of hulls gently knocking against fenders. They were sights and sounds that refreshed the spirits in a life, currently, of increasing complication. With reluctance and a heavy heart, she pulled away from the harbour and her fleeting daydream. Ted was poorly and needed her.

Since her boys had virtually left home, and Alistair's business and golf commitments had become increasingly time consuming, Ted was often her sole companion in the large family house. She loved him dearly but needed more social interaction. The occasional job in the charity shop was proving insufficient, so she had looked for a voluntary job in the town and found a suitable post as a part-time assistant in the primary school. Three days a week in term time between ten and two o'clock, she could be found happily helping in the classrooms in whatever capacity the class teacher required. It was never a chore for Anna to mingle amongst the youngsters, supplying stationery and equipment, helping with the spelling of words, or asking them to sit nicely at their desks. She loved every minute. Sometimes, on days when Alistair didn't take Ted to his office, she would take him to school and he would sit obediently in the entrance porch, a sucker for all the pats and strokes along his furry back that the children grew fond of giving. They weren't frightened by his poorly eye which had now developed into a full-blown cataract and showed as a white background in his pupil. If anything, as far as they were concerned, it made him even more adorable. And Ted wasn't about to turn away adoring fans.

The town's close-knit community was in most part a consequence of the sparsely populated region it occupied along the north Norfolk coastline. It wasn't a place of industry, or of commerce, or indeed of any particular agricultural crop. It was just quietly rural. And so, it was unsurprising that one day, in the staff room over a cup of tea, Anna was to learn about the teacher who had helped one of Anna's fellow countrymen to speak English during the war. Anna was, of course, familiar with the story of Arne's arrival in Norfolk by boat and the subsequent help he had received from the townsfolk especially the Drews, but knew little about the teacher who had given up so much of her time to help Arne with basic English. At the time, she had been a youngish widow with a young son, about the same age as Arne. She had retired at sixty but had died tragically while on a coach trip when a bridge had collapsed. Anna had nodded that she knew about the accident because Alistair was a construction engineer who had been called in to give an expert opinion at the public enquiry. According to one of the teachers whose teaching days had overlapped with hers, the son had become a financial journalist on a respected weekend national. He had been very close to his mother and had been devastated by her early death as she had, for so long, been his only close relative. When the public enquiry failed in his opinion to prescribe a path for adequate compensation for the twenty-three victims, or indeed provide some sort of memorial to recognise their untimely deaths, he took it upon himself to delve into affairs and expose in print any wrong doing he might find. Periodically he had articles published about the heavily criticised concrete company and its directors. It was a sort of bingo moment when he was able to prove that Arne, the Dutchman his mother had taught, was not only a lobbyist for that very company receiving regular and ample payments for doing so, but that he was also aware that they engaged in certain malpractices. It made good copy, and such a red rag to a bull stuff was never going to end until he had unearthed every possible detail of negligence by the company and by its directors and associates. He entered a murky world of white-collar crime where participants were frequently guilty by what they failed to do; failure to adhere to regulations laid down to protect the general public from those who would seek to cut financial corners for their own benefit. His focus on Arne led him in many directions and while the unfolding stories were finance-based, his editor sanctioned his intermittent articles. What Anna didn't already know about the bridge tragedy was the depth of feeling still alive amongst the families of the victims some three years after the accident, and that the teacher's son had made a point of keeping them up to date with his research to expose everyone who had had a hand in causing the disaster. And it was by this channel that Anna was to learn about the existence of Stella and Little Marilyn; innocent parties themselves, their relationship with Arne putting them under the son's spotlight too. And in a conversation with a retiring dinner lady whose aunt had also died at the scene, it came to light that the victims' families had set up a support network which now met periodically for social purposes, or on a "when the need arose basis" when the son had new information to impart. An invitation was extended to Anna to attend one of their social meetings as Alistair's late father, the rear admiral, had been instrumental in overseeing Arne's safe and comfortable stay in their town.

'I don't think we've met before,' said the journalist when he encountered Anna. 'I'm David.'

'And I'm Anna,' she replied smiling. 'I listened with interest to your accident update and to your amusing anecdotes of newspaper life in the big city.'

'But unless I'm mistaken, you're not one of the bereaved family members.'

'That's quite correct,' agreed Anna, rather formally. 'But

I have a connection with someone who I believe is regarded as being indirectly central to the accident.' The journalist raised an eyebrow and Anna continued, 'Arne Visser.'

'Arne Visser. The man who flits in and flits out of the drama like a bad penny, but who is never present to be tied down.'

'He seems to attract trouble,' admitted Anna cautiously.

'Do you have personal experience of him?' David asked.

'Yes and no,' replied Anna, not wishing to bring up the subject of the attempted escape in wartime with her brother in Arne's boat in nineteen-forty. 'My experience of Arne is mostly through my marriage to Alistair after the war. His family provided him with board and lodging for several months.'

'And now?' inquired David.

'Well, he does seem to keep turning up in our lives like the bad penny you mentioned.'

'In any specific setting?' pressed David.

'Well,' repeated Anna, 'currently, he seems to be making waves at the golf and country club.'

'In what way?' asked David, a puzzled expression on his face.

'Best to speak directly to my husband,' said Anna, wary of getting the facts wrong and falsely incriminating Arne. It was an opening that the journalist would definitely explore as past experience had shown that one thing so often led to another. Trouble at the country club, it sounded promising. 'Alistair, my husband, is the captain there,' added Anna. Even more promising thought David.

'I believe he has a holiday home in the vicinity,' said David apropos of nothing in particular.

'Yes. A cottage on a river estuary giving access to the sea, yet a location close enough for him to enjoy playing at several of East Anglia's main golf courses.'

'Does he stay there often?'

'I've no idea. Why do you ask?'

'He has unpaid bills on his London flat.'

'Oh. Maybe ...,' she trailed off. She knew nothing about unpaid bills in London, but it was the sort of thing that Arne did. He would be acting totally in character, and leaving a familiar trail of unresolved problems in his wake. 'I must go,' she said suddenly, remembering the need to feed Ted before Alistair arrived home and would want to take him for a walk before having their own dinner.

'I'm glad to have met you, Mrs. Drew,' said David. 'I'm sure there will be questions that will come to mind later that I will wish I'd asked you. I presume you know about his adult daughter named Stella, but you may not know about his recent addition, Little Marilyn.' It might have been a remark that would normally have stopped her in her tracks, but somehow a fifth sense had told her it was coming.

Over dinner – still a formal meal even for just the two of them – with damask linen and a table centrepiece, Anna plunged into the latest life and times of Arne Visser.

'Not him again,' said Alistair grumpily.

'Sorry, darling, but yes, him again.'

'But why? Haven't we had our fill of him?' It was a subject that could be relied on to cause a volatile reaction in Alistair.

'Fine, fine. I'll hold my tongue,' said Anna immediately. 'At least until the second course anyhow.'

'Okay, you win,' said Alistair, a smile creeping slowly to his lips. She always got the better of him. She'd been through the school of hard knocks and he was no match for her.

'When I visited Jens in Bern, I learnt about Stella. She was Eva's friend. You will recall, darling, that I told you she was Arne's adult illegitimate daughter. Eva had become very friendly with her because at the time they were both pregnant and both their husbands served in the diplomatic corps. It was a sensitive subject for Stella then.'

'Sensitivity is not part of Arne's repertoire.'

'Regarding Stella, maybe not, but regarding Little Marilyn almost definitely yes.' But Alistair had to wait until after dinner coffees in the bay window before his wife elucidated that situation.

'Do I really need to know about her?' he asked, pre-empting his wife's wish to put him in the picture.

'Possibly not, but you do need to know that Arne is very likely her father, and that he is almost certainly complicit in the falsification of her birth certificate.' Alistair groaned; more intrigue of a dubious nature. What possible concern was it of his? But when Anna proceeded to explain that the name recorded as Little Marilyn's birth father was one of Arne's business partners in the holiday company, and that there were question marks of fraudulent behaviour hanging over him, Alistair realised that information about Little Marilyn was indeed relevant. According to David, the journalist, her name could be used in vain; without her knowledge and without her approval.

'Hard to give considered consent when you are an under five-year-old.'

'That's what David said.'

'Presumably, he was anticipating her name being used to cover the real power behind the throne. A cover up.'

'Exactly that,' agreed Anna, 'he was warning that illegal actions could be taken by others sheltering under her name. And in any fallout, Arne would make the headlines again, Stella would be upset again, and we would be fed up again too.'

'Hmm,' mumbled Alistair, putting on his reading spectacles and grabbing a pencil and writing pad. 'I need to make some notes and draw a flowchart showing possible ramifications. This may not appear to affect us personally, but we know from experience that whatever Arne does, innocent or not, we somehow seem to get caught up in it.' They exchanged knowing glances.

'It's shameful,' said Anna after a pause, 'that the bridge tragedy families have no place to go to remember their loved ones.'

'I agree. They need some sort of memorial. Even a small plaque by the side of the replacement bridge could suffice. You could donate one. Have you thought of doing that?'

'Actually. Yes. But I'm not sure that I'm the right person to do so. My links with the accident are tenuous. I think it would be better coming from the school on behalf of their former teacher who died.'

'Yes, that would make sense. But we could pay for it. A small tombstone by the side of the road with an engraved plaque to all of those who lost their lives,' said Alistair. 'Yes, I believe that would fit the bill well.'

'Would you propose it to the school's governors, please? It would be better coming from you.'

'Of course, and I think I ought to have a word with David to find out exactly what he knows and what he anticipates might happen.'

Matters moved swiftly after Alistair contacted the school. One of the governors remembered the teacher, and all the governors thought it would be an act in keeping with community spirit to provide the bereaved with a place of memorial. Small though the cairn might be, and undoubtedly in an area noisy from traffic, it would be a place of significance for them and a recognition that their loved ones had not been forgotten.

On the morning of the unveiling, a group of mostly middle-aged men and women accompanied by a handful of older grandchildren huddled together for moral support in inclement weather. The vicar of the local parish – the accident had happened some miles away from Wells-next-the-Sea – had been asked by the group to read out all the names of the victims in his eulogy to them. As he mentioned each name, a relative in the group held up his or her hand in a form of acknowledgement of filial duty and respect being finally discharged. David, in his role as the group's figurehead, rather than as that of a financial journalist, was asked to remove the cover from the cairn. The group came forward in their ones and twos to read the inscription and to tap the granite stone with a kissed finger. It was a touching scene, but one that also marked the end of a chapter. As a group, they could now move on.

Alistair had arranged for a mobile refreshment canteen to serve food and drinks in a nearby lay-by. The chatter amongst the group – some had travelled considerable distances to attend as they no longer lived in the area – was positive and cheerful. Anna, like any good hostess, made a point of talking to everyone. Very slowly the bereaved relatives drifted away; back to their cars and their homes in other counties and other parishes. The local rag had sent a cub reporter to cover the short ceremony. Anna assured each family that she would do her best to forward to them any article printed. As the mobile food van shut up shop and prepared to rejoin the open road, all who remained were David, Anna, and Alistair. It was the chance that Alistair was seeking to confirm with David in private his thoughts about how Little Marilyn's name could be used dishonestly to cover illegal activity by others.

'There are many routes to dishonest commerce,' said David. 'The inventiveness of deceitful traders is remarkable. I have long since ceased being surprised by how they wriggle around the law for their own ends. But what exactly is your connection with such shady deals? Why is it of interest to you?'

'It's the proverbial long story,' said Anna, stepping in with a reply when she saw how her husband was struggling to find an adequate answer to David's question. 'To the casual observer it may appear that we have no meaningful connection with the subject on which you report in your respected Sunday newspaper. But that's not actually the case.' Anna pressed her thin lips together and continued reluctantly, 'it's a wartime story about one of my compatriots.'

'You're Dutch,' said David, immediately grasping that the very slight mispronunciation of the occasional word was not some slight regional variation but due instead to English not being her mother tongue. 'You speak English almost faultlessly.'

'Thank you. I was a teenager surviving in a war-torn land when the Allies arrived and I soon recognised that learning English would be an essential for future living. Luckily, I met and married Alistair, and later, with three young sons, I had every incentive possible to speak the language well. They didn't hold back on correcting me whenever I made an error.'

'I can well imagine,' said David. 'I wish I had the time to hear your story but I must get back to my work in London. I have my own family to support and copy makes money.' They gave him a lift to Peterborough station so that he could catch a fast train back to London. On the way, an invitation was extended to enjoy a drink together when next Alistair was on one of his working trips in the capital. 'I'd like to keep in touch and one day hear the proverbial long story.'

'All off the record, I trust,' said Alistair.

'Absolutely.'

What David didn't know about concrete wasn't worth knowing. He could have been lauded as a world authority on the subject and spoken at conferences, or held seminars, or answered questions correctly on quiz shows about aggregates and binding agents, superplasticisers and stone chippings, steel reinforcing rods and mix quantities. After the loss of his only living parent, he was making it his life work to know everything there was to know about the construction material, just in case, or maybe on the off chance, that he could prevent a similar accident from depriving a family of a loved one. Several years on from the tragedy, the sudden loss of his mother was still having a profound effect on him, although he bravely kept most of the hurt and upset to himself. His wife and young family could never have guessed the gnawing feeling in his soul as he started each new day without his dear buddy, or the effort he had to make to silence his thoughts of the past and to concentrate on the future, such as looking forward to sharing a drink with Alistair when next he was in London, and learning about Anna's "proverbial long story." But matters did not quite pan out as planned, and it was in Alistair's offices in Norwich that they next met.

'I'm grateful for your clever idea,' said David on arriving in the workspace occupied by Alistair's engineering company. Referred to as an office, it was technically a laboratory with modern office facilities. 'I've made concrete my hobby,' continued David, a twinkle in his eye, 'but it was forced on me really, I had no option. However, I know little about the construction of bridges that the concrete supports. So, your invitation came as a welcomed surprise and a good reason for another train journey up to this lovely neck of The British Isles.'

'As you see,' said Alistair with arms outstretched to point in various directions, 'the place we call "the office" is more of a workshop than a conventional administrative space. Sure, my partners and I each have a small, private office and the clerical staff have a separate and spacious room to themselves, but on the shop floor itself there are areas for model making, design testing, drawing boards, storage for sample materials and a large platform cum table top to lay out our proposed designs and run them through a few basic tests. Soon computers will be available and take on much of the tedious and repetitive work and make many of our present procedures obsolete. It will be progress of sorts, but without the social interaction that humans bring to the party.'

'To an outsider, I guess that everyone's own, individual workspace has an air of intimidation. I know mine does with the constant chattering of typewriters, loud voices on telephones, cigarette-smoke laden air, and a general buzz of staff all working to deadlines.'

'We must be calm and considered in engineering. Deadlines can come and go, penalty clauses can be invoked, but in the end if the product is not right, it cannot be taken to market,' explained Alistair, 'and you've seen the direct result of inadequate attention to detail and deficient safety checks.'

'Wilful corruption, that's the bugger we're all up against. Believe it or not, the press tries hard to get its stories right. Journalists may be allowed liberties to sensationalise, but accuracy is their editor's holy grail. Many a young correspondent has been told by his editor to go away and come back with his copy when the facts are correct.'

'I see similarities between our professions,' remarked Alistair, 'and the vital need to check facts and figures. If we get something wrong in engineering then failures of construction can occur costing lives and hundreds and thousands of pounds and cause inconvenience to the public, and if *you* use dubious information then you can ruin a person's reputation in a trice and be sued yourself for libel.'

'I deal in facts flavoured with a little speculation,' agreed David, 'whereas you deal in figures without any margin for error. In this regard we are Jack Sprat and his wife.'

The child's rhyme of the husband and wife who together had licked the platter clean was followed by a hands-on demonstration on the display table of the type of bridge construction that had given way so dramatically because of a faulty component. With various cardboard models, Alistair demonstrated the forces at play when the four-by-four slammed into the base of the bridge pier, and went on to explain that in normal circumstances the pier would have held firm. 'But the concrete and its reinforcing rods failed because the companies involved had supplied materials which did not meet the minimum legal standard.'

'A criminal act,' stated David, 'but one that so far, in the eyes of the victims, has not been adequately punished. The company concerned has used every trick in the book to squirm out of its responsibilities. Redress is a word they don't recognise. As far as they are concerned, they would rather pay lawyers to find legal loopholes to absolve them of responsibility than to admit their fault.' The distaste in David's words was obvious to any listener.

'It wasn't just the concrete that failed,' announced Alistair, moved by the palpable depth of David's hurt. 'In my opinion, although it never came out in the public enquiry because of insufficient evidence, the reinforcing bars were also of a sub-standard quality.' He paused for reflection before adding, 'the company that supplied the steel bars had links with the concrete firm.'

'In what way?' asked David, immediately interested.

'Arne Visser was paid to help lobby for local authority contracts on behalf of each company.'

'The subject of your wife's proverbial story, I seem to recall.'

'A common factor, it seems.'

'Can you expand?'

'It's her story to tell, not mine. And it is just as heart-rending as yours.' David said nothing. There was strain etched on Alistair's face. He could only hope that Anna would tell him her story one day. Ted padded into the room and broke the tension. 'Another casualty of Arne Visser's wayward behaviour,' said Alistair flatly as David stared at Ted's wonky eye. 'Come on, Ted, let's walk David to the station to catch his train home.'

Anna had suggested to her husband that David might like to have an early dinner in Norwich before catching a later train home. She would have made her way into the city by bus and local train to join them. When Alistair rang to tell her that David had to get back to London as scheduled, Anna felt relieved. She had pondered on the wisdom of her decision to mention to David that a story dating back some three decades or so to wartime, was at the root of the Drew's involvement in the bridge fiasco. Did she really want to stir up old memories of when she was called Annaliese? She would have been far younger than David when she cruelly "lost" both of her parents. But what good would it do to rehash memories from those harsh times? Arne was a flawed character, but he was not all bad. He had genuinely loved Pieter, and probably unreservedly in the same way that David had undoubtedly loved his mother. Life could be cruel.

* * *

The golf club milieu was not one that Anna enjoyed. She suspected that it was not one in which Alistair was truly comfortable either. An inadequate golfer was the way in which he described himself, and from the few strokes she had seen him make, it seemed an overly generous description. But she knew her role and was present supporting him at social functions and on important golfing days whenever duty required.

The golfing grapevine was still in full swing following the seniors' championship. Anna became skilful at parrying members' requests for clarification of the facts surrounding "the affair at the dogleg," as it was becoming known. Much as she would have liked to help, her answer was that she knew nothing about golfing matters except that her husband was spending a lot of money over the bar buying drinks for members; a reply which never failed to raise a titter with the would-be conspirator. At home, the atmosphere when golf was mentioned was far from cordial.

'I enjoy your club social events,' Anna stated one evening. 'The eating, the drinking, the dancing, and getting to know other golfing wives. But I'm getting fed up with being asked about the affair at the dogleg.'

'Me too. I'm just as fed up with it as you, but I can't escape it. I'm club captain, the buck stops with me. I must clear up the mess.'

'But why? You are only indirectly involved.'

'It's not that simple. I can't wash my hands of events that occurred whether or not I was directly involved. I must show that I am upholding both the rules of golf and our club local rules, and if a member fails wilfully to do either, then whoever it concerns must be sanctioned and be seen to be sanctioned otherwise the good name of your average golfer for sporting behaviour is tarnished.'

'Even poor old Ted is embroiled,' said Anna in frustration. There was no worthy reply to Anna's statement. Alistair was beginning to wish that Ted had not sniffed out Arne's presence at a thousand paces and gone bounding after the golf ball that landed out of bounds. But Ted was a great sniffer and Arne wasn't a person he was going to forget easily.

'One thing led to another,' said Alistair hunching his back as if that gesture explained everything. 'But the bottom line is that Arne knowingly cheated. And when I realised that his playing partners suspected the same, then I had no option but to do something about it.' Anna shook her head and muttered something incomprehensible.

'So, *you* were the source of the non-attributable leak.'

'I was, and I have no reason to feel guilty about it,' retorted Alistair raising his voice.

'I wasn't trying to make you feel guilty.' She didn't like it when he raised his voice. Nor did Ted. 'Simmer down, darling. I'm sure you did the right thing. And what punishment have you meted out?'

'I banned him for thirty days for another misdemeanour. Wearing golf shoes in the lounge bar is strictly against clubhouse rules. He'd been warned several times not to do so but took no notice.'

'Hmm,' murmured Anna weighing up Arne's sentence. 'Doesn't sound much like a penalty for cheating.'

'An action has been taken and that's what counts. It sends a signal to the membership that he is being sanctioned. Those who suspect the rumours that he had cheated were true, will understand that the ban has nothing to do with his shoes. It was to do with cheating, but for legal reasons, even with evidence, it would be a thorny road to tread.'

'I suppose that's the best solution,' said Anna sighing.

'He won't try that trick again in a hurry. And he's intelligent enough to realise why he's been banned.'

'But not intelligent enough to care.'

A letter from Jens arrived and diverted Anna's attention from golf club affairs, bringing a welcomed detente in atmosphere in the Drew household. Finally, her brother had come up with, he declared in his hastily penned note, a viable plan to donate Henrik's gold coins anonymously to the good cause they had selected. He had a few days leave due and asked if he and Eva and their daughter could come and stay with them. Anna was overjoyed at the prospect and caught the last post of the day with a quickly scribbled reply in the affirmative.

Anna had long forgotten about how much paraphernalia a toddler generated. The family was collected at Norwich station by Alistair after work, and he was still unloading the car with her brother's luggage long after their young daughter had scampered around in the rear admiral's library and made friends with Ted. Exchanges of news followed, bedtime for the very young soon followed, and after dinner for the adults, it was a gentle wind down of a hectic period. Plans for the following day, Saturday, involved a walking tour of Wells for Alistair and Eva, with or without a pushchair for her daughter, and with Ted on a tight lead. From a landlocked country like Switzerland, the change of scenery to a pretty coastline with leisure activity on the sea to watch and enjoy, would be the perfect start to a few days of relaxed vacation.

The decision to be made about the coins was, Jens reminded his sister, one for the two of them alone to make. Eva still knew nothing about Henrik's inheritance and he wished that situation to remain unaltered. Alistair's thoughts on the merits and practicalities of their solution would be listened to carefully but he would not be responsible for the idea itself.

'Okay,' said Anna immediately the others had left the house for their outing around Wells. 'What is your plan?'

'It involves the use of the diplomatic pouch,' answered Jens, also keen to get matters underway. 'I have given it serious thought.' Anna looked bemused; Jens smiled. 'Did you know that even in the mid-nineteen-seventies, there are still people working as diplomatic couriers?'

'For security reasons, I presume.'

'Exactly. Your country's government sends out sensitive instructions to one of its embassies in a far and distant land and knows that the contents of what they have sent will be seen by no other eyes that those of the senior embassy staff.' Jens paused. 'It won't remain this way for much longer. Computers will take over in the next few years and send encrypted information electronically. But for now, no better method to guarantee secrecy has been found.'

'Don't tell me, Jens, that you intend to simply wrap up the coins and send them off to our seat of government in The Hague with a handwritten note asking them to please refurbish a lighthouse of their choice somewhere along the Dutch coastline with the proceeds from the sale.'

'Don't be silly. That would be asking for trouble. It would be the end of my career too. No, what I have in mind is far more subtle than that, although I must admit that in essence, it is almost my plan.'

'Explain, brother dear.'

'Well, the diplomatic pouch passes through many hands on its journey from government building to embassy. It is, in fact, only secure in the period when in transit from place A to place B with the courier. Much of its content is mundane. Some papers are marked "Strictly confidential" and make their way to me, as ambassador, without the sealed envelope being opened. Material which is deemed to have a lower grade of sensitivity is seen by various senior staff. Small packets arrive in the bag too. They are usually addressed for the attention of a named member of staff.'

'Packets. What kind of small packets?'

'Small packets containing all sorts of things. If they pertain to official business then they are usually items of contraband: wadges of bank notes for bribes, or an illegal beefing up of embassy staff safety equipment such as a small handgun. That sort of thing. But private packets are not uncommon either; someone has unexpectedly run out of a vital medication that is not obtainable in the country in which they are working and the easiest way to bridge the gap whilst they are awaiting fresh supplies from an official source, to stick a month's supply in the pouch. Or, more promising from our point of view, is the scenario when someone mislays something of real value, or perhaps more importantly to them of sentimental value, while attending a diplomatic or trade function and only realises it after they have returned home, which may be to another country.'

'Far, far away,' said Anna. 'So, it's not just one way traffic.'

'That's right. Packets normally go from base to satellite, but not always. The situation I'm reminded of is one where a guest at a trade fair removed her rings when washing her hands and mistakenly only replaced the wedding ring after drying them. Her engagement ring was found by a member of the embassy staff and returned to her via the pouch.'

'The gold coins would make a small and very heavy packet and would be going against the normal direction of travel,' said Anna thoughtfully. 'But presumably, any secure box they were put in would be bulky.'

'Not necessarily. It doesn't have to be made of steel or hardwood. You can get small lockable bags made of a special fabric material called Kevlar which is almost indestructible and impenetrable, and takes up comparatively little space. It would sit easily in the diplomatic pouch, and be just as secure as a proper box.'

'But how could you protect anonymity?'

'Anonymity is tricky, but safety is relatively straightforward.' Anna looked expectant and Jens explained how the two-key box trick worked so that the sender could have faith that only the intended receiver could access the contents.

'That sounds complicated.'

'Not really. A bit long winded, perhaps, but not complicated.'

'So, after placing the coins in the bag you would lock it and send it off marked for some particular person's attention.'

'That's right. The person who receives it has a key to the second lock but not to the first, hence the bag cannot be opened. That person locks the second lock and returns the bag to the originator who unlocks the first lock and sends the bag back to the designated receiver. As the box is now only locked by the lock to which he or she has a key, then the bag can be opened.'

'It *is* complicated,' protested Anna.

'But it is that very complication of to-ing and fro-ing that helps mask the identity of the sender and receiver,' explained Jens. 'It's the way anonymity can be preserved.'

'I can't really see how,' said Anna looking perplexed. 'If you put something in the diplomatic bag and send it to someone named, let's say John, and John returns it to you, and you complete the cycle by sending it back to John, where is the secrecy in that? If anything, it seems to me to make the sender and receiver more obvious to anyone wishing to discover their identities.'

'If I did it like that then of course it would,' agreed

Jens. 'On its cycle there and back and there again, different names and different addresses will need to be used in order to make tracing difficult.'

'But how can you do that?'

'In the case of the engagement ring,' said Jens, 'it was sent back in error to our embassy in Budapest instead of Vienna, and awaited collection by the female delegate to the automotive trade fair in Bern. It had journeyed back to our hub in The Hague, then out to Budapest, where it awaited collection for some time before being sent back to the hub and out again to Vienna where it was finally picked up. At various stages of its journey, different people will have handled the ring and in the minor chaos created, the facts of what happened will have become blurred.'

'And you think you can set up a similar trail?' asked Anna sceptically, wondering if her brother's confidence in his proposed system was misplaced.

'I do. It's work in progress at the moment, but I am confident that I can organise a route that will protect our names as the source of the gold coins.'

'And who is the final recipient? It can't be the council on Vlieland Island. They might put two and two together and realise that the black tin box that they had given to Henrik contained more than they realised.'

'That would never do. A long and damaging dispute over ownership with absolutely no chance of keeping affairs and personalities under wraps. That would be anathema to us.'

'So, who is going to manage things at the other end?' persisted Anna.

'Ilse.' Anna went quiet and after a pause, Jens continued. 'I would trust her with my daughter's life.'

'She was Henrik's friend and shared so many tough times with us. But she's also Arne's sister, and it seems from what David has told us that Arne is in debt big time.'

'Ilse may be Arne's sister, but she was also Henrik's true friend and nothing will change that.' Anna fell silent again. She was weighing up factors. 'I've already contacted her,' continued Jens. 'I was recalled recently to The Hague for business discussions. Before returning to Switzerland, I arranged to visit Ilse in Leeuwarden. We hadn't met since Henrik's funeral in Wells.'

'You told her about the legacy?'

'Yes. She was alone. We exchanged family news at first. Her family are well and Ilse is still enjoying working in the finance department of the manufacturing company she joined with her late sister before the war. She has recently been promoted to a more senior position. And family life for Ilse is good. I was happy for her.'

'And so am I. I've always got on well with Ilse. So, you told her the story of the black tin box.'

'Yes. Everything that was relevant,' confirmed Jens. 'At first, she was taken aback, but later thrilled when she discovered that Henrik's loot could be used for some useful purpose in our home region. She was sure her father would approve of what we had in mind. Pieter and Frieda, and her older sister would have been proud. A modernised lighthouse would be a sort of gravestone to them.'

'No mention of Arne?'

'None. But she had some interesting comments to

make about our plan. What to do with the coins when she finally receives them.' Anna listened attentively as Jens carried on. 'She hasn't lived in Harlingen since the end of the war. Very few people there would know her by sight.'

'And in thirty years, from being a youthful adult to becoming a middle-aged mother of three, your appearance can change drastically.'

'Right. No one would stop her in the street and ask if her father was Pieter Visser.'

'So, what has she suggested?'

'She will remove the coins from the two-key pouch and place them in a modern cash box which she will purchase. She will ask her youngest son to hand the box in at the police station in Harlingen. A letter, marked for the attention of the senior policeman at the station, will be attached to the box. The boy will hand it over the counter and scamper away as soon as it is in police hands and before he can be questioned. After posting a letter in Harlingen, Ilse and her son will return to Leeuwarden where they live, and nobody will be any the wiser as to their identities.'

'What will the letter say?'

'It will give a full description of the contents of the box: the number of coins, their dates, etcetera. The letter will also inform the senior police officer that the coins are a gift made anonymously to the regional council and that the donor's fervent wish is for the proceeds of their sale in an auction house to be used to upgrade and modernise one of the lighthouses dotted along the region's north-west coastline. The letter will also inform the senior officer that an exact copy of the letter he is reading has been posted to a national daily in Amsterdam, and that doubtless the press will be in contact very soon.'

'It will make headlines,' remarked Anna, 'that's for sure.'

'Not just in the press, but in all the media. Harlingen will be besieged with reporters and correspondents wanting to get the full story. And that is the beauty of it, because none of the coins will be able to go missing while in police custody because the press will know precisely how many were handed in.'

'Whoa. Ilse's really come up with a great idea,' agreed Anna, 'if her son really can scamper away quickly. It will be headlining news for months.'

'And the regional council would have no other option than to use the money for the purpose that had been chosen. They wouldn't dare do anything else with the glare of the media focussed directly upon them.'

'And we can sit back and watch the events unfold,' said Anna with a sense of relief. 'Have you purchased a two-key box?'

'Not exactly, but I have procured one,' replied Jens.

'What does that mean?'

'It means that I have a suitable secure bag, but you mustn't ask too many questions less I incriminate myself,' said Jens, 'and before you ask, yes, I have given a key to Ilse.'

'So, what are you waiting for?'

'If you are in agreement with what I propose, and I believe you are,' said Jens looking his sister directly in the eye, 'then I want you to tell Alistair that a workable plan has been concocted.'

'But not to burden him with the details, I presume, of something he doesn't really need to know.'

'Exactly that. It's an all-Dutch affair. You, me, and Ilse.'

'It's an all-Dutch *wartime* affair,' corrected Anna. 'And I shall be glad when it's all over.'

'Done and dusted is the English expression. But first I must carefully plan the journey of the two-key box with a few experiments so that I can't be implicated as the original sender.'

'Nor Ilse as the final receiver.'

They strolled down to the marina with Ted leading the way. Business had been concluded and hearts and minds could rest peacefully for a while at least in the knowledge that matters were within reach of a finale. Led eagerly by Ted, Anna showed her brother the school where she now worked part-time and recounted her meeting and subsequent acquaintance with a journalist whose mother had been a teacher at the school but who sadly had been killed in the bridge tragedy. Jens didn't understand the link until Anna explained that the journalist's mother had taught Arne basic English.

The following day, with Jens departing with Alistair to London on one of his working trips, Anna and Ted made a meandering return home by car from Norwich station. It was a thoughtful woman who stopped the car along a quiet and wild part of the northern coastline, and Ted sensed her profound melancholy. Just like a recurring nightmare, the sadness she felt from barely knowing her parents surfaced from time to time to haunt her. She was just one of that unlucky cohort of young children whose parents were taken from them in their formative years. It was the war that was to blame for her loss of roots. Her memories of them were few, and faded with every passing year. She didn't know their values, apart from hard work, or their ethics, and could only guess at the courage they must have shared to uproot themselves from their families to start a mixed-religion life together. Jens was her allegory; the personification of her abstract thoughts. What she saw in him was just a hint of how life could have been with her parents. Memories of highs and lows as she grew to know them well. How it would have been with her mother by her side as she married Alistair, or her father cradlings her newborn sons.

Ted flicked his tail to tell her he had urgent matters to attend to, and the moment of nostalgia passed.

Chapter 9

ALISTAIR

The telephone on Alistair's desk rang shrilly as if it wouldn't accept being left unanswered. Alistair cursed. He was in the throes of a complicated computation and didn't wish to have his concentration disturbed.

'Alistair Drew speaking,' he said reluctantly after lifting the handset, and waited for the caller to identify himself.

'Hallo, Alistair. Apologies if I'm disturbing your train of thought, but I believe you ought to know the soon-to-be breaking news regarding the bridge tragedy,' said David. Alistair put down his pen and calculator; he was all ears as he mumbled down the line to go-ahead. 'There was a fatal road traffic accident just before dawn this morning on the northbound carriageway of the motorway to Leicester.'

'Oh,' said Alistair, not understanding how this related to him.

'You are probably wondering why I am telling you this, but it is linked to the bridge tragedy.'

'I see,' replied Alistair, wondering how on earth it could.

'It relates to a lone biker. He was dead when the police found him.' Thoughts stirred in Alistair's mind. A tale about a lone biker was familiar. 'He had a note on him,' David went on, 'a suicide note.'

'Oh,' repeated Alistair without any intonation in his voice. 'I still don't understand why I need to know.'

'You will when the suicide note is printed. It explains the biker's reasons for taking his own life. There will be widespread coverage on this evening's six o'clock news programmes and tomorrow's newspapers will be full of it.'

After David had hung up, and his news had sunk in, Alistair was left amazed by the speed of the media's information flow. Their tentacles appeared to spread out in all directions leaving no stone unturned in their quest to convey every minute detail they had discovered. He hurried home from the office to catch the early evening television coverage, surprising and delighting Anna who had become accustomed over the years to his normally tardy home coming.

'We must watch the news,' said Alistair immediately, explaining David's call earlier in the day. 'Something to do with the bridge accident is likely to be screened.'

'Gosh. We certainly must watch that,' agreed Anna. 'Who told you?'

'David. He rang me at work.' They fell silent as the familiar opening sequences and music of the nationwide news programme played out, followed by the day's main headlines. They looked at one another when the fourth headline was displayed on the screen as "Church biker atones to his God." There was just time for Anna to nip to the kitchen and make herself a cup of tea and for Alistair to pour himself a small whisky from the decanter in the library. Perched, rather than seated on the sofa in front of the television, they could only speculate about the bizarre fourth headline of the day. Finally, the presenter, a well-known broadcaster, turned to the item about the death of a biker. Reading from the autocue, he reminded viewers of the horrific accident some three years previously when a lone rider, swerving dangerously across a carriageway caused a motor vehicle to plough into the base of a bridge pier. The pier collapsed and a coach full of passengers passing across the bridge at the time broke through the side railings and plunged headlong down as the tarmac under its wheels broke up. In all, twenty-three lives were lost, but despite a nationwide hue and cry, the biker was never traced. A couple of images of the accident were then flashed onto the screen to show the sombre scene.

A video clip then followed of the mangled wreckage of the motorbike – believed to be a powerful Suzuki, but legal for road use in the United Kingdom – before cutting back to the studio presenter who announced that the dead biker, a man in his mid to late fifties, was pronounced dead at the scene, and that there was no other party to the accident. A spokesperson for the local area police – Cambridgeshire constabulary – was then invited to read a prepared statement.

'In the early hours of this Friday morning, officers attended a road traffic accident on the motorway at junction nine,' announced the senior officer, a woman wearing uniform with insignia on her epaulettes denoting the rank of assistant commissioner. In a clear voice and with a measured speed she continued, 'when the scene was attended at approximately seven o'clock this morning, the driver of the motorbike was found to be dead, although the accident is believed to have happened shortly after midnight. After completion of general scene of accident forensics, the body and mangled remains of the motorbike were removed for further investigation and the northbound carriageway of the motorway was reopened.' She turned over to the next page of her statement, and looking ahead steadily at the assembled press, carried on. 'On inspection, the corpse was found wearing a religious collar under the black leathers, and subsequent enquiries and evidence show the man to have been the vicar for the parishes of Filmore and Hurtley.' She briefly looked up from her text to confirm that the correspondents were still paying attention, before continuing. 'In addition to the normal personal effects, a handwritten note was also found on the body explaining why he had taken his own life.' There were gasps from the media; this was high-octane stuff which would fill many column inches and take many "on air" minutes to broadcast. 'I have a transcript of that crumpled note and I intend to read it to you.' In an instant, the sound recordists' microphones were pushed to the fore as they strove not to miss a single word.

Despite her ordeal which was already palpable to the assembled press, the assistant commissioner continued determinedly, reading verbatim from a photocopy of the note, which she told them would be issued later as a handout to all media representatives.

'To whom it may concern,

My death is the result of a pre-meditated act to commit suicide. No one else was involved in the act, and I was not persuaded by anyone to take my own life.

Three years ago, because of my reckless driving, I was the indirect cause of the bridge tragedy which resulted in the death of twenty-three innocent people. For several hours after I had made a dangerous and foolhardy driving manoeuvre on a dual carriageway where I was responsible for causing a car to swerve violently to avoid contact with my motorcycle, I was unaware that the car had ploughed into the base of the bridge pier. I was travelling at speed in what can only be described as daredevil mode, and the rush of noise on my helmet from the wind prevented me from hearing any sounds that may have arisen from the car slamming into an immovable object.

On reaching home after a day out with my biker friends, I was shocked to hear a report on the local radio station, that a bridge had collapsed earlier in the day on the road along which I had driven home. Switching to the television, I caught a late evening report with images of the catastrophic damage and with a coach seemingly hanging in thin air. But it was not until a correspondent, speaking into a microphone whilst he did a piece-to-camera, mentioned that the police were trying to trace a biker in black leathers and black helmet who the driver of the four-by-four claimed caused

297

*him to swerve, that the awful truth dawned on me
that I was the cause of this domino effect.'*

The assistant commissioner moistened her lips ready to be able to clearly articulate the final, emotional paragraphs of the biker's confession. She was dreading having to do so, but determined to make a good job. She was a woman who would not be found wanting.

'My faith should have been sufficient to guide me along the path of righteousness, but I succumbed to the sins of mortal man by putting self-preservation ahead of truth and justice. After I had failed to contact the police in the days following the accident, I found it increasingly easier to justify not notifying them that I might be the person they were trying to trace. Weeks passed, the hue and cry died down, media coverage dwindled to the occasional article, and I thought I could carry on with my ministry. But I was wrong. The burden of being the cause of so many deaths has come to haunt me. That I played no active or willing role in causing the deaths is of no consolation for the grief I have caused and continue to cause amongst the families of the victims, the family of one of my own parishioners included. The Book of Exodus expresses the principle of reciprocal justice in "an eye for an eye" punishment, and I must accept that as a fair sentence. I can no longer stand in the pulpit and address a sermon of care for one's fellow man with conviction in the knowledge that I have robbed so many of their loved ones. I can no longer live with my guilt.'

The policewoman was addressing the throng from the steps outside the constabulary's headquarters. So poignant was the moment that scarcely a noise other than her voice could be heard on the busy corner normally bustling with pedestrians and motor traffic. With a slight quiver in her voice, she reached the last sentence. *'I am truly sorry for the pain I have caused. Signed, "Geoffrey Arthur Stowman."'*

She told the assembled crowd that as she would not be taking questions until a more in-depth investigation of the circumstances had taken place, consequently, that concluded the day's briefing. She turned on her heels and walked back into her headquarters leaving the press to mull over the handout and to speculate about other details. Alistair switched off the television feeling deflated. Anna conveyed she had no sense of jubilation that the person who had triggered the appalling sequence of events had been found, and they both wondered what David would make of the news.

It wasn't long before the media were postulating a range of theories. With the departure of the officer, small groups started forming to dissect the latest information about a story of, essentially, greed that simply wouldn't lie down. The new evidence of the discovery of the person who had unintentionally initiated the catastrophe was a further twist in the sorry saga of dead bodies and unhappy families. But for the greed of the company supplying the concrete, said one correspondent, the story would have been of a tragic but simple road traffic accident with two killed and the culprit yet to be apprehended. But instead, chipped in his photographer, it was one of mass manslaughter with the culprits trying to make excessive profits untouched so far by the sanctions of the law. He made a face to mark his disapproval. Culpability, said another journalist had been borne in full by a middle-aged biker who after a day out with his biker pals and a few plates of shared fish and chips, culminating in a crocodile formation ride through some country lanes, had been injudicious enough not to rein back his exuberance to ride home in a gung-ho manner. It was a terrible waste of life most agreed, before splitting up to go their separate ways to file copy.

David's reaction was sombre. The revelations about the ecclesiastical biker seemed to make the tragedy even more tragic by conferring a sort of inevitability on the miserable mess. Normally he would have seen the funny side of a vicar biker whose helmet bore broad bands of deep purple to mark his trade, but not right now. Nerves were still raw and no jokes along those lines made him laugh. He would go to Geoffrey Arthur Stowman's parishes to try to get a taste of the man, and hope that his present mood would improve.

Geoffrey Arthur was a widower in his early fifties with an only child, a daughter, who lived in Scotland. She kept in regular contact with him and made the journey south from the borders to north Cambridgeshire whenever she could which was every few months or so. He was in good health and always busy looking after his flock in the two parishes. He had been a widower for almost a decade, and although he had had opportunities to remarry, he had chosen to rekindle his love of biking rather than to tie himself down to a new wife. He had a sense of humour that was not always understood and appreciated by womenfolk, but one which was usually at one with his biking mates who called him "Vic." He didn't usually wear a dog collar under his leathers, but when he bought his latest helmet and was given the opportunity to customise its colour, he had chosen to have two deep purples slashes applied in the rough shape of a cross to compliment the metallic background black.

In former times, the vicarage in Hurtley had been a fine house with extensive gardens, but had slowly fallen into its present shabby condition as funding from church covenants and the government were reduced in line with congregation sizes and the prevailing attitude to secular living. However, it was still popular with the parishioners who used it extensively for local fund-raising activities, and it made a comforting venue for poorly souls who due to sickness or bereavement, could open their hearts and offload their grief and worries to their own compassionate and kindly parson.

When David visited Hurtley, he found that Geoffrey Arthur had a loyal following of regular churchgoers who held him in high esteem. They were naturally shocked at the recent events but refused to budge from their high opinion of their clergyman no matter what he might or might not have done. According to most, his intentions were always honourable and if he had slipped momentarily by riding his motorcycle rashly, then his God would understand and pardon him. David was sufficiently wise to keep his own counsel by not mentioning the ruined lives that he had indirectly caused, but had to wait until he met Geoffrey Arthur's daughter before he could get a real flavour of the man.

'It was the small cairn by the side of the bridge,' said his daughter, when she and David were walking along a winding path through shrubbery that once must have been spectacular when in bloom but was now overgrown and in need of some radical pruning, 'that was the final nail in his coffin, if I can put it that way.'

'Why so?' asked David.

'He rang me and told me that he had seen it. Apparently, it had only recently been laid. There was tension in his voice as he spoke. We were separated by about three hundred miles but there was no mistaking his faltering words. He said that when he saw it, he had stopped and read the inscription, and then said a prayer.' David nodded. It couldn't be easy for his daughter to recount a conversation with her late father so soon after his death. 'He knew then,' she added, 'that further life would be meaningless.'

'He was a man of the cloth,' said David as gently as he could, 'and he would have been aware that suicide is considered a sin.'

'Yes,' she agreed. 'It was why he had such a heavy heart. He didn't want to go against the gospels' teachings but he couldn't see an alternative.'

'He took all the blame himself when in driving fast he had done nothing more than countless numbers of drivers do on our roads,' ventured David. 'It all went horribly wrong for him.'

'But he would have had remorse every single day of

his life for his actions. And that remorse would have been a life sentence. If my mother had been alive, she might have pulled him round to a different way of thinking. To realise that he could still do his ministry even though he considered himself tarnished. She would have told him that having sinned himself, he was even better placed to understand those who needed help and to give them succour in their moment of need.'

'Life's not easy,' remarked David, stating the obvious.

'Even if you have a strong faith, it's not easy,' agreed Geoffrey Arthur's daughter. 'But what is your interest in this saga?'

'My mother was one of the twenty passengers on the coach who died.' An awkward silence ensued. They shook hands and David thanked her for her time. They were both wounded parties; a cherished parent had left the scene before time. When asked what sort of story he would submit for printing, David appeared ambivalent. He would have to give it serious consideration, but in his heart, he knew he would find it difficult to produce an article with a cutting edge. Geoffrey Arthur's daughter was yet another victim and so was Geoffrey Arthur himself.

David's wife and young family relied on his adequate salary for all the "good things" life had to offer. A senior journalist with a good track record – even though it was well known that you were usually judged by the quality and success of your latest report – could afford to offer his partner some regular luxuries and pay for his children to enjoy plenty of out-of-school extra-mural activities.

But David wasn't quite your average hard-nosed hack. He had a well-developed moral compass. Often, he had shared an empathy with the subject of his report such that the old mantra "print and be damned" had never been one to which he had adhered. Was there anything worthy in trashing the life and times of "Vic the biker" for his possibly only serious real error in a life devoted to helping others? David pursed his lips and wrung his hands and wondered how his meeting with the editor would pan out.

'Your article verges on the sympathetic,' declared his editor after having read the fifteen-hundred-word piece destined for a centre page spread. 'When did articles of the "kind" ilk sell massive numbers of newspapers?'

'They do when they chime with the attitude of the ordinary man and woman in the street,' replied David, stoutly supporting his work.

'May I remind you,' said the editor removing his half-eye spectacles and lighting up an evil-smelling cigarette, 'that the ordinary men and women in your virtual street do not buy our paper, and they never have.' He was right, thought David. Their average reader was centre-right with disposable income and a tendency to want punishment meted out in proportion to the crime. 'But I will indulge you this one more time as you have brought a very topical issue to the fore: liability.' David waited silently whilst the kindly headmaster ticked him off. 'You have managed to bring the concept of personal accountability to the party,' the editor went on, 'and even in this particular case, a hint of financial accountability too. In a story about death and disaster, that was clever.'

'The only accountability there has been so far,' said David, taking a seat unbidden by the editor's desk after the sham ticking off, 'was from the biker who knew right from wrong.'

'So, what do you want to do?' asked his editor deeply inhaling a drag on his cigarette, 'go after the concrete company directors full tilt?'

'We need a whistleblower to trap one of those bastards,' said David with feeling.

'And you want me to come up with some sort of ransom money for spilling the beans, I suppose.'

'Deeds matter, but money talks,' stated David matter-of-factly.

'I hope you can trap all the bastards, David, without bringing our newspaper into disrepute. Remember that.' He mulled over the editor's lingering instructions for several days on how best to approach a prospective whistleblower, and then he contacted Alistair.

Alistair wasn't surprised when he received the telephone call from David; he had been expecting it.

'I imagine that you have been following the story of the vicar,' he started without any preamble.

'And I imagine that you have followed it even more closely than me,' replied Alistair. 'What further news have you?'

'The biker was essentially a good person who took more of the blame than he should have. I've been up to the vicarage in Hurtley where he lived and I've spoken at length with his daughter.'

'A moment of madness on his bike, I suppose.'

'Something like that,' agreed David, 'but one with a very heavy penalty.' After a lengthy pause, David resumed. 'The real sinners have yet to pay a penalty commensurate with their blame. My article in the weekend edition will focus on the way in which company directors can hide behind commercial laws to mask their wrongdoing.'

'Do you have a plan to bring them to justice?'

'I'm working on it. I need a whistleblower in the concrete company. Someone who knew that cost cutting would affect safety.'

'How will you do that?'

'I'll start with former employees,' said David. 'Check them out and try to ascertain the reason for them leaving. Then move on to the current employees if that fails.'

'How will you get the information about past and current employees,' asked Alistair.

'There are ways and means. A press pass opens many closed doors.'

'I understand,' replied Alistair. 'You will have your sources.'

'I do, but I would be grateful if you learn anything during your normal business that you consider remotely connected to PerfectMix Limited, that you pass it on to me. Diverse pieces of data, when assembled, can paint an interesting and unexpected picture.'

Driving home from the office, Alistair's thoughts turned to whistleblowers. It was a subject he knew little about, and somehow, he felt grateful for that. What he'd read in the press over the years was of a system that was fraught with difficulty, and one that was often reported to end in tears with the whistleblower achieving little positive in rectifying wrongdoings and ending up, for his pains, ostracised by all involved. As his mind drifted from the road ahead to such deep thoughts, he appreciated how easily he too could cause an accident; a corner taken too tightly, driving a shade too fast, a moment's loss of concentration. On the narrow, twisty roads of his home county, accidents could happen in a heartbeat. Quiet roads could become quiet killers so very easily. The more he learned about the late Geoffrey Arthur, the more empathy he felt for him, and he guessed that David felt the same way too. It was easy to hate a person who showed no respect or consideration for others, but almost impossible to do so for someone who so patently did.

'Will the enquiry be reopened?' asked Anna when her husband recounted the gist of David's telephone call.

'I doubt it. It doesn't change the dynamics of the accident. The concrete issue occurred regardless of who drove into the bridge pier or who caused the driver of the four-by-four to do so. Geoffrey Arthur could be considered to have been unlucky.'

'But perhaps it will affect the coroner's verdict of how the victims died.'

'Yes, that's a possibility, but I suspect that they will stick with the original verdict: death by misadventure. I hope so as manslaughter would be grossly unfair to the vicar.'

'And to his daughter. Who would wish her to live with that tag round their neck?'

'I guess that's why David is so keen to find a whistleblower.'

'To divert attention from the biker.'

'Yes. But mostly to ensure that the people responsible for the carnage have their day in court and receive a punishment in keeping with their offence.'

* * *

The grey cells in David's brain whirred. They were working on overtime. He was using every slither of information he had, and every trick in a journalist's book to find an Achilles' heel in PerfectMix Limited. Once he found a weak point, he would dig in the knife and twist it violently, and watch the blighters squirm. He savoured the thought, but so far, no real progress. He hoped his dream wasn't wishful thinking.

His erratic working hours made the little time he had to play with his children very precious. But switching off from work commitments was not always easy. It was an innocent remark made by one of his five-year-old twins that set him thinking along different lines. A character in one of their weekly comics – he was keen that they should read the written word rather than just sit passively watching a television programme – was named Womble. It made him think of Little Marilyn. And then the penny dropped. One of the directors of BAV Enterprises was listed as George Wremble. Wremble wasn't a common surname, and yet there were two Wrembles listed in the company's Articles of Association as directors, Victor and George. Victor and George, he repeated to himself, not Victor and Little Marilyn, not even Victor and Gloria. Who on earth was George Wremble? As he mulled over the conundrum it became increasingly apparent that a return to Somerset House would be necessary.

Wording his request to one of the counter clerks very cleverly – a tried and tested method used regularly by private investigators – he was able to ascertain that on the day of Little Marilyn's birth, a death had been registered in the name of George Wremble. David's heart skipped a beat. Could the death certificate show that George was Little Marilyn's twin? He requested a copy of the certificate and waited patiently for it to be supplied.

In the large, open plan space which formed the newspaper's shop floor, ranks of desks were positioned between the square-shaped structural pillars holding up the floors above. It was a noisy environment in which to work with the incessant chatter of the typewriters and the sporadic thumps and grunts of the telex machines. The office was normally buzzing with people hunched over their desks or standing in small groups discussing how the day's news was panning out. There was never a moment in the day when nobody was about with whom to talk over an idea or to share a joke. Although impersonal in many respects, the office had a friendly feel. David was one of the few to keep a personal memento on his desk top; a photograph of his mother at her retirement party. In a neat frame, it was always kept angled towards his chair. When he could see her face full on, he felt bathed in the warmth of her smile. He wasn't yet ready to let her go, but he would one day.

The editor spent long hours secluded in his office with weighty decisions on his mind, but every day, on principle, he made a couple of circuits of the shop floor to keep in touch with his staff. Seeing David working at his desk at an hour of the day when he would more usually be at home with his twins to read a bedside story, the editor strolled over and sat down at the adjoining desk.

'How's it going?' he asked, referring to David's story. 'Seeing you here at this hour suggests that you have uncovered some useful facts.'

'I'm exploring a new channel of information,' replied David.

'I get it. You want to remain a bit tight-lipped until you have something definite to offer.'

'That's about it,' agreed David. The editor made a move to continue his amble around the shop floor passing the time of day with whoever was present and had the time for a brief chat. 'Before you go,' said David, 'I need to know that the funds are available to support my lines of enquiry.'

'Ah, the euphemism for slush funds. I did wonder when that would rear its head.'

'Well?' said David in an enquiring tone.

'I'm sure I'll find sufficient to cover your needs providing that you're not out to make someone a millionaire overnight.'

'I'll certainly need to consult a forensic accountant, and very likely the services of a private investigator too.'

'Expensive,' said the editor with a knowing nod. 'If the story looks promising then the funds will be available.' David nodded in gratitude. He might only need the bluff of a whistleblower as confrontation of the facts, coupled with some threats of prosecution, might just be sufficient for the wrongdoers to offer voluntary compensation to the victims' families.

The idea of confrontation was also on Alistair's mind. It wasn't what he wanted to do. Lord, no. But it was beginning to look unavoidable. The golf club gossip just wouldn't stop despite the punishment that Alistair had handed out. He had been too lenient with Arne according to many members including his committee. That he had meted out the penalty quickly, quietly, and effectively counted for nothing. He had been too lenient and that was that. A ban of a short period for some trumped up violation was not the serious sort of punishment that cheating warranted.

'How did they know he had cheated?' asked Anna one evening when Alistair was looking particularly fed up, 'when you had been to such pains to keep it secret.'

'It had happened before, apparently. Nobody liked playing with him. If you were marking his scorecard and you questioned the number of shots he had taken on the hole, then he would flare up into a temper and make the remainder of the round uncomfortable for the other three players.'

'Thank God I don't play golf,' said Anna. 'All the moaning and groaning that goes on. How can that be a pleasurable pastime?'

'I'm beginning to think the same myself,' replied Alistair sighing deeply. 'But it doesn't settle the issue, and it's an issue that won't lie down until our members are happy that Arne has got what they feel he deserves.'

'A total ban, I presume,' said Anna rubbing the back of her neck and blowing out hard against her closed lips.

'How many more months of your captaincy have we got left to endure?'

'A total ban right now would be like a death sentence for Arne. He has money worries including an unpaid bar bill at the club. The rumours that he is strapped for cash are probably true. We know from the newspapers that his holiday company is financially in dire straits, and David said that his flat in London is unoccupied. Kicking a fella when he's down…', he trailed off.

'Shaking your head,' pointed out Anna, 'at the thought of taking an action you consider to be below the belt, will get you nowhere. If he deserves to be banned, get on and ban him regardless of any extenuating circumstances.' Anna fell silent as if struggling with a deep thought. 'Over the years, I've come to realise that Arne's action when he dumped my brother and me into the sea off Vlieland Island was the right course of action.' Alistair could see the emotion welling up in Anna and patted her hand gently. 'If he had let us join him on the crossing, none of us would have survived.' Alistair frowned. He had never heard his wife speak in support of Arne. They were coming up for their silver wedding anniversary and yet in all that time she had never had two good words to say about him. What she was saying now was not unambiguous. If he skirted around the situation for whatever justifiable reason, he would just be adding to future difficulties.

'I take your point,' said Alistair. 'Engineering courses through my veins. I can grapple with a tough technical problem enjoying the challenge and knowing that if I persist, I will eventually find a workable solution. If only human situations were that simple.'

'But they're not. We've been lucky, three mostly intelligent boys who have been sensible when asked to moderate their behaviour. We haven't had to cope with the difficulties that Arne's character throws up. You may take my point in being strict, but I need to take yours by realising that you intend him no harm.'

'For Arne, image is everything,' commented Alistair. 'It's how he makes the money he needs to pay his bills. Rob him of his image and you rob him of his life. I must settle matters decisively I know, but I cannot and will not destroy his ability to live his life the way he wants by some form of overt character assassination. I already feel slightly ashamed of the "unattributable leak" that I stage-managed.'

'You shouldn't feel like that. The situation was not of your making.'

'I'll meet him face-to-face and will tell him that he is banned from the golf and country club for the foreseeable future, and if he stays away and keeps a low profile in our region then we won't do anything to exacerbate the situation.'

'What are the odds of Arne keeping a low profile?' asked Anna. 'Not great, I suggest.'

'Maybe he'll do his old trick of escaping to sea for a few months whilst the pressure eases.'

'He might be too old to do so,' said Anna thoughtfully. 'A middle-aged man with a string of debts taking to the high seas whilst someone clears up the mess. Seems an unlikely scenario for the next glamorous episode in his life. And where will you have this meeting?'

'If he's not living in his flat in Pimlico then he must

be hiding from the debt collectors in his holiday cottage near here. That's where I'll go unannounced and take him by surprise.'

Alistair had been told that the holiday cottage, nestling quietly near a bank of Oulton Broad, had easy access to the sea near Lowestoft. From the road, the unpretentious building appeared to blend in well with the scrubby landscape in both size and colour. It was unremarkable being neither shiny bright nor dowdy. Just a modest one-storey building looking neat and tidy in the morning sunshine. There was no drive or obvious parking area so Alistair brought his car to a halt on the grassy verge alongside the boundary wall. If Arne had a car at the cottage, it was nowhere to be seen. The only clue as to whether he was at home was the tip of a boat mast which could be seen rising above the lowest part of the cottage's roof on its far side.

Dressed in casual clothes on Anna's advice – his task would be easier according to her if he was wearing the style of clothing that Arne wore for messing about on boats – he walked up the narrow path of flag stones and knocked on the front door without pausing. In his heart, he was dreading facing Arne but it was a task that had to be done. There was no response to his first knock on the front door and when a second and third knock also failed, Alistair made his way around the side of the house to the back garden. For such an unassuming dwelling, it had a broad area of land which splayed outwards on either side as it approached the water. Alistair realised that it wouldn't have been easy to hear a knock on the door from the water's edge. He called to announce his presence, but there was still no reply. He inspected the sailing boat moored at the bank's edge, but likewise, there was no activity to be seen there. A large shed, masked behind some thick bushes, came into view as he fully explored the property's backyard. The sound of tools being used drifted out through its open double doors. Alistair cleared his throat and called out Arne's name distinctly, and a tall man with a full head of hair emerged into the sunlight.

Apart from brief encounters at the golf club, the last time they had met properly was at the road bridge before the disaster; the same morning that Ted had sustained his eye injury. On that day, Arne looked suave in his dark suit, white shirt, and expensive shoes, and he had a bullish air about him. Today he was wearing workman's dungarees over an old T-shirt, and his mien was decidedly less bullish. Indeed, he had a somewhat hangdog expression. If it was true, thought Alistair, that his financial situation was troubling, then it was mirrored in his face.

'Good morning, Arne,' said Alistair boldly. 'I hope you don't mind my arriving here unannounced.'

'What brings you here, Captain?' replied Arne. Out of formal clothes, Alistair looked very different, and it had taken a few seconds to register with Arne that his visitor was Alistair Drew.

'An unpaid bar bill, for one,' said Alistair, 'but is there somewhere we can sit as I need to discuss with you your continued membership at the country club?' Arne bristled. His hitherto downbeat look changed to one of steely recalcitrance.

'Only on the boat,' said Arne, adding sarcastically, 'I don't keep armchairs in my workshop.' Clearly Alistair was not going to get an invitation into the house. They walked down to the boat and scrambled aboard. Seated in the cabin, Arne was in his element but Alistair was not; a boat was not his comfort zone.

'And a total ban at the country club for the foreseeable future, for two,' said Alistair holding his nerve.

'Why?' asked Arne, staring unblinkingly at the man delivering the sentence. 'You are not just the messenger; you are also the judge.'

'I'm not here to beat about the bush,' said Alistair angrily. But he wasn't on any account going to mention the word "cheat." 'The members have taken exception to your behaviour on the golf course. They don't consider it in keeping with retaining your membership, and I agree with them. I am not here to trade insults. And I am not here to justify our reasons. Your annual subscription is a little overdue and you have a large, outstanding bar bill. Membership is terminated forthwith.'

'You can't do that. There are laws that prevent you from taking such a high and mighty stance.'

'There probably are,' agreed Alistair, 'but there are also people at the club who could easily trash you name, and you have a variety of outstanding debts that could also topple you. If you agree to sever links with the club, then those voices will not be heard and your outstanding bar bill, in the hundreds of pounds, will be paid off on your behalf. Your image will remain intact. Think about it carefully before you consider legal action.' Arne knew it was a proposal he could not ignore, but he neither accepted nor declined the offer. 'I shall take your silence as acceptance of my terms,' stated Alistair. 'The matter is now closed as far as the golf and country club is concerned and I shall stamp down hard on any tittle-tattle I may hear.' Arne looked crestfallen but remained silent, and against all odds, Alistair heard himself say, 'Good luck, Arne. I hope things sort themselves out well for you.'

'Do you need help off the boat?' Arne asked.

'No,' said Alistair hauling himself onto the bank and turning to face Arne for a final time. 'We wish you well.' Arne looked quizzical. 'My wife, Anna, and I wish you well,' he added by way of explanation. Long after he had slammed the car door shut and bumped down off the grassy verge, Alistair still felt the distaste of kicking a man when he was down. He wished Ted had been with him so that they could have given each other their version of a hug. It would have made him feel better.

Long after Alistair's departure, Arne was still sitting in his boat. He felt rooted to the spot. He had churned over his entire life and realised that apart from Stella, he had failed to build anything of substance. He had been at this point before in his life, several times in fact, and always been able to surmount his problems, but this time felt different. He wasn't sure he could. His confidence in himself had eroded. And there was something else, Alistair's wife. He'd only seen her at a distance, either at the golf club or at an embassy "do" in Bern or on a train, but there was something about her that kept nagging at his mind. Had he met her before? He wasn't sure.

'The boat,' demanded Anna, 'what's it like?'

'You know even less about boats than I do,' replied her husband over a late lunch, 'so why do you want to know about Arne's boat?'

'Is it his and is it valuable?'

'I don't know is the answer to both your questions. Why do you want to know?'

'I just wondered if he could use it profitably.'

'Profitably? I don't get your meaning.'

'If he owns it and if it's considered valuable then he could either sell it to pay off some of his debts or he could sail away in it to some promised land to try and start again.'

'I didn't really pay much attention to it,' explained Alistair, 'I obviously had other things on my mind, but I do recall that it looked good.'

'If you could have stood back and looked at it for a few moments, you could have admired it. Is that what you mean?'

'Yes. A bit like a good-looking car. Classic lines, that sort of thing. I believe it was all wood, and it did look sleek.'

'I wonder what happened to the boat in which he crossed the North Sea at the beginning of the war.'

'You surely can't be suggesting that they are one and the same. No, that's not possible.'

'Why not?'

'It's just not possible. My knowledge about boats is limited but I know sufficient to know that they need constant maintenance.'

'And if they are kept out of the water, stored in a

large barn or somewhere similar, then presumably they wouldn't deteriorate. Sort of wrapped up and set in aspic for the duration.'

'It's thirty-five years since he made the crossing. It can't be the same boat,' said Alistair shaking his head. 'The rear admiral would have known what happened to it, but I don't recall.'

'You could make some enquiries at the marina.'

'Clive, the harbour master at the time, is long since dead. I doubt very much if one of his successors knows but I could ask.'

'Well do that, because if it's the original boat then it's likely to be worth a pretty penny at auction,' said Anna. 'It could at the same time solve Arne's insolvency and give him back some pride.'

'I suppose so, although it's a long shot, but he has got a large workshop at the cottage. Being wood, he could probably make any new parts he needed. I don't know, all this ado for a man we despise,' grumbled Alistair.

As predicted, Clive, the harbour master at the time when Arne had sailed across the North Sea in nineteen-forty, and who had impounded his boat on arrival, had died shortly before the death of the rear admiral in the mid-nineteen-sixties. At the time of the crossing, Clive's son had been seconded to war work at a naval dockyard in Scotland and was not able to further Alistair's investigation into what had happened to the wooden vessel after his father had impounded it. Alistair remembered seeing it beached on some dry land along with all the other small, leisure vessels that normally filled the marina making it look such a jolly place. He also remembered the incident with the cat when out walking one early evening and how furious Arne had become when he discovered a moggy giving birth to her litter while curled up in a warm and secure nook on his beloved boat, and how he had literally thrown them out without regard for their safety. For Alistair, it had been a moment to take stock of his hero, Arne, and question whether he was all the good things he thought him to be.

Discussing affairs with David over the telephone – an exchange of information relating to all matters concerning Arne and or the bridge tragedy, was now a routine occurrence – David was able to suggest another person to contact. The husband of the former head teacher at his mother's school had been a local councillor for many years and was now, in his retirement, a keen historian and guardian of local information. Apparently, if anyone remembered what had happened to all the small boats after the cessation of hostilities, he would be the most likely person. And when Alistair did contact him, he was rewarded.

'Many boats were reclaimed by their proud owners despite the evident wear and tear that they had suffered during five long years of being beached,' said the historian. 'Some owners decided to have them taken straight to the breaker's yard as they were either too far gone or needed repair materials that were simply unavailable while the country was getting back on its feet.'

'Understandable, but what a shame,' replied Alistair down the line. 'To some of them, their boats were like precious pets. They must have missed them greatly during those five awful years.'

'By spring of nineteen-forty-six, only two were left unclaimed. They looked sad sitting on dry land just the pair of them as if they had no home to go to.'

'Unwanted,' echoed Alistair. 'I was serving in the military overseas at the time and wasn't around to see them.'

'One fell literally to pieces in high winds on a stormy day in late April and the council removed the wreckage. The owner never came forward despite repeated attempts to trace its holder.'

'And the other?'

'The other was sold,' said the historian. 'Nobody had ever enquired about it, and as it was still in reasonable condition, the parish council took the view that selling it would relieve them of any further burden of responsibility.' Alistair was stunned and made no reply. 'Are you still there, Mr. Drew?'

'Yes. I'm still here and very grateful for the information. I don't suppose you know who bought it.'

'I don't offhand, but there's bound to be something in the recorded minutes of the relevant council meeting about the sale price and the name of the buyer. I don't have access to those records any more but I could enquire on your behalf.'

'I would be grateful if you would. Thank you,' said Alistair replacing the receiver carefully on its base unit as if it was a piece of delicate China.

Alistair cast his mind back to the excitement Arne's arrival in Wells-next-the-Sea had caused, particularly to how it had galvanised his late father into action. The rear admiral had taken a good look through his telescope at the small yacht that had been towed into the marina by the naval coastguard. He had then rushed into his library and started thumbing through the pages of back copies of a monthly sailing magazine that he read regularly. Neatly stacked in piles in chronological order, although extremely dusty as the house cleaner was under instructions not to move a single thing in the library, Alistair remembered the yelp of delight when his father had found the copy he was looking for. The front cover showed a wooden yacht made by the Visser Boat Company of Harlingen. Just launched on the market, it was small in size but big in ambition and it was targeted at the middle classes. With magazine in hand, the rear admiral had hurried down to the marina to show the picture to the harbour master and compare it with the real thing.

'When you had that great sort out of the library with Henrik,' Alistair asked his wife as casually as he could, 'do you remember what you did with the rear admiral's back copies of his sailing magazine?'

'No, I don't, but I can guess that they were chucked away,' replied Anna. 'Our concentration had been on books not on magazines, and if I remember correctly, there were several piles of various magazines and newspapers stacked on the floor.'

'Oh, pity.'

'You look disappointed. Was there a particular magazine that you wanted?'

'I've got a feeling,' said Alistair, 'that the boat I saw at Arne's cottage might just have been the one in which he crossed the North Sea.'

'The original? Whoa. That would be a turn up.'

'Much more than that,' said Alistair thoughtfully, 'but more to the point, a potentially very valuable asset.'

'Do you want me to check the library shelves for it? Your father may not have put it back in the same pile if it was so important.'

'That would be helpful,' he replied putting on his jacket, calling to Ted, and hurrying out the front door on his way to the office.

Edition number eighty-three was printed in April, nineteen-thirty-eight according to its slightly crumpled cover. Anna had found the magazine jammed in a thick tome of maps between its last page and the hard cover. She too had given a yelp of delight on finding it. Alistair would be pleased, but she was not quite sure in what way it would help. She had never seen an image of the boat prior to finding the magazine and on the ill-fated night that Jens had led her along the dike to stow away on Arne's boat, it had been too dark to see anything other than its rough outline. But she could stand back now and admire its sleek and ergonomic lines, and understand in small part what all the fuss had been about. It would have been a design ahead of its times, and would have turned many a nautical head in its heyday.

When Alistair returned home that evening and the magazine was held up in front of him as if it was part of a prize fighter's purse, he was as happy as he had been for some time. Other troubles appeared melted away while he described its importance to his wife.

'Well, is it the same boat or not?' asked Anna eventually.

'Looks the same,' replied Alistair guardedly.

'But you're not sure. You said you'd clambered onboard and sat talking to Arne for some time.'

'True. But at the time my concentration was on the matter of Arne's finances and barring him from the country club, not on anything to do with the boat.' Anna gave him her well-used look of exasperation and ambled off muttering to herself that she might have wasted her whole day on a fool's errand. He followed her into the kitchen and clasped her by the shoulders in an attempt to defuse her annoyance. 'If I cast my mind back to the incident with the pregnant cat, and how we looked over the gunwale of the beached yacht to find a litter of suckling kittens in a safe nook in the cockpit, then I can see similarities of design between then and now. But I would have to see the boat again to have any certainty of it being the original.'

'And how can you do that? And what purpose would it serve?'

'I'm still figuring out the answers to both those questions, but I'm confident that something important will come from them.'

'But don't watch this space,' stated Anna tersely.

For Anna, it was a mostly sleepless night. She would have liked to have tossed and turned but that option would not have been fair to Alistair, so she lay as still as she could while planning in detail her visit to Arne's cottage. When the detail was complete to her satisfaction, she must have relaxed and dozed off shortly before the sun rose. She awoke in a startled manner and found a note from

Alistair on the blanket telling her to enjoy the lie in for as long as she wished, and that Ted was accompanying him to the office. She looked at the bedside clock. It was almost nine o'clock and from the noise emanating from outside the bedroom window, she realised that the gardener was already about his horticultural duties. She cursed. She had wanted to rise with the larks and make Alistair a special breakfast as she'd been unnecessarily beastly to him the previous evening. He was doing his best and she should have supported him fully.

The plan was simple in concept, but would be audacious in execution. She would have to hold her nerve because if she got it wrong, her action would serve no purpose and would stir the situation beyond any reasonable chance of achieving harmony. And some form of harmony with Arne was what was needed.

She dressed carefully to promote a relaxed demeanour expecting Arne, if he was at home, to be wearing casual attire too. She wondered for the umpteenth time if he had recognised her as the young Annaliese of pre-war times. If he had seen her together with her brother at some stage between his escape from his homeland and the present day, he would have noted their facial similarities; their Catholic and Jewish parents providing a pool of gens relatively unsullied over the centuries by interlopers.

Having taken the decision not to tell Alistair of her intended trip to the cottage, her first task when getting up was to contact a friend she had made when working at the charity shop. She would need a lift to the cottage as it was in a rural location not served by trains, and very probably by only a sparse bus service. Her friend, a lady with time on her hands and no real hobbies, was overjoyed to learn that she could pass her day chauffeuring her chum through the byways of Norfolk, enjoying a paperback novel while Anna was visiting her friend in the cottage, and stopping off for a cream tea at one of the roadside cafés on the way home. They parked on the same spot of grassy verge where Alistair had left his car a few days previously. After telling her chauffeur friend that she expected her visit – a metaphor for not having to discuss or reveal the reason why she was there – to last at least an hour and possibly longer, Anna shut the car door quietly and walked boldly up the narrow path to the front door. Her first knock was answered by the still good-looking man she knew as Arne Visser.

'I've been expecting you, Annaliese,' he said, instantly stealing her thunder. 'Come in.'

'We must talk,' said Anna, somewhat crushed by Arne's opening greeting.

'I know. But not on the doorstep. We'll go down to the boat.'

He cast off before Anna had a chance to object. The wind was light and the water smooth as the boat headed slowly in the direction of the estuary.

'How long have you known?' asked Anna defiantly, refusing to be phased by the apparent loss of control over her mission.

'Not long, Annaliese.'

'Same boat?' she enquired after casting her eye around the cabin's interior.

'Same boat,' he agreed after a few moments of hesitation.

'I'd never fit into the locker space now, but I absolutely know that this is the boat you sailed out of Harlingen harbour all those years ago.'

'And the same boat from which I handed you down to your brother standing in the sea on the shore of Vlieland Island.' He trimmed the sail and adjusted the tiller and then said, 'Why are you here?'

'Why are you asking when you already know the answer?' demanded Anna, having regained her aplomb. Arne appeared to fiddle again with the steering whilst considering his reply. 'Well?' repeated Anna.

'You're here to sit on the moral high ground and wag your finger at me as a lost cause.' It wasn't a reply that Anna was expecting, but it was a fair summation of what she had intended to do and she had to change tack.

'If you leave a trail of destruction in your wake, what can you expect?' They both half-smiled at the nautical term used so appropriately. 'Your daughter, Stella, won't like it. And if Little Marilyn was old enough, she wouldn't like it either.' Arne flinched. 'Yes, I know about her too.'

'So, is it some form of blackmail you have in mind?' he asked.

'How would your long chain of debt, or your illegitimate daughters, or you cheating at golf, or your collapsing holiday empire, or even your association with a company responsible in part for the bridge accident, how would that lot chime with your public? Not very well, I imagine.'

'So, it is blackmail,' said Arne.

'Yes, you're dead right. But I am not here to exacerbate, I'm here to resolve.'

Anna's friend was whiling away the time reading a gripping novel. It wasn't until she had finished a lengthy chapter that she noticed the passage of time. Almost two hours had elapsed since Anna had got out, closing the car door quietly behind her. She was sure that Anna had mentioned that she expected her visit to last about an hour. Although not overly disconcerted, she decided to give her friend another half-hour or so before knocking on the front door herself to remind Anna that they had a long drive home. She didn't want to miss their planned stop for a cream tea and chat to which she was looking forward.

On the boat, the passage of time had yet to register with Anna. She had struck a deal with Arne and was now content to watch the light breeze fill the sails as Arne guided his vessel towards the sea. A glance at her wrist watch brought her back to the reality that her friend was waiting for her and might become alarmed. She was already overdue.

'We'd better turn back,' said Anna, realising her error.

'That's dependent on tide and wind,' replied Arne laconically. She was in his territory and could not call the shots. Had it not been for the sailing boat with an outboard motor, Anna might have arrived home at a very late hour. Arne would have tacked across the river mouth skilfully in adverse conditions using every draft of wind and stream of current to arrive back at the cottage had they not received the helpful "ahoy" message that they were welcome to hitch a lift upstream and let the outboard motor do the job of towing them along.

Almost an hour overdue, Anna's friend was still

sitting in the car wondering what else she could do; her knock on the front door apparently achieving nothing but indecision. Scrambling into the passenger seat full of apology, and suggesting a change of date and venue for their chitchat, Anna was keen to get home before Alistair and Ted arrived back from work. He was a modern man and open to change but with a core of Victorian discipline passed down from the rear admiral that she needed to respect. The basis for a happy partnership was respect, and although he never exploded with anger when riled, she was always unnerved by the silent option he generally took in such moments of annoyance.

With Ted walked and fed, and their own evening meal in the oven, Anna announced her trip to the cottage.

'Before you jump down my throat,' said Anna, using a recently acquired English idiom, 'I want you to know that I did what I believe to be the right thing.'

'But I'd just been to see him,' protested Alistair immediately. 'Why on earth did you have to interfere?' It wasn't a question; his remark was rhetorical. And Anna knew she had a great deal of explaining to do.

'You went to see him to tell him what he couldn't do and to tell him to shove off and leave us alone. I went to see him to tell him what he could and should do and to plead with him to stay on good terms with his daughters and sister. Your visit offered him no solution to his problems of debt, but mine did.'

'You're interfering in matters you don't fully understand,' replied Alistair evenly but with a hint of chauvinism in his voice. 'It wasn't your place to meddle in a subject I had already sorted out.'

'But that's the point, Alistair. You hadn't sorted it out. You had left him with no options.' She paused before continuing in a more conciliatory tone. 'He's not the same as us, he's not down to earth, he's practical and intelligent but without any common sense, his head is in the clouds, and quite frankly, he needs someone to guide him through life.'

'He's nothing but trouble,' retorted Alistair unsympathetically. He'd had a tiring day at work and didn't need a lecture from his wife over the dinner table. 'We'll speak about it tomorrow when I have more time.'

The roast meal was hot but the atmosphere in which it was consumed remained frosty, and Anna knew she had to carefully prepare her arguments for the following day. Arne needed help and no amount of harsh disciplinary talk would solve his problems. He needed a mentor and she thought she knew who that should be.

The following morning was Saturday. Anna awoke at her normal hour, just in time to notice the presence of the lingering darkness of an early autumn day fade away into full daylight. From the hall, she heard some murmured instructions followed by the click of the front door lock closing as Alistair and Ted left for their habitual start-of-the-weekend walk. It was the walk they loved the best, with few people about and the harbour to themselves. She would have some time to herself now to collect her thoughts and structure her case, and accept that she was responsible in large part for the frosty relations of the previous evening.

On their return, long before they reached the front

door, Anna heard him whistling as he and Ted walked up the path to the house. 'Did you have a nice walk?' she asked, smiling.

'A good brisk walk to chase the demons away,' he replied, brushing back a lock of windswept hair. 'It was invigorating.' Ted stood between them sensing with relief that the previous evening's tension had passed. 'We're both looking forward to a big breakfast.' Anna sighed. How lucky she was to have married such a well-adjusted human being, and what a good thing it was that she had prepared a full English breakfast.

'Tell me what you agreed with Arne,' said Alistair, wiping his lips and putting down his napkin. He had consumed every morsel on the plate packed with the unhealthy, fried offerings that constitute a full English, and was now on his second mug of coffee.

'Okay,' responded Anna, 'but we need to recognise that what we know about the inner Arne is very little indeed. And most of what we do know comes via Eva who is still very friendly with Stella. And Stella and her mother, Coco, know far more about him than anyone else in the world.'

'I'm not sure about that, but carry on,' urged Alistair.

'Your mother died some years ago. You and your brothers arranged a funeral and then you buried her. Later, your father died and you buried him too. Jens and I also had parents. So did Arne. We loved our parents just as much as you loved yours. But we had no funeral and we didn't bury them. You see, ours is a shared story of unfinished business. We have never laid them to rest and that's a situation that taints a life in a way that you couldn't possibly imagine. It is an unending burden that we will carry through the rest of our lives.' Alistair waited for his wife to continue. She was speaking from the heart. 'I can share the burden with my brother. I grew up with him through hard years and know him well. Arne has a living sister who he barely knows as he was studying in Germany from his mid-teens onwards and then escaped across the sea to England.'

'So, he has never really known Ilse.'

'He never had the chance to get to know her personality in the way that I know the character of Jens,' agreed Anna. 'He has no one with whom he can share his particular burden.'

'But unlike you, he does know what happened to them, although he might wish he didn't.'

'I've pondered on that very question so many times over the years. Would I have wanted to know what happened to my father and mother, or have I been unwittingly better off not knowing all the terrible things that could have happened to them? To this day, I've never heard a single story of those events of yesteryear playing out well for any family. And Arne's story is just one such: father shot by firing squad and dumped in front of the town hall for helping the resistance, and his elder sister shot at point blank range for trying to retrieve his body.' Alistair's chin quivered. He knew the story well but when it was starkly juxtaposed with the respectful send-offs that he and his three siblings had given their parents, it highlighted the drama involved. 'Pieter represented the love of Arne's life,' continued Anna, 'the centre of his universe and like Jens and myself, he has nowhere to go to mourn his parents and to express the grief that he still feels more than thirty years after Pieter's death. He needs help to offload his burden; he can't manage to do that on his own.'

'Are you saying that he needs psychiatric help?'

'I believe so,' replied Anna solemnly. 'He can't shed his grief on his own. He needs a confidant to show him how to do so.'

'A counsellor?'

'Or a bosom friend. Just someone he can reply on and who won't judge him for needing help. But the equally pressing matter is one of his increasing indebtedness. Sources of income have dried up and he has taken shelter at the cottage pretending that they don't exist.'

'Head in the sand mentality,' muttered Alistair, 'which can only result in a worse scenario. What can we do about it, Anna? And is it up to us?'

'Probably not, but we will have to point him in the right direction and cross our fingers tightly that that will succeed.'

'I know of a debt management agency that could take control of his financial affairs,' said Alistair. 'It is very discreet.'

'Very discreet but very expensive, I fear.'

'Tactful, circumspect, judicious, yes, all those things, and it would be very expensive if you hadn't been to university with a partner in the agency. I'm sure there's a deal to be done to reduce the fees to a reasonable level if you are able to convince Arne of the necessity for dealing with his debts. I don't think I would be able to convince him of that, but I'm sure you could,' said Alistair. 'Speaking in your mother tongue would it give it extra gravitas.'

'Would he be given a sort of "monthly allowance" to run his life? He'd hate that.'

'There may be no alternative. Or, even worse, he might be declared bankrupt.'

'Oh, no. That would be awful,' said Anna clasping her neck. 'I'd hate to have to tell him that. It could dent his pride permanently. There would be no way back from that.'

'But that might be the reality of his situation, and why employing an expert to manage paying off his debts in a structured way is important.'

'How I could deliver that message, in our mother tongue or not, I just don't know,' uttered Anna looking extremely anxious.

'You'd find a way. I know you would. Especially if you've already convinced him to seek some sort of therapy for his unhappiness.'

'I'd never thought of it like that. Unhappiness. Yes, that's the right word,' said Anna thoughtfully. 'I'm beginning to think that he isn't mentally unbalanced, he's just very unhappy. In the same way as the bridge tragedy families were unhappy until a plaque was erected near where the accident occurred, and then suddenly their collective gloom was lifted as they had a special place where they could remember their loved ones.'

'And finally, they could move on,' added Alistair. 'But could Arne's deep-seated unhappiness really be cured by just a simple memorial stone? It seems improbable to me.'

'There must be remembrance plaques all over Holland commemorating the wartime dead,' said Anna engrossed in thought. 'Whether there is one in Harlingen, I just don't know. My only visit to Holland since we married, was when I accompanied Henrik to Vlieland Island for his presentation. Jens might know though.'

'But even if there is one, and whether Arne knows of its existence, maybe it's just not personal enough for him. Generic but impersonal.'

'And Frieda's suicide was triggered by a lack of tolerance for being born German. So, there certainly wouldn't be anything for remembering her.'

'You could ask Ilse,' said Alistair. 'She's bound to know. How is it that she could deal with the loss of her parents in such cruel circumstances, but Arne cannot?'

'We all have contrasting personalities. We excel at different things and have weaknesses in different areas. And maybe the fact that Ilse and her sister were living with us through those tortuous years has a bearing on how she's been able to cope with the grief of losing her parents and her sister. She was able to share her anxieties in a way that Arne was not.'

They had been sitting steadfastly at the dinner table throughout their soul-searching conversation. Both had ideas floating about in their heads, but as Alistair quite rightly said, they needed to sleep on them. They would be refreshed in the morning and would make better decisions about the future course of events.

Whereas the dinner conversation was lengthy, the breakfast conversation was brief. Sleep had uncluttered their minds and shown a definitive pathway ahead. It was obvious, they both agreed, to use Henrik's gold coin money in an alternative way. Yes, a small contribution in his memory to the government department in charge of lighthouses would still be a splendid idea, but the vast bulk of the sale of the coins should be used for another purpose. There was no need to formalise that purpose in words as both knew that it should be used for the reconstruction of the Visser Boatyard of Harlingen.

After an exchange of letters with Ilse, Anna travelled to Harlingen to spend a few days with Ilse and her family. The boat passage across to the Hook of Holland demonstrated the power of the sea and she shivered at the thought of so many brave young men risking their lives in unseaworthy boats to cross the North Sea to safety three decades previously. She sat back on the train marvelling at the flat countryside passing before her eyes and with seemingly every square inch being used for agricultural purposes. Changing at Amsterdam, she was thrilled to have a couple of hours to wander around the city centre and see the sights; she had never been there before and found the frenetic activity of its inhabitants and traffic exciting. The long journey north to the main regional town passed through towns she vaguely recalled from geography lessons at school. Ilse and her husband were present to greet her when the train finally pulled into the terminus. They still lived in Leeuwarden, which was not too far away by car. But it was not until the following day that Anna felt able to discuss with her the plans that she and Alistair had formulated.

'We're still happy living in Leeuwarden,' said Ilse, 'and we don't regret returning from Perth. Our five years in Australia were amazing, but we couldn't adjust to the vast distances between towns and cities. We felt lonely there. The letters from Henrik were a reminder that friends are more valuable than vast, empty spaces. And I enjoy my job here. But you came with something in mind. My brother, Arne, I presume.' They both half-smiled and Anna moistened her lips as a prelude to what she wanted to say.

'Arne is in trouble,' she started, 'he is in debt and without any steady income. Alistair has a friend whose company specialises in sorting out such matters. But there is another, more profound problem; one that is far less easy to rectify. His heart is heavy because he can't shed the grief of losing his father, and as a consequence, everything he does in life is shallow and ill-considered because nothing means anything to him.'

'All that matters to him is his love for Pieter,' cut in Ilse. 'He did love Frieda and he did love my older sister but it was his father who he knew best and who he truly loved.'

'I'm glad you realise that because until he can bury his grief, he can never have a fulfilled life,' said Anna sadly.

'I saw so little of him in our childhood. When he was very young, if he wasn't at junior school then he was at the boatyard or out on the water with Pieter. Then he was away at senior school in Germany and only returned home for a few weeks before sailing for England. I love him simply because he is the only remaining member of my Visser family, but I know him little.'

With the family at work, the two women drove to Harlingen. They would stroll the streets of what had once been their home town and which they had known in both good and bad times. Memories would be jerked, raw feelings would surface, and perhaps some heads would nod in acknowledgement to passers-by if recognition of times past dawned. The town square, the house where Ilse grew up, the former site of the chandlery with the flat above where Anna and Jens were born and where Henrik had worked for so many years, the railway station where Ilse and her sister had caught the train every Monday morning to their book-keeping jobs in Leeuwarden, and finally, the site of the boatyard where the Vissers had settled when Ilse's grandfather had led his family to their first permanent home away from the sea.

Chapter 10

ILSE

1975

The two women stood silently gazing at the still vacant space where once in a bustling boatyard, leisure vessels had been designed, produced by master craftsmen, and sold to customers all over the world. In a semi-derelict form, it had survived the war, but not the peace that followed. The patched up boatyard had continued into the early nineteen-fifties, but without sufficient funds to make permanent repairs to the war damage, the building became unsafe and had to be pulled down.

'Let's walk farther along the dike to where Arne had moored his boat in preparation for a swift departure under cover of darkness when the Germans entered Harlingen,' said Anna. 'Jens led me by the hand and I counted the paces as we made our way tentatively along the bank for fear of slipping into the water. I can't remember the number now but I was only nine at the time and had to take two paces for every one Jens took.'

'Were you very frightened?' asked Ilse.

'No, not really. It had all been such a rush, I barely understood what was happening to me. A German in uniform was spotted in the town and it sent all the inhabitants into a spin.'

'I remember that too,' said Ilse, 'my mother was crying and my sister was comforting her, and there was no sign of Arne. We were waiting for my father to return home from the boatyard. When he did, he brought news which caused Frieda great heartache. Arne would not be returning home. We all knew what that meant.'

They stopped when Anna thought they had reached the spot. 'I was an innocent thirty-five years ago,' she said, 'but it took less than a month for me to learn the horrors of war. My parents were gone, my home was barred, my life could never be the same.' Ilse sighed deeply; the sigh of shared experience.

'You just had your brother left.'

'But unlike you,' said Anna, 'my brother was with me to give love and support throughout that tumultuous period. You and Arne were separated by the North Sea and had no contact.'

'I still had my parents then, and my own home,' pointed out Ilse. 'And I lived in the knowledge that if Arne had survived the crossing, he should be safe.'

'He survived the crossing, he survived the war, but he hasn't survived the loss of his father,' said Anna bluntly. She had worried about suggesting that Arne's only real love was for his father, not for her, not for his other sister, not for his mother, not even for his daughters. For them he had affection certainly, but for Pieter it was unadulterated love. 'I hope I'm not being hurtful,' she added simply.

'Of course not,' replied Ilse, putting her arm around Anna's waist as they made their way back to where the boatyard used to be. Ilse was tall and blessed with the same full head of blonde hair as her brother, but her personality was kind and grounded. 'Like me, my sister and mother both appreciated that there was a special bond between Pieter and Arne.'

'I grew to love Pieter, too. And Henrik, of course. Those were special times when we helped one another to keep going. But now we must help Arne.'

'Because he can't himself? Is that what you're saying?'

'In essence, yes. He has flitted from one thing to another in his life so far without making any meaningful connections with people. He's missing a person or a strand through life that has meaning for him.'

'The boatyard,' said Ilse without hesitation, 'and a male figure to whom he could be loyal.'

'That sums it up exactly,' agreed Anna. 'We need to provide him with a way forward from the mess he's in.'

'Jens spoke to me about Henrik's unexpected inheritance,' ventured Ilse. 'I presume you know all about it.'

'It is a subject that has permeated our lives ever since we discovered the coins. Dear Henrik's inheritance has been on the tip of our tongues constantly since then. It's a frustrating subject but a happy one as it gives us the opportunity to both remember him and to do a good deed with it.'

'I agreed to help Jens by finding a way to get the coins anonymously to an auction house in Amsterdam once I

341

had received them through a two-lock box system that he had described. The money raised would go to the council with specific instructions to upgrade a lighthouse along our coastline. I was happy with that idea,' said Ilse.

'But since then, we have found Arne in this parlous state of indebtedness and despondency such that Alistair and I feel that Henrik would approve of an alternative plan for the proceeds of his unexpected wealth.'

They had arrived back at the space once occupied by the Visser boatyard. Either side of the unoccupied area structures had sprung up over the course of the years and businesses relating to the dike, the water, the sea, and sailing in general could be seen to be flourishing. The creation of jobs and the associated esprit de coeur that they engendered had restored life back to the bank.

'It looks like a broken notch in a fly wheel, a missing tooth in a dentition, a gap in a row of marching soldiers,' remarked Ilse, 'the space should be filled.'

'That's what Alistair and I think too. We think it should become the new Visser boatyard and that Henrik's money should be used to build it.'

'It would bring further prosperity to the town undoubtedly, but what role would Arne play?'

'Sadly, we can't replace Pieter,' said Anna, 'but we can provide him with the very strand that can accompany him through the rest of his life.'

'The boatyard was his life, that's true,' replied Ilse, 'but after the war when he returned here briefly, he turned down the opportunity to rebuild it with my help.'

'So, you're sceptical that it might not be a long-term interest for him?'

'Not exactly. You know him better than I do and I'm sure you're right that Arne does need a lifetime purpose, but his love of the boatyard was because Pieter was there. Not only did he love Pieter, he also respected him.'

'He looked up to him,' said Anna, a little lost for what to say next.

'I fear that a thread through the remainder of his life would require more than just the boatyard. It would require someone there for him to respect.' Ilse ran her fingers through her flapping blonde hair as the wind got up. 'Respect may be more powerful than love,' she added insightfully.

'You're probably right,' agreed Anna. It was a nuance that she and Alistair had failed to consider.

'My son,' said Ilse, 'like my husband, is an accountant. He is also a very keen and proficient sailor having learnt to sail at school when we lived in Perth. He is Arne's nephew, but possibly more importantly, he is Pieter's grandson. He doesn't bear the surname Visser but in all other respects he is a member of that clan.'

'So, if he was involved there, it would still be the Vissers of Harlingen,' said Anna with a twinkle forming in her eye. 'But would your son wish to work there?'

'He has a good job already, and one with career prospects, but accountancy can be a soulless occupation. To run a boatyard would be much more fun.'

'But would Arne be prepared to be second best? I somehow doubt it.'

'I think Arne would remember a childhood story told by our late grandfather about his son Pieter, our father. We would have been very young at the time, probably seven or eight, but it was a story that made a deep impression. Grandfather was the first in our line of Vissers to settle his family away from the actual coast. He brought them inland a kilometre or so, but it represented a huge move. He started the boatyard and worked night and day to give his family better chances in life. As Pieter became a teenager, he recognised special qualities in him. In that epoch, academic maritime studies were in their infancy. A new course started in Bremerhaven, the first of its type, and Grandfather sent him there using his hard-earned savings. Three years later, aged about eighteen, Pieter returned, and Grandfather almost immediately put him in total charge and started working under him. He had recognised in Pieter, a person of integrity and high principle in addition to his wide range of nautical skills. Pieter would be able to lead through respect.'

'So, your grandfather stood down in favour of his still very young son. A brave decision to make.'

'Arne will remember that story just as well as I do,' said Ilse. 'My son is in his early twenties but shares the same laudable principles as Pieter. When Arne recognises that, which I believe he will, he may feel as our grandfather did, that taking a back seat and giving over the helm to that person is the right thing to do, as everyone associated with the boatyard, including himself, would benefit.'

'There would be no loss of face in making way for someone more suited to the task ahead,' agreed Anna, 'and the responsibility for running the boatyard would be on your son's shoulders, allowing Arne to do the very thing that he and Pieter enjoyed, being out on the water putting new designs through their paces, tinkering with the construction to get the best out of the boat, coming up with solutions to problems and making the vessel outstanding in its class.'

'The bond of uncle and nephew could grow as powerful as that between Pieter and Arne,' said Ilse.

'And that would be the very thread through life that Arne needs. His adult daughter, Stella, would be grateful that finally her father was on a steady footing and out of mischief. But whether we could claim that plot of land,' continued Anna, 'will presumably be at the will of the council who may have earmarked it for something else.'

'But it is our land,' exclaimed Ilse. 'That's why its lain fallow all these years and never been redeveloped. My grandfather bought it when he moved the family to Harlingen, and it was passed down to Pieter when Grandfather died.'

'But how can you prove it?' demanded Anna who looked shocked at the news. 'So much official documentation was destroyed by the bombing during the war that unless you have proof yourself, you have little chance of your claim being upheld.'

'Before the war, my sister and I worked in Leeuwarden. We were employed as trainee bookkeepers which made Frieda very proud. We loved it there and travelled home only at the weekends. When Pieter reckoned that war was inevitable, he asked us if it would be possible to store a bundle of his important paperwork in their fireproof safe, as there was no secure place in the boatyard, it being mainly constructed out of timber. We asked, and they agreed, and the bundle of papers were put in the company's safe.'

'Did the safe survive the war?' asked Anna eagerly.

'The safe did and most of the building too, although I'd completely forgotten about Pieter's bundle. A lot of distractions happened in those years and the following early years of peace. You married Alistair and moved to England to live, I married the boss's son and moved to Australia where we started a family before returning to Leeuwarden. When my father-in-law died prematurely, my husband inherited the business and became extremely busy and I had to look after the family mostly on my own. It wasn't a time when a bundle of old papers rang a bell.' Anna nodded. She knew all too well the hectic pace of family life. 'It wasn't until the factory building was redeveloped some years later and a new system for the protection of valuable documents was introduced,' continued Ilse, 'that the contents of the old safe were fully examined and my husband brought home a package marked "belonging to Pieter Visser." Even then, I wasn't overly curious. Memories of the war and the death of my parents and sister were still raw and it was territory that I didn't wish to revisit.'

'You preferred not to disturb sleeping dogs.'

'Yes. Eventually I did flick through the documents in a desultory way half-hoping, I think, that I wouldn't find anything to tug at my heart strings. It was only when the council started making proposals to rent the area for warehousing that I decided I should look more closely at my father's documents.'

'What did you find?'

'A sepia photograph of my mother and father taken on their wedding day in Germany, with my mother's family in the background. It was a joyous moment,' said Ilse, the emotion evident in her haltering speech. 'The bulk of the package consisted of technical drawings with annotated measurements that Pieter would have drawn up painstakingly on his drawing board, but in addition, there were odd documents about this and that, including one that related to our rented house in Harlingen, and another detailing the purchase by my grandfather of the land along the dike dated just after the first world war.'

'Gosh. Then you do have actual proof.'

'I produced the evidence of ownership to the council who conceded that it did not belong to them. With the death of my grandfather, then my father and mother, and finally my sister, its ownership trickled down to my brother and me.'

'So, you and Arne are joint-owners,' said Anna, stunned.

'That's right. Although I imagine that Arne knows nothing about the land ownership because the last time I saw him, shortly after peace was restored, the relevant documents were still in the safe and were to remain there for several more years before being brought to my attention.'

'Oh, my goodness!' said Anna, using one of her favourite English exclamations. 'It's hardly credible.'

'It may not be worth much in terms of monetary value in a land sale,' Ilse went on, 'but it would be very unlikely that the council would not endorse the re-establishment of the boatyard that had earned such a fine reputation over many decades and which had brought prosperity to many of the town's inhabitants.'

'But joint ownership could complicate matters. It might be better,' said Anna reflectively, 'if Arne believed that your son was the sole owner. Arne's acceptance of his new, calmer lifestyle might be easier to tackle if he believes that your son is in total charge.'

'I see what you mean. Obscure possible complications for the good of all parties.'

'Something like that,' agreed Anna. 'If we can take care of Arne's debts, then he won't need to raise money from a sale, and in the fullness of time, upon Arne's death, the half portion of land ownership would revert to Arne's daughters.'

'A complication for the next generation to sort out, not us,' said Ilse laughing.

It was difficult to turn their gaze away from the plot of land; it had a mesmerising effect on them. Images of the simple, pre-war wooden building, images of the wartime damage caused by the bombing, and their own imagination of how it might soon look. They could see in their mind's eye the bold lettering painted on the structure's front proclaiming "Vissers of Harlingen."

'Arne would be paid a salary,' said Ilse, 'a generous one.'

There was a fond farewell at the terminus. Ilse kissed Anna goodbye and walked along the platform waving until the train had left the station. She didn't doubt Anna's motives, but she doubted her brother's compliance. Pieter and Frieda's failure to discipline Arne's unruly behaviour while expecting good conduct from their daughters, was to blame. Before he had been sent off to Germany, more correctly to learn self-discipline than for maritime studies, he had been almost out of control. Her mother knew it, but Pieter refused to see the truth.

That ownership should skip a generation and go directly to Stella and Stella's baby half-sister, and to her own son, made absolute sense, but only if Arne played ball. And there was the problem of how to ensure that. What did seem necessary was a closer scrutiny of Pieter's documents, particularly the technical drawings. She wondered if he would have owned intellectual rights of the vessels he'd designed pre-war. If so, then it was more than possible that they had value, even four decades on. She stood stock-still at the end of the platform; her body frozen while her mind churned with possibilities. She became aware of someone enquiring if she was all right and replied that she was fine, and had just been momentarily lost in deep thought. But as she walked away, she muttered to herself "more questions than answers." What was clear was that the path forward would be very dependent on her own son's wishes; he had a good job already but running a boatyard would prove far more fulfilling in the long-term and would combine his hobby with his work. She would put it to him and they would go through her father's drawings together.

For centuries, the language spoken in northern Holland was a mixture of provincial languages and regional dialects. With the proximity of Germany, it was hardly surprising that the inhabitants of West Friscia had a good working knowledge of German. But after being roughed up by two world wars, the government and the population preferred to look westward to The British Isles and the New World across the Atlantic Ocean, and consequently the teaching of the English language from a young age became a standard feature in school curriculums. Ilse's children had a head start being born in Perth and although still very young when their parents decided to return to their homeland, they had a decided Australian rhythm and twang to their speech. In amongst the "odd" documents in Pieter's bundle of papers were several handwritten letters in English, the gist of which were complimentary about the design and handling of his latest small, leisure cruiser. Mainly from the eastern seaboard of The Americas, but also from Ireland, countries around the Mediterranean basin and South Africa, each correspondent wished to express his delight in the purchase of a boat which did everything that the advertising claimed it could. There were three letters from a purchaser named Erik Hag. They differed from the rest as they were written on headed notepaper: Erik Hag & Son, Shipwrights of Hampton River, Virginia. Ilse read the letters carefully dated late nineteen-thirty-seven and passed them over to her son to read. The first was one of fulsome praise for the new vessel's splendid appearance as per the front cover of the latest edition of Monthly Sailing and the review therein of its technical data. The second was to make a firm order for the wooden boat, and it outlined a method of payment and specified various shipping details. The final letter, dated April nineteen-thirty-nine, confirmed the safe arrival of the new vessel in Virginia and alluded to how thrilled Erik Hag's young son, Chuck, had been taking it out for the first time onto the broad river. His own shipwrights expressed admiration for the high level of technical expertise and ingenuity used in the production of such a stunning craft and the writer wished to enquire whether they could do a deal to build the new vessel under licence for distribution to customers in The Americas. Erik Hag went on to say that his company were not designers of boats, although he had hopes that his teenage son might one day become a future designer, but were craftsmen in the building, repairing and maintenance of river and sea-going boats and in that regard enjoyed a good reputation amongst the recreational boating fraternity, not just in their state of Virginia but along the whole of the eastern coastline.

'That would be a reasonable proposition,' said Ilse's son, using his business brain. 'The sale of production and distribution rights in North America would have tremendous value.'

'But did Pieter reply? And if so, what was his decision?' replied Ilse.

'There is nothing in Grandfather's papers to answer your questions, Mother, but you could contact Erik Hag and ask him directly.'

'If he's still alive, or his son Chuck who is probably about my age,' said Ilse. 'Yes, I could do that.'

'And you can tell him that we have the actual blueprint for Pieter's most iconic boat,' added her son, 'although, of course, methods and materials have moved on dramatically in the last forty years, that nowadays most recreational sailors have never put a foot into an all-wooden boat.'

'But it would have little commercial value now, I suppose. Who wants the blueprint of a boat, sleek and good-looking as it undoubtedly was, and technically ahead of its time, when it's made out of materials of yesteryear?'

'Probably only a boat aficionado. Or a collector, maybe,' conceded her son. 'There are people around who collect the strangest of things.' Nothing stranger than gold coins of a previous century, thought Ilse, but the words did not escape her lips. 'Why don't you use the telephone, Mother? The latest transatlantic service uses a co-axial cable and offers direct-dial for the first time. And there is a telephone number on the letterhead.'

'But the letterhead is almost forty years old,' protested Ilse. 'The number has probably been superseded, and anyhow it's easier to compose your thoughts and present them in a structured way in a letter.'

''I'll try dialling it from the office tomorrow.'

'And if it works,' said Ilse graciously, knowing that she would have to give in, 'I'll ring tomorrow evening which should be early afternoon in that part of the world.'

The transatlantic connection worked perfectly. Within seconds of dialling the number, Ilse heard a clear voice with an American accent announcing that she was through to Hag & Son in Hampton, Virginia. When she asked to speak to Erik Hag there was a momentary pause until the female voice told the caller that she was being put through to Chuck.

Chuck had sounded like an affable bloke, Ilse later told her family, and had explained that his father, Erik, had retired and was now old and frail. He was smart too, as he discerned immediately that Ilse's English was spoken with a Dutch accent. He knew the accent well, he had told her because his father as a young man had entered the United States as an immigrant from Holland and had never "lost" his accent, and by way of further cordiality had told her that he himself had served on merchant convoys for the free Dutch during the war.

When Ilse switched to the business of the day, aware of the high cost per minute of the new-fangled service linking them, Chuck became serious. Ilse's explanation for the call to enquire whether Chuck's father had entered into an arrangement to build and distribute in North America, a wooden sailing boat with a small cabin, was met with incredulity, or as Chuck described it "he was gobsmacked." Was she related to Arne Visser was his first of many questions. But with her husband pacing up and down the hall and the expression on his face plainly showing concern about the escalating costs as the minute hand on his watch kept rotating around the dial, Chuck's questions had to be politely left for another day. An exchange of airmail letters ensued allowing questions to be set out clearly and fuller answers to be provided until finally, frustrated by the stilted pace of correspondence, Chuck took the decision to book a seat on the daily New York to Amsterdam flight.

When they met at the airport at the pre-arranged meeting point, and Chuck's first action was to doff his hat to her, Ilse knew that he was a man with whom she could do business.

Chapter 11

JENS & ARNE

At some time, agreed Jens, the all-Dutch affair had to include Arne; it was just a question of gauging when. The right time and the right place, had been Anna's summation following her meeting in Harlingen with Ilse. To Alistair, logic dictated the meeting place to be his family home in Wells-next-the-Sea, but he was adamant that neither he nor Ted would be part of the conspiracy. Host their meeting, yes, contribute to their deception, no. He and Ted would cast a blind eye over any information they learnt inter alia. There was a buzz in the air from the moment Jens and Ilse arrived. Both had sneaked a few days away from work and their families to be present. Jens came with some vague ideas which the girls rejected in favour of their own which were far more realistic and which they had thought through.

Arne was still living at the cottage, Anna reported. Alistair's university chum had taken control of his finances which David had found to be in a far dodgier state than at first thought. The flat in Pimlico was up for sale and although it would net a tidy sum, there would be little equity left after the mortgage and utility bills were paid off. Still, it would be a welcomed breathing space whilst getting to grips with his other debts. And the question of his intellectual property rights to Pieter's designs should be explored as to whether they had any monetary value. For three reluctant sailors whose knowledge of nautical affairs could be written on the back of a postage stamp, they had correctly supposed that in modern day materials the iconic boat design would still have commercial legs. Lastly, according to Anna, Arne's general mood was one of day-to-day survival without thought for the future and which Jens likened to their shared experience when living together through the occupation. The "just get through the day mentality" would serve him well, but could not be allowed to last for too long.

As a prelude to the rebuilding of the boatyard, Ilse proposed that they set up a meeting between Arne and her son. It should be at the actual site in Harlingen and would give her son the opportunity to express his ambitions for its future. She felt sure that her brother would be impressed by his nephew's ideas and his plans to work with Arne, and from that little acorn mutual respect could grow. They would also erect a temporary plaque as a monument to all those associated with the boatyard who were victims of the war, and which would, in the fullness of time, be incorporated permanently into the fabric of the new structure. Anna nodded her head vigorously at this suggestion. Ilse then went on to give news of a meeting she had had with a man named Chuck who had an important shared history with Arne. Not only was Chuck the owner of a boatyard, handed down from his father who was Dutch by birth but who had emigrated to the United States in the early part of the century, but he had also served on convoys during the war with Arne, and in more recent times, they had come to some sort of business arrangement to build similar models of *the* boat featured on the front cover of a nineteen-thirties edition of Monthly Sailing. Anna and Jens had never previously heard about Arne's association with a man named Chuck with whom he had apparently deep, shared experiences spanning several decades, and they were agog with wonder as Ilse recounted Chuck's tale. Would Chuck be interested in helping with the regeneration of Pieter's boatyard? Yes, you bet he would. Moreover, with three daughters each uninterested in inheriting his business, Hag & Son, Chuck himself would be open in principle to consider some form of tie-up with a well-managed Vissers of Harlingen. It would all hinge on his confidence that Arne's nephew was up to the task and that Arne's actual involvement was confined to testing designs for seaworthiness, as he too was aware and nervous of Arne's lack of self-discipline. And when probed by Anna and Jens, Ilse had said that she believed Chuck to be a trustworthy individual.

With a realistic scenario of how the future could look – the last thing they wanted was a fanfare for Arne's arrival at the boatyard - they focussed on the method to ignite the plot. Clearly, an anonymous act of benevolence could not be made to a commercial entity such as a private boatyard. Jens didn't have the answer, but the girls did. Still under lock and key in the rear admiral's old safe, the coins would not encounter a single diplomatic pouch in their journey to their final destination, although clearly the council offices in Harlingen could now only be a staging post in a bigger picture. The splendidly thought-out chain of events that Ilse had already outlined for ensuring that not a single coin could be "lost" in transit as both the police and a television station would be involved, would now be made redundant by their change of plan. Anna was particularly grateful that her brother's part in the plot would be greatly reduced thus not bringing into question, she believed, his status as an ambassador. Reduced to the role of a back-seat player, she could see from the relief on his face that the burden had been taken from his shoulders, but nevertheless he queried their plan to take the coins to Harlingen by sea. Certainly, the less he knew the better, and that was okay by him. It wasn't a rebuff, he told himself, and anyway Eva could read him like a book and there would have been no chance of convincing his wife that he was a complete innocent in the matter. He had no misgivings, only the wish that the whole wretched thing could be over and done with so that he could get back to his important work promoting his country and helping his fellow countrymen in times of need when they were abroad. A slightly dull embassy life in Bern suited him fine, but a newspaper article highlighting the soaring trend in sales of high-end properties in London to overseas purchasers of dubious standing who were often as not just seeking a sanctuary for their money, mentioned one likely forthcoming sale: Arne's flat in Pimlico. Another apartment in his block was in the throes of being sold to a Middle Eastern owner of a stud of racing horses and would be occupied each year only during the short periods of Epsom racing and Wimbledon tennis, and Arne's property could go the same way. The article's purpose was to focus the attention of Londoners on how their city was being transformed into a dormitory for the foreign super rich, but it had unexpected consequences as it was spotted by one of the directors of BAV Enterprises, namely Barry, who was still livid at the financial impact on the group's holiday companies caused by Arne's abrupt departure. With extensive wracked-up debt, the holding company, much against Barry's wish, had needed to bail out Arne's individual company if it wished to control who poked their nose into its business, and with a director named George Wremble on their company listing who had died within a few minutes of birth, Barry certainly did. All had been quiet on the Arne front for many months, too quiet in fact for Barry to relax. He tapped the blunt end of his pencil on his blotter several times, raised and lowered his eyebrows as if the action was part of a daily exercise regime, and considered various future plans. He snorted in disgust of Arne's actions preventing him from any chance of taking BAV Enterprises public; his dream of heading a public limited company was over. But Arne would not be forgotten. Any titbit of scandal or possible wrongdoing surfacing in the press would be considered as a lever for recovering the company money he had had to use to cover Arne's company's insolvency, and the sale of the apartment in a fashionable location in London was one such.

But whereas for Barry, the gone-to-ground caused anxiety, for Stella the lack of contact from her father had come as a blessing. Her children were still far too young to question why the handwriting on their birthday cards from their maternal grandfather were so like that of their mother's. Stella was just happy that her family was currently free of awkward disruptions. Ever since her first meeting with David, the financial journalist, at the café in a Lyon back street, they had kept in touch. It was David who had alerted her to her father's debts, and more recently, to the fact that his finances - lock, stock, and barrel – had been taken over by an up-market debt management company which sought to help its "clients" to pay off their debts and get back on their feet again. He had suggested that her father would have been put on a fixed monthly allowance after the ratio of Arne's assets to debts had been calculated, leaving him little margin to swank around town. The cottage with its large workshop and proximity to the open water could prove the antidote to his usual excessive living. The thought of her father feeling lonely or outcast stirred in Stella an innate feeling of protection. He was, after all, her father and she didn't wish him harm or to be unhappy. She crossed her fingers that he had the fortitude to get through the imposed hard times intact, or that some helpful asset might turn up out of the blue to shorten his financial sentence. It was almost certainly a forlorn hope, but hope allowed Stella to "deal" with her father's circumstances more effectively than without. She had no reason to feel a sense of guilt; he had brought upon himself any problems that he was encountering. But. Yet ….

* * *

From the moment he entered it, the workshop proved to be an oasis of calm and contentment for Arne. It was his natural home, standing there surrounded by all the things he truly valued: his boat, tools for working wood, stout benches on which to place parts undergoing modification or repair, a north facing window allowing a natural light to stream in and illuminate his benchtop with soft, but powerful shafts coming from the sky rather than directly from the sun. Any artist would be content with such a fine studio, and in his own way, he too was an artist.

Chuck had made it all possible, and while he worked happily at his bench most days, Arne grew increasingly grateful to the laid-back American for allowing him to transport "The Frieda" back to England. He had paid his friend a nominal sum for the unseaworthy pile of timber that had been stored for many years under a tarpaulin in a corner of the Hag & Son boatyard, and once its use as a template for the production of updated versions of the basic design – everything must be larger for an American market, as Chuck had once told him – had been fulfilled and its purpose served, it was transported by freighter and road to his newly acquired cottage. Ever since, he had worked happily on its restoration, at first in dry dock in the workshop, and later when all the major renovations had been completed, out on the water at its mooring. Now he was administering the last finishing touches. He applied the gold-coloured paint with a steady hand with long, careful brush strokes for the verticals and short dabs for the horizontals. When he had finished, he stood back and admired the lettering: The Frieda. It looked good, and it transported him back to another era in time which made him catch his breath. He could recall precisely his feelings of ambivalence then. By crossing the North Sea in his boat, he would win his freedom but it would be at the price of missing his father during the years of hostilities. Had he known then that he would never be reunited with Pieter, he would have sacrificed his freedom for the love of his father. Seemingly from nowhere, the tears rolled down his cheeks and clouded his vision. He hadn't cried in years, but now he was weeping like a kid in a totally uncontrolled way. Everything was a blur except his increasing dislike of Alistair. How dare he come to his cottage and perch himself on some moral high ground and speak down to Arne as if he were some sort of crusader coming to rescue an untouchable. Alistair had never known hardship the way he had. He had more in common with Annaliese and Jens than the holier than thou Alistair who had never put a foot wrong in his life. He could accept admonishment from Annaliese, even from Jens, and would try to comply with their wishes. Despite his vow made so very long ago never to look back with regret, he had always regretted offloading them on the sandy shore of Vlieland Island. The only comfort from that shameful act was confirmation from Annaliese when she visited him recently at the cottage that Pieter had never known the full story of what his son had done.

Arne stood for quite some time gazing at his boat. He had completed the restoration of The Frieda and she looked good. He sighed deeply. Time had slipped by so effortlessly as he had moved from one aspect of restoration to another, and his contentment had grown with every passing day.

He wished he could turn back the clock and extend that contentment for many more weeks or even months. But tomorrow would be very different with the arrival at the cottage of his sister and one of her sons. He had not seen her for decades and had never met his nephew. And they would be accompanied by Annaliese. What it was all about he didn't know, and didn't really care to know, but he would listen.

The interruption to his daily routine by their presence – people he had known since boyhood yet still strangers in many respects – was less disconcerting than he had imagined it might have been mainly due to the person he had never met before: his nephew. From the workshop where they had been introduced and exchanged cordial salutations, the pair had quickly escaped to the boat and cast off within minutes. Ilse and Annaliese stood at the open workshop door watching with approval as the boat glided away silently from its mooring, the two men aboard already absorbed in the intricacies of steering it towards the sea. A nod of their heads in unison and the exchange of a conspiratorial smile between the women was reassurance that their plan had every chance of working. Arne would show his seamanship skills but be cast under the spell of his young nephew whose enthusiasm for the world of recreational sailing would enthuse him too. By the time they returned, not only would the beginnings of a tight bond exist between uncle and nephew, but his nephew would have told Arne about his future plans for the boatyard and asked him to be part of the new Vissers of Harlingen. As Arne in his youth had attracted so many admirers by his aura, so he in turn would now be trapped by the mere presence of his quiet but charismatically talented nephew.

By the time the men were back, having spent several hours together out on the open water, the women knew that the nephew would have convinced his uncle of the value Arne would bring to the development and testing of the new designs the boatyard would build. For Arne it was a flashback to the hours he had spent as a young boy out alone on the Wadden Sea with just his father for company, putting Pieter's designs through their paces. Lost in thought, the nephew reminded him that although he did not bear the Visser surname, he too was a Visser and it was his great grandfather who had relocated the family to Harlingen and built the original boatyard along the dike. He was a Visser through and through and would learn on the job how to successfully manage the new boatyard. He had never lived over one, the young man told Arne, but as a very young lad living in Perth, he had fully embraced his chance to learn how to sail at his school classes, and since those days he had enjoyed it as his main hobby. There was much that Arne could teach him, and he would be a willing student, but together they could make a successful team and he urged Arne to give the opportunity real thought. But Arne didn't need time to reflect on that. This was an opportunity not just to immerse himself in what he loved, but it was also an opportunity to come in at last from the cold and to be part of the sequence of Vissers who had made a purposeful mark in the region of north-west Holland. He didn't enquire where the money was coming from to finance the rebuild, or their right to claim the land as their own, but if he had, well prepared by Ilse, his nephew would have had all the right answers. Clearing the site ready for the new, and installing a memorial plaque to Pieter and all his former employees who had lost their lives during the second world war was all that Arne needed to know to make his decision.

Chuck's arrival at the family home in Wells-next-the-Sea signalled the prelude to Anna and Ilse's grand plan. He was the important key to unlocking the series of events that would ultimately result in success or failure. Arriving in London with his wife for a touring holiday of several of Europe's famous capital cities, he had journeyed up to Norfolk for a couple of days ostensibly to reunite with a wartime crony. In fact, his overnight stay with the Drews, as well as setting the train of events in motion, would also be for Chuck the start of a period when he would have to be continuously mindful that he was carrying in his breast pocket the most precious of Henrik's gold coins: the jackpot coin as they were now terming it; the single coin that Alistair's friend had reported back was worth to a collector as much as all the other coins combined. The King William I five-guilder coin of eighteen-fifteen that had great rarity value because of the small number minted in the early years of his reign. In handing over the coin that Chuck had agreed to take back to the United States with him, Anna had told him that at the time of the discovery of Henrik's booty, and the subsequent valuation via one of Alistair's friends which identified one coin as having a potentially huge value in relation to the others, she and Jens had awarded it no special care as the value of their intended gift to Harlingen Council would be immaterial to them. However, since the very moment its value was brought to their attention, it had been separated from its peers and kept in the safe in a small silver snuffbox that had belonged to Alistair's grandfather. Discussed at his previous airport meeting with Ilse, Chuck had come prepared, the casual jacket he wore having a small, secret inside pocket with a zip.

When Alistair took Ted out for a walk, he wittingly gave them the space and time for a final recap of the plan they had hatched to rebuild the boatyard. He didn't wish to know the details; knowledge in this case was not power, rather it was trouble and a burden. And Alistair and Ted didn't want either.

'Just go over your plan, please Chuck,' said Anna directing proceedings on behalf of Ilse and Jens who had arrived earlier in the day before Chuck.

'My wife and I are setting out to enjoy the historical and cultural scenes of five capital cities, starting in London with a visit to Hampton Court and an evening concert at the Royal Albert Hall,' responded Chuck in his natural slow drawl. 'We have plans arranged in Paris, Rome and Vienna, and when we arrive at our final capital, The Hague, we will do something off the cuff before flying home on a flight via New York.' Lightly touching his breast pocket, he continued. 'Apart from when in a hotel room, the coin will always be on my person. It is gleaming now, but by the time I have rubbed it numerous times with grubby fingertips, it will blend in with all the other small change I have in my trouser pocket leftover from the other countries visited. If the customs official asks me to turn out my pockets, I shall have no qualms.'

'And then,' said Anna.

'A private transaction with a collector. A person known to me. Discretion guaranteed as both parties to the deal wish to remain faceless.' Chuck looked around at his co-conspirators before continuing. 'The coin will remain in the collection until the collector's death. After that, well, who knows,' he said, shrugging his shoulders. 'But it will never become attributable to one of us.'

'And the sale money?' asked Jens.

'It surfaces in the guise of a large donation from an unknown benefactor to the newly created company "Vissers of Harlingen" for the rebuilding of the boatyard to modern day standards.'

'Is secrecy of the benefactor also guaranteed?' enquired Jens.

'Absolutely,' confirmed Chuck. 'No amount of ferreting by persons with forensic skills to follow money trails will succeed in uncovering the source.' There was something steadying about Chuck's slow drawl. Ilse was right, thought Anna, he was a man with whom you could do business.

'Very well,' said Jens taking charge, 'we can move on to the planned discovery of the other coins.'

'We've already decided that they need to be found in the cashbox in which we originally found them,' said Anna.

'And sealed in by bitumen in exactly the same way as it was discovered?' asked Ilse.

'That would certainly add to its authenticity,' agreed Jens, 'but if you can't open it and therefore can have no idea as to its contents, why would you hand it in to the council?' There was no easy answer to his question and for a while it appeared to be a stumbling block until Anna suggested the simple solution of just saying that they didn't know to whom it belonged. Sure, it was found on Pieter's land but whether it had belonged to him was another question and one they couldn't answer. It was either the council or the police, and they had thought the council was the more appropriate choice.

'Yes, that would work,' said Jens, 'playing the innocent and not knowing if the concept of "treasure trove" would apply if the cashbox was found to contain something of value. But who would seal the lid?'

'It would have to be Alistair,' said Anna somewhat reluctantly. 'With Henrik's help he found the way to unseal it, so he is the only person who knows how it can be done. And only a thin layer must be applied so that it can be opened without too much difficulty. Pity really as I was hoping to spare him further involvement.'

'So,' said Jens, 'the coins must travel from here to Harlingen in the sealed cashbox, and I can think of only one person who has a reasonable chance of safely delivering such a bulky item: myself. I can put the cashbox in my briefcase together with a handful of diplomatic documents and if I give the appearance of being on official business, I would be very unlucky to encounter a customs official who wants to go through its contents.'

'That's probably correct,' agreed Anna, but it was clear from her facial expression that she was worried about her brother doing so. 'You risk your job if you are caught,' she warned him, 'the job you love so much.'

'There's no other way,' he replied, and Ilse nodded in agreement.

After that, the sequence of events and its participants in the charade of uncovering the hidden box whilst the construction crew was preparing the new footings, and the method of its subsequent transfer into the hands of officialdom, fell neatly into place.

When they gathered unheralded as a group at the site of the old boatyard some weeks later, everyone had fulfilled their allotted task including Arne who had spent many hours at the bench in his workshop designing and then carving out of oak a suitable commemorative plaque to all those who had been employed in the original boatyard since its founding in the early part of the century, but who had perished as a direct result of the occupation and the bombings. Anna had indicated that it would serve as a temporary memorial until the construction of the new boatyard was complete when they would commission a permanent plaque in brass or in stone to be displayed in a prominent position at the entrance to the building. She would arrange a service with a blessing to which the families of the fallen would be invited.

Her words haunted Arne as he worked at his bench with chisels and gouges, planes and handsaws, rasps and files. He had never had anywhere to go to mourn the absence of his father; the loss had left a deep wound in his life that had never healed. Countless times over the years he'd cupped his face in his hands as if afraid to look beyond his lonely world without Pieter. But soon there would be somewhere to go to express his grief and to tell Pieter how much he missed him. It was the start of a dawning that he could soon lay his grief to rest.

Memories came flooding back for Ilse too; Arne was not the only Visser haunted by the past. She too had dark skeletons in the cupboard that from time to time continued to tweak her senses but which over the years she had fought hard to control. While doing a recce of the site of the old footings alone one previous evening in the decreasing twilight to find the best spot for Jens to bury the cashbox for discovery by the construction crew, she too had felt the weight of her personal history being slowly and gently lifted off her shoulders. The relief was palpable and her tears were of joy not of sadness. After identifying a suitable location where Jens could dig a shallow hole with a small hand tool and rub the cashbox in the loose soil extracted to integrate it into its new position at an edge of the former building's footprint, she stood silently in prayer. Her son would lead the Vissers away from harm and into a new era of accomplishment. As his great grandfather before him had relocated his family inland from the seashore, so her son would quietly but firmly lead his generation into the seismic changes of the new world order.

As the group departed walking quietly away, Anna turned her head to look back at the plaque that Arne had attached to a wooden post. It stood out proudly at knee height above the ground, the gold lettering shimmering in the autumn sun. Jens squeezed his sister's hand; he knew where her thoughts lay. She would be thinking that everyone now had somewhere to remember their dead except them.

'We mustn't mind,' he whispered. 'Our prayers will be heard wherever we make them, I promise you.'

'I make them all the time,' she said quietly.

'So do I.'

The news of the "discovery" broke not long after the heavy machinery brought on site to establish foundations fit for modern boat building, slipways and parked cars had begun their excavations. The cash box was soon jostled out of its shallow grave as the excavator tracked its way across the site, its rotating cab allowing the arm with its fearsome-looking bucket to easily reach every sod of earth to be shifted to provide a level surface. Dumped in a large heap, the spoil grew in height and area as successive bucket loads were added to the pile. It was only as the heaped-up spoil slithered downwards in mini avalanches as fresh spoil was added to the pile that someone noticed something sticking out forming an unexpected shape. On examination by one of the labourers it was found to be a grimy tin box which he had handed over to his site foreman who scratched his bristly chin and indicated that he would have to refer a decision about what to do with it to his boss. In the absence of her son, the real boss – all part of Anna and Ilse's plan – Ilse caught the train into Harlingen to meet the site foreman who had told her over the telephone that he couldn't open it but that something was in it because when he shook it, it rattled.

The staff at the council offices didn't appear to be terribly interested in the "find." Apparently, the discovery of odd bits and pieces on building sites had become commonplace, and to date, said the head of one of their departments with jocular intent, no gold coins had been found. Ilse's legs wobbled at the reference to both "gold" and "coins" and she was glad to have been behind a stout counter to hold onto something solid until the shock wave passed, she told Anna later that evening when she telephoned.

'They really didn't have the time or staffing to waste on such matters, he told me,' Ilse said, 'so I went to the police station instead.'

'Ooh,' said Anna, fearing the worst.

'As luck would have it, a young officer there was able to identify the material holding down the lid,' Ilse started. 'He was familiar with tar because his father worked on the railways. With the tip of a menacing-looking knife produced from a cupboard of confiscated weapons, he scored a line in the tar, and with one powerful yank, the lid flew open.'

'Ooh,' repeated Anna, imagining what was coming next.

'After the coin tray was removed, the two small bags were revealed,' Ilse continued, gulping with excitement. 'They were removed by one of the officers who loosened a drawstring and let the contents spill out. There was a deathly hush as the realisation dawned on them that this was a hoard of valuable coins.'

'Do go on,' urged Anna, 'the suspense is practically killing me.'

'All hell let loose after the stunned silence was broken. The young officer looked bemused but his elder quickly decided to ask the most senior officer on duty to come and have a look at, what he said, might be gold coins, and I agreed, adding that they looked very old.'

'A bit of acting on your part.'

'The situation called for it, but I wouldn't wish to have to do it again,' remarked Ilse. 'I was afraid of a quivering voice letting me down.'

'And then?'

'Things moved fast,' recounted Ilse. 'I had to give a lot of details of how, when and where the cashbox was found. I said I didn't know to whom it belonged but it was found on land owned by my family. The number of coins were counted and I was given a receipt but was told that as the find would probably be deemed as "Treasure Trove" it would be unlikely that I would be allowed to keep it. Apparently, most countries have laws which regulate what must be done when something precious is found.'

'Then so far so good,' said Anna in a more confident tone. 'What we expected really.'

'Yes, they kept to the script of what we had anticipated,' agreed Ilse, 'but I hadn't envisaged that I would have to hang around there for almost three hours.'

'But you got the job done just as we'd planned, and now we can sit back calmly and await any ripples it might have caused. It's in their hands now, not ours.'

Ripples started appearing almost immediately as word got out that a hoard of gold coins had been dug up on a building site. Correspondents of the local and national press were on site at daybreak the following morning, soon to be followed by television crews with reporters, microphones in hand, trailing long cables as they moved about the site pointing to the general area in which the cashbox was assumed to have been buried. As there was little there to see except a motley group of construction workers gawping at the media presence, programme directors switched back to the television studios for in-depth analyses by experts.

'The coins are of the purest form of gold,' started the numismatist brought in to the studio at short notice. 'They were minted in the first half of the nineteenth century and are of the value of either five or twenty guilders from the reigns of William I and William III. They are in good condition and rare, and therefore of high value.' When asked by the show's presenter whether they would have formed part of a larger collection, the numismatist was ambivalent. 'Maybe or maybe not,' he replied, 'but usually a keen collector would seek greater variety. Rare though they may be, none were minted in the early part of either reign. The first three years when the numbers produced were small would have had a rarity value greatly in excess of those minted later in their reigns. Maybe whoever collected them wanted to hold them for their intrinsic value too. You can't go wrong with gold and it is very transportable.' And an easy commodity to hide from the tax authorities, thought the expert without saying so.

With the departure of the expert, the programme's attention turned to how the contents of the cashbox were accumulated. Ilse and her son were glued to the television set. This was likely to be the weakest part of the story and open to speculation. Would the theory that it was Nazi gold stashed away over the period of the occupation and hastily buried before the Allied liberation find favour? Or was a citizen of Harlingen trying to find a safe place to hide them after being bombed out of his home? A wide range of opinions were canvassed but no better storylines emerged. And when the cashbox came under scrutiny too, and was found to be of a pre-war make, the scenario of occupation forces robbing banks and hiding the loot to be retrieved at a later date, before fleeing back in disarray to their homeland, became increasingly plausible. In the absence of any person with believable credentials coming forward to claim the booty – the police had to deal with the usual string of halfwits with unfeasible stories or known criminals trying it on or attention seekers who had all the facts wrong – after a certain period of time it became accepted that whoever had buried them must have been killed in the war before he could return to unearth the cashbox. Ilse and her son let out sighs of relief that nothing to throw them off course had arisen, and that permission to continue with the boatyard's new foundations was granted.

The closing chapter in Anna and Ilse's plan played out in exactly the way they had envisaged. Treasure Trove was cited in every paragraph of an official document explaining why the local authority was the only body that had a justifiable claim over the coins. Ilse sent newspaper clippings of related articles to Anna and Chuck – with her translations for Chuck whose father was far too old to do so himself – explaining how the decision had been reached and that, after considerable pressure from various Dutch bodies representing the country's heritage, the council had donated the coins in their entirety to a museum in

Amsterdam. A smile of satisfaction spread across their collaborators' faces. Their plan had worked perfectly. Henrik's legacy, minus one very important piece had been successfully returned to the nation and would soon be on display to hundreds of thousands of museum visitors. The missing piece had been transferred anonymously to a private collector for an agreed extraordinarily large sum which, via a series of complicated and untraceable bank transfers had ended up in the asset column of a newly created company, Vissers of Harlingen, thus permitting work to start in earnest on the construction of the new boatyard.

It was springtime by the time the last nail was hammered in, the last screw was turned, the last bolt was tightened, the last locking mechanism oiled, and the last piece of wood given a final sanding. The boatyard was complete and stood proudly along the banks of the dike ready for business. Invitations to the grand opening had been mailed, and on the special day bunting adorned the entrance. There were sadly no memorabilia of the former yard to display in the entrance foyer, but Ilse's son had commissioned an artist to produce a large poster of Pieter's iconic design that had featured on the front cover of Monthly Sailing back in the late nineteen-thirties. It was a nod to Pieter, but also to Arne who had sailed that very boat across the sea to freedom.

As promised, Anna had found a mason to carve Pieter's name into a large rock of granite. It had taken several trips back and forth to Holland to discuss the preparation of the face of the stone, and the size and font of the lettering. It would be a memorial that no employee, guest, or visitor could fail to notice as they entered the modern version of Pieter's boatyard, and which caused many male visitors to doff their hats. It had been a poignant moment for Arne as he stared at the granite stone for the first time, but strangely unemotional. He had made his peace with his father's death some months previously when he had hammered home the post holding his hand-carved wooden plaque, allowing the inner emotional turmoil that he had carried with him for so long to be dispelled.

But for Ilse it provoked feelings that she hadn't realised she had carried with her but suppressed for so very long. To the astonishment of her husband and adult children, their grounded and practical wife and mother, kneeled and wrapped her arms around the rock, clinging to it until her husband gently disengaged her fingers from the stone and helped her stand up. Arne watched from the sidelines and noted for the first time that he was not the only person to have been emotionally affected by the loss of their parents. Ilse may not have outwardly displayed her grief, but it was there nonetheless and in one brief moment when she let the mask slip, she had laid bare her pent-up torment for all to see.

The arrival of Chuck and his family diverted Arne's train of thought. He looked as American as any American could look with crew cut hair, bold check shirt with a button-down collar and worn with a black string tie. With his wife on his left arm and his three vivacious daughters extending in a line on his right arm, his presence in Harlingen did not go unnoticed. The two men warmly embraced and Chuck congratulated his fellow ex-convoy mate on taking up the post of technical director in the new firm. After presenting his family in the well-rehearsed and jovial manner to which they had clearly become accustomed over many years, Chuck was taken aback when Arne responded by introducing his own: Ilse his sister and her family including his nephew who was boss-designate, and then Stella his daughter and her family who had flown in from Lyon especially to celebrate the event. Chuck stood back momentarily lost for words. Arne had never previously introduced him to any of his family. He looked at Ilse and she smiled as if to convey the message that Arne really had changed, and by the way, their meeting at Amsterdam airport when Chuck flew in from New York, was still their secret and would always remain so.

The afternoon was full of introductions and guided tours around the different workshops housed within the boatyard's perimeters before finally the managing director and leading light, Arne's nephew, speech in hand, took the stand to address his guests. He started by reminding them that he wasn't just Ilse's son, or Arne's nephew, or Pieter's grandson. He was the great grandson of the original boatyard's founder; a man who had taken an extraordinarily audacious decision to move his tribe away from the actual coastline for the first time in centuries. And in the intervening years, they had honed their skills and together with wisdom and tenacity they had designed and built futuristic vessels of high quality which had provided worthwhile jobs for local families. Despite the ravages caused by two world wars, the young managing director went on to say how proud he was to be part of that long line of Vissers, and that his intention was, together with his assembled team of talented workers which included offspring of some of the original master craftsmen, to achieve as much as his forebears in the world of recreational sailing. He reminded them of the poster of his grandfather's most iconic boat and that Vissers of Harlingen would seek to emulate designs of such outstanding quality even with modern materials. Finally, he reminded his audience that based purely on anecdotal evidence, the baton of leadership and responsibility over the course of several generations had been exchanged without murmur or conflict or regard to age when the holder recognised the wide range of qualities of his successor. And he was confident that with a workforce of gifted individuals it would not be long before a boat from their yard would again feature on the front cover of Monthly Sailing.

The prophesy of a press feature in the coming years arrived sooner than anticipated and came in the form of a "new start-up business" assessment by David, the financial journalist, which was of great interest to two of his readers in particular; Arne's former business partners, namely Barry and Victor.

'Where did they get the money from?' asked Barry, shoving the newspaper article under his partner's nose.

'Is Arne in trouble again?' responded Victor, donning his reading spectacles.

'Vissers of Harlingen, according to the journalist, have a load of unexplained dosh in their asset column, and just in case you've forgotten,' snarled Barry, 'Arne is Arne Visser.'

'No, I hadn't forgotten,' replied Victor with real feeling, 'but give me time to read the article fully.' The deliberate removal of his spectacles which he set down on Barry's desk, sides neatly folded in, to precisely align with one of the margins of its leather inlay, gave Victor a few more seconds of thinking time. Oh, how he wished he would never have to hear about their former partner again, but there was some inevitability about it. 'Have you tried searching its origins?'

'Of course, I have,' said Barry dismissively. 'No joy. Dealings all wrapped up like a set of Russian dolls.' Victor frowned and replaced his spectacles to enable him to reread the article.

'Do we need to know the source of their finances?' asked Victor not unreasonably. 'What's it to us?'

'I'll tell you what it is to us,' said Barry impatiently, 'it's not being taken for a ride.'

'And you think we are?'

'There is something fishy, that's for sure. I'd like to wring that work-shy layabout's neck.'

'Why bother with him anymore,' replied Victor. It was a statement not a question. 'We've recouped his losses in the holiday sector, and it's questionable whether we would have got it off the ground without him. Maybe we should be thankful for his brief input.' Victor's utterance was entirely in keeping with his plodding persona which could drive Barry mad with frustration.

'I just don't want him to think that he's got one over on me by making me use some of my hard-earned money to pay off his debts. As my old man used to say,' said Barry, playing his Cockney card, 'you can never have too much money, and I think you might be beginning to realise that too.' Victor recognised the remark for what it was: a home truth. Little Marilyn was becoming expensive and costs were ramping up as her private school fees mounted.

For Jens, the grand opening of the second iteration of the boatyard had come as the culmination of a whole range of difficulties and obstacles that had beset him since his teenage years. For a quiet well-mannered boy, short in stature and generous by nature, the steely inner core he went on to develop over time would never be apparent to an outsider.

As a young boy growing up in Harlingen, the chandlery had been at the heart of his world. Living over one of the most important shops in town with his parents, life had been vital with the daily comings and goings of fisher folk and local sailors and the news, gossip, and interaction that their presence brought. And when his sister had been born, her seven-year-old brother had rejoiced at her arrival with the prospect of an even happier family life. That the war appeared to dash all his hopes as it indeed dashed the hopes of so many of his fellow countrymen, would prove a lifelong burden for many but not for Jens.

Back in the embassy in Berne, doing the job he so loved, his thoughts drifted to his sister. Even as a young girl she had always given him as much comfort as he had given her protection, and yet all he had offered her when she became overcome with emotional pain for the absence of a memorial for their own parents, were words. Nice words certainly, but just words. And if he was truthful, he too had never quite been able to lay to rest his parents' deaths. But sitting quietly at his desk with the day's business transacted and the embassy staff on their way home, it occurred to him that he could use his diplomatic skills to do a good deed for Chuck, and allow Chuck to do one in return for him.

At the opening of the new boatyard, Chuck as a boatyard owner himself, had been his unofficial guide explaining how the modern equipment operated and giving an insight into the logistics of boat building. During their enjoyable tour, they had exchanged potted background histories of their links with Arne and his family. Jens learned that Chuck's father was Dutch by birth and had emigrated to the United States just after the end of the Great War and that Chuck himself, as part of the free Dutch forces, had served on convoys with Arne during the first two years of the second world war. Born and reared in the United States, and like so many fellow first-generation Americans, Chuck was immensely proud of his European heritage. His "roots" in Holland were his link to his ancestors; that was where the history of his family was to be found and where truly his heart lay. Reflecting on what he could do for Chuck, Jens' initial thoughts centred around some form of official documentation that could be framed and hung on the wall showing an honorary citizenship with the country he still regarded as his homeland. And he would be able to show that the bearer of his particular passport was not just a person of the new world as his roots had grown and been refined in the old world for at least a dozen centuries before the discovery of the new world.

Still seated at his desk, his attention slipped to the framed photograph of his wife and daughter which occupied a position just next to his pen set. Family snaps pre-world war were luxuries that were usually few and far between, and in his case, almost non-existent since in the hasty departure of his parents from the chandlery dictated by the Germans, he guessed that his father, for the sake of reassuring his wife, must have made a futile attempt at normality by grabbing a few precious family photos and some small trinkets to take with them to the camp. Chuck, in the new world probably had more memorabilia than he had in the old world. But the chandlery, although it no longer existed in its previous location or under his family name of Leesen, was still his connection to his parents, and he guessed his sister felt the same. He could certainly use his diplomatic skills to obtain an impressive certificate, which even in honorary form he knew would be valued by Chuck, and in return, his musings had sparked an idea of how Chuck could help his sister.

One year later, almost to the day of the grand opening of the boatyard, Jens and Anna were invited to attend the annual prize-giving of the school in Harlingen they had attended in their youth. In the intervening years it had expanded and moved location as the town's footprint grew in size and in number of inhabitants. Now located away from the dike on the town's eastern flank, it boasted a series of interlinked modern buildings with recreational facilities and a myriad of student amenities. Anna had queried with her brother the reason for their invitation, and he had mysteriously replied that all would be revealed.

It was a day for parents to be proud of their offsprings' achievements. Anna sat dutifully next to her brother applauding at appropriate times from their seats at the front of the assembly hall, but still unaware of the reason for their presence.

'It won't be long now,' Jens said, whispering in her ear.

'What won't be long?' she asked, whispering back.

'Until all is revealed.' He had a bright countenance but she noted that it was tinged with sadness.

Suddenly, to Anna's astonishment, the school's principal welcomed onto the platform and introduced to the assembled parents and students, Chuck Hag from the United States. Apparently, Mr. Hag's father was Dutch by birth and had lived in their region before emigrating to North America, and that there was surely a chance that his father had attended the school in whatever form it existed in those early years of the twentieth century. The principal went on to say that Mr. Hag was very proud of his Dutch forebears and wished to formally mark the esteem in which he held them with a philanthropic gesture. He would donate an annual bursary which would be awarded to the student the school considered most worthy of financial help to permit learning at a higher level. The assembled throng were rightly impressed, but it wasn't until Mr. Hag himself addressed them in English that the full bountifulness of his donation became apparent when the polite clapping turned to rapturous applause.

'You see,' said Chuck addressing the audience in his normal, slow, deep drawl and informal manner, 'I may have lived all my life in the amazing and wonderful state of Virginia, across the ocean and many thousands of miles away, but it is here, in Harlingen that my roots were formed.' He paused and looked intently at the many faces staring back at him. There was no apparent fidgeting in the audience. 'Our roots are tempered and fashioned by decades and centuries of habits and practices passed on and improved by our forebears as the actions of each generation become ever more sophisticated.' He paused again to take a sip of water before continuing, 'at some stage we need to take a long look back and appreciate what they have done for us. They have given our lives meaning by setting the stage for further advancements. And in addition, they have provided us with a beating heart around which we can muster in times of strife and uncertainty.' Jens and Anna were as spellbound as everyone else in the hall; their gaze glued to Chuck's face. 'Let me give you an example,' said Chuck. 'In the days long, long ago, when my father lived in this area, jobs and commerce centred around living off the sea. There were simple fishermen, ferrymen who plied across the Wadden Sea to our offshore islands, boat builders and designers, and men who maintained the dikes. But at the heart of all those workers was the chandlery. Anna couldn't prevent a sharp intake of breath which Jens sensed rather than heard. 'It was the chandlery that was the beating heart for all those people. A shop which was small and simple, even rudimentary by today's standards, but which had a profound effect on all those who were engaged in maritime affairs.' Jens knew what was coming and squeezed his sister's arm. 'For many years the chandlery was owned by Mr. and Mrs. Leesen. They built it up into the beating heart of the town by hard work, diligence, and honesty. What wartime adversity befell the proprietors we may never know, but the legacy they left behind shines on and is a powerful reminder to us all that the effort we each put into making our way in life should also include striving for the benefit of our fellow man. I am proud of my surname Hag but I am equally proud to have some connection with the Leesens, and for that reason I wish to name the award the "Leesen Bursary." Their chandlery may no longer exist in physical form but their humanity lives on in their son and daughter, Jens, and Annaliese, who I have asked to present it.'

'So, you see dear sister,' said Jens, 'we do now have somewhere to remember our parents. It is right here, and it is every year.'

Chapter 12

TED

1985

Their walk along the exposed beach pathway, seldom encountering another human or dog, which led to the sheltered marina and back through the narrow and familiar streets of Wells-next-the-Sea, was one of Alistair and Ted's favourites. They had done it together hundreds of times and loved it. As a puppy and young adult, Ted had invariably jumped up onto the harbour wall and surefootedly navigated along its twists and turns, looking back at his master from time to time for reassurance. From the town, they would proceed home slowly up the only real slope of significance in the area with its wide grassy verges where Ted often stopped several times to poke his nose into the wild vegetation to explore interesting smells, before completing the final leg up to Alistair's family house with its wonderful views out to sea.

Ted had been doing the walk in one form or another since his puppy days in nineteen-seventy, sometimes accompanied by Anna, or Henrik, or even the gardener, but mostly with Alistair. But while Alistair was a fit fifty-something-year-old, Ted was in the latter stages of his life. Anna had noticed it, but not Alistair. She wondered whether that was because he chose not to notice it; he didn't wish to accept that his great friend was nearing his terminal point. But today when they got home, Alistair remarked for the first time that Ted seemed to be reluctant to do the full walk and kept pulling on his lead in the direction of home.

'Do you remember when we went to the breeder's kennels to collect him?' she asked over the dinner table.

'Yes, I do,' replied Alistair. 'It was fifteen years ago but it seems like yesterday. We only got him because of the constant nagging and pleading by our second son. He promised us faithfully that he would always look after Ted.'

'It didn't happen,' sighed Anna, using the latest popular phrase. 'But it worked out for the best as the two of you were made for one another.' Alistair nodded, but looked uncertain. 'Ted's grown old,' Anna went on sympathetically, 'he needs shorter walks and longer rests.'

'I suppose so,' agreed Alistair, but with an obvious unwillingness to face the facts. 'I could ask the vet to prescribe a tonic for him,' he added more cheerfully. 'Ted will be in great demand for strokes and cuddles when the family arrive next weekend. We will want him to be on top form for that.'

Over the washing up, Anna wondered if the vet would tell Alistair the truth that Ted was dying. She hoped so as her husband had his head firmly in the sand on that score, and she didn't relish the idea of having to do so herself.

Ted was in his usual welcoming place on the wide porch as family and friends arrived for a long weekend: Jens and Eva, Ilse and her husband, Chuck and his wife. He almost seemed his normal inquisitive self with his pricked ears and wagging tail, but when they went inside the house Ted didn't follow them into the grand reception room with its stunning vista out to sea. Instead, Ted curled up in the soft blanket that lined his basket and closed his eyes. The chatter, the noise, the different smells, the comings, and goings; it was already proving too much for him. Jens went to look for him when he noticed his absence from proceedings and found Ted enjoying a nap. Crouching down, he noticed the grey hairs on his snout and the sagging skin around his neck. Ted was looking old, and he had to admit, decidedly frail. He stroked his back tenderly and uttered some words of encouragement to the sleeping dog before offering help to his sister who was preparing the midday meal single-handedly.

Alistair would lead a walk around the marina after lunch for all those interested, to showcase all the advantages of living in his part of the world, and would point out to all and sundry where precisely Arne had made landfall on his famous crossing forty years previously to the day.

Although Alistair had greeted and treated his guests in his usual cordial and carefree manner, he had done so with a heavy heart. The previous day he had consulted the vet.

Ted had been helped up onto the examination table where he stood quietly as if bemused and unable to comprehend what was happening. He was in a completely passive state and unable to play any active role in proceedings. Alistair's heart broke to see him so subdued.

'He's not in pain, Alistair, but his systems are shutting down,' said the vet. 'As you can plainly see, he is nearing an end-of-life stage.' The brutal facts hit hard. Alistair gulped, then cleared his throat, but said nothing. 'The time has come,' the vet went on in a kindly voice, 'to let Ted go.' Alistair cleared his throat again, and fought back his emotions. 'Bring him in next week when your visitors have left.'

'If he's not in pain …,' Alistair trailed off.

'Then why put him to sleep prematurely?' said the vet finishing off Alistair's question.

'There's no need to answer that,' said Alistair glumly. 'I must do whatever is best for Ted.'

The invitation to Arne to attend the Drews' gathering had been down to a bold move suggested by Anna and endorsed by his daughter Stella. By all accounts, he was a changed man, and it was time for a fresh start. Splitting his time between Harlingen and the cottage, he spent most of his days out on some body of water testing designs and coming up with solutions. Sceptics might have wondered how long this would last, but Arne's contentment appeared real. Stella and her husband had collected him from the cottage and they had arrived in the Drew household one day later than the other guests, but as a family rather than as Stella and her husband plus Arne.

The magnificent house on the hill was the perfect setting for the occasion; a flashback to gracious living in a previous era. With sufficient bedrooms to accommodate everyone in style, and with large reception rooms to cater for all tastes, the ambience was one of languid well-being and the house was full of happy chatter. Anna had arranged a programme of events for the four days, with a visit to Holkham Hall, a walk along the high cliffs at Sheringham, a football league match at the stadium in Norwich, and a visit to a craft fair. With outside caterers known for their exceptional cuisine providing dinner in the rear admiral's library which had been especially kitted out with a long table that seated eleven diners, it would be a grand finale to remember.

Arne's presence in the house was at first somewhat stilted. Alistair recalled well that back in war-torn Britain, since his eldest brother had already settled in a distant land, the rear admiral had allotted the room to Arne for the time he was detained under house arrest pending the wartime authorities deciding what to do with him. Anna had asked her husband which bedroom Arne had occupied for the period he had lived with them, and it had taken some winkling out from a slightly begrudging Alistair who was not truly at ease with welcoming Arne back. He still could not quite divest himself of Arne's former image. Stella's presence eased the small talk into meaningful conversation, but it was Ted who allowed his master to finally relax. Sniffing around the guests' feet in one of his rare sorties from the wicker basket, he seemed to enjoy the pats and tickles that his presence generated. Alistair stood back and wondered how Ted would react when he came to Arne. Would he remember the incident at the bridge when Arne kicked gravel in his face, wounding Ted badly in the eye? Or chasing after the out-of-bounds golf ball that Arne failed to acknowledge was cheating?

'Did he pass the Ted test?' enquired Anna, watching the scene unfold.

'He licked Arne's hand and wagged his tail, so I would say he has passed the Ted test,' replied Alistair. 'Good old Ted, not harbouring any grudges. A gentleman to the end.'

Alistair's golf had not improved during his period of club captaincy but through necessity his speech making had; he had turned into a confident raconteur. As he stood at the head of the table, he was able to describe with humour the history of the rear admiral's library. In the convivial atmosphere of good food and fine wine, it was not difficult to enthral his audience of family and friends with the history of the special house on the hill. He told them how privileged he felt to have grown up in such surroundings and how lucky he had been to have three much older brothers who had "bummed off" to different parts of the globe leaving Alistair to inherit something that had always been at the core of his life. The library, he recalled to his guests, had been the domain of his father. Under lock and key from the rear admiral's wife and children, entrance to the room had been strictly by invitation only. Hundreds of books lined the three walls and stacks of magazines and old newspapers were obstacles around which to navigate on the occasions when entrance was granted. The cleaner's job was impossible since the rear admiral had embargoed moving anything and her resulting light touch with a feather duster, often on tiptoes, left the room as dusty and musty as when she had started. Notwithstanding the imposed limitations, the library had featured prominently in the history of the house. Alistair recalled how it had been used as a depository for naughty children, a place of learning from the wide range of subjects lining the shelves, a hidey-hole when the rear admiral was wanted in the kitchen by his wife to help, a place of joy when he had found the copy of Monthly Sailing illustrating the radically new Visser boat design, and amongst the hundreds of dusty books, the English/German dictionary with which he and Arne had held their first conversations. From stories of the past, Alistair stepped seamlessly into the present by reminding his audience how the regenerated boatyard had brought family and friends together over the last five years in a way they could never have imagined. Separated by the Atlantic Ocean, no one could have guessed that in a joint venture, the new futuristic designs of the two privately-owned firms could have attracted so much attention and received so many accolades. In a commercial union that satisfied both parties, long-term goals of retaining their independence and preserving a family interest could be achieved. The future, Alistair concluded, was rosy and as they were sitting in the library, he bid them all to join him in a toast to the late rear admiral. Amongst those "in the know" – Anna, Ilse, Chuck, and Jens – a discreet wink from Alistair acknowledged that their mission to distribute Henrik's legacy had been successfully achieved.

With the departure of the guests, the gardener started work behind the large shed. In a position that offered a view out to sea, with spade and rippling muscles, he dug out a rectangle where they would bury Ted. The following morning Alistair urged his enfeebled dog to stand up and make his last walk to the car. His soft blanket had been arranged on the back seat and the gardener gently lifted Ted onto it. Anna gave Ted a final cuddle; she was in an emotional state as Ted sensed that it was his last hurrah.

It was only a short car ride to the vet's practice on the edge of town. Alistair chose to go alone with Ted; a few more precious moments for the two buddies to be alone together. The staff were waiting when he arrived to help him get Ted out of the car. In what seemed like no time at all, Ted had been given his relaxation drug and was laying on his blanket on the operating table. After the vet administered the overdose of barbiturate there was just time to exchange one last loving look between master and dog before Ted's eyelids closed for the final time. When the vet checked that Ted's heart had stopped beating, Alistair had to steady himself against a chair. He had a glass of water in the waiting room while the nurse wrapped the soft blanket around Ted's body and took him out to Alistair's car.

Alistair's phlegmatic British character was on display at Ted's burial. In the presence of Anna, and with the help of the gardener, they carefully laid the bundle which was formerly Ted into the prepared resting place. Whilst the gardener replaced the soil and Anna put some large cobbles around the grave's edges, Alistair read out a prayer. Calm and dignified, he shook hands with the gardener and thanked him for his help before the burial party of three went indoors for a cup of tea.

The gardener normally whistled as he strode down the drive on his way home, but not today; he would miss Ted too.

'Will you get another dog?' asked Anna.

'I don't think so. There could never be another Ted.'

'Never say never,' said Anna softly, but Alistair was gazing out to sea lost in his own world and didn't hear her advice.

A few days later the postman delivered a small package. It lay on the hall table until Alistair returned home from work. Anna surmised that the handwritten address was in the style of continental script, and when Alistair unwrapped it, a wooden plaque expertly carved in the shape of a curled-up dog and bearing the name Ted, was revealed.

Chapter 13

LITTLE MARILYN

1990

From behind a set of sliding doors of one of Oxford Street's pre-eminent department stores, a young woman emerged into the bright daylight. Designer carrier bags swung from her slender shoulders as she walked without a care in the direction of a chic restaurant just off the main thoroughfare to meet her latest beau. Money had never been a problem for Little Marilyn; her doting parents were a soft touch. With a company director as father and an accountant as mother, the concept of having to make ends meet had never been anything with which she had had to grapple.

Not far behind her, but maintaining a careful distance apart and using skills he had observed and learnt from other investigative journalists during his career, trailed David. She was an easy target to follow with no sense of the people in her immediate vicinity, and no sense that in order to expose a fraud, someone might be interested in what she did and who she met. When Little Marilyn stepped into the restaurant and gave a winning smile to the maître d' who ushered her over to the table where her friend was sitting, she had no idea at all that she might be providing David with another piece of a jigsaw puzzle which would help him answer serious questions about the source of funding of BAV Enterprises and its criminal use of naming Little Marilyn's twin who died at birth as one of its directors. From across the street, David observed her entering the posh eatery. Prices there were beyond his pocket and he knew that any reference in his monthly expenses to eating there as a necessity whilst following up a lead would cause his editor to choke with laughter. It would be a long wait David knew, but one he weighed as worthwhile, and he was not disappointed when eventually the couple left together in a taxi for an address he overheard in Pimlico.

The editor's office always looked a mess. David, a neat and tidy man himself, had never seen it in anything other than disarray. The fug of the cigar smoke and the full ashtray that the office cleaner appeared never to empty, and windows that he failed to open for an injection of fresh air, added to the general disorder.

'So, what's the state of play now, David?' asked the editor in his usual avuncular manner. 'What's little Miss Whatsit up to?' David found his reference to Little Marilyn somewhat grating since she was probably the only innocent party in the deception.

'I'm not a betting man, but if I was,' David replied, 'I'd bet that she has no idea that Victor is not even her adopted father, and that she is in fact the daughter of Arne Visser.'

'Whose new company,' cut in the editor, 'is doing rather splendidly in the world of boat building, thank you very much.'

'Whether he's her father or not, she knows how to spend his money,' stated David.

'Not an unusual skill for teenagers and young people. They seem to master the art of spending their parents' money without any formal training.' David smiled; his young family had also mastered that craft.

'Pimlico,' announced David, moving the conversation on. 'Arne's former flat. Guess who owns it now?'

'If I was a betting man,' said the editor sitting back in his swivel chair with its frayed cushion and burn marks on the wooden arm rests from ash falling from the tip of his cigars, 'and I sometimes am, I'd guess that you are about to tell me that it is owned by a person who is dead. Could it be the elusive George Wremble who never saw the light of day because he died at birth?'

'Exactly that,' confirmed David, who was just a little miffed that his editor had stolen his thunder. 'George Wremble is not only a company director, but he also appears to own a flat in a posh part of London.'

'George Wremble aka who?'

'Right now, I don't know,' admitted David. 'And it could be George Wremble also known as a whole string of other aliases. But the answer to that question would undoubtedly resolve the mystery of who is funding a lowly-ranked company that seems to go from strength to strength without the infrastructure or the level of business acumen and experience to suggest it is being generated in-house,' replied David. 'It's the reason why I'm here now asking for the assistance of a forensic accountant and a private investigator. There are some things that a humble journalist like me just cannot do.'

'Expensive,' responded the editor. 'Does your story really merit such expense?' he asked with raised eyebrows and a penetrating gaze. 'Put it this way, David, would you be prepared to pay for them yourself?'

After several weeks of costly surveillance, it was clear that Little Marilyn was a regular visitor to the flat in Pimlico, but the purpose of her visits, other than the wholly innocent reason of having been invited to spend time there with friends and acquaintances, was still unclear as no one of newsworthy identity had been logged entering the building's well-maintained foyer and taking the lift to the fourth floor. It seemed to be a dead end and despite his convictions that the flat was in some way central to a white-collar crime, David had to accept that further monitoring was out of the question. There was no obvious good news either from the forensic accountant whose tracing of a single, large injection of cash into BAV Enterprises had also hit the buffers. David was temporarily stumped; he had no leads to explore. He had, however, a boss to placate over the costs his paper had incurred pursuing his whims. It was an uncomfortable position. With nowhere else to go, Barry, the double ex-bankrupt and the brains behind the firm came more urgently under his microscope.

* * *

'She's a money pit,' remarked Victor to his wife as they sat down in front of the television to eat their supper. There was a hint of bitterness in his voice. 'And let's face it, she doesn't seem to want to spend much time with us.'

'Take the money and run,' replied Gloria trying to stay loyal to her daughter, but sharing a kindred spirit with her husband. 'She doesn't think we are good enough for her any longer.'

'All her hoity-toity friends she met at the expensive schools we paid for by working our socks off. And now we are not good enough to be seen out with her.' Gloria's deep sigh said it for them both. Years of loving, adoration even, only for them to feel that they had been carelessly tossed on the scrapheap when they were no longer willing to meet her demands.

'The car was the last straw,' stated Victor, putting his supper tray aside. He couldn't eat a thing; his insides felt all knotted and the gastric juices weren't flowing. 'Wanting a Porsche runaround for her twenty-first birthday and going off in a huff when I refused.' It was a strange world, thought Gloria. Little Marilyn had brought husband and wife together in a way that she could never have envisaged. She no longer found Victor boring. She was beginning to see and appreciate his strengths. They were coming together as a real partnership. Victor took Gloria in his arms and for the first time in years, they held one another in an embrace of true affection.

'We must let her go,' said Gloria eventually. They had been sitting on the sofa holding hands for quite some time ruminating on the way forward. The span of their joint outburst of emotions – unusual for their normally placid personalities – had passed and their thinking brains returned. 'She's not like us and never will be,' continued Gloria. 'She's like Arne and carries the same fatal flaw as him. In her mind, she is the only person who counts.'

'And bugger everyone else,' added Victor. 'But how can we cut her loose?' The question was rhetorical as both knew that the implications of doing so were to expose the crime they had committed in registering Victor as her biological father.

'I'm sure we could weather the storm *together*,' said Gloria. 'Some uncomfortable public exposure in the papers maybe, some hours of community service at worst as a penalty for the infraction, and maybe even some sympathy from those in a similar position.'

'Yes, you're probably right. Non-custodial sentences can be overcome, but we are party to something far more serious and that would definitely come to light under the scrutiny stirred up by the falsified birth certificate,' agreed Victor. 'Barry is as much a thorn in our sides as is Little Marilyn.'

Throughout the night during intermittent bouts of slumber, Gloria's workaholic brain was processing the facts. When she awoke fully at daybreak, she quickly scribbled them down before she could forget. Slipping on her dressing gown, she made two mugs of strong tea and called her husband downstairs for a conflab across the kitchen table.

'These are the facts,' she started in a business-like manner. 'To the best of our knowledge, my daughter doesn't know that you are not her father. You've been too loving and too generous all these years for her to question why she is tall and blonde and not short and dark like us. But we are both agreed that the time has come to introduce her to her father, Arne, and to pass any remaining responsibility we may owe her, onto him. She has reached the age of majority and is no longer a child.' Victor nodded. 'I propose that the next time she's at home we sit her down and give her the facts of her life. And suggest that she may wish to start a new life with him.'

'And if she declines?' asked Victor rubbing his chin, 'what then?'

'She won't decline, of that I am certain. We'll offer her a golden handshake and that will be that.'

'But she's your daughter. Can you really erase her from your heart?'

'I don't like her, and any remaining bond I have with her dwindles with every passing day. She has never loved either of us, and it's hard to have empathy with such a person whether or not she's your daughter. I don't wish her harm, but ...,' Gloria broke off, bereft of other words to describe her feelings.

'And Barry,' asked Victor, 'what do we do about him?'

'We leave him.'

'What? Just get up and go?'

'Exactly that. Let him face the music. We've played no active role in the George Wremble saga. That is entirely Barry's baby.' Victor sniggered; he was developing a sense of humour.

'And just how do we make our living and pay for the golden handshake you mentioned?'

'We have sufficient skills between us to make a good

living as financial management consultants in our own business,' replied Gloria reassuringly. 'We're still young enough to start again and old enough to impress our future clients with a wealth of experience.'

'I don't doubt that we could make a success of our own company, but with virtually no savings and a mortgage to service, how could we survive in the early days until the business started making money?'

'I was coming to that,' said Gloria with a mischievous grin. 'I'm not a smart accountant for nothing. And what Barry probably didn't know, or didn't remember, is that I'm also a Chartered Company Secretary, so I know my way around the rules of company law.'

'You spotted a loophole?'

'Not so much a loophole as an opportunity to put aside future directors' fees where they couldn't be accessed by Barry and used for other purposes. Apart from his dodgy moves, Barry's knowledge of company law and how it works is limited. It wasn't difficult to baffle him with a bit of general babble, and although my intention was only to ring fence a pot of money to pay off our creditors if the company floundered, it can now be used as our nest egg. We may not be able to afford a villa in Spain sometime soon, but there will be sufficient in the kitty to get us started.'

'And Barry's villa in Spain may turn out to have been built on sand. All hype and no substance.'

'Some flak will come our way of course when BAV Enterprises fails, but the brunt of it will be directed towards Barry for his criminal use of a dead person's name as a director. The public won't like that.'

Gloria brought their chapter of parenthood to a conclusion by saying she hoped that whatever Little Marilyn did on her frequent visits to the flat in Pimlico, life would work out well for her. Victor was ambivalent. Over the course of the previous fortnight, he had stood near the block of flats and noted her arrivals and departures. On one occasion she had swept close by him but never noticed him. He had trudged back to the underground station with tears in his eyes; the apple of his eye seemed to be unaware of his existence. It was a cruel world.

* * *

Little Marilyn had always hated her name. Why her soppy parents kept referring to her as Little Marilyn she had no idea; she'd asked them a thousand times to desist, but if anything, it had reinforced their annoying habit. She hated Wremble too. Her school friends teased her that it was a good name for a mole living down a hole but not for a person wishing to be taken seriously. So, when parents and offspring bid each other farewell, it was her opportunity to start afresh, and it came to her that just a small change was all that was needed to improve matters greatly. From that moment she chose to be known as Marilyn Little.

Her boyfriend, the latest owner of the flat in Pimlico, treated her well and as a couple they were seen in all the right places wearing the latest fashions. With trendy coiffeurs and manicured finger nails they rubbed shoulders with the swingers of the day. Life was all she dreamed it to be until her boyfriend fell under the spell of a more mature and glamorous woman. The daughter of an ageing American multi-millionaire, Marilyn found that she was no match for his new woman. With nowhere to go and no regular income, Marilyn signed up with a model agency. Tall and blonde was exactly what they were looking for, and temporary accommodation was soon organised.

Marilyn was soon in demand; her rangy looks were just right for the burgeoning recreational market which was making a killing out of the sale of designer clothing ranges for every conceivable pastime. And when she started featuring on the front cover of various sporting magazines wearing these ensembles, other, more exciting avenues of modelling began to open. A boatyard in Holland that was soon to launch its latest design in the seagoing, small cabin cruiser class, came up with an innovative idea for its advertising campaign. Arne Visser, former sailor extraordinaire and a consultant for the boatyard, would sail the new vessel out of its home port of Harlingen and make its way south hugging the western coast of Europe before traversing the Atlantic Ocean to repeat the same along South America's eastern seaboard as far south as Buenos Aires. Stopping for a few days at selected ports en route with busy marinas, photo shoots marrying clothes especially designed for sailing with the trailblazing boat design would be arranged at each port with the chance for local sailing enthusiasts to clamber aboard for detailed inspection, and to discover its virtues with short runs outside the harbour walls. With a company salesman following the itinerary and timetable to take orders at each stopping point, the unadventurous advertising plans that had held sway for so long, would be jettisoned in favour of something far more dynamic.

When Marilyn's name was put forward by the agency as the ideal person for shoots in Jersey and Cadiz, there was instant acceptance that she would be the perfect model for the job. For Marilyn, however, the prospect of meeting her biological father was not just daunting, but also unsettling. Since the denouement of her parentage, she had never once made enquiries or sought to meet her father. She knew little about him other than he was Dutch and that he sailed boats. Sailing wasn't her world and didn't interest her. That he was Dutch was neither a positive nor a negative; it was just information that failed to excite. And she was in demand and beginning to make a good living. What could a father who had never played a role in her life except to get her mother pregnant offer? Not much in Marilyn's estimation. If she did agree to go, and the thought of turning down such an exciting offer was dreadful, any contact with her father would be on her terms, not his.

Jersey was cool but bright in the pale June sunshine. She stood on the timber deck in various poses directed by the experienced fashion photographer, a woman with all the necessary credentials to produce exactly the type of images of their clothing that the fashion house required. It turned out to be a long and tiring day for all concerned including the backroom staff who ensured that after each change of outfit, Marilyn's make-up and coiffeur were still immaculate. They had use of the boat for one day only and had to make every second count. Tired on the short flight home, the agency crew all agreed that modelling was far less glamorous than the public believed. There had been no sign of Arne in Jersey, although Marilyn felt aware of his presence in the background, but at Cadiz things were different.

Buoyed by initial results in their first port of call, the clothing and boating partnership looked forward to further success in the warmer climes of southern Spain. Marilyn approached the trip with greater confidence too. She hoped that Arne would remain in the shadows, but she was prepared for any encounter that might arise. She knew him but he didn't know her, and she had no intention of losing that advantage.

Now, modelling bikinis, shorts, nautical tops, sun hats and warm wraps for cooler evenings, Marilyn was the perfect model to display the garments at their best. Watched from the quay by small huddles of locals and tourists, the day's shooting did not go without recognition or applause. With additional lighting set up for some twilight shots, a couple of classic design, figure-hugging, slinky evening dresses in non-crease materials that could be rolled up and easily stowed away in a locker was the final triumph of the day. According to the fashion house, not only was it the start of one-stop shopping for everything a woman needed whilst out sailing, but it was the chance every girl crewing on leisure boats would yearn for. After days of physical exertion at sea, it would be the chance to show off their femininity.

Marilyn knew that any confrontation with her father would occur on the second day of shooting when both parties to the joint advertising experiment wanted action images. Stills were fine, but images captured showing sea spray cascading over the gunwales, the vessel heeling in the wind, a billowing spinnaker, and all with a super model in the background dressed in the latest fashion hauling in the sheets or with a firm hand on the tiller, would have more impact on the viewer. Sales, the companies anticipated, would rocket.

A tall man with fair hair greying at the temples stretched out a hand to help Marilyn board his vessel; no one else would join them. A cinematographer, especially hired for the day at enormous expense, would capture pictures and film from a motor launch running alongside Arne's boat. The shots would be dramatic in a stiff breeze and they would capture the moment perfectly.

Alone on the boat with Arne, Marilyn's resolve would be tested. He had a faint smile on his lips as he cast off and headed out of the harbour closely followed by the motor vessel carrying the gaggle of film crew. Using a megaphone, the film director conveyed instructions to Arne on course and actions required. Arne shrugged his shoulders and shouted back that the weather and currents would dictate what would happen, but his comments were lost in the wind. Marilyn relaxed. Arne knew what he was doing and the film people would have to accept whatever he managed to serve up. And in a thrilling chase, Arne manoeuvred his boat frequently across the path of the oncoming chaser and pulled out of direct hits amidships at point blank range with ease as if his boat was no more than an extension of his hand which could be whipped away in an instant.

The evening was a time for celebration. Back on dry land, a review of the action shots obtained had more than satisfied both company representatives. An amble through the town's historic streets and alleys followed: eating and drinking at tapas bars favoured by the locals. By the time the group arrived back at their lodgings near the waterfront, most celebrants were worse for wear, and with the prospect of an early morning flight home, disappeared quickly to their beds.

Marilyn had drunk sparingly throughout the social ritual of going from one bar to the next; bitten on previous pub crawls in her late teenage years, she had not forgotten the ignominy of being out of control of mind and body. Arne too had long since lost the taste for excessive drinking. By a natural process of last man standing, they came together. Marilyn gave her thanks and said her farewells to the tall man leaning on the iron railings along the water's edge.

'Won't you join me for a quiet coffee before going up to bed?' asked Arne.

'Well,' said Marilyn procrastinating over her reply. It wasn't an invitation she sought. 'Why not?'

'Did you enjoy being out on the water in a sailing boat?' he asked.

'It was hair-raising.'

'But did you enjoy it?' he asked again.

'I was concentrating on doing my job,' she replied evasively, 'and trying to follow the director's instructions.'

'I'm surprised if you could hear what he had to say over the roar of his motors,' said Arne. 'Wretched things, motors.'

'But people with lots of money buy boats with motors. So, why are you trying to sell a boat without one?' Arne thought about her comment but made no attempt at a reply. It was late but a nearby coffee bar was still open. They drifted in and sat on stools at the counter.

'Would you like to learn how to sail?'

'Why are you asking me?' asked Marilyn looking puzzled.

'Because if you did, and if you had your own boat, then you would realise the joys and freedom of being able to sail the seas without the smell of fuel in your nostrils, or engine grease on your hands, or a relentless noise in your ears. Just you, the boat, the winds, and the currents. Living off your own wits and trusting yourself. And time to ponder the universe.'

'Or, being cold, wet, miserable, and scared. No, I don't think sailing is for me. I'd rather have an engine to fire up to take me back to dry land.'

'Shame,' muttered Arne. 'You have all the physical attributes to make a fine sailor.'

'Where do you go next?' enquired Marilyn changing the subject.

'São Miguel. The largest island in the Azores archipelago. A male model is booked to come on board for the clothing photoshoot.'

'So, several days at sea, I presume.'

'Yes. Almost a thousand nautical miles from here to there. Several days at sea without company,' replied Arne. Marilyn wondered if it was a teasing remark; were they sparring with one another? She did not know.

'And from there?'

'I traverse the Atlantic from north to south.'

'On your own again?'

'Maybe, but I shall be giving a daily update by ship-to-shore telephone to a radio station in Holland,' replied Arne. 'Position, speed, weather, how the boat is handling, any winged or marine creatures that I've spotted. That sort of thing. All part of the publicity deal.'

'And how long will that take?' asked Marilyn, not prepared to question the "maybe."

'An Atlantic crossing east-to-west is usually straightforward outside the hurricane season when the trade winds are favourable. Then, generally it can be as little as two to three weeks. But I'm doing a traverse from the Azores to South America, not the standard crossing from the Canaries to the West Indies. It makes a difference,' he said, indicating to the barman that he wished to pay. 'When conditions are settled and you can skirt around bad weather with the help of radar, you can speed along at fifteen knots, barely needing to retrim the sails from day to day. The aim is to get to Buenos Aires in time for their grand regatta in November when the whole place will be a frenzy of activity.'

'Great publicity, I guess.'

'The best possible,' he replied.

But their conversation wasn't over. Instinctively both knew there was more that needed saying. They walked slowly along the deserted quay, the gently lapping water making a soothing sound on its stone walls. Did Arne know who she was? Did she like him or detest him for never being in her life? Her jumbled thoughts were spared as Arne broke the ice.

'I'm going to repeat in reverse the journey I made about twenty-five years ago when I sailed from Buenos Aires to Southampton via the Azores. I was in a single-handed race and had every chance of winning. But after leaving the mouth of the River Plate, I realised that I had a stowaway; a young woman, a political activist, who was evading the brutal regime in power in Argentina at that time. She had fled at a moment's notice when thugs had banged on the door of her father's house demanding that she be handed over,' Arne recalled. 'Living near the waterside, she must have jumped on my boat in a hurry to hide herself not knowing that I would be putting to sea later that evening. I was sailing a larger class of vessel with more places to hide and when I got back from celebrating my last evening out in a city for some time, I failed to notice her. Out of sight of land, she suddenly sprang out of the cabin and confronted me.' He paused. They sat down on a bench. The only light was from the moon. 'Her name is Coco,' Arne went on. 'I offered to put her ashore on a sandy beach on the Uruguayan coast but she was too het up to make a rational decision and she stayed with me all the way to the Azores.'

'You got to know her during the long passage.'

'Yes. And she got to know me. We were both running away from something.'

'She, from a military junta, and you from what?' asked Marilyn pointedly.

'From the death of my father near the end of the war in Europe.' They watched the sky as a cloud passed across the moon partially obscuring the light. 'She was young and beautiful and we became intimate. Your half-sister

413

was conceived just south of the Azores.' The information smacked Marilyn between the eyes. She gasped; he'd known all along that she was his daughter.

'How?'

'How what?' How did I know?'

'Yes. How did you know?' she asked, still gasping, 'that I am your daughter.'

'My adult daughter, Stella, told me.'

'But how did she know? I know nothing about her, or how she knows about me.'

'I think you should let her tell you herself,' said Arne. 'She will be joining me in the Azores and accompanying me on the passage south. Just like you, she knows nothing about sailing but she's got pluck. Why don't you come too? A father and his two daughters; a certain recipe for getting to know each other's bad traits.'

* * *

Stella and Marilyn arrived at the small international airport in Ponta Delgada on the same plane. Since the introduction of the service a mere three years earlier, the scheduled weekly flight from London Stansted had always been jam-packed. From different seating rows, the two women had eyed each other as potential half-sisters, but sharing the same thought that what they were about to embark on, may not have been their best decision. With instructions to stay away from the boat whilst publicity filming and interviewing were under way, the half-sisters would have ample time to come to terms with one another. Initially, meetings in the hotel restaurant were awkward

414

and frosty, neither woman prepared to carelessly blurt out her feelings towards her father. A cautious approach was adopted by both until Marilyn forced the issue by demanding to know how Stella knew of her existence.

'Via the editor of a national newspaper,' replied Stella truthfully but laconically. Marilyn looked bemused and Stella realised that she had to put some flesh on the bone. 'The "old" Arne had the knack of creating confusion and gossip wherever he went. When I married into a family who could trace their lineage back to the sixteenth century of service to the monarch, publicity of any type became anathema. Arne's playboy image did not blend well with my husband's job as diplomat. As a family friend, the editor kept us abreast of any newsworthy items likely to surface in the public domain. It was not so much the birth of a second child born out of wedlock that generated displeasure, but his consequential lack of care and responsibility for the newly born.'

'So,' demanded Marilyn angrily, 'how old were you when you discovered that he was your father?'

'I knew for some time before I approached him, and I only did so to beg him to avoid future controversy. Since then, we have had an on-off relationship until recently. He has finally come to terms with the loss of his father who he adored. He is now a "new" Arne and ready to love again. Give him a chance.' Marilyn looked sceptical but said nothing.

They left the harbour on a sunny morning some days later. Arne had warned them that space would be at a premium; two bunks, three crew, and limited stowage already crammed with either food or safety equipment. Apart from a few necessities, a change of clothing was all that was permitted. He would provide the correct footwear.

The girls watched silently as he steered the vessel onto the exact south-easterly course he had planned; one which would avoid the Atlantic hurricane basin. Later in the day he started providing a commentary of the actions required to sail the vessel safely. Tomorrow, there would be lessons, hands-on experience, and a whole new sailing nomenclature to master. One person would always be on watch. Discipline was essential for safety. Tomorrow afternoon after their midday meal, he would sign in with the radio station and give his first live report.

By the end of the first week, a daily routine to allow best use of the limited space had been established. The half-sisters had picked up the rudiments of sailing in benign conditions, and they had reached much warmer southerly climes. Becalmed several times with little to do, conversation became more voluble. From different standpoints, discourse moved from polite and restrained to frank and bitter opinions with no subject off-limits. Questions were asked, fingers were pointed, grievances were aired, disturbing revelations were made, voices were raised, tempers frayed, and tears were shed as the "full truth" according to the individual was laid bare. Although uncomfortable for all, these periods of tension with its release of negative energy allowed a bonding to begin and a spirit of adventure to seep into their passage to South America.

Arne's radio reports became a highlight of the day with contributions from both his daughters. The

Dutch station reported a high level of interest in Arne's communications as hundreds of armchair sailors plotted their daily positions and gave their forecast for the number of nautical miles the boat would cover during the next twenty-four hours. With cheery news from their sponsors of the positive effect their passage was having on sales, all seemed set fair for The Frieda II and its occupants.

The first time that Arne failed to sign in did not arouse concern, but when he failed to make contact on the second successive afternoon, alarm bells rang at the radio station. Someone suggested a radio malfunction as the cause, and not to get unduly agitated. Another suggested that they had been steering a course well away from the hurricane zone, and the weather in that vicinity had been unexceptional. Yet another suggested that with three people aboard, if Arne had been injured or fallen sick, one of his crew would have sent out a mayday call. However, when the usual time came and went on the third afternoon without any radio communication, the station's director felt it prudent to inform the coast guard of their fears. Alerts were made to shipping in the area to search and rescue, if possible, but the vastness of the ocean made it a near impossible request.

The media were soon involved with the emerging story. A boat lost at sea or overdue in port was always a newsworthy item, and in this case especially so since the sailor on board had been famous in his younger days for some audacious maritime exploits. Whilst there was no hard news to report, the media concentrated on speculation about the newly-designed boat's seaworthiness and the wisdom of carrying two passengers on what was, essentially, a one-man vessel. In addition to being novice sailors, the two passengers were also his daughters. One expert offered the opinion that the boat might have been swamped by a large wave as it would have sat lower in the water due to the extra weight of the women. Others scoffed at the thought that an experienced sailor like Arne could make such a basic mistake. But with no detail to extrapolate into an ongoing story, media attention faded.

For the Visser boatyard of Harlingen, it would be a double tragedy if the vessel and its crew were not found. The loss of the founder's grandson would be a hammer blow to the company, but the long-term ramifications of being unable to prove that the vessel was seaworthy, or that the design, into which they had poured their expertise over so many months, was trustworthy, would be even more stark. The managing director knew instinctively that control of the future was now out of his hands.

Gloria monitored the news relentlessly once she learnt that Marilyn was on board. According to the model agency, she had quit her job with them to go on a sailing adventure with her father to South America. Victor too, was in a state of agitation. Neither had been able to maintain the pretence that Marilyn meant nothing to them. In a roundabout way, they had Marilyn to thank for allowing them to "rediscover" one another. Gloria fretted that Marilyn had no one other than them to take the necessary steps to apply to the court to have her declared missing presumed dead. Victor knew that anything they did would have to be done discreetly.

Alistair sat in the bay window with the folded newspaper on his knees. The article he had just read about Arne was like an obituary. It offered no hope of survival. He felt on edge. If Ted had still been alive, master and dog would have gone for a brisk walk to clear the despondency that Alistair felt. Instead, he went out into the garden and stood at Ted's grave. Arne wasn't a bad man he told Anna when she joined him.

* * *

Coco stood in the street staring silently across at the space that had formerly been her parents' house. The domestic dwellings of yesteryear had long since been replaced by bars and restaurants as the citizens of Buenos Aires enjoyed a more liberal political regime. After some moments of contemplation, she retraced the route she had taken down to the harbour, when running for her life. She stopped at a point she believed was close to where she had jumped into Arne's boat and hidden under a pile of sails in the hope that she would elude the regime's chasing thugs.

Now, it was the day when Arne had told her that he expected to sail into the harbour with his daughters amid a joyous welcome, and she had promised to be there to greet them. It would be a happy day Arne had assured her; the day when they would announce that they had married secretly before Arne had left Harlingen on his long marketing cruise to the southern hemisphere. They were to enjoy it together, just the four of them: Arne, his wife, Coco, their daughter, Stella and Arne's daughter,

Marilyn. But six long weeks had passed without news of The Frieda II or its crew. No boat, no wreckage, no bodies, no indication of what had happened, and the search and rescue called off. There was a general acceptance that both boat and occupants should be considered as "missing, lost at sea."

Coco bit her lip. On the brink of family harmony, happiness had been cruelly snatched from her grasp. Her hand felt for the small medallion on the chain around her neck; Arne had given it to her on their wedding day. Adapted to swing on a slender chain, it was a five-guilder gold coin depicting King William I of The Netherlands and minted in eighteen-fifteen.

This book is printed on paper from sustainable sources managed under the Forest Stewardship Council (FSC) scheme.

It has been printed in the UK to reduce transportation miles and their impact upon the environment.

For every new title that Troubador publishes, we plant a tree to offset CO_2, partnering with the More Trees scheme.

For more about how Troubador offsets its environmental impact, see www.troubador.co.uk/sustainability-and-community